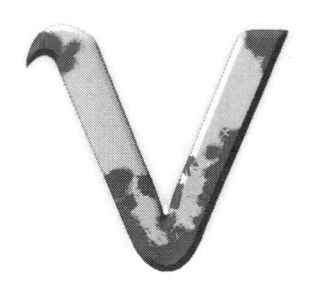

Valenfaar:
The Crimson Plains

James McLean

This is a work of fiction. Any resemblance to people or places, real or fictional, are entirely coincidental.

Copyright © <2023> <James McLean>

All rights reserved.

ISBN:
9798412183589

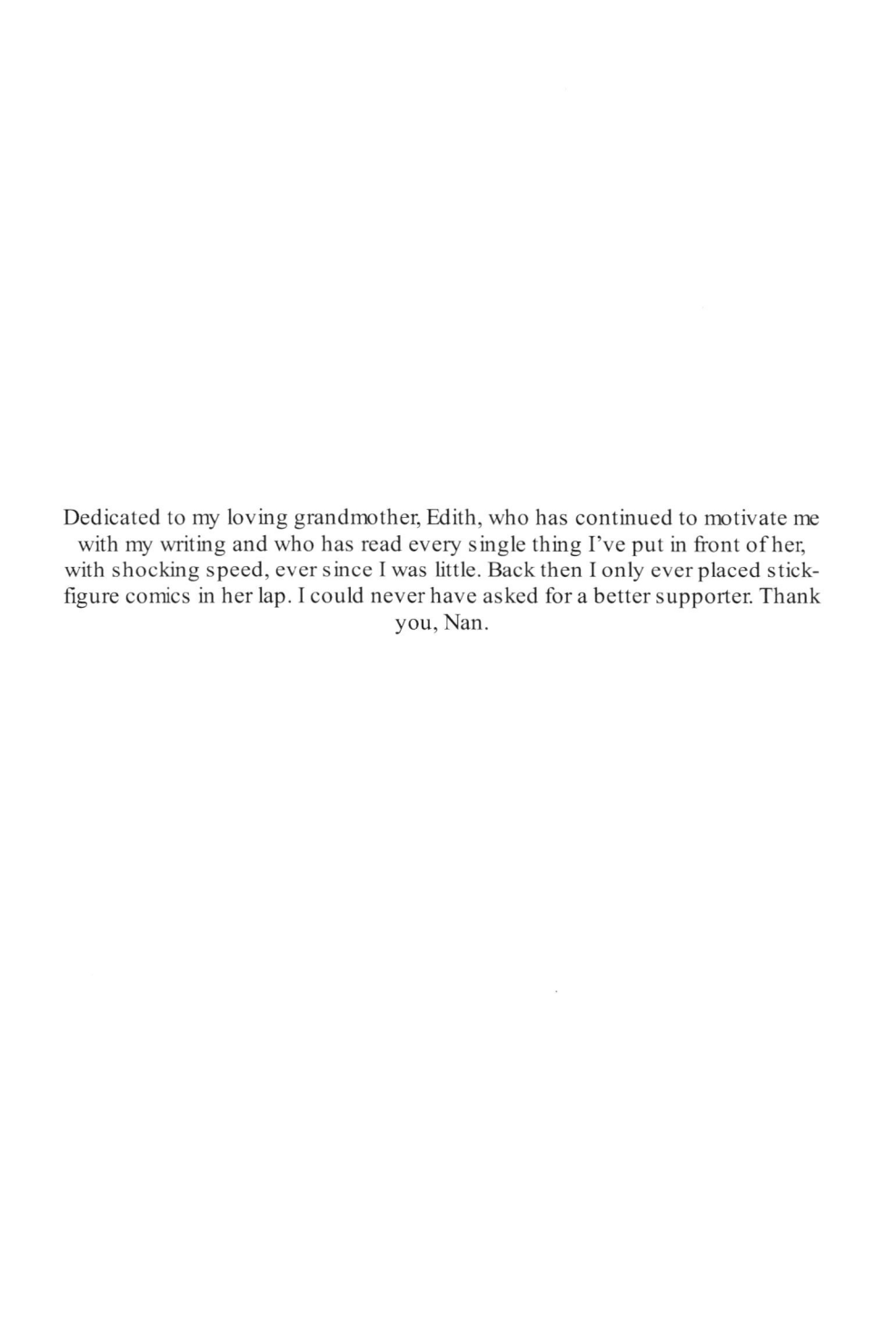

Dedicated to my loving grandmother, Edith, who has continued to motivate me with my writing and who has read every single thing I've put in front of her, with shocking speed, ever since I was little. Back then I only ever placed stick-figure comics in her lap. I could never have asked for a better supporter. Thank you, Nan.

Prologue

500 cycles ago ...

The Tall Plains had been something of fierce rumour and mystery for Gren's people for many suns. For each and every sun, their warriors and scouts would wander into the golden land and never return. Gren was determined to find out who or what had taken his people, and to find out whether they were alive or dead.

The rumours spoke of a great ring of stone, reaching for the sky that seemed to stretch on almost endlessly. The rumours continued, saying that within this great stone ring, sat a magical being that could erupt fire from his hands, twist a man's arms without laying hands on them and could even touch the emotions of others. Gren knew what all of it was: piss-vomit. It was nothing but piss-vomit to him and his men. He was the best that his people had to offer and they would all know the truth upon his return.

There wasn't a version of the rumours in his sharp mind that told Gren the being with invisible powers existed, not a single version, no. He knew their men were captured and killed by the Talls. Roaming savages that stood far taller, and smelled far worse, than any man that Gren had seen. Their black roars were likely the last things his men and women would have ever heard and he would make sure to avenge each and every one of them.

He hefted his large, two-handed axe into his hands, sunlight gleaming off the blades, it was the largest his people had ever made. No one had been able to wield it but him. It stood as tall as he was, just shy of six feet. "Lef, keep a blade drawn, boy," Gren called behind him, "the Talls will be ahead. Look." He pointed a finger to the horizon.

The tall stalks of golden grass that lay like a sheet across the Tall Plains were beginning to stand erect, compared to their surroundings. A large mass had been through this way, the grass was only just beginning to recover, and further ahead nature struggled to keep taller still.

"We keep marching," Gren spoke through the silence, his voice coarse, "come."

They walked for three more days before they saw the pillars of white smoke on the horizon. The fabled ring of stone stretched and reached to the sky on their right, almost infinite in its size as it stretched out forward and back from the travellers. They were approaching the land of piss-vomit invisible powers and the Talls.

"All of you keep your blades drawn, we will find the Talls by day's end. Come."

The dozen men in his command followed him forward, through the trampled and wet grass, each step plaguing them with dread.

Sure enough, before the sun had reached its highest point in the sky, Gren stood at the borders of the war camp that would belong to the Talls he had been seeking. They had grown in number. He had expected to find twelve, maybe fifteen, at most. But here he found close to fifty, by his best guess. Their green skins were bright under the hot sun, the grass golden around them like the coins of home. How far he was from home, half a sun away he guessed, but he had finally arrived. There was only one way to win this now, he needed to challenge their leader to a duel, and win. His group would surely lose in open combat.

Thankfully, Gren, nor his men, needn't try too hard to get the leader's attention. This larger Tall walked out from their crude leather-like camps, taller than the rest by a full head. It looked at them as its four nostrils flared. This one looked calm, collected, and almost smart.

Gren stepped forward, his eyes absorbing every bit of info he could of his foe. The bone armour it wore, still streaked with blood and bits of flesh, made the Tall look almost undead. This did not matter to Gren, he needed to kill it, and he needed to kill it this day.

The creature stepped forward, its hands empty, its only weapon the foul grin upon its face. The yellow teeth felt evil in the creature's skull, felt like malice, with deathly calmness. The horror didn't exchange a single word with Gren, they knew what was expected of them. Hoisting his axe up, Gren met the Tall in single combat.

The fight hadn't gone on long before the warrior found himself cast into the dirt, his nose broken and bleeding, his jaw dislocated. Groaning, he crawled for his axe and could see the smear of his own blood on the shaft. No, he couldn't fail here, there was no way. He, Gren, the best warrior of his tribe, would not fall to a monster such as this. But it did not matter, he realized, as he pulled his body through the dirt; his men had been surrounded during the battle. Even if he had won the duel, they would have all been killed in the end. No. Failure was not an option. Gren cast the doubts from his mind. Stubbornly, he crawled forward, one broken arm dragging underneath him.

How would he wield the axe with one arm? The thought was quickly shoved aside, he would deal with that problem when he got to it. He groaned and roared as his foe dug its heel into his leg, just above the knee. Gren ached as he looked over his shoulder to face the monster above him. He could hardly acknowledge the open-handed strike that would have him seeing stars.

By the time the stars in his vision cleared, his men were dead, throats slit and heads scalped. Their eyes glazed over in one final picture of fear. Gren cleared his head and looked up at the Tall he had fought. It held the double-bladed axe in its hands, staring down at him, level and calm. The eyes of the beast spoke to the warrior: "You were never meant to conquer me. You were to gift me this weapon."

As much as the warrior wanted to disagree, the way the time and events had woven themselves together had him reluctantly admitting this simple fact. His own gaze, pained and broken, sent its own message: "You're right."

Chapter 1

Endless fields of golden grass stretched out over the horizon and the soft evening glow of the setting sun rested upon the tips of the Halo. Valenfaar would be plunged into the night once more, only to awaken again the following day, as it had done for the last 500 cycles.

In the tall grass, Rel stood, her slender silhouette outlined against the orange glow of the sky behind her. Her ebony skin glistened with sweat in the evening heat as she plodded her way through the plains, moving towards her fellow Plain's Strider, Nef.

Nef was a good man, average height with a slender frame, and dark green eyes. He had proven time and again out in the plains that he could handle himself, and keep those of Valenfaar protected. He was assigned to Rel two cycles ago, when he had first arrived in Plainsview, after getting into a fight with a man from the Sovereign Guard. Nef had been hesitant at first with his assignment, and with good reason, he was partnered with the Plain's Master, Right Hand to Saffron, the Plain's Warden. For a new recruit, he was faced with incredible expectations for no other reason than the fact that he had been a troublemaker.

So far, the young Plain's Strider had impressed both Rel and Saffron, earning him constant patrols in the Endless Plains, and earning himself the privilege of many trips into the Central Cities for days of rest. Though to Rel, she had rarely seen him take his rest days, oftentimes offering to cover patrols for other striders, and offering them the time off instead.

Rel approached and cleared her throat to get Nef's attention. The young man turned to face her, seriousness in his gaze. "Plain's Master," he said, giving her a slight nod. "I see a tower of smoke on the horizon, out to the east. That's not normal."

The Plain's Master sighed, and pulled back her golden yellow hood. Her blackened skin was harsh against the tall golden grass of the plains, sweat beaded on her forehead.

"No, not normal at all. Traders don't usually come from that direction, they're usually more southward, closer to Ajwix." her voice was soft and serene, calming, she had been told, and she took great pride in that. Oftentimes, she would be called upon to ease dying Plain's Striders in their final moments, if their families could not provide them with the comfort they deserved.

That thought saddened her: she knew that if she had been deathly wounded in the plains, she would want nothing more than to see her dear Ashlin again and to stare into her piercing blue eyes for one final moment before moving to her place in the Soul Spire.

"Want to take a peek?" Nef said, a playful grin playing at his lips.

Rel snapped out of her trance. "Lead the way, strider. You know this section of the plains as well as most. If not better." She returned the grin.

The two striders pulled their hoods above their heads and began to move through the grass, their cloaks of matching colour brushed softly through the foliage. They were not impossible to see, not while moving, but they would be much more difficult to spot.

The shadows of the sprawling mountains behind them stretched ever onward towards the smoke, quickly enveloping them in darkness as the sun gently lowered itself behind the Halo. The mountains were of great benefit to Valenfaar: a gigantic ring, encircling the country, with only one entrance: Plainsview.

Plainsview was the portal to Valenfaar. It was a sprawling town of 75,000, with a complement of 10,000 guards, not including the 200 Plain's Striders that worked to keep the town safe from threats beyond the Halo.

The bustling Outlier City was almost a Central City; the population and large wooden walls, and the fact that it was the outermost city in all of Valenfaar however, kept it from being titled as such. Only cities with a population of more than 150,000, with great stone walls residing in the country's middle, were titled Central Cities.

Regardless, Plainsview was held in incredibly high regard amongst the nobility of the land. It kept threats out and kept trade, and diplomatic relations, alive as striders worked as security for convoys and envoys both. Ensuring safe passage across the Endless Plains, and to the country of Ajwix with their Great Metal Cities.

The smoke on the horizon began to fade into the darkening sky, beginning to blot out the occasional stars that would flicker into existence once again.

"Nef, wait," Rel put a hand on the man's shoulder. "Let's rest here for the night, we can hardly see the smoke as it is. No sense wandering in the dark."

"Yes, ma'am."

The two of them gathered up several strands of long grass each, tied some off for makeshift twine, and tied them around bundles of more grass. The straw pillows they made in the plains were never comfortable, but their hoods and the fact that it was better than the dirt, would make them bearable for the night.

The stars glistened above, among a cloud of strange glowing dust that stretched further into the world beyond than anyone could imagine. Rel watched as a small blue star twinkled against the darkness. It reminded her of Ashlin, the gorgeous glint she would have in her eye every time Rel came home from a patrol, happy to see her lover was safe. The Plain's Master felt lucky to have her. They were criticized for not liking men, from time to time, but the two of them cared not for the constant jabber of judgemental people. They were happy with each other, and to them, that was all that would ever matter.

The night came and went without a word, and come the morning, the smoke could still be seen directly to the east with the bright morning sun glaring through.

Rel turned to the sleeping man beside her and nudged him with her foot. "Get up. We need to move."

The strider grumbled lazily as he woke to see the Plain's Master staring down at him.

"Ugh," he groaned, "these pillows are awful. Has my neck feeling something fierce." He sat up, shook his head, then rose to his feet twisting his head from side to side. Nef turned to face the smoke in the distance, it hadn't moved. Whoever was supposedly camping, hadn't moved, and the simple fact the entire Plains weren't ignited in flames, told them it wasn't a wildfire either; it was controlled. "Alright," he said with a stretch. "Let's get going."

The two striders used their long knives to sever the makeshift twine holding their pillows together and cast the strands into the grass. It would be almost impossible for anyone to know where they had settled. Within moments the grass they had slept on would prop itself upright, as their pillows lie scattered amongst the endless yellow, never to be identified by anyone other than another Plain's Strider.

Rel and Nef continued towards the smoke, allowing it to grow ever closer to them. The sun nearly rose halfway to its peak before a strange structure began to take shape, showing a tip above the tall grass. The striders crouched low and spread out, Nef circling to the right.

The tip of the structure grew more detailed as Rel approached. She heard the crackling of a fire and could smell the smouldering of meat as she drew near. She moved a gloved finger between two strands of grass, and pulled one of them aside, allowing her clear vision into the camp.

There was a small clearing, made for the camp itself. The grass was cut short, and stools of a strange white wood were situated around the fire pit. They were oddly large, and rather grimy compared to other stools she had seen. Rel looked to the tip she had seen before, and brought her gaze down from the uppermost part, down to the foundation.

It was a small tent, and much like the stools, it was slightly larger than anything a typical man would need. Once more, the strange white wood had been used as supports, with a kind of pink hide used as fabric. Something about the materials seemed familiar to Rel, but she couldn't place them.

The Plain's Master worked her way around the border of grass, occasionally looking into the camp to see if there was anyone there. To her knowledge, she couldn't see anything useful and had assumed that Nef would be seeing much the same. Slowly, she emerged from the grass, and stood tall, leaving her hood up. No more than a few metres to her left, Nef did the same.

The Plain's Master raised a finger, indicating silence was still needed: they hadn't checked the tent yet. Carefully, Rel removed her short sword and long knife from their scabbards and inched towards the structure. She poked her knife through the flaps of the hide and pulled it open. She breathed a sigh of relief as her gaze ran through the hovel. No one was there. At least not living.

Inside, skulls and swords made of white wood littered the ground. The soil was soaked with blood, and small metal instruments, similar to tools used for carvings.

"What in the depths of the Soul Spire is this?" Nef asked, his eyes wide at the gore that marred the ground.

Rel inched forward without reply, sheathing her weapons. She knelt and picked up one of the wooden swords by the hilt and held it up. She looked it over closely and felt the smoothness of the handle. It hadn't felt like any wood she had ever seen. There was no grain to it, no roughness. She ran her fingers along the blade and brought them up to the tip. Turning the weapon over, she saw a spatter of blood on the other side. Her eyes widened and she dropped the sword, a sudden realization slamming into her gut; a battering ram that threatened to drive the breath from her lungs.

"Shit!" she whispered.

"What is it?" Nef asked, worry in his gaze.

"This isn't wood, Nef," She passed the weapon to him. "It's bone." Quickly, Rel reached her hand out to feel the hide covering the tent. The pink material felt all too familiar to her: skin.

"Fuck!" She pulled her hand away sharply and looked at her partner. "We're leaving. Now."

"What is it, Rel?" Nef asked as he followed her back into the camp, dropping the sword behind them.

"Not now. We need to get back to Plainsview and get word to Saffron. He'll know what to do."

"But what is i-" he was cut off as Rel's hand fell over his mouth.

She raised her finger to her lips, then pointed to the east, just above the grass. The silhouette of a head poked out, towering higher than the average man by almost two feet. She moved her finger from the figure's head, back towards the grass, in the direction of the Halo.

Nef nodded silently and moved hurriedly into the grass, his feet a whisper. They kept low and fast for much of the day until the sun began to set. It hadn't occurred to them by the time they set up for the night, but neither of them had eaten throughout the day.

Once they were ready to close their eyes, the two striders drank from the water they had left and nibbled at the salted meat they carried. The food wouldn't last them more than another day, but that was alright. By nightfall on the morrow, they would be back in Plainsview with loved ones in their arms, and full bellies to help them sleep.

Nef broke the silence. "So what in Esmirla's Rains was that Rel?"

She looked back the way they came; she hadn't dealt with those things before. She wasn't even sure Saffron had. Usually, they were a problem for the

Sovereign Guard, and usually, they sent the Pale Bull. But out here in the plains? This was new to Rel, and it didn't add up, not with the little information she knew.

"Rel? You there?" Nef asked.

"Thregs," she said, her tone flat.

"Wait, what?" He sat a little straighter. "Are you sure? Out here in the plains?"

The Plain's Master turned to look her partner in the eyes. "You ever hear of something else seven feet tall with equipment like that?"

The man shook his head.

"Exactly," She took a sip of water, draining her sheepskin. "We get back to Plainsview and tell Saffron. He'll know what to do."

"Alright, you're the boss. You think they'll move their camp tonight?"

"I sure hope not." Rel leaned back and placed her head on another grass pillow. "Rest. We have a decent range ahead of us on the morrow."

"Yes, ma'am," Nef laid his head down and closed his eyes.

The Plain's Master kept her gaze on the stars above, thinking of what she had found in the camp earlier that morning. Who or what had the Thregs killed to make those weapons? Traders, hunters, other striders, animals? It was impossible to tell. But Thregs had never been reported outside the Halo before. She wasn't sure, but as Rel watched red stars streak across the sky, east to west, she felt in her gut something was awry. She closed her eyes and thought of Ashlin in all her beauty, her lover and best friend. Pale of skin, and bright blue of eyes, a beauty if there ever was one, with a stubbornness to match her own.

Dreams flooded Rel's mind that night, dreams of her lover, of her childhood, and of the life she led in Plainsview. But those fantasies were quickly dashed by nightmares of what she had seen that morning. In her nightmare, Ashlin had been murdered and torn to shreds by the Thregs while Rel remained pinned, her face planted firmly in the dirt. She couldn't see the Thregs, but she knew Ash had her throat slit, and her arm pulled from the socket.

She watched as the Threg's massive green hands carved away the flesh and muscle from her lover's arm, and fashioned the bone into a dagger. Rel awoke with a start. She sat up quickly and rubbed her eyes. She was breathing heavily, it had all felt real. But thankfully, the nightmare was just that: a nightmare and nothing more.

Rel turned her gaze to her partner, he was standing, his hood raised, with a pale finger pointed to the east.

"Um. Rel?" he said shakily.

"What is it?" she said rising to her feet.

"Is it just me, or is that smoke a lot closer than it was yesterday?"

Rel turned her gaze to where her partner was pointing, and sure enough, the smoke had moved: it was no more than a kilometre away. The Thregs had covered nearly as much distance as they did, in seemingly half the time.

"Nef. Let's go. Now."

With that, the two striders took off towards the natural stone wall that protected Valenfaar.

By the time the sun had reached its peak, Nef and Rel were already coming upon the entrance to Valen's Passage. A natural valley, six kilometres in length, that worked as a natural passageway from the Endless Plains to Plainsview. The striders arrived at the mouth of the valley, out of breath and covered in sweat.

"Rel," Nef huffed, "Rel, I think we can slow down now. We covered a lot of ground. Let's walk the valley; enjoy it while we can."

"You know I don't like to be late, Nef." she retorted.

"Late?!" he said exhausted. "We covered a day's worth of travel in a quarter that time. It should be nightfall by now, but it's hardly Sun's Peak! We couldn't be late if we tried."

Rel slowed her pace to a march, she looked over her shoulder to her tired partner. "Fair point," she admitted. "Alright, we'll slow down. But if those Thregs come sniffing up our asses, it's on you."

"Noted," Nef said between breaths.

The two of them walked through the valley at a more leisurely pace than they had at the mouth. The large dirt road they travelled weaved between large boulders, trees, and the occasional pond. Here, unlike the plains, the grass was green, with the large white trunks of birch trees breaching the ground and reaching for the clouds.

The base of the mountains were gradual slopes covered in mud and sediment, before jutting straight into the air as if a wall of stone. Following the wall upwards, a passerby could see, through the treetops, white, snow-capped peaks piercing the world like spears, trying to reach the stars themselves.

The pale birch trees began to fade from sight and give way to darker, and thicker ash trees as they began to wade into the swamplands. Past the valley mouth, the swamplands began, a result of heavy rainfall hundreds of cycles ago that washed mud and soil from the mountains and into this particular branch of the passage, creating the bog, and giving life to a smaller ecosystem within the valley itself. It was here that insects and reptiles ran rampant, enjoying the humidity, and wetness the swamps had to offer. Rel hated it here, it threw her hair into tatters every time she made the journey.

The Plain's Master reached up under her hood and felt her hair, it was beginning to frizz.

Great. She thought.

She wanted to look her best when she saw Ash after her patrol, and she hated it when she had to do her hair at the barracks before seeing her: it took too much time. But to her, Ashlin was worth it.

Moisture began to well in Rel's boots, she grimaced at the feeling as her toes squished through the muddy waters. She hated wet feet; the swamps were the one part of her patrols that she absolutely hated, and it showed no signs of getting any better. It was wet, dank, humid, and smelled awful. Nothing like the dry air of the plains that she had grown all too fond of.

An insect buzzed near Rel's ear, she swatted it away. But not soon after, the buzzing returned in her other ear, and again she swatted. This continued for some time until finally, Nef's hand shot out and he grabbed the cretin, crushing it in his fist.

"I never could understand why you don't just kill these things. Gwendall knows you have the reflexes to catch them."

"They serve a purpose in these forsaken swamps. Though annoying, they do something to keep things survivable here."

"You may be right. But I doubt they'll miss one here or there." Nef wiped his hand on his trousers, leaving a smear of red on the fabric.

Rel looked over at him as he cleaned his hand. "That all depends on the one you kill."

"True enough," he said, still focused on his hand.

More time passed, and the sun moved wistfully in the sky, until finally, they crossed the swamps, and made their way through some hills and fields. There was room for several small towns to be founded, but the Highfolds had traditionally left it as natural as possible, to show the vast diversity of lands that their country had to offer to its visitors.

Finally, the wooden walls of Plainsview greeted the two striders, sixty metres tall, and made of dark oak. The walls stood strong and were constantly repaired to keep their town looking as presentable, and protected, as possible.

It was often argued why the entrance to Valenfaar was protected with wooden walls and not stone, like the Central Cities. The answer was simple to anyone that knew the lay of the land. To the west, towards the centre of Valenfaar, stood myriads of small mountains, with pathways worming their way throughout, high and low. The nearest quarry for mining the stone needed to build suitable walls, laid beyond these mountain passes, and made the journey too difficult for anyone trying to cart stone to Plainsview. It had been attempted, but each attempt was met with failure and loss of life.

"Halt! Who approaches?!" a voice called from atop the wall.

Nef stepped forward. "I am Plain's Strider Nef, and this is Plain's Master Rel. We are returning from the plains, and carry urgent news to be delivered to Saffron with all haste!"

"What kind of news?" the voice asked.

"News too important for the likes of you," Rel replied, removing her hood.

The silhouette of a man poked his head out over the wall and took a look at the woman.

"Alright, Rel. Whatever you say." The head disappeared. "Hey, you there! Yeah, you! Open the damn gate!"

The large wooden doors creaked open on their hinges, revealing the town of Plainsview on the other side.

"Good to be home," Nef said as he did after every range.

"That it is, Nef. That it is." Rel agreed.

The two striders walked through the large wooden gate and into one of the several smaller squares of Plainsview. It was here, in this very square, just before Valen's Passage, that every Plain's Strider graduated from Trainee, and where at every day, the striders would meet before deployment, to pray to their gods, and say goodbye to their families. Every venture into the plains could be life-threatening. Plenty of bandits and outlaws made the fields their homes, as would the occasional predator, though these were rare.

The area of Plainsview they entered was known as "Valley's Gate." The name was simple and to the point. This was a staple of the striders, all their names were kept short in the field, to keep things quick, cohesive, and sharp. Even Saffron had his name shortened to Saff, when out on duty. It was a happy coincidence, however, that Rel's name was naturally short, picked by her parents. She had been told her name meant "Blade of the Goddess." Though she wasn't sure if she believed that or not, as Esmirla was a mage, and wasn't known for carrying a blade. Regardless, the meaning-filled Rel with a sense of pride, as if she were meant for a higher purpose in life. Time would tell she supposed, as it did all things.

Quickly, Nef and the Plain's Master moved through the endless streets of Plainsview, towards the central square. It was there, ahead of them, a gigantic willow tree, with vines of white-green leaves reaching towards the soft dirt. The tree's bark was a soft, almost magical grey. Its roots were hidden under a simple stone ring, bordering the centrepiece as if it were a painting in need of a frame.

Rel glanced quickly at the tree, it stretched higher into the sky than most buildings in town, and much taller than that of any other willow tree she had ever seen. Rel liked to think it was for this reason Plainsview was founded. It was a remarkably large town after all, so it only made sense to her that it would have been founded around a remarkably large tree.

On the northern side of the central square, sat a wooden longhouse, cloaks of green and yellow stretched along its walls, much like flags. The building looked remarkably normal, save for the garbs used to decorate it. This was where the striders operated, a simple wooden longhouse, with a large courtyard in the rear of the building for training. Rel had asked Saffron why the striders kept such simple accommodations and didn't try to show their status with something a little more grandiose.

The warden's answers always came back the same: "Our true home is out there in the plains, Rel. That is where we show our status. No one knows those fields as we do, and no one has been able to survive out there as long as we have. You best remember that."

Once again, and much to Rel's disappointment, Saffron had been right. Most people baulked at the fact the striders were able to stay in the plains several moons at a time, no one seemed to care about their longhouse, it was always about the Endless Plains and the sheer amount of unknown that could be waiting at any moment in the fields of yellow-gold grass.

Nef walked up to the longhouse first and pushed open the door. Within was a rather simple wooden room with paintings of the plains hoisted up along each of the four walls, a simple wooden bench below them, allowing visitors a place to rest and wait if they were coming to visit. Two doors stood along the northern wall, Nef walked up to one and knocked. It opened with a crack, and a small brown eye peered through at them.

"Names?" the voice said.

"Rel, and Nef," Rel replied.

The door opened further, revealing the short, slender form of Kol, his dirty blond hair a frazzled mess as if he had just gotten out of bed. "Good to see you two," he said, looking up at Nef and Rel. "You're back earlier than I expected though."

Nef opened his mouth to say something, but Rel cut him off. "Yes. Urgent news for the warden. Is he here?"

"When isn't he here? Don't think he's too busy right now though. Want me to check?"

"Yes."

Kol left the two striders in the smaller room for a few moments. It was here where the portraits of all the former Plain's Wardens hung, from Keetlyn the First, all the way to Saffron, the current warden. It had always been a silent dream of Rel's, that one day she would see her own portrait hung on the wall. But once again, only time would be able to tell if that dream would come to fruition.

Footsteps vibrated along the floor, and Kol entered back into the room from beyond. "Alright, Saff is ready for ya. Head on in."

Rel and Nef paced through the myriad of corridors and rooms that paved their way to the warden's office. The longhouse was much larger than it appeared from the outside, but only the striders would be the ones to know that particular detail, as they were the only ones permitted past the first room.

Finally, a large door with a metal ring for a handle presented itself to them, Rel reached out, grabbed the ring and pulled. The door creaked with age as she opened it, Nef stepped through first, then herself.

"Rel, Nef," a guttural voice greeted them. "I hear you have news for me?"

Saffron, the Plain's Warden, the figurehead, and leader for the Plain's Striders sat behind his desk, quill in hand, scribbling onto a piece of parchment, regularly dipping it in the nearby inkwell to refresh it.

The warden wasn't an attractive man, his skin was boiled red in colour; a side effect of spending most of his natural life under the sun of the plains, where most people would have tanned, bronzed, or darkened, his skin burned. His hair was a ring of incredibly thin long hair, reaching down past his shoulders in bedraggled clumps. His cheeks were jowls, hung loosely on his face, pulling the skin down from his large, dark eyes. To top it all off, Saffron looked as if he had been perpetually sweating; because of this, and his various other features, many people took to calling him Saffron the Squid, as he looked much like a squid fresh out of the water. The warden didn't like this name and forbade the striders from using it.

"Yes, sir. We do." Rel said calmly.

The warden looked up, his large eyes darting back and forth between the two striders. "Please, take a seat." some spittle flew from his mouth and rested on the desk.

Nef moved forward first and sat down. He leaned back comfortably as Rel took her seat next to him.

"Well," Saffron said. "You're back early. I'm assuming there is good reason for this."

"Yes, sir, there is: we came across a Threg camp in the plains. A little more than a day's walk from here. No more than three or four of them living there, by my best guess."

"Thregs?" The warden looked confused. "Surely you jest?"

"No, sir, she does not. We saw them just before we left." Nef confirmed. "Definitely Thregs."

"And you are certain? You saw them with your own eyes?" The warden put down his quill and leaned back in his chair, arms crossed.

"Well, somewhat sir," Rel said, leaning forward, her elbows on the desk. "We were low, and the sun blocked out most of their features. But they were definitely Thregs. I've never seen a man that tall, never mind several of them together at once."

Saffron separated his arms and put his palms on the table. "So you saw silhouettes? Is that right?"

"Yes, sir," she said. "But I have no doubt in my mind. The camp was made of human flesh and several sizes of bones. There isn't anything else alive in all of Valenfaar that uses those kinds of materials for tools."

Saffron closed his eyes, and let out a long, deep breath. "Rel. If you weren't my Right Hand; if this had been anyone else telling me these things. I'd have them sent to the magister immediately to be examined. But it is you I'm hearing these things from. It is you, that is telling me there are Thregs in the plains. For the first time in recorded history." He opened his eyes and looked at her. "I'll give you four more striders, take them into the plains at first light, find those Thregs, and end their lives. Then, look for more camps, but do not engage. My best guess would be the ones you had seen are the closest to the Halo, and thus, the biggest threat. Are we clear Plain's Master?"

"Like the skies over the plains, sir," Rel responded confidently.

"Good. Now get some rest. You leave at first light, remember. Go. Both of you."

Nef and Rel rose from their chairs and left the room. By the time they were in the shade of the town's willow tree, Nef looked to the Plain's Master.

"See you at first light?"

"See you then, Nef." They nodded towards one another, then went their separate ways, heading home. Oh, how she wanted to see Ashlin.

Chapter 2

Ashlin toiled away over the small hearth in the middle of the home she and Rel had made theirs. As she stirred the small pot of elk stew, she couldn't help but wonder if Rel was safe. She loved Rel and knew that she was given the position of Plain's Master for a reason, none of the striders could match her skill in the field, or in combat, but Ashlin was still worried for her lover's safety, she couldn't help it. It was a bad habit of hers, but regardless, it probably would never change. The day she stopped worrying about anything, would be the day she died.

Ashlin made her way over to a small pewter bowl that sat just across from her, she retrieved it and came back to the pot. Taking the ladle, she scooped out some of the broth with browned chunks of meat inside, and splashed it into her bowl, grabbed a small spoon from nearby and ate a mouthful. The taste was rather bland: she had forgotten to add the usual black pepper.

"Oh well," she said to herself. "Can't be bothered now." She fed herself another mouthful.

Behind her, she could hear the front door creak open, she whirled her head around and set her eyes on Rel's slender figure. She swallowed hard, and dropped her bowl, spilling stew and meat onto the wooden floor.

"Rel," she gasped as she stood, "is everything alright?" Ashlin walked over to her lover and held her. "Why are you home so early?" She stood back, holding Rel by the shoulders. "Did something happen to Nef?"

"Ash. My darling. Please, calm down. Stop overthinking. Everything is fine... more or less."

Ashlin's head tilted to one side. "More or less?" She put her hands on her hips, thumbs forward.

"Yes," Rel leaned in and gave her a quick kiss on the lips. "Nef and I are fine. Nobody is dead, and nobody is injured. We had to get back quickly, to report to Saffron."

"When you and Nef are out there and need to get back quickly, there is usually something wrong. What was it?"

"Ashlin, love, please calm down." Rel picked up the pewter bowl and the spoon from the floor. "We found a Threg camp. First time in our history one has been spotted outside the Halo. They didn't even know we were there."

Ashlin's eyes shot open. "Rel, Thregs? You know what those things are capable of. You've heard the stories."

"Yes. But they're just stories. We think there were four. Six of us will be leaving tomorrow to deal with them. Nef will be with me. It'll be fine."

"You're going back out in the plains tomorrow? When?"

"First Light," Rel said with a sigh.

Ashlin wore a look of anger and annoyance. "I don't like this."

"You don't have to."

"Excuse me?" Ashlin's eyes lit up with fire.

"Sweetheart, I love you. I don't like this either. But Saffron gave the order, I don't have a choice. Besides, I need to protect you, keep you safe, and if Thregs are looking to poke around in Plainsview, I need to help stop them. You would do the same in my position, and you know that."

Rel was right, Ashlin would do the same thing, she probably would have left the instant Saffron had given the order, get the job done sooner, and make sure Rel was safe. It pained her to see Rel take the dangerous jobs while she worked the market, and kept things liveable. She wouldn't be able to change that though, it was the way their lives had worked out. Rel was recruited to be a strider when she was very young, cycles before the two of them had ever met. And Ashlin herself had been a merchant's daughter before she lived in Plainsview. It was the way their lives had worked out, Rel was a warrior, and Ashlin, well, she was a vegetable and meat merchant, working for the shops around town, helping to spread their business and earn them some more coin.

"You know you're wrong when you're right," Ashlin said with a defeated grin on her face.

Rel laughed.

Oh, how she loved the sound of that laugh.

"And I'm wrong when you're wrong too, my dear." Rel placed the pewter bowl down on the dining room table. "Now come here, my love. I've missed you, and I'm only here for the night." The Plain's Master held her arms out wide.

Ashlin walked over and embraced her lover, holding her tightly. She took a deep breath in, and let the smell of her flood her senses. She exhaled, then looked up.

"I love you," Rel said, beating her to the line.

Ashlin grinned. "I love you too." She gave Rel a quick kiss. "How long will you be gone this time?" she asked reluctantly, not entirely sure if she wanted to know the answer.

Rel paused for a moment and chewed her lip. "If we're lucky, half a fortnight. If we're not, a full fortnight. We need to clear the camp we found, then scout to see if there are any more."

Ashlin began to feel tears well in her eyes, she shook them away. "Please be careful, Rel. You've never dealt with a Threg before, have you?"

"No."

"Have any of the striders?"

"Not that I'm aware. If any of them have, it probably would have been Saffron. But he's not the same warrior he once was. Still commendable to be sure, but not nearly as agile."

Ashlin sighed again. "I don't like this Rel." She looked to the floor, then back up at the beautiful face above her. "Can you promise me something?"

Rel looked at her, with sincerity and concern. "That depends on what it is."

"Promise me you'll come back home safe. I don't want to lose you."

"My love, I can't promise that," She paused then added: "But I can certainly promise you I'll try." She grinned and gave her another kiss. "Now, you forgot the black pepper in the stew again didn't you?"

Ashlin could feel her cheeks warm with blood as she blushed. "No."

Rel raised an eyebrow.

"Maybe," She grinned widely, showing her teeth playfully before laughing.

"You bloody fool," Rel said with a grin. "You know it's no good, without the damn pepper!"

"I'm sorry."

"No, you're not. There's nothing to be sorry for." The strider gave her another quick kiss before moving through cupboards. "And you probably weren't going to add any once you realized, were you?" She held out a small wooden container, with a dark letter "P" burned into it.

Ashlin shrugged, playing dumb. She knew Rel loved it when she did this.

The Plain's Master walked over to the pot, opened the small wooden container, and took out a pinch of black pepper. She sprinkled it into the stew, then repeated the process a couple more times.

"Think that's enough?" Rel asked.

"Guess we'll have to try it and see!"

They grabbed another couple of pewter bowls and wooden spoons. Once they had sat down on the floor next to the hearth, Ashlin scooped out the meat and broth and placed it into their bowls for them. They both took a bite and scrunched up their faces. They inhaled through their noses sharply, fighting back the urge to sneeze.

With a hard swallow, Rel blurted: "Too much pepper! Too much pepper!" She waved her hand in front of her face, squinting.

Ashlin swallowed then laughed, her lover joined in the uproar.

"Let's find something else to add to this shall we?" The strider rose from her seat and began rifling through the cupboards again.

Ashlin stayed where she sat and just watched her. The memories they had together floated through her mind as she gazed upon Rel. She traced her figure with her eyes, from her dark, straight black hair, to her strong shoulders, petite bosom and slender waist. Rel's buttocks were round and firm, and her legs long and strong. Ashlin bit her lip as a playful thought came through her mind.

And tonight my dear Rel. I'm going to have my way with you for as long as I can handle.

Chapter 3

First Light came faster than Rel had anticipated, the night before was taken up with much less sleep than she would have thought. She and Ashlin had been rather "appreciative" of each other's company and made sure that their time had not been wasted.

Though she hadn't slept as much as planned, Rel still felt refreshed, as she often did when leaving home to go to the plains. As much as she loved being at home, and spending time with Ashlin, Rel had been in and out of the plains more times than she could count. Ever since she was a young girl, even before she was recruited into the striders by Saffron, she would wander out into the plains against her father's wishes and run through the tall grass, oftentimes pretending she was an elk, or a wolf, or a Plains Strider.

It was funny to her, thinking about how she would pretend to be a strider, and how she was next in line for Plain's Warden. It made her happy to think of things that way, a dream that she had since she was a child, coming true in every way. Not many people had stories like that, but she did.

The Plain's Master stood in front of Valley's Gate with her bow slung over her back, the flat quiver of arrows tucked under her cloak, her long knife and short sword sheathed on her hips. A couple of the men and women of the striders would customize their gear, or use pieces passed down from their mentors, or family. But Rel liked to keep things simple: the standard-issue gear was well crafted and held its sharpness just fine. It felt right to her. Would a day come when she used a more personal tool? Maybe, but she had yet to see that day even start approaching.

With her back to the gate, Rel looked out over the square in the early morning light, there wouldn't be too many people out this time of day, the farmers on the western side, they would already be in the fields, but as for the merchants and common folk, it was unlikely.

A single figure strode out from the compact building towards the centre of the village. A familiar figure, hood pulled over their eyes, and their yellow-gold cloak flapping behind them. Nef pulled his hood down when he saw Rel.

"Rel! Figured you'd be here first," he called from across the square, "don't you ever sleep?"

Rel waited for him to get closer before responding, once he was five paces in front of her, she smiled. "On occasion. Though it's hard when I know I have to look at that nose of yours in the morning."

Nef laughed. They would joke about the crookedness of his nose. Rel had broken it in a sparring match long ago. At the time, Nef felt as if he were lacking in hand-to-hand, compared to the other striders, so Rel had offered to tutor him late at night, when no one was around. On their third session, Nef had misread a feint, failed to move his head out of the way, not expecting Rel's knuckles to make contact. They did, and his nose paid the price for it. Even through the pain, Nef still found the strength to laugh at himself, and how stupid of a mistake he had made. He made an assumption and would be reminded of it by the woman who gave it to him.

"One day I'll get you back," he said with a mischievous grin. "Just you wait."

Rel laughed. "That'll be the day I *let* you, Nef. So, are you ready for this?"

"Yes ma'am," the strider said. "And yourself?"

"Of course."

Each strider was to prepare themselves for every range. Ensuring they had enough food and water to last them a couple of days before needing to search for more. Because of the nature of the plains, finding elk, wolf, or other food could be difficult. As such, each strider had conditioned their body to function off of as little food as possible, oftentimes pushing the boundaries of starvation, and only carrying small stores of salted meat with a sheepskin sack of water.

The striders travelled lightly, they were the most acrobatic soldiers in all of Valenfaar, and as such, travelled with very little. They were to move quickly, in and out of the grass without being seen, and if they were seen, to make that sight no longer than a blink. In and out, fast as the wind and blend back into the plains from whence they came.

Many common folk were often heard spreading tales of how the striders were born of the plains and of Esmirla, and that they could transform themselves into the golden stalks on a whim, to blend into the scenery. These were all lies, of course, the striders were human, just like anybody else, they were just talented at their jobs.

"Kol should be here soon," Nef said. "Hopefully with the others. We should be out the gate by now."

"Agreed," Rel said flatly. "Though Kol always was one to sleep in. Lazy turd he is."

The other strider snorted in amusement, then brought his gaze up. "Ah, there he is."

Rel looked forward to where her friend was staring, sure enough, there was Kol, with three other striders behind him. All of them donned their hoods and cloaks, bows strung over their backs, quivers tucked under the cloak, and blades at their sides. They were ready, late to depart, but they were ready.

Kol strode up to the two striders, a grin on his face. "Well good morning to you, fine folk. Sleep good?"

"Let's go," Rel said coolly. "We're already late."

She turned and called to the men atop Valley's Gate. "Alright, open up, we're leaving!"

A brief nod, followed by the creaking of wood, gave the affirmation that her order had been understood.

"Plain's Striders, move out. We'll go over the rest of the details in the Valley."

They all nodded silently, with the exception of Kol. "I'll take that as a yes, I suppose," he muttered audibly, flicking a strand of dirty blond hair from his eyes.

Rel grinned. Kol was considered her Left Hand, and Nef her Right, but that hadn't stopped her from giving them a hard time when they needed it, it was the feeling of comradery that she shared with her men that made them appreciate her as both an officer and a friend. It was something that they had come to reciprocate, chastising each other for mistakes in the field, wounding each other during training, or just making fun of each other in general. They were soldiers and they had a duty to do, but they would make sure to have fun when they could, keep things alive, and keep things feeling right in the world, even when nothing seemed to be.

The half dozen scouts marched through the gate, and with a low creak, it closed behind them.

"Alright," Rel said. "What did Saffron tell you?"

A fair-skinned woman named Hera, towards the rear of the group spoke up. "Saff told us we 'sposed to be huntin' Thregs. That right?" her northern accent was thick.

Nef nodded. "That's right. Rel and I found a Threg camp, by now, we suspect it should be within the day's march. Located not far out of the Valley."

"M'kay," Hera said. "Anythin' else we should know 'bout?"

The Plain's Master turned to look at Hera. "Once the camp is cleared, we're to fan out and look for more. Not to engage, only scout. Are we clear?"

"Yes'm." she agreed.

Silence greeted the striders as they marched from grass to swamp, and back to grass again. Kol had cursed through the swamplands as insects fluttered around him, like vultures to a corpse. Rel's Left Hand hated insects, this she knew, as time and time again the young man would complain endlessly about the small critters. How they were always buzzing, never accomplishing anything but annoyance. From one ear to the next, they would hover, constantly leaving the poor man swatting at them. There had been one positive side to Kol's relationship with the insects: he kept them away from everyone else.

The mouth of Valen's Passage opened to them widely, revealing the golden sea of tall grass ahead of them. A single plume of dull grey smoke rose in the distance, stretching into the sky as if reaching for the clouds. The pillar looked nearly identical to the one from the previous day, but this time it was closer. Not the quick leap the Thregs had made before, a much smaller move. But a move closer to the passage regardless.

Thregs were vile creatures, using flesh and bones from anything they could kill to make their tools and wares. This wouldn't be so bad normally, as humans do much the same. But the Thregs preferred to use humans more than anything else. It was rare, or so she was told, to see Thregs using wolf pelts, or bones for their tools, or even elk and spraven. Why they preferred humans, Rel hadn't the slightest clue, she had only ever seen Thregs once, the rest of her knowledge resided in the rumours and ramblings of tavern drunks.

"You thinking what I am?" Nef said, turning to face her.

"That they're closer?"

The man nodded, his neatly kept brown hair starting to dampen with sweat from the early summer sun. "Yeah. Not good."

"Agreed," The Plain's Master turned to her striders. "Alright everyone, they are a quarter day's march from here. We move fast, and we move low, stay within earshot of each other, but do not be seen. If we can't see each other out there, nothing else can see us either. Are we clear?"

Everyone nodded.

"Good. Move out."

With that, everyone lifted their yellow-gold hoods, crouched low and began to move through the strands of grass, letting their bodies meld with the scenery, melting and weaving between the stalks like wind and water. This was their home, not their shacks back in Plainsview, but the grass in which they ventured day after day. The plains were as much a part of them, as the blade was a part of a sword. And it would be from these Plains, that they would strike, to defend the Valen people from those who would wish it harm.

Rel moved quickly and quietly, feeling the soft press of dirt beneath every footfall, the tall grass moved and slid around her body with every movement. If she strained her hearing, she could make out the faint plodding and rustling of her fellow striders nearby. By her best guess, they were only a quarter of the way there. Soon, she would halt her movement, and listen for the others to do the same.

Moving quickly and quietly through the grass was a great benefit of their training, but it still took a toll on their bodies, even after cycles of training and practice. If they pushed themselves too long, and too hard, their bodies would give out in a fight, making it hard to stand. And that wasn't great for their life expectancy, a small break every now and again did a lot for the body and mind, allowed them the opportunity to regroup and recover, and that was good for their life expectancy.

Once they were halfway to the spire of smoke, Rel felt the burning in her legs telling her to stop for a few moments. She slowed her pace and strained her hearing. She heard the pacing of the others begin to slow as well. Gradually the Plain's Master came to a halt and knelt in the dirt, she heard the others stop their momentum. They were moving in a large line, a wave through an ocean of gold. Rel had entered the grass first, and therefore, would be the furthest on the left, with Nef on her right, and Kol on his. The line would continue travelling this way until they had surrounded the encampment that was their target.

A few long moments passed by, and Rel began to move forward again, waiting to hear the soft rustling of Nef, not far off. Sure enough, he had taken the signal and began moving as well. She picked up the pace, and before long, they were back to moving at full speed. The spire grew thicker with every step.

All around her, Rel watched as the reeds of grass whizzed past, with small webbed patches of Dead Man's Root sprawling along the dirt. The Root wasn't actually a root at all, it was a type of fungus, but it was named as such due to its appearance. It was thick and reached into the dirt like the roots of some unseen tree. It was light turquoise in colour, and a lot of smugglers and traders would harvest the fungus whilst traversing the plains, and sell it for obscene prices back in town. Dead Man's Root was a narcotic, and a heavy one at that. It had been given the former part of its name because most men who used the drug died from an overdose.

It always started the same, chewing the root, letting the blue-green slime coat their tongue, and foam from their lips. It didn't take long for men and women to add the Root to their meals, mead, and ale, for a quick high. This was the deadly part: once Dead Man's Root was mixed with alcohol, its effects and potency multiplied horrendously. Almost always causing an overdose, and causing the user to suffer a seizure, and heart attack simultaneously. It was incredibly rare that anyone had survived the ordeal. Most of the time, if someone had survived, they would be left partially brain dead, a shell of their former self. Out of every hundred men and women that would overdose, maybe six of them would survive, and maybe one of those would still be able to live a normal life afterwards.

Rel hated the Root, she had witnessed many good men fall victim to its vices, and throw their life and money away, chasing a turquoise fungus that promised them a temporary escape from the horrors of the world. But those men had always become too greedy, wanting that temporary release to be permanent, to forget all the pain and suffering. She supposed, that in a way, they had gotten what they wanted, it was too bad they weren't alive to enjoy it.

A few more breaks, and countless steps later, Rel and the others approached the border of the camp. Beyond the grass, the sounds of chewing and grunting filled the dry air, the inhuman sounds sent a jolt up Rel's spine. They all kept quiet, and the Plain's Master could envision with her mind's eyes, where her soldiers were situated around the camp. Rel positioned herself carefully and peered through two stalks of grass.

Sitting on the ground, near the central campfire, sat four Thregs. Their skin was green and covered in scales, not much unlike an alligator, or crocodile. The hair that sat atop their head, was thin, long strands of black, that fell down to the shoulders. Their faces looked to be the worst part: the eyes were large and dark, sitting above a long wide nose, with four vertical slits along the bridge. Rel assumed these slits were nostrils. When the Thregs opened their mouths to eat, they revealed large yellow, and brown teeth, rotted and misshapen. Their tongues licking at the meat in their hands between each bite.

The tongues were the strangest parts of their bodies: they didn't have anything that resembled normalcy, instead, it was a bundle of thick black strands, almost like hair that lashed outwards with each bite. The sight caused Rel to shiver. The Thregs were awful. One stood, and the sheer height of the creature put a lump into Rel's throat. It easily stood seven feet tall, its arms and legs long and lanky, but still bristling with muscle. She had noticed that they weren't wearing many clothes, a simple torn cloth wrapped around the waist, hiding what she assumed to be genitals.

Reality snapped back to her. The rest of the squad would be waiting for her to start the attack. By now, they would have all taken up their positions for an ambush, waiting for Rel to take the first shot before moving in. The Plain's Master unslung the bow from her back and moved her cloak to clear her quiver. She had a dozen arrows. She didn't plan on using them all, she preferred her blades more than her bow, but still, a dozen arrows weren't many, she would have to make her shot count.

Reaching over her shoulder, Rel grabbed the first arrow and nocked it on her bowstring, she raised the weapon from where she was crouched, letting the arrowhead breach the grass. She looked carefully and saw another arrow, on the opposite side of the camp do the same. Rel grinned at the cohesion her striders held in the field.

The Plain's Master pulled back her bowstring, the recurve bow bent and curled under the pressure, but never creaked. She kept her tools in good working order. The bow raised slightly, she aimed for the neck of the standing Threg. Taking a deep breath, Rel released. The arrow shot out the grass and whipped through the air. It impacted the Threg's neck with a low thud. Another arrow shot from the opposite side of the camp dug into the shoulder of one of the three sitting Thregs. A miss, the shot didn't make its mark.

The three Thregs stood, rage filling their eyes, swords and clubs of bone in their hands. The Threg Rel had shot still stood, it reached its massive hand up to the arrow, gripped the shaft with gnarled fingers, and yanked it free. It threw it to the ground and looked at the ebony woman. Her eyes widened as she nocked another arrow. She pulled and released. The arrow caught the Threg in the chest, and again, the creature pulled it out and tossed it to the dirt.

Rel let loose a sharp whistle, and like lions stalking their prey, the striders erupted from the grass, drawing their long knives and short swords. The Plain's Master tossed her bow to the side, drew her weapons and moved with speed towards her target. She closed in fast, letting her powerful legs throw her forward with each step. The Threg looked her over, and with an angry scowl, swung the bone sword in its hand. Rel ducked, and sidestepped, avoiding the first swing. In her right hand, she swung her own sword, trying to cleave into the green scales of the Threg's stomach. The creature twisted slightly, avoiding the cut.

Turning to face her opponent, Rel readied herself, her long knife held in a reverse grip in her left hand, sword held upright in her right. She waited. The Threg stepped closer and swung at an angle. Rel twisted and avoided the blow. The creature swung again, from the opposite side this time, and again, the woman avoided the cut. This continued for a dozen heartbeats before Rel found her opening.

The next swing cut horizontally, from left to right. Rel twisted past the blow and brought her dagger down, piercing the scaled skin of her target's sword arm. Much to her regret, however, the Threg didn't drop its weapon. Instead, it turned its head to stare at her. Its mouth opened wide as it snarled, the strands of its tongue splaying saliva and spittle into her face. Rel saw something move, its other hand began to rise up, clenched in a fist, looking to find a target.

The Threg began to turn, its fist starting to gain momentum. Rel braced herself for the impact. But much to her relief, the Threg's body snapped around the opposite direction, an arrow jutting out from its left shoulder. The beast looked to its new attacker: Kol stood, with his bow drawn, a sly grin on his face.

"Fuck off, you scaly cunt!" he yelled.

Rel's eyes opened wide. "Kol! Behind you!"

The dirty blond man looked over his shoulder, just in time to avoid a club to the skull. He ducked, threw down his bow and drew his blades.

Rel turned and focused on her own foe. She pulled the knife out of the Threg's arm and swept up behind the creature, letting her agility carry her momentum. She stabbed her knife into her foe's back, and pulled down, trying to split the Threg open. The skin was too thick. The weapon didn't budge. She wasn't strong enough.

She had an idea: using all her strength, Rel hoisted herself up, using the knife like a climbing hook. Throwing her sword to the ground, the Plain's Master jumped as she pulled, launching her body into the air. She removed the weapon on the ascent and at the apex of her leap, Rel brought the blade over her head. As she fell, the Threg turned to face her, a look of amusement in its gaze. The long knife plunged between the eyes of the seven-foot-tall monster, splattering the Plain's Master with dark black blood. The body fell to the ground, Rel on top of it, breathing heavily. She took a moment to look around, to finally see how the others were faring.

Nef was struggling with his foe, deflecting what little blows he could, and countering when timing allowed. The Threg had several cuts on its body, all oozing thick blood. Though her Right Hand was struggling, it looked as if the man would win his duel.

Hera was looking in not as great a position. Her hood had fallen, and her hair was soaked through with sweat, she moved raggedly away from the club her opponent wielded. Cutting each dodge too close for comfort. One of the others had noticed this and came to help. The strider moved with grace and launched himself into a slide, cutting at the Threg's legs as he slid. The beast dropped its club into the ground. There was a loud shriek as the strider's legs were crushed beneath the weapon, then his knee, his hip, and his chest. The

Threg had beaten the man like they were tenderizing a steak.

Hera's eyes opened in a frenzy, and she sprinted towards the killer. The creature's eyes rose with its club, catching the woman in the chest. The thin leather armour she wore did nothing to protect her. Rel watched as Hera's chest sank inwards, and blood spewed from her wheezing mouth.

The Plain's Master removed her knife from the Threg that lay beneath her, she grabbed her short sword from the dirt and ran towards the monster that killed two of her striders. As she ran, she could see Kol and the other strider working together to take down a Threg. They moved with skill, both lashing out with their weapons at the tower of an enemy. The Threg fell in sync with Nef's own target but not before Kol's partner took a club to the back of the head.

One left. Rel thought to herself.

The Threg turned to face her and swung its club, Rel dropped and slid along the ground, raking her knife and sword at the inside of the Threg's legs. Black blood spewed out as she slid, bathing her in gore. The Threg tumbled. Rel turned sharply and launched herself to her feet. In three quick steps, she was over the top of her enemy before it could roll over to face her. With a grunt, the Plain's Master thrust the tip of her short sword into the Threg's skull.

The battle was over, Hera and the other two striders were dead. Half her squad. Leaving only herself, Nef, and Kol.

"Fuck!" Kol yelled, "By Gwendall's Blade, what the fuck was that?!"

Nef stood, his eyes glazed over, staring at Hera's body. "They were vicious. I've never seen anything like it." He wiped spit and sweat from his mouth.

Rel didn't know what to say; there wasn't anything she could say that they weren't already thinking themselves. None of them had faced Thregs before. It took the three best striders in Valenfaar, and three others, to kill... what? Four Thregs? If there were more in the plains, Saffron would have to call on Alistair Highfold for aid. It would be more than they could handle, that much she knew for certain.

Kol walked over to Rel and put a hand on her shoulder. "Rel, what are your orders?"

"We scout for other camps. From now until Moon's Peak, in five days. Then we meet back here, and head home." she said while shaking her head.

Nef snapped back to attention. "We're continuing with the mission? Are you crazy?!"

"Nef, listen," the Plain's Master said.

"No, this is ridiculous. You saw what those things were capable of. We're dead if we find more!"

"We are not to engage. We don't even need to get close, Nef," she replied flatly. "We look for more smoke. If we see it, we report it. No need to get any closer."

"They'll still kill us, you know. If not today, then by the end of the summer. Who in the depths of the Soul Spire is Saffron going to get out here for help?"

"Look Nef, I don't know. But if we turn tail now, and retreat back to Plainsview, and more of those things are out there, we need to know. We need to tell Saffron. Those things could rampage through Plainsview with a quarter of the town guard's number. And you know that as well as I do." Rel turned and focused her brown eyes on her friend.

"You know she's right, Nef," Kol said reluctantly. "And I'm not happy to say that."

Nef raised his head and looked at the two of them. "Fuck," He shook his head. "Alright, Let's get moving then."

Chapter 4

Standing atop the white walls of Valen in the midday sun, Alistair Highfold looked to the ever-expanding horizon of green grass and trees. He was lost in thought, letting the sun bathe him in warm light. He enjoyed it atop the walls, letting the wind blow his problems away, for a few fleeting moments at least.

Alistair Highfold was Valenfaar's Arch General. The chief of military and tactics in the country. Every armed soldier, guard and otherwise, was under his command, with one small exception: his brother Varen, and his own elite unit of men were out of Alistair's reach: the Sword of Magus. The unit was an oddball group, but they yielded results quickly and efficiently, oftentimes working to support Alistair's own men.

Valenfaar had been living peacefully for many cycles, the rebels that rose due to lack of protection had been quelled, and existed as small camps of bandits who were more likely to die of starvation than in combat. Alistair had seen to that himself: he founded a volunteer unit that would work to a suicidal extent to exterminate them. He had made it very clear that the Sanguine Aegis was a suicide unit. Much to his surprise, the unit excelled in the field. The men who volunteered for the duty were relentless, they had the rebels take everything from them, family included and showed them no quarter in return.

One man had risen to prominence within that group, his anger becoming the bane of the rebel's very existence: Garridan Lethar. An older and talented soldier, he had served the Guard longer than most men would ever live, but he had been ruthless during the rebellion, killing surrendering rebels, prisoners, and occasionally his own men. Had he not been part of the suicide unit, Alistair would have had him tried for war crimes. But the man was of more use to him alive, and there was something in his gut that told the Arch General he would be needing him again.

The sound of hurried footsteps on stone forced Alistair to turn around. A messenger in light leather and green cloth jogged over.

"At ease!" Alistair called.

The younger man relaxed and walked the rest of the way. "Message for you, sire," he said between huffs of breath.

"From who?"

"Plain's Warden, Saffron, sire. From Plainsview."

Alistair raised a blond eyebrow, *What does the old Squid want?*

"Do you have the parchment with you?"

The messenger had regained his breath. He shook his head. "No, sire. It's back at the Keep. Your father told me to leave it there, anything from Saffron could be important. That's what he told me, sire."

"Very well," the Highfold chewed his lip for a moment. "Where is my brother?"

"Which one, sire?"

"Varen," Alistair started to walk towards one of the many lifts lining Valen's southern wall, he motioned for the messenger to follow.

"He should be at the Grand Church. Attending to his duties, sire."

"Good. Accompany me off the wall. Once we're on ground level, seek out my brother and tell him to see me in the war room, if it isn't too much trouble."

"No trouble at all, sire."

"I didn't mean you," Alistair gave the messenger an accusing look. "I meant my brother."

The other man blushed, his cheeks a rosy red. "Ah, my apologies, sire."

The two men stepped onto the wooden lift and pulled on a taut rope that ran parallel to the machine. The wood shuddered and creaked as the lift operators began to lower the platform.

Most of these devices lined the walls of the Central Cities, but most of them had small bells to signal when its occupants were ready to descend. Those walls were smaller though, usually by more than a quarter kilometre. Valen's walls stretched nearly a kilometre in height, so the usual bell that would have been used would have been difficult to hear, from the bottom. Instead, Valen's lifts used a taut rope, connected to a bell at the bottom instead of the top. When the occupants pulled the rope, it rang the bell at the bottom, signalling the operators that someone was waiting to come down. It was a simple workaround, and Alistair was happy for this, as was his sister, for it was cheap to fix, and promised not to invade Valenfaar's coffers.

With a low thump, the lift rested on the stone bricks of Valen. Both Alistair and the messenger vacated. The younger man broke into a jog in the direction of the Grand Church, whilst the Highfold wandered his way to the nearby stables. He found the small cluster of wooden buildings and asked the stable hand for his horse. Moments later, the tall brown stallion, clad in crimson-gold armour strode out with a march of pride. Alistair grinned at the beast and ran his hand along its neck. He mounted up with ease as his honour guard joined him atop their own mounts.

His honour guards were good men, meant to protect him on a battlefield, and in the streets, wherever the common rabble of the Valen people would be, and where they could possibly attack. Atop the walls of Valen he had not needed his honour guard, soldiers lined the walls, and the common folk were not permitted entrance, it was even difficult for a commoner to get within 100 meters of the wall without being descended on by guards. Down in the streets, however, commoners outnumbered the Sovereign Guard, and an assassin could be lying in wait in an alleyway or any street. Alistair's honour guard knew this, attempts had been made on his life, but none had succeeded.

The hooves of their horses sounded off the stone roads with a rhythmic glopping, signalling anyone who stood in their way to move. The looks Alistair would receive from the Valen people as he rode down the streets were often that of awe or wonder. He had been blessed with his mother's good looks, that much was true. But he accredited most of these looks of awe to the way he carried himself, the way his father had taught him. To look like a man with a purpose, and to walk a certain way: with his head held high, and his back straight; to bear a gaze of confidence and purpose everywhere he went. He liked to think he had mastered this appearance, to look like a man of importance, whether he was one or not. Thankfully, he was a man of importance, he was the military might of Valenfaar, and even his armour displayed that title.

The plates of gilded iron and scarlet cloth painted him as if he were Gwendall himself. He even wore a replica of the ceremonious scarlet cloak that the ancient deity had worn when he was alive. This was common for the Arch Generals of Valenfaar, his predecessor had worn a cloak of similar likeness, as had the one before him, and so on. The armour, his posture and his looks granted Alistair the full title and appearance of royalty. He was a Highfold to the bone, and everyone he rode past knew it from a glance.

After a long ride within the city, the Arch General arrived at the stables for the Highfold Keep. He dismounted with his honour guard and handed off their mounts to the stable hand. Moments later, he heard the familiar sound of his brother's voice behind him.

"Ah, Alistair, I was wondering when you would arrive." Varen approached him, wearing robes of light and dark blue, lined with golden stitching. "Took you long enough, dear Brother." The High Priest held out his arms for an embrace.

Alistair stepped forward and held his brother. "You arrived here quickly. Did my messenger reach you in record time?"

"Messenger?" Varen stepped back from the hug and looked at his brother, a playful smirk on his face. "A messenger never reached me. Where did you send him?"

"To your damnable church." Alistair grinned.

"I haven't been at the Church all day, I've been here, toiling with personal errands. I saw you approaching from the Keep. I thought I would grant you the pleasure of my company on your way in."

The Arch General laughed with his younger brother. "I suppose the messenger will be on a merry chase won't he?"

"The merriest!" They laughed once more before turning to face a looming stone gate, it creaked open slowly and rested loudly once ajar. The two Highfold brothers stepped through, and it closed behind them.

Ahead of the brothers rested a monolith of white stone stairs, granting them passage to the Highfold Keep at the top of the hill.

"So, you were requesting my presence?" Varen said curiously.

"Yes, I was. I wished to meet you in the war room. I have some things I wish to discuss with you." Alistair rested his hand on the hilt of his sword as they ascended the steps.

"Hm, a strange coincidence."

"How so?"

"I too require a discussion with you. Something that could be of dire importance to the country, and my church." Varen plodded up the stairs methodically as he had done hundreds of times before.

"Dire importance?" Alistair asked. "And you need my help?"

"Of sorts. Yes. We will go over the details in the war room, best not have unseen eyes on us for this."

"Agreed."

The Highfolds strode up the stairs and into the Keep, working their way up and to a small door sitting down the hall from the massive shadewood entrance of the throne room, where their parents undoubtedly sat. Two royal guards stood next to the war room's door, large gilded spears in hand, and short swords on their belts.

With a nod, the two soldiers opened the door and allowed the Highfold brothers entrance. The war room was small, with a round wooden table in the centre, a replica of Valenfaar etched into it. The war room itself was not meant to be large. Only big enough for Alistair and his immediate circle of generals, half a dozen in number.

Once in the chamber, Alistair turned and leaned against the table, crossing his arms. "You said you need my help?"

Varen started, seemingly lost in thought. "Yes I do ..." he trailed off.

The Arch General raised an eyebrow. "And are you planning on telling me what you need my help with?"

"Yes, yes," Varen wrung out his hands mindlessly.

"You seem nervous. What is it?"

The High Priest's eyes turned and stared deep into the Arch Generals. "Mother and father cannot find out about what knowledge I possess. Not until I know for certain. I must have your word."

Alistair nodded. "You have my word, Little Brother."

Varen took a long sigh before regaining his posture. "I might have found the Children."

The older Highfold stood straight, no longer leaning on the table, his arms hanging down by his sides. "Varen, are you sure?"

"Positive. The location matches the rumours. A room deep inside an Outlier City's catacombs, large and faceless, grey and deathly." the High Priest recited the old rumour nearly word for word.

"Varen," Alistair said slowly. "Are you sure?"

"With Daylen as my witness, I have no reason to doubt it."

Alistair pondered on this for a moment as he eyed a scroll of parchment on his war table, sealed in yellow wax: the Seal of the Plain's Warden.

"Alright," he said finally. "What would you have of me?"

Varen grinned, letting no surprise show in his expression. "I need close to 100 soldiers. Volunteers will do, for the bulk of the forces. But I want at least two full squads of reputable men in the group. Doesn't matter which ones. And I need them sent to Wreath's Burrow with all haste."

Pondering for a moment, the Arch General quickly assembled the plan in his mind.

"I'll give you the men you require. I have an officer who has been rather eager to prove himself recently, he'll lead the expedition. The bulk of your forces will be volunteers, I will only provide you with the minimum trained soldiers you requested. Two squads worth. But they will be well-seasoned and worth triple their number. Spearpoint Force, and the Sanguine Aegis."

"The Aegis, your suicide squad? They have yet to die if I recall correctly."

Alistair nodded. "Aye, you recall correctly. Which is why they are going with you. With luck, we'll be rid of Garridan Lethar and the rest of his band of misfits."

"I never did understand your quarrel with that man," Varen said, crossing his arms. "He's always gotten the job done."

"With too much blood spilt, aye. Regardless, we will call for a meeting of Valen's Sovereign Guard in half a fortnight."

"Thank you, Brother," The High Priest turned to leave the room.

"Before you leave," Alistair said. "There was something I wished to discuss with you."

"Yes?" Varen said over his shoulder.

Alistair quickly reached over to the parchment from Plainsview and broke the seal. His eyes hurried over the words, taking in their knowledge.

Thregs? In the Endless Plains?

"We may have a problem over in Plainsview. Or we may not," He shrugged. "It's still too early to tell. But, if it turns out to be something serious, can I borrow the Sword of Magus? I may need your captain's talents."

Varen laughed. "Jo-een taking orders from you? That'll be the day." He paused for a moment. "But, if the time arrives, and they aren't on church business, you may borrow their blades. But, *only* if they are otherwise unoccupied. Is that alright?"

The Arch General nodded. "Thank you, Little Brother."

"No, thank you. With what you have given me, Brother, we shall change all of Valenfaar for many cycles to come. Long after our family has entered the Soul Spire."

Chapter 5

It had been three days; three days of sun, heat and grass, with little food or water. It had been three days since the botched attack on the Threg camp, and it was beginning to look like it would be another three days until he was back in the valley and heading home.

Kol wasn't the kind of strider to prefer the plains. He knew them, and he knew them well. Well enough to earn him the unofficial title of Rel's Left Hand. He was talented, sure. But he hated the sun and the dryness of the air, throughout the plains. It was because of this, that he had cursed when Saffron told him he would be heading out for a few days with Rel and some others. Something he had secretly hated doing. The sun and heat always chapped his lips, and if there was a strong wind, it would dry out his eyes into a blinking red mess, much like that prisoner back in Plainsview.

Over the past three days, he had turned up nothing. Kol had circled around the Halo, following the mountains north. He hadn't spotted any smoke stacks or signalling fires, nor had he spotted signs of travellers passing through the grass. He had found plenty of Dead Man's Root, that was certain. Enough to allow him a life of luxury should he ever decide to harvest the blue fungus and sell it in one of the Central Cities. That far in the country, he could make a sizeable fortune from the Root: you couldn't find it within the Halo. Maybe one day he would consider this more heavily, as for now though, he needed to focus on the job ahead. Thregs in the plains were a bad thing, he couldn't explain how he knew it, but something in his gut told him it was so. Something very bad indeed.

#

The stone peaks of Valenfaar's Halo had begun to fade away a day ago, behind the tall yellow-gold grass of the Endless Plains. Nef had made sure to keep them at his back, and the sun at his front as he travelled, so as to not get lost.

Three days ago he set out from the Threg camp, heading eastward, towards the Wixen country of Ajwix, in search of more. And so far, much to his relief, he hadn't found much of anything. A couple of batches of Dead Man's Root, a few small hares, and a fox were all that greeted him in the grass. No signs of camps, hunting or travel to report. It had been a dull three days, especially after the action with the Thregs, but it gave him a lot of time to think. Time to think about himself, Rel, Ashlin, Kol, Saffron, the striders, Plainsview, and life in general.

Nef was always lost in thought when he didn't need his focus elsewhere. He never obsessed over anything, he just liked to think. About what made Saffron, Saffron. How he had made his way up the strider's chain of command, and how he had aged so horribly. Would he be left to the same ageing? He had been out in the plains for countless days, letting the elements of nature take their toll on his body. Would he, one day, also look like a squid? He doubted it, or he tried to doubt it.

A sign of movement on the horizon caught the strider's attention. Towards the east, where the sun had risen, a silhouette moved against the sky, something large, something tall. Nef's heart slammed in his chest. He had to get a closer look.

#

Rel sat in the tall grass, gnawing at a small piece of rabbit she had shot the day before. She had cooked it slowly over some dried grass. She risked the smoke stack alerting others in the plains, but she had needed to eat. She kept the fire small and kept it brief, limiting the amount of smoke that would waft into the air.

She wondered how her men were faring. Nef would probably be alright, he was her Right Hand for a reason. He was a solid warrior, a dependable ally, and emotionally strong. But Kol was different: her Left Hand was younger, less mature, and more prone to making rash decisions. It also didn't help that he hated the plains and preferred to do menial work within the city instead, or running guard duty for some of the other soldiers. He tried to keep it a secret, Rel knew this, but the pained look in his eyes whenever he looked upon the Endless Plains left little to be misunderstood. He hated the plains and almost everything about them. But he did his job.

Rel had made him her Left Hand in the effort of turning this around, hoping that the title and recognition of his skills would help him walk a little taller, and with more pride when out for a ranging. She had yet to see this happen, and it had been two cycles since she appointed him. Hera had almost made her Left Hand, but one night the woman had gotten into a drunken brawl with a guardsman; Atlas, she thought his name was, right before he left town with one of the tavern maids. Rel couldn't remember the other woman's name, it had been too long, and too foggy a memory.

The memory of Hera flashed through her mind, like a stalk of grass falling to a farmer's blade. A sudden jolt of imagery, then the memory faded away to the back of her mind. Hera was dead, chest crushed by a Threg, three days ago. It had been horrible, the crunch of bone through leather, the spatter of blood exploding from her lips. The Plain's Master wondered what had been her final thoughts. Did she think of home? Her lover? Or would it have been something so simple, but so utterly important to her? Something like a promise, or a plan to a loved one that would never be fulfilled. Rel couldn't be sure, and she hoped she would never find out.

#

The silhouette that Nef had seen had grown much larger now. As he approached, so too did the shadows. Still tall and lumbering, but he couldn't quite make out what he was looking at. They didn't look like Thregs. He quickly traced out the shadow's pathway in his mind, and moved out of the way, just far enough that he could be within earshot of any conversation.

"Any information was good information," his father had always told him. "Take in everything you can, and deduce from what you know."

Many long moments stretched by, and the familiar sounds of a horse's hooves plodding on soft dirt graced the air, followed by the creaking of wooden wagon wheels. Nef continued to wait, not wanting to reveal himself too soon. Before long, the caravan had been atop him, three large wooden carriages, pulled by horses, cloths draped over the top of them, hiding what wares they may have been carrying.

Once the final carriage had passed, Nef moved into a position directly behind them, pulled the bow from his shoulder and nocked an arrow. He stood tall and called out: "In the name of Valenfaar, and the Endless Plains, who is it that dare cross this land?"

The caravan slowed to a stop, and a man with pale skin and a long black ponytail leapt from the centre carriage, his hands raised, a dagger on his belt.

"Ah, friend. Ajwix we hail from. Come to trade. We bring many wares for Valen people." his accent snuck through, and his Valen seemed to stutter, forgetting the occasional word.

Nef kept his bow ready, not willing to take any chances. "Tell me. What wares do you bring?"

The man kept his hands raised, a look of professionalism on his face. "We bring trinkets, weapons, armour. All for your people. We wish no harm. Not many of us here. Three trader, twelve guard."

"Where are your guards?"

The man grinned. "They stay with wares, in carriage! Four men to each. I leave them there unless trouble."

Nef lowered his bow, and slung it back over his shoulder, he placed the arrow back in its quiver, only four left, best not to waste any. "Alright," he said. "I'll escort you to Valenfaar."

The man lowered his hands, he rested one on the hilt of his weapon. "Who are you, to escort us? Friend, soldier, bandit?"

Bowing his head slightly, the Plain's Strider explained: "I am a Plain's Strider from the Valen town of Plainsview. We act as guards for the Endless Plains and escorts to those that dare cross it. I promise you safe passage into our country and the lands that lay within." He looked up and matched the Wixen's eye.

"And besides, if you do have twelve guards, I doubt I'd want to quarrel with them."

The trader laughed and waved for Nef to follow. "Come then, friend. Let us travel!"

The strider followed. "What's your name?"

"Name?" the man asked. "Markos, Man of Many Wares they call me. But Markos is good, yes?"

Nef nodded. "A pleasure to meet you, Markos. My name is Nef."

"Ah Nef, the pleasure is mine. Tell me, how long to Valenfaar?"

"Three days," Nef said, climbing aboard the middle carriage, Markos taking a seat next to him.

"Good," he said. "Then we sell!"

Chapter 6

The entrance of the valley had a gradual fade from the yellow of the plains, into the soft green of shorter grass. Rel had been waiting for a day before Kol came back from his circuit north.

"You find anything?" she asked.

"Nothin'," her Left Hand said. "Not a damn thing. Not even a trader. It's barren out there."

"Same here," Rel sighed, "absolutely nothing."

They were sitting up in the branches of a tall oak tree, waiting for Nef to arrive from his range eastward. It had been six days since they encountered the Thregs and set out from the camp. Rel would be willing to give Nef another two days at most to make it back, before heading back home. She knew Kol wouldn't mind waiting here, at least the entrance to the valley had shade and some runoff water from the mountains.

"You think he'll make it back?" her Left Hand asked.

"I do," the Plain's Master said. "He's always at home in the plains. Even the Thregs didn't stop him. You saw that."

"Aye, I did. But something doesn't sit right with me about all this. Why were there Thregs *here* of all places? They've never been out here before! Not for as long as the striders have existed, anyway."

Kol was right, something was very wrong, even Rel couldn't deny that. As much as she wanted to; Thregs hadn't appeared in the Endless Plains, not once since the striders were founded, and they were put into place before Valen had been founded. If they had existed, no one had found them.

"You're right," she finally said as she grabbed the sheepskin of water at her side.

Kol watched as she drank. "It doesn't add up. There were only four of them. Don't people usually find Thregs in groups of twelve or so? Why such a small number?"

Rel placed the cork back into her sheepskin and looked at her friend. "Look Kol, I feel the exact same way you do. I don't like this, not one bit, something isn't right out there. But it's not me you need to convince. We'll need to convince Saff, and then he'll need to convince Alistair." she sighed, swatting at a fly. "Keep that head of yours thinking though, we need to force Saffron into a difficult position. The more unanswered questions we have, the more pressed he'll be to do something." She smiled and placed a hand on the young man's shoulder.

Kol returned the expression. "You know I'll be thinking out loud quite a bit in the meantime, right?"

With a chuckle, Rel nodded, her dark hair bouncing playfully. "I'm counting on it."

Both of them saw movement in their peripherals. They turned to see a large silhouette on the horizon, obscured by heat waves from the midday sun.

"You see that too?" Kol asked.

Rel nodded, pulled up her hood, and leapt from the tree. She landed with a soft roll before rising to her feet. Kol followed in a crouch next to her. Without words, the two of them separated, moving to opposite sides of the dirt road. Rel climbed into the thicket of another oak, while she saw Kol hunker down behind a tree trunk, rooted into the earth.

The two striders waited patiently while the silhouette grew closer. Until finally, they could see what it was that had them so on edge. A caravan of sorts. Three carriages donned with cloth coverings. As the second carriage passed by, Rel heard a familiar voice.

"Alright you two, come on out!" Nef said playfully. "They're just Wixen traders, not here to harm us." There was a pause. "And they have us outnumbered. Four to one."

Rel dropped from her perch to the left with a soft roll and Kol emerged from the trunk on the right. A pale man, with a long black ponytail, spoke. His Valen was choppy.

"Friends of Nef?" he asked.

"Yes. They're my friends," Nef answered, "striders, like me."

"Ah, this good," the trader said. "They will escort us to your home, yes?"

"Yes, yes they will," he confirmed.

"Excellent!" the trader looked to Rel. "You, dark woman. You can ride on front carriage. And you," he looked at Kol then said, "dirty boy. You can ride in back carriage."

They nodded and mounted up onto the wooden benches at the front of the carriages. Rel could hear the Wixen man call out from behind her.

"You two have names, yes? I am Markos, Man of Many Wares."

Looking over her shoulder, the Plain's Master called back. "A pleasure, my friend! I am Rel, Plain's Master!"

"Ah, so you are the one in charge, yes?"

"You would be right!" she called back.

"And you, dirty boy," she heard Markos say, "name?"

It was hard to make out, Kol was too far behind her. But Rel could just understand what her Left Hand was saying.

"The name's Kol!" he replied. "I'm Rel's Left Hand!"

"Ah, I see! So we have the Master and the Left Hand. I know your name, but do you have a title?"

Rel guessed the trader was speaking to Nef.

"I'm her Right Hand," she heard him say.

The man laughed. "A woman who wields two young men as weapons, eh? Something fearsome that is!"

Rel grinned: the man had no idea how fearsome they truly were. The three best striders in all of Plainsview, in all of Valenfaar! Saffron's most elite. She liked to think that any of them would have given the old Plain's Warden a run for his money back when he was still young. Though she couldn't be too sure. He was the Plain's Warden, he had survived the Plain's longer than any of them had been alive, and was given his position for a reason.

Though riding the carriages took slightly longer than it did on foot, being able to sit through the valley was a small luxury that Rel was happy to take advantage of. The man on the reins next to her hadn't said a word. She assumed he didn't speak the Valen tongue and knew only of his own language. It was said that the Wixen were a stubborn people, refusing to learn languages from other cultures unless a person were to travel abroad constantly, or for diplomacy. By the looks of it, this man who accompanied Markos, either saw no need to learn the language or had decided he didn't want to. Rel was fine with this; a little peace and quiet was nice.

Before long, they had arrived at the entrance to Plainsview. The gate was sealed tight, and the guard atop called out to them.

"In the name of Valenfaar and the Highfold Family, who requests entrance into our town and into our country?"

Both Rel and Markos stood simultaneously, but the Plain's Master held a hand up towards the man. Not a rude gesture, a way of saying it was best if she vouch for him.

"These are traders from Ajwix, under the escort of me and my men. They are safe to pass into Plainsview." Rel announced.

There was a brief pause before the man above answered. "Yes ma'am!"

He disappeared for a few moments, then the gate creaked open. Once the opening had grown large enough for the carriages, they began to move again. Rel pointed to the man next to her which way to go, and which corners to take to find the town centre, where Saffron would speak with them, and inspect their carriages before allowing them into the markets.

Finally, they arrived outside of the longhouse. Rel dismounted, as did Nef and Kol. They met at the front door, Markos hot on their heels.

"This does not look like market," he said confused. "What is this?"

Nef stepped towards him. "This is the town square. Your carriages, wares, and men are to be inspected by our superior, Saffron. Then you'll be taken to the markets."

The trader frowned, he looked displeased but didn't argue. When a trader came to Plainsview from outside the plains, they were to succumb to rigorous inspections. The security of the country came first, no questions asked. The last thing the striders needed on their heads would be a malicious infiltration from a foreign country. It had nearly happened once before: a rogue element of deserters from Ajwix made it through the gates of Plainsview under the guise of traders and managed to make their way towards the Central Cities. Once they had arrived in Valen, their carriages were revealed to contain explosive powders. The deserters attempted to blow open a way into the Royal District of Valen, to attack the Highfold family.

Rel wasn't sure what the bandits planned to do once they had breached the District, as they would have been outnumbered immensely, and she supposed she would never find out; that information died with the infiltrators. Cullen Highfold and his spies had found out about the plot ahead of time and quickly summoned the Sovereign Guard to deal with the problem. The crisis was averted, but the king and queen had some rather harsh words for the Plain's Warden.

Kol gave a quick nod towards Nef and Rel before disappearing inside the longhouse. Markos maintained his look of displeasure, but otherwise stood quietly, waiting patiently for the young strider to return.

"So, Markos," said Nef. "What brings you to our realm?"

The trader looked up, his eyes searching the strider for a hint to his intentions.

"I seek to be wed." he finally said.

Rel cocked her head. "You came to Valenfaar to wed? Why not marry in Ajwix?"

"You do not know?" Markos replied.

"Know what?" Nef took a small step forward.

"For a Wixen to be wed, one must become master at craft."

"So," Rel said. "You need to become a master at your profession? In order to wed?"

"And have children," Nef interjected, "I've heard about this somewhere before. The Wixen are stubborn when it comes to continuing bloodlines: they prefer to have folks who are experts in their fields. Blacksmiths make buildings of metal, hence their metal cities, swordsmen win champion titles, hunters hunt legendary game, and so on."

"Yes yes," the Wixen said. "That is right. I must sell my wares."

"Well, that should be easy," Rel said, crossing her arms.

"No no. Not so. I trade everything! Guards, horse, carriage, clothes. Everything!"

"Huh, well that is certainly interesting," Nef admitted. "We'll still need to inspect everything you have though, Markos."

"So, Markos?" Rel asked, "Why do they call you the Man of Many Wares if you are not a master tradesman?"

The foreigner chuckled from deep within his throat, it came out more like a grumble. "Man of Many Wares is not just Markos. Man of Many Wares is every Wixen who trade! All of us! Not just Markos!"

"Interesting," Nef stepped forward again and eyed the man with suspicion, trying to tell if he was honest. Eventually, Rel assumed he was satisfied as he stepped back to her side.

Her Right Hand had a tendency to be wary of travellers, especially those that came from outside the Halo and across the plains, they never sat right with him, and Rel was never sure as to why. He had to have a reason though, Nef was never the man to operate away from gut instinct, but she was never able to pry the reasoning for his paranoia from him.

Before long, the door to the longhouse opened as Kol stepped out with the Plain's Warden no more than five paces behind him.

"This is the man?" Saffron said, spittle flying from his jowled lips.

"Yes, sir. This is him. His name is Markos. Says he is here to trade."

"Hmph," the warden huffed as he walked up to the Wixen.

It was hard to miss, but when Saffron was sitting at his desk, it was easy to forget how large he actually was. He stood six feet tall with a belly that had consumed a few tankards of ale too many. In front of Markos, the man looked much larger than he usually did, the skinny, scrawny trader looked as if a reed compared to the Plain's Warden.

"So, you're Markos?" he asked.

"Yes yes. Markos, Man of Many Wares." the trader answered, a hint of defiance in his voice.

"Well, Markos. It is a pleasure to have you in our fair country. I need to inspect your wares. My colleagues here informed you of that, did they not?"

The Wixen nodded.

"Good. If you have anything you wish to declare, you may do so now, before we begin our inspection."

The trader hesitated for a moment before clearing his throat. "Yes. But moment, please." He walked to the rearmost carriage and dropped a fist on the side of each carriage three times. There had been a slight rumble of footsteps before thirteen men left the wagons.

"I count thirteen, here," Nef said, hand resting on the hilt of his sword. "You told me you carried a dozen guards, and last I checked, that meant twelve."

"Yes, yes. One not guard. This man scholar. He pay for passage." Markos rested one hand on the back of a rather short man in light blue robes. The sleeves hung low enough that he could sit his hands inside. Like Markos, this man was pale of skin and dark of hair, but his eyes seemingly glowed a faint green instead of the pale blue of the traders and his escorts.

"His name Varden," the trader said, patting the man on the back once more. "He come to learn about Valenfaar."

The scholar nodded, his mouse-like features bathed in sunlight. "He speaks truthfully." he finally said, in perfect Valen. "I have come to your country to learn more about your people, and to study one of the many mysteries that only Valenfaar seems to possess. I apologize for the subtlety of my entrance, it was not my wish, but my friend Markos thought it would be best if it wasn't known I was present."

By Gwendall's Blade, most people in Valenfaar didn't speak such perfect

Valen. His accent and knowledge of the language seemed to rival that of the Highfolds. Rel was impressed. This man was clearly no soldier, nor bandit or spy. He had to have dedicated cycles of his life to learning the language alone.

Saffron had raised an eyebrow. "And what would that mystery be?"

The scholar grinned inwardly at the thought of what he was about to say. "The shadewood trees," he finally said with an air of admiration. "Too little is known about them. I wish to achieve mastery of my scholarly studies and learn of the shadewood tree and its secrets. With your permission, of course."

The warden chewed his lip for a moment before answering. "Fine. But you do not leave Plainsview without my or Rel's saying so. Are we clear?"

"Absolutely," the man answered serenely, "I thank you for your hospitality."

"Don't thank me just yet, Scholar. Wait until we find you some quarters. They won't be pretty, but it'll be something to rest your head." Saffron turned to face Markos. "But first, we need to see your wares, and your men."

The inspection took until dusk. Markos didn't carry anything worrisome. He brought with him several ornate weapons, though none more practical than an average sword or dagger, accompanied by exotic armour and jewellery. One piece of weaponry had caught Rel's eye: a dagger with a hilt as black as night, white etchings of vine wrapping it to the base of the blade, which had been made of a cardinal-red metal. It was thick at the base, but twisted and rose upwards, becoming two forked tips, resembling that of a snake's tongue. Rel almost tried to haggle the man for it, but decided against this; the weapon would be expensive, and not too practical. She hoped though, that someone worthy of such craftsmanship would purchase it.

Markos would fetch a fortune in the Central Cities, Rel and the others had told him as much. Many of the people of Plainsview didn't carry much coin. But to this, the man objected and insisted on staying for a while, in order to sell what he could.

"A Master of Wares can sell anything, anywhere!" he had said.

Rel supposed he was right but she didn't expect to see many of his wares leave him before he made his way towards the Central Cities. Until then, however, she would have to report to Saffron regarding their lack of findings in the field, and see what he wished to do next.

Chapter 7

Alistair stood in his war room, talking to the shadowy figure of his brother Cullen, somewhere in the room behind him. His brother was the Spymaster for Valenfaar, and as such, preferred to remain unseen, even to his own family. This was fine, Alistair supposed, he had always felt a certain wave of calmness wash over him when his brother was around.

"Cullen?" the Arch General asked.

"Yes?"

The voice seemed to come from nowhere, and everywhere all at once. Alistair couldn't place where in the room his brother had been speaking from, and any time he turned to try and find him, he would come to find nothing, not even a muddied footprint.

"I've received another letter from Saffron."

"Ah, yes. The Squid. How does he fare?"

"They've found Thregs in the Endless Plains. He seeks aid."

"I see," a low hum reverberated through the room. "And what is it you would suggest? Why do you call me here, to your war room? Surely you don't wish me to aid them, I am not the warrior you think me, Brother."

Alistair chuckled. "No no. It is not you that I wish to send as aid. Though I will be asking you to head that way: I require information."

"Ah, now you are speaking in familiar terms, dear Brother."

The voice came from behind Alistair. He turned to face his brother, a flutter in his stomach. Only to find nothing once again. Then, Cullen's voice reached out from all around him.

"What information do you seek?"

"The Pale Bull. Where is he?"

"Of course!" Cullen said. "Saffron has, what could be, a Threg problem. So you wish to throw the one thing that can scare a Threg his way? The Pale Bull, the good Bronwin, Shield of Northwood!" the Spymaster chuckled, almost vibrating the floor. "The man is an absolute brute. You of all people know this especially well. Are you sure he is the answer you seek?"

"Who else would you suggest?" Alistair asked, crossing his arms.

"Why not that Garridan fellow of yours? Him and his Aegis?"

"No, he'll have another assignment shortly. Just tell me where Bronwin is."

"He resides in Sun Spire, in the barracks."

Alistair nodded. That *was* lucky, it was the closest Central City to Plainsview. It would take Bronwin the better part of a moon to reach his destination. "Thank you, Brother. I will send word at once for his immediate departure. If there is a Threg problem at our borders, he'll be the man to quell it."

"Yes, this is true. But," Cullen said, curiosity seeping into his words. "You were to ask me to head eastward?"

"Yes. I need you to keep an eye on the Pale Bull and his men. Relay anything and everything that happens directly to me. Is that to your abilities?"

A chuckle bounced from wall to wall. "Of course, Alistair! I already have men in his employ. My eyes are everywhere, what I know, you shall know."

"Thank you, Cullen. Now tell me, where have you been hiding in here? It has been driving me to the depths of the Soul Spire since you arrived."

The answer to his question came from the closing of the war room door. His brother had left already, wordlessly and out of sight. The only clue to his departure had been the intentionally loud volume of his exit.

Alistair shook his head, it had been too long since he had actually seen his brother, and even longer since he had seen his face. At a young age, Cullen had gone to Ajwix to train with a Spymaster. He had returned just before the Highfold election, in which their family had won, nearly twenty cycles later. It was a bizarre feeling, to know your brother, yet not know him, or what he looks like at the same time. It had also made sense to him. If no one knew what the Spymaster truly looked like, he could blend into any crowd without hazard, he could be anywhere at any time, and even his own siblings would be none the wiser.

The Arch General left the war room and began to make his way through the maze of halls that were the Highfold Keep, dark marbled floor and white-marbled walls clashed against royal blue and crimson red banners, sunlight shone through each window, bathing the halls in warmth.

As he travelled, the royal guards nodded in affirmation towards him, he always nodded in return. Alistair was a firm believer that if he were to command, he would show his men the same respect he wished to be shown. As a result, all his men were treated as a general in his eyes. And to him, they had all earned that respect; a man's life was priceless, and the fact that his men put their lives on the line for not only their country, but himself, had gained them the respect they deserved, and in turn, he too had earned theirs.

It hadn't taken long, or at least it hadn't felt like it had taken long before Alistair reached the treasury. He nodded to the two royal guards at each flank of the door, then pushed it open. Stepping through, Alistair let the warmth of candlelight wash over him. The treasury was really his sister's office. It didn't house the gold and treasure of the Highfold Keep, instead, that was kept elsewhere in Valen, under incredible guard; the only people who knew where it was located were the Highfolds themselves and the guards that defended it.

And, Alistair resented to admit, a certain thief who had broken into it once, and only once, before he was captured.

Sitting behind her desk at the far side of the treasury, sat Maryam Highfold, Alistair's sister. Maryam was the youngest of the four Highfold children, but she did her duties with honour and with pride. She always had a knack for acquiring coin and finding the best ways to put it to use. This was why she had been named Coin Master.

Alistair looked over to her as he made his way closer, she looked to be buried in her work, scrawling down what he assumed to be numbers onto various pieces of parchment. The quill in her hand darted from parchment to inkwell with practised precision. Maryam was a gorgeous girl, slightly heavier than the average woman, but by no means considered fat, or overweight. She kept her long black hair tied into a braid that rested at the small of her back.

The Arch General let his footfalls grow louder, vying to get his sister's attention. Finally, she started and looked up. Her blue eyes met her brother's, and a grin spread across her features.

"Alistair! I had forgotten our appointment." She rose from where she was seated and moved around her desk, making her way closer with open arms.

Alistair embraced her, and let the scent of her perfume fill his senses.

"I am so sorry," she said sincerely.

"Sweet Sister, it is alright, there is no cause to apologize." He held her by the shoulders and gave her his best brotherly grin.

"Of course there is, dear Brother. It is not like me to forget such things." Her gentle smile turned into a frown. She looked back up, renewed vigour in her gaze, her smile returning. "Enough glumness," she said. "What is it you wanted to speak about?"

Alistair looked concerned. "I need to arrange an expedition for our brother Varen. He requires 100 men to travel west. I've already reached out to my officers regarding two units. But I need to know if we have the coin to outfit eighty volunteers," He paused then said: "Roughly."

Maryam tilted her head to one side, candlelight flickering in her blue eyes. "Oh, Alistair. I've shown you our budget for the volunteers. It is not well."

Nodding slowly, he answered. "I am aware. But Varen insists this is of critical importance, and that it could change our country for many cycles to come."

"If our brother deems it of such import. Then why does he not send his mangy lapdog to deal with it?"

The Arch General chuckled. "Mangy lapdog? I haven't heard Jo-een called that before." He shook his head with a grin. "Regardless, he feels the Sword may be best used later in this expedition if his suspicions are correct."

"And what does Varen suspect?"

"The Children," Alistair said flatly, almost surprised at how quickly he confided in his sister. "He wishes to scout Wreath's Burrow. I'd imagine he'd deploy the Sword of Magus if they turned out to be real."

The Coin Master's eyes grew large with excitement. "The Children?! Such a find could yield magical secrets this world has never known! The opportunity for economic growth would be immense!" She looked to think for a few moments, then spoke, "I'll get you the coin you need to outfit your volunteers. No problem there, I'll subtract some costs from Sun Spire's volunteer forces, to make up the difference here. They have no need for volunteers at the moment, anyway."

"Thank you, Maryam. I will send the men out within half a fortnight. Have our quartermasters handle the equipment once it is purchased. They are more than capable."

"Of course," the Coin Master said. "All will be well, I promise you."

Chapter 8

In his office, Rel stood across from Saffron. Her disbelief oozing into her words. The note Saffron had received from Alistair left her mouth agape.

"He's sending the Pale Bull here?"

"Yes, Rel. He should already be on his way, and should be here before the next moon."

"This is insanity, Saff. The man is a brute, an absolute monster!" frustration fuelled her words like a fire.

The Plain's Master had met Bronwin once before, when Thregs had been sighted near Plainsview, from within the Halo. They had disagreed several times regarding the use of men's lives. Plainsview had lost nearly two dozen guards during his involvement, but he hadn't cared. To the Pale Bull, soldiers were tools, and if they broke, he would find more. No striders had even come close to encountering the Thregs at the time, much to Rel's relief, as they were outside of Bronwin's command. This time, Rel had a distinct feeling, things would be different. Thregs had been spotted in the Endless Plains, who better to aid the Pale Bull than the Plain's Striders themselves?

"I am more than aware of what he is like," Saffron said, raising a hand. "But he is the most efficient soldier we have that is capable of dealing with Thregs. He has never failed to quell them."

"But at what cost? How many men?"

"Listen," he said with a fatherly tone, putting a stop to her rebuttal. "I know you don't see eye to eye with him, and I can't blame you. But he is considered Alistair's Right Hand. We need to follow his orders." He looked at her, sympathy in his eyes.

Rel placed her hands on her hips. "What do you mean by 'we'?"

"He'll have command of the striders, once he's here."

A cooling flood of heat and anger flooded the Plain's Master's body. Her heart felt as if it had frozen for several heartbeats, her body buzzed with anger and anxiety, fire coursed through her veins.

"Sir, with respect-"

Saffron cut her off with another raised hand. "Rel. No. There is no room for negotiation here. Once he has arrived, we are at his disposal. Whether we like it or not. And if we disobey, we are likely to be tried for treason." Saffron paused, remembering something from cycles long past. "And you know the Pale Bull prefers to do that himself."

A short, angry snort signalled Rel's agreement.

"Thank you, Rel. You are dismissed. Check on Markos, then get some rest. You've earned it." Saffron grabbed his quill ceremoniously and went back to scribbling on parchment.

Wordlessly, she nodded and turned to leave. She would bring Ashlin with her to the market, she could use the company, someone who could calm her nerves.

Stopping at her own door, Rel opened it and looked through her home. She found Ashlin, broom in hand, sweeping the floor, a bucket of water with a rag sitting within laid in the corner. It looked to Rel that her lover had dedicated herself to cleaning their home today.

"Rel, my sweet," Ashlin said, her blue eyes glittering with her lover's arrival.

"Ashlin," Rel said with a muted smile. She walked over and gave her a kiss. "I need to stop by the market before I finish my duties for the day. Would you care to join me?"

"Of course, just let me finish sweeping, I'm almost done."

It wasn't long before Ash had finished, and they had left into the sprawling streets of Plainsview. The dirt road beneath their feet guided them towards the hustle and bustle of the market square. It was here where Ashlin would normally work, running errands and selling goods for the various merchants of the town. She was a freelance tradeswoman, Rel always thought. Offering to sell goods for a portion of the profits.

Markos stood with his servants, guards and carriages near the centre of the market square. The sun was beginning to set, and many of the other merchants had already left for the day, taking what wares they had left with them. A crowd had grown around the Wixen, many villagers eager to see what the foreigner had to sell. Many of the people, men and women alike, left without purchasing anything, their hands empty and bare, a look of discontent on their faces. The prices were too high, she assumed.

They pushed their way through the crowd, many of the prospective buyers giving them room upon seeing the Plain's Master.

"Rel," a familiar voice called, "you have come to see wares, yes?" Markos greeted her excitedly.

The crowd fell silent.

"No no, Markos. I am merely here to check up on you. How has everything been so far? Any trouble?"

"No no," the man said. "No trouble. Only coin!" he held up a small sack. It jingled as it swayed. "But people here poor. How can I sell wares?"

"You don't have to stay here forever, Markos. You can head west if you like. To the Central Cities. Many of the rich live there, in a city called Valen."

"Valen?" the Man of Many Wares asked.

"It's our capital. You'd turn a steady profit there, I have no doubt."

"How far?" He was like a child told of secret treasure.

"It should take you two moons and a half to reach it. You need to work your way around a mountain pass, Gwendall's Spear, then through another Central City, Sun Spire. After that, it's a clear shot through easy roads."

The Wixen scratched his chin as he thought about this. "This good. This very good. I leave at first light then. Head to Central City, Valen."

Rel smiled, she enjoyed the foreigner, but she would be happy to see him on his way, it would be less for her to worry about.

"Would you care for an escort to the base of Gwendall's Spear? I can arrange for some of the striders to accompany you."

"No no. I have guards. Only ten now, two sold!" He held up another bag of jingling coins, a triumphant grin on his face.

Rel chuckled at the childlike excitement. "That is good Markos. My offer still stands, however. Just let me know if you change your mind."

The call of a man interrupted the exchange, and a guard with a small sack ran towards the trader.

"Markos!" he called, "Markos, Markos!" A guardsman came forward, heaving in his leather armour. "I have the coin. Nobody bought it, did they?"

The trader turned to face the guard, a smug grin on his face. "Ah, you, boy! I still have the weapon you seek. Here."

Markos turned and unbuckled something on the side of the carriage directly behind him, a small, but thick, wooden hilt, two or three hand spans tall. Attached to the hilt sat a chain, extending out two metres. Markos held the hilt in one hand, and the chain aloft in the other, at the end sat the blade of a sickle. The weapon looked to be more showy than practical, but Rel admitted it looked rather interesting.

"Well, that's a weird-looking thing," Ashlin whispered to her, "why would he buy that?"

"He's a low-rank guard," Rel answered, "I think he's looking for something to help himself stand out. To get noticed."

"Oh, he'll be noticed alright. The second he cuts his own foot off with that thing. How would you use that anyway?"

"I haven't the faintest clue, my love." but she had a vague idea, one that began to slowly unwind in her mind like a spool of twine.

The guard had moved forward now, his breathing still rapid, but calmer than before.

"Five silver valens." Markos said, his smug grin glued to his face.

"Deal," the guard said, handing the trader his pouch of coin.

Markos opened the pouch and inspected its contents. He looked satisfied, then handed the weapon over to the man. A smile blossomed on his face.

"Thank you, Markos. Thank you," he said desperately.

"No!" the Wixen said. "Thank you, friend! On day of my wedding, remember you, I will." Markos turned to the fading crowd before him. "That is all!" he called, "I leave at light, live wonderful lives, may you all." He nodded to Rel with respect. She returned the gesture.

Turning her attention to the guardsman still standing there, the Plain's Master took a step forward, Ashlin at her side. "Guardsman!"

The man looked at her frantically, he hadn't noticed her before. He quickly snapped to and stomped his foot into the dirt.

"Plain's Master Rel!" he announced, "I did not see you there, ma'am!"

"At ease, guardsman. What is your name?"

"Corduvan," he said relaxed. "It's Corduvan, ma'am."

"And why have you acquired that, er, weapon?" Rel raised an eyebrow as she nodded to the strange tool.

The guard hesitated before answering. "Ma'am, I hope to learn something new, other than swordplay."

"And who is to teach you?" Rel hadn't noticed it at first, but she had been standing straighter, her hand on the hilt of her shortsword. An air of absolute authority permeated around her. Corduvan seemed smaller than he had previously.

Again he hesitated. "Um, no one ma'am. I was hoping to teach myself."

The Plain's Master raised an eyebrow. "And if you should lose a foot playing with your new toy?"

"A fault of my own ma'am, no questions asked," he answered confidently.

"Alright, Corduvan. But I want to see what you've accomplished." Rel paused to think. "Twice every fortnight. Are we clear?"

"Like the skies above the Endless Plains, ma'am." he beamed a smile.

"You are dismissed, get back to work." she grinned back at him.

With a quick nod, the guard took his weapon and went back the way he came.

"Why do you want to see him practise?" asked Ashlin, who was watching after Corduvan.

No matter how tall Rel felt, she always felt level with Ashlin, she was always able to bring her back to reality.

"If I let him go into battle with that thing, I don't know what kind of harm he could cause. I'd be inviting him to wedge that blade into any one of us. At least with this, I can confiscate the weapon if he proves to be careless."

"Rel, he paid good money for that. He spent about a moon of his wages on it." she frowned.

Rel looked down at her, with a face as if to say: *what, really?*

"Don't worry," she finally said, after a moment's more thought. "I'll compensate him. He won't go broke because I took away his toy."

Ashlin smiled. "You're a good woman." She paused and looked up, her pale blue eyes shining in the evening glow of the setting sun. "I love you."

"And I love you, my dear. Now come. Let us head home. I need the rest."

"Of course."

Later that night, Rel and Ashlin found themselves on the roof of their home, tangled in each other's bodies. Ashlin's head sat upon her lover's chest looking up at the stars.

The Plain's Master raised an arm, the loose cloth of her tunic falling slightly. "Look at those," she said with wonderment.

In the sky above them, in front of the Night Cloud that hung beyond their sky, a smattering of red stars streaked across the black, from east to west, glowing a crimson red.

"I've never seen those before," Ashlin said, sitting up. "They're beautiful."

"They are," Rel agreed. "Some say they're good luck, that the next day will bring nothing but joys."

"I hope they're right. It would be nice for this whole talk of Thregs to disappear for a bit, wouldn't it?"

"I couldn't agree more." Rel sat up and kissed her on the cheek. "Now come to bed. We have our duties tomorrow."

"I'll be right there," she said. "I want to watch them a little while longer."

As Rel lay in bed, she closed her eyes and pondered over the day. The Pale Bull would be in Plainsview soon, in less than one moon. She crossed her fingers under the covers, hoping that no more news of Thregs would come. That the one sighting was nothing more than chance, that the Pale Bull wouldn't have a need for the guards or her striders, and that he could settle the matter, if there was one, with his own troop.

She could hear Ashlin's footsteps on the roof above her, followed by the sound of her climbing down. The front door opened and closed gently, then the lock slid into place. Moments later, Ashlin was in the room with her, naked and crawling into bed. She climbed on top of Rel and began to kiss her. Her lips were soft and caring, with emotion in every touch. Rel moaned at the feeling of her kiss as it travelled down her body.

Chapter 9

The morning after Alistair and Varen had deployed forces to Wreath's Burrow had started with bad news: another parchment from Saffron stating there were more sightings of Thregs in the plains, and paired with those sightings, were the fatalities of four more striders. They cleared out the camp, but none of Saffron's men had survived the encounter. Allegedly, he had to send another patrol out into the plains to follow up with the lost warriors, only to find them lying in pools of their own blood, the bodies of Thregs close by.

The Arch General was thankful, Bronwin would arrive there within the fortnight, and he would begin dealing with the situation. One thing was certain though, two camps of Thregs, that far east, for the first time in recent history, couldn't be a coincidence. He had to do something, and Bronwin would be the man to see it through.

Alistair wrote out his reply and handed off the parchment to a messenger for delivery via spraven. His reply had been simple: *"Do not engage any further Threg camps, observe, scout and track, Bronwin will be there soon, all forces will be under his command."*

Alistair turned and rested against his war room table, he crossed his arms. A familiar presence graced the room, how he knew he was there, the Arch General didn't know, but he knew it nonetheless.

"Cullen," he said. "Do you have anything to report?"

"Ah, you've grown more aware since we last met. Tell me, do you know where I reside, at present?"

"You know as well as I do, that I haven't the faintest clue."

A chuckle echoed through the room, vibrating the walls.

"Now, Cullen. Any information?"

"Bronwin should arrive at Plainsview in little less than a fortnight, I estimate." He paused. "Eleven days. If my reports are accurate."

"Is the accuracy of your reports ever in question?"

The reply came slyly. "Never," Another chuckle. "Now, I have things I need to attend to. Should you need me, I won't be far."

"Travel safely. We will speak again soon."

The door to the war room slammed shut once more.

Valenfaar: The Crimson Plains

Alistair hoped Cullen's report would be correct, which would put the arrival of Bronwin at Plainsview in sync with the arrival of the Sovereign Guard forces currently heading to Wreath's Burrow. A happy coincidence.

#

Plainsview: a not-so-small shit hole of a town, filled to the brim with wannabe guardsmen, and overly glorified rangers: the Plain's Striders. The Squid had a good hold on the town, but he wasn't firm enough. From where he stood, Bronwin could see the smokestacks from the town's homes over the horizon, he would be there before Sun's Peak on the morrow. He dreaded that moment, where he would set foot through the pathetic wooden gates of the town, and march up to the boiled man known as Saffron: the Plain's Warden.

The old Squid was insufferable, both in appearance, and attitude. He acted like some grand warrior; as if he had done something worthy of a god during his service. The man wasn't even Sovereign Guard, he hadn't pledged his life to the realm of Valenfaar. Instead, he and his little clubhouse of useless acrobats had pledged themselves to fields of grass. To act as over-glorified doormen to a country that Bronwin himself, had dedicated his entire life to defending from the Thregs. The sorry excuse for soldiers that waited for him, were nothing more than hollow re-imaginings of his own men.

How many men had the Pale Bull lost? He wasn't sure, but the number had to be in the hundreds. Each death was justifiable, every man had given their lives in service to their country. To Bronwin, it wasn't his fault, as the commanding officer, that those men died under his command. He was a commander, a man to wield the tools that were soldiers. Tools would break, get lost, or be stolen, but they could always be replaced. His men were no different, they were his tools, just as he was Alistair's. At the drop of a hat, any one of them could be ordered to give their lives, and any one of them would do it, himself included. Alistair wasn't stupid enough to order Bronwin to his death, he needed him, and if he knew what was best for the country, and his position, he would make sure the man was kept alive.

"Bronwin, sir," a gruff voice came from behind. "Camp is set, the men are beginning to settle in for the night. We should do the same. Going to be a busy day tomorrow."

The Pale Bull turned to face the man talking to him: Algrenon, his most loyal soldier. "Good. See to it that you rest. I do not look forward to seeing the Squid again."

"And you, sir?"

"You beginning to worry about me, boy?" Bronwin turned, his gaze piercing the air between them.

Algrenon took a step back. "No, sir. Not at all."

"Good, keep it that way." He turned back to the horizon. "Now get out of my face."

"Yes, sir," the man said before stepping away, his footsteps soft in the grass.

Fucking Plainsview, the last place in Valenfaar he wanted to be, and he would be there soon, putting an end to the petty bullshit they couldn't handle themselves.

#

It had been a busy ten days, but on the eleventh morning after the star shower, an air of anxiety filled the town. Nef had been working harder than usual since that night. A strider returned from the plains the morning after, with reports of a Threg camp beyond the Halo. Almost directly east, not far from where the first camp had been found. A hunting party had left immediately, and after five days, had not returned. Nef led the manhunt for their striders: they had found them dead, killed in battle, but with neither side victorious, all participants laying in pools of their own blood.

Four striders had fallen at the hands of two Thregs. The tall, lanky creatures were littered with arrows, stab wounds and cuts slashed throughout their bodies. Had it not been for their size, Nef wouldn't have been able to recognize what the creatures were through the hail of injuries. He wished, however, that he could say his own kin were in better condition. But they weren't.

Two of the striders had their heads smashed in, their faces completely unrecognizable. Had their bodies not been intact, Nef wouldn't have been able to even tell their gender. The other two striders were ripped open, entrails bathing the ground in crimson pools. He could have sworn some of the wounds looked as if they had been gnawed at, but he wasn't sure. He shivered at the thought.

The rescue team, if you could call them that, had entered the camp with an eerie silence. They hadn't spoken, merely took in the sights. The Thregs died of blood loss. They had survived the battle, but not the aftermath. Nef was, he guessed, happy about that. At least they weren't alive. The rescue team had buried the striders, then recited the Strider's Endless Range, a way to release the fallen rangers of the oaths they had taken in life:

"The Endless Plains, our land, our duty.
Valen's Passage, the door, the Valley.
We stand to protect, hold fast to defend.
We are the Plain's Striders, the men and women that comb the land.
To protect those that would fall by the harshest hands.
Your ranging is complete, your oath is done.
Go free our brothers, sisters, and leave as one.
A new duty awaits you in the Soul Spire.
May you serve, with freedom, and a lively fire."

Nef had always thought it a kind of silly poem, but the message was clear. He often wondered himself, what duties would befall him in the afterlife, if any. Did they have Plains there, outside the Spire? Would he be assigned to range in the afterlife? He honestly couldn't be sure, but part of him hoped this would be the case. He always felt a sense of belonging when out in the plains, like he was doing something right, and this was the way forward for his story. He often wondered if he was mistaken with this thought, and he often told himself there would only be one way to find out: to keep living his life the way he enjoyed it.

Right now, he wasn't enjoying it. Since the Wixen trader, Markos, had left Plainsview, heading west, he had been stuck babysitting the scholar that decided to stay behind. This man, Varden, could be *very* annoying. Nef had been assigned to keep watch over him during his day-to-day proceedings, and for the most part, the strider found these days absolutely laden with nothing to do.

How many of his friends had to sit with a foreign scholar in a library, in absolute silence, while the man read and cooed over almost every book he came across? The only time there had been actual conversation, Varden had used words that Nef could hardly begin to imagine had meaning. They seemed the Valen tongue, but they seemed so long that Nef could have sworn he was stringing together the alphabet in different orders. Who used such large words? What was the purpose? He recalled one time he had begun to gain an understanding, after pulling an explanation out of the scholar.

"Hmm," the Wixen had hummed. "This man's stories are utterly superfluous," he said as he tore his gaze away from the book he had been reading.

Nef had raised his eyebrow. "His stories are *what?*"

"Superfluous."

"That ... doesn't help. You do realize, answering my question with the *thing* that made me ask the question, doesn't really help, right?"

Varden had chuckled smoothly. "Nef, my friend. I apologize. You are correct. I am so used to being around other scholars, I often forget that not everyone carries as vast a lexicon as I."

"Carries a what? A latex thong?" *What in the name of Esmirla was a latex thong? What was latex?* The scholar had to have been making up words to mock him.

Varden had raised an eyebrow. "Now what are you going on about? When did you last clean your ears? I said, *lexicon*. Think of it as a kind of library. In this case, a library in my mind." He tapped a finger against his temple. "The more you learn, the more you know, the larger your lexicon."

"I see," Nef had said. "That first word you used, superflounder?"

"Superfluous?" The scholar had corrected.

"Yes, that one. What does that mean?"

The scholar smiled at him. "Put simply, it means: useless, not needed."

"Then why not use those words?"

"Well, I like the way superfluous sounds, how it feels to say, especially in your language. Here, try it! *Superfluous.*"

"Sooperfluid." Nef had tried.

"No no, close. Not fluid, fluous. Think of it like a bird. 'The bird flew.' Flew is the sound you want there."

"Superfluous," Nef had managed to say with a grin. "Superfluous!"

That memory still made the strider smile, and he tried to learn a new word from the scholar every other day. It had been going well so far. It had started with superfluous, then moved to lexicon, menagerie, aromatherapy, and psychology. He had learned a great deal, and every day he tried to use each word once or twice, to help them set in. This had been the only redeemable part of his new babysitting job: he was learning things. But everything else felt dull and dry, sitting in the grass while the Wixen pulled out weeds, tasted their roots, spat them out, cursed and then tried another one, only to repeat the process.

This morning, however, was following the same routine. Varden had plucked another green weed out of the grass in one of the town's many gardens. He studied the root closely, took a bite of it, spat the hunk of white-brown substance onto the ground and then swore to himself.

How many roots can this man taste? Nef thought as he watched, *He's been through a dozen already, this morning.*

"Hey, Varden," he finally asked, "why are you always shoving that shit in your mouth? It seems superfluous."

The scholar smiled broadly. "Ah, you're improving you-"

"Lexicon, yes." The strider interrupted. "Now please, enlighten me."

"Well, my eager beaver."

Eager beaver? What in Esmirla's Breath was a beaver?

"I'm happy you've asked. To you, these weeds all seem the same, like there is no difference from one to the other. But if you look very closely at the leaves, and at the roots, you'll see small differences. Here. See?"

The scholar held out the root he had just taken a bite out of and handed it to Nef, he then reached down and grabbed one from earlier.

"If you look closely, you can see that even though the leaves of these two look identical, the roots on the one you have there, have small, straight, hair-like fibres coming off of it. Where this one here: the fibres are curved and curled. It's small, but it is different."

"Okay," The strider agreed. "They're different. Sure. But why taste them?"

"To see what properties the roots have! You see, many roots contain healing properties, and they usually taste acrid and bitter in these parts. Some roots can be poisonous, which can be rather sweet. Thankfully I haven't found any of those yet. And others, well they simply do nothing to us. But then you also have the Dead Man's Root, which isn't really a roo-"

"Yes, yes I know. It only looks like a root but is actually a fungus. You can find it out in the plains, if you look hard enough."

"Oh yes, I know. I had found plenty on my journey."

Nef raised an eyebrow. "You did?"

"Oh yes. The Root is quite strong. I think I may have partaken in some rather questionable practices with some of Markos's bodyguards on one occasion. It's all a blur really, hardly a memory."

"Oookay," The strider quickly avoided the topic, shifting uncomfortably. "You said some of these roots could be poisonous, what if they are? It could kill you."

"Well yes. But I would get a first-hand chance to study the symptoms of the poison. And I have you here! I trust you would seek me proper medical aid should I fall ill?"

"Yes, of course. It wouldn't look good on me if I watched the person I was protecting poison themselves, then do nothing about it."

Varden frowned. "Is self-preservation your only concern?"

"Self, what?"

"Preservation: preservation is to keep something the same, to keep something safe. If you preserve yourself — self-preservation — you are keeping your image, reputation, and physicality intact and safe."

Once again, Nef raised an eyebrow.

The scholar sighed. "Do you only care about yourself?"

"No, not at all. I'm a strider, I'm here to protect millions."

"Am I among those millions?"

"Well, yes. Of course."

"So you would save me, for the sake of self-preservation, and to protect my life?"

Nef smirked. "Yes. I would preserve both my image and your life. It's a win-win."

Varden smiled widely. "You are a quick learner. Now here-"

The sound of a bell, ringing through the air, interrupted the Wixen. Someone had arrived at the town's gate, a force of soldiers, judging by the frantic ringing.

"C'mon, let's go take a look." Nef and Varden rose from their seats in the dirt and jogged towards the westernmost gate.

When they arrived, a large assembly of villagers and striders had arrived. Nef looked around quickly, he saw Rel and Saffron on top of the gate, speaking to somebody below them. Kol remained on the ground, waiting with the other striders.

"Wait here, I'll be right back."

"Take your time, I'll be taking some notes," Varden said, pulling out a small book of parchment.

"Kol, what's going on?" Nef asked, running over to his friend.

"Oh, hey Nef," Kol muttered, "I think it's the Pale Bull. Not sure though." He looked to where Saffron stood and pointed a finger. "They know for sure though."

Almost on queue, the Plain's Warden turned to the striders below. "Striders, form up!" Saffron's voice boomed and cut the chatter in the air.

The group of rangers hurried into position, five lines of ten. Fifty of them total, the other striders were on duty elsewhere. Regardless, for the striders to assemble in anything resembling an official manner, meant someone important was on the other side of the gate.

Rel and Saffron descended the stairs and made their way to the front of the formation. Nef and Kol standing behind them, in the centre of their line.

Rel turned to face them. "You two alright?" Her face was wrought with worry.

"Yeah, we're fine," Nef replied, "what about you? You don't look too good."

She grinned sadly. "I'm not. But I will be … I hope."

The creaking of the wooden gate forced their attention forward. As it opened, the gentle sight of hills of green grass, and the occasional birch tree melted into view. Slowly, a large group of men, soldiers, short and tall, slender and muscular filled the void, their armour a pale steel grey, with the head of a bull embroidered in black on the chest plate, some wore helmets, many didn't.

In front of them stood a man, larger than any Nef had ever seen. He marched through the passageway and in front of the striders. His own men falling in behind him. It had to be him; the legend himself. Nef's heart began to beat faster. Was he really going to meet *him?*

Bronwin stood tall over everybody, a tower amongst hovels, a mountain amongst homes! He was revered as the Pale Bull and the Shield of Northwood. He had carried his titles for many cycles, and for good reason.

The striders before him knelt in respect, their gaze never breaking from his own. Nef could feel the group's collective stare taking in the sight before them, his hair was cut short, as was his beard, both were speckled with grey as if peppered with snow. His large shoulders mimicked that of a bull.

Nef could tell, easily, that Bronwin stood more than seven feet tall. So tall, that even some Thregs would have to glance upwards to see the entirety of the warrior. He was a true soldier, the one people read about to their children from books. But the Pale Bull was *real* and he was standing in front of them.

"Plainsview!" he boomed, his voice an avalanche cascading through the silence. "I am Bronwin, the Pale Bull and Shield of Northwood! You and all of your forces are hereby under *my* command, by the order of Alistair Highfold himself! As of this day forward, you will answer my summons, or be dealt with appropriately!" He paused for a moment, letting his voice echo into the distance. "Plain's Striders," He looked around at them all, Nef's stomach fluttered as Bronwin's gaze passed over him. "You may rise, and carry about your duties. All I ask for today is that you stay out of my way, and that of my men. Are we clear?"

The striders all nodded in agreement, even Rel and Saffron had nodded from their knelt positions at the front of the group.

The striders rose from their formation, spreading out, back into the sprawling streets and alleyways of Plainsview. Only four had stayed behind: Saffron, Rel, Kol, and Nef. The four best striders that Plainsview had to offer.

"Bronwin," Saffron said, his jowls jostling with each syllable. "Welcome to Plainsview, it's our pleasure to have you."

The Shield of Northwood raised an eyebrow. "I'm sure it is, Saff. But let us be clear. I don't want to be here longer than I need to be. I will help you with your little problem, then me and my soldiers will be on our way. We have other things that we'd rather be doing. Am I clear?"

"As clear as the skies over the Endless Plains. What shall be our first steps?"

The Pale Bull snorted. "The prison. I'm to see the prison. Some of your prisoners may prove useful to me." His boulder of a head looked over one shoulder. "Algrenon, get the men ready for a patrol of the Valley."

"Yessir."

Algrenon didn't have much going for him in the way of physicality, but his face made up for that. His features were sharp, and defined, his eyes like needles, always probing for some unseen weakness. He kept his dark hair long, tied back into a ponytail, and had grown a dark, pointed chin strip on his face. Algrenon waved to the men and began moving to the eastern side of town.

"Rel," Saffron turned to face her. "Could you take Bronwin to the prison?"

"No," Bronwin interrupted. "You will take me, Squid. Nobody else."

Rel paused with her mouth open, not sure what to say. Was she shocked that she had been turned down, or was she surprised that someone actually called Saffron 'Squid', to his face? Nef wasn't sure.

"Ah, yes. Of course. My apologies." Saffron waved for the commander to follow him, leaving the trio of striders in silence.

The western gate closed with a shudder.

Kol spoke first. "So that's the Pale Bull, eh? Bit of a turd isn't he?"

"You have no idea," Rel shook her head, exasperated. "This will be a long job, you boys have my word."

Nef stayed silent, not sure what to make of the whole situation when a third voice broke the air.

"So *that* is the Pale Bull, is it? What a behemoth of a man!" It was Varden, his eyes wide, following the departing warrior. "I wonder if he'll let me stay close? The Wixen historians would love to hear a first-hand account of the Shield of Northwood."

"Your people have heard of him?" Nef asked, turning to face the scholar.

"Of course! Almost half of this world has heard of that man. His stories of strength are things that could only be thought of in children's songs. But they're all real. Every single one of them. And he's right here, in front of me. Fascinating."

Nef saw Rel roll her eyes, disapproval staining her delicate features. "C'mon boys," she said. "Let's get something to drink."

Chapter 10

The Squid led the way towards the prison, leading the Pale Bull through busy, dirty, streets and past merchant stalls that reeked of refuse and body odour. How could these people live like this? Did they not seek the comforts of the wealthy in the Central Cities? Half of these people looked as if they only bathed once or twice every *moon* instead of the near-daily washings of Bronwin and his soldiers.

They passed a curious-looking beggar on the side of the road, his nose half cleaved off, one eye clouded white, and missing three fingers on his left hand. Bronwin hoped the man had seen better days, but to be honest, he wasn't all too sure. Something about the way the beggar sat, made it look like he was happy with his situation.

After crossing much of Plainsview and its unfortunate denizens, the prison rose up in front of them. A tall four-story wooden structure, thick iron bars — nearly touching — were placed in every window. Guards patrolled its borders, and three men stood watch at the entrance, one to either side of the door, and one in front of it, hands on the hilts of their swords. Bronwin brought his own hand down, onto the head of his flanged mace, strapped to his side, he tightened his grip on the tower shield he held in his left hand. He didn't trust anyone in this part of the country, especially those that were armed.

Saffron, in all his boiled glory, walked up to the guardsmen and nodded. The man in front of the passageway returned the gesture, then stepped to the side. Pushing the door forward, both men stepped through and into the prison that awaited them.

Much to Bronwin's surprise, the prison was quiet. He had grown accustomed to the wailings and rantings of madmen from Sun Spire. But here, the prisoners almost seemed content. Just living their day-to-day lives next to a bucket of their own piss and shit.

"We'll have to leave our weapons here," Saffron said as he unbuckled and pulled out his blades. "My men will keep a close eye on them, don't worry."

Raising an eyebrow, the Pale Bull looked down at the Plain's Warden. "Surely you jest?" his voice reverberated off the wooden walls. "You wish for me to leave *my* tools with a man I do not know?"

"Yes, I do," Saffron said defiantly, his posture straightening. "I know the man, and you know me. Whether or not you like me is a different matter. But the town guard can be trusted." He paused. "Now, I understand you've been given command of, well, everything here in Plainsview, myself and my striders included. But going against our established rules and customs, would not work in your favour."

Saffron and the words he spoke angered Bronwin, but he did speak with some semblance of knowledge. He huffed in agreement and handed his mace and shield over to the other guard. Saffron did the same with his weapons.

"Thank you," the Plain's Warden said with a nod. "Now come, you wanted to see the prisoners."

"Aye, they may be useful for my plans."

"Do you mind if I ask how?"

"Fodder, bait, might even arm a couple. It may save a few of my men's lives."

Saffron stayed silent, not replying. They walked past and looked into each cell; Saffron recalling the deeds that had placed them in their confines. It was remarkable at how well the Plain's Warden could remember each and every man's crime.

More than a few thieves had three fingers cut from each hand. They would be useless if given a weapon, but they would make adequate bait if needed. There were some rapists and murderers on the second floor of the building. The Squid had told him their cocks were severed and the wound cauterized. A tight bronze band had been placed around their testicles as a constant reminder of their crimes during confinement. A few men writhed and moaned at this in the corner of their cells, but none of them were outwardly violent.

If these men were to be used, they would be fodder for the Thregs, rapists had no place in society, Bronwin would gladly send them to their deaths if he was given the chance.

The third floor of the prison held foreign criminals, those coming in from the Endless Plains, with either illegal merchandise or the intent to harm Valenfaar and its people. Some had bronzed skin, their heads bald and their eyes a shade of golden yellow. Hailing from beyond Ajwix, in the lands owned by Gillian of the Battle Axe, a warlord with a sprawling empire.

Though the Valen people had never been directly in contact with the warlord, they had heard many tales of him, and his country from those that escaped. These foreign criminals, hailing from a country ruled by a warlord, would be useful with arms and shields placed among them. Bronwin smiled at one of the prisoners, a man of muscle, his skin nearly golden. The prisoner shied away and looked out between the bars of his window.

Finally, they arrived at the fourth floor, the part of the prison reserved for bandits. The thought behind this particular piece of segregation, or so Saffron had said, was to discourage their comrades from orchestrating breakouts. The fourth floor was the least accessible and would give the town's guards more than enough time to coordinate a response and thwart the rescue attempt.

This floor of the prison had been louder than the others: the bandits were conversing with one another from their cells about which groups they belonged to, and how theirs were better, the crimes they committed, the kills they had made, and so on. The Pale Bull would arm these men if he needed to.

Bronwin and Saffron had reached the back of this floor before long, peering into each cell as they went. At the far end sat a man, his eyes narrow, squinting at some unseen object. He sat with his back against the wall in the rear of his cell, quiet. Not saying a word.

"What did this one do?" the Pale Bull asked.

"Technically, murder. I guess."

"You guess?"

"Aye, it was rather confusing that day. The guards still aren't too sure as to what happened. But the one thing they could agree on was that this man was responsible. He's been here for a few moons now. He'll be conscripted by the end of this cycle."

"Does he have a name?"

"Not that we know of. He stays quiet about it all."

Bronwin snorted, then turned his back, and looked to another prisoner. There were sounds of shuffling behind him.

"Oi!" a gruff voice chirped. "They call me Dry Eyes!"

Bronwin started; a man with a title? Those were few and far between in Valenfaar. He held two different titles himself, the Pale Bull, and the Shield of Northwood. Anyone with a title had a history behind them. Who was this Dry Eyes, what did he do to earn this namesake? Bronwin pondered as he turned to face him; perhaps he had plucked the eyes from his victims and dried them in the sun, to be used for ... something, jewellery maybe?

Regardless, the bandit was standing, his hands clasped around the iron bars of his cell. His eyes were red and his beard unkempt. A scar ran down his cheek, and another along his scalp. He had seen combat, more than a few times.

Feeling hopeful the Pale Bull strode to the bars. "And you, Dry Eyes. Who are you?"

"I'm the greatest bandit that ever was, I am."

Bronwin raised an eyebrow. "Are you now? How many men have you killed?"

"Dozens! No, 'undreds! No. Dozens of 'undreds!"

"Is that so?" The commander's hope started to falter.

"Aye! 'Dry Eyes!' They would always say, ' 'ave mercy! 'aven't you killed enough?' Spat in their face I did, sure as shit. Then slit their throat." He drew his thumb across his neck.

"And who said this to you?"

The bandit hesitated, glancing to the side. "A person I killed! Doesn't matter which one!"

Bronwin leaned in, his own hands on the iron bars of the cell, he towered a foot and a half over Dry Eyes. "Oh, it does matter, you petty *bandit*." he spat. "Who told you to have mercy?"

"Er, uh," he stammered, "I, uh."

"Was it a child?"

"Uhhhh, no."

"A woman?"

"Um, no."

"A man?"

"Um, no?"

Bronwin was taken aback, a smidgen of hope returning to him. "A Threg?"

"Never 'ave seen a Threg I 'ave."

"So who, or what, told you to have mercy?"

The prisoner finally stopped hesitating. "Alright, fine! Twas a bird!"

"A bird?"

"Aye! A bird! An old man I robbed taught 'is bird how to talk. Damn thing wouldn't shuddup. Not ever." Dry Eyes blinked, then blinked again, and again before squinting back at the commander.

"So, bird-killing, is that what landed you in here?"

The bandit laughed a raspy chortle. "Naw naw. Not at all."

"So how did it happen?"

"It was my boys and me!" he said proudly as he puffed out his chest. "We came to rape the horses and steal the women!"

Bronwin raised an eyebrow. "*What?*"

"Oh, that ... didn't come out right, you see we-"

The Pale Bull held up a hand. "Please, spare me the details. One last question for you, bandit."

"Alright."

"You bear a title. That's rare. Especially for a bandit. Why do they call you Dry Eyes?"

Again he stammered. "It's because I have dry eyes." He blinked his red eyes rapidly again, then squinted.

Bronwin sighed heavily and turned away from Dry Eyes. He was utterly useless, Valenfaar's worst bandit if ever there was one. He would be fodder, a frontline meat shield.

"Ey!" the idiot bandit shouted, "I'm legendary! Best bandit there ever was, I am! Dozens of 'undreds killed! You will remember me, you pile of meat, you will remember the name Dry Eyes as it is sung in songs for many cycles to come!"

Songs? Bronwin thought. *Children's rhymes, mocking tunes, and ridicule. But not a bard's song you dry-eyed fool.*

#

Rel sat with Nef and Kol at a corner table in the local tavern, the Strider's Respite. The tavern's owner Deeanne — also known as Dee — was an absolutely lovely woman, as long as you kept on her good side. Rel had watched the woman chase out soldiers from her establishment in a yelling, violent, flurry of insults. Each of those men had deserved it: they had harassed her servers, reaching out for their bosoms or skirts.

One instance of this had gone differently than usual. A soldier: Atlas, Rel recalled, had stood up to his fellow soldiers. They had harassed one of the servers: a woman by the name of Olenna. An absolutely lovely person that Rel nearly had a fling with, many cycles back. But that one night, Atlas rose to his feet in defence of her. Rel had noticed Dee pursed her lips at the sight, her gaze casting daggers through the room, waiting to see what would happen. And much to everyone's relief, the situation defused itself harmlessly, and Atlas ended up leaving Plainsview with Olenna happily in tow.

The Plain's Master wondered how Olenna fared, it had been a long time since she had seen her. Oh, the stories she would have for her, of what had been happening in their hometown. Maybe one-day Rel would get the chance to see her again; that would be nice, they had practically grown up together. Now, she sat with two other close friends, Nef and Kol, her Right and Left Hand. Here they were, sitting in a tavern, sipping at their Plain's Mead, while the Pale Bull gallivanted around and took charge of their daily duties. What a shit show.

Taking a large mouthful of her mead, Rel placed her tankard down and looked to her friends.

"I don't like this," she said. "I can't stand that rhenhardt."

Kol nodded along, his mead already hitting him hard, he stayed silent as he swayed.

"How bad is he really though, Rel? I mean, he's often been called Alistair's Right Hand, just like how I'm yours. And Alistair seems like a fair man."

She shook her head. "He's a fair man, sure. But I doubt that he knows of everything Bronwin does."

"He's never failed a mission though. Even against the Thregs! And let's face it, we know what those things can be like."

A frown graced the Plain's Master's face. "He's never failed a mission. But have you seen the death toll that man comes with? Dozens, Nef. He throws soldiers at the problem until it's fixed."

Nef took a dreg of his tankard, then placed it down loudly. "I've heard those rumours too. But I'm also told that most of those men are prisoners: rapists and bandits, men who would be shunned for their crimes. Most of which deserve death. At least the way Bronwin sends them off, he's giving them an honourable end: defending their country or serving their sentence with a sense of bravery. Is that really so bad?"

"They could have it worse," Rel reluctantly agreed. "He uses prisoners, who may, or may not be, worthy of living, but he also uses men that aren't his. Units loaned to him from other commanders. He sends them out onto the front lines, next to prisoners, and gets them butchered. It's disgusting." She signalled a server for another tankard with two raised fingers. "He'll be doing the same with us."

"Alright," Nef nodded. "That's fair, but answer me this," He looked at her with clear certainty. "If you were leading an attack on an enemy, and were given, let's say, Spearpoint Force, to use, along with the striders. Would you not want to keep *your* striders safe? Your friends, and comrades? You would likely put Spearpoint forward in the lines wouldn't you?"

Rel grimaced: he had a point. She could see the reasoning was sound, even logical. It was only human to protect those closest to you.

"Agh, damn you Nef. You already know the answer to that question."

"So. You would only put us on the frontlines if absolutely necessary then?"

She nodded.

"He's not as bad as you paint him, Rel. He is still human, remember." He grinned slyly and took a small sip of his drink. He placed the tankard with a light tap.

A heavier thud shook the table a moment later. Kol had passed out, unable to hold his alcohol, his forehead pressed into the table.

"Did you see him eat anything today?" Rel asked, as the server — a dwarf — sat another drink next to her. "Thank you."

The server nodded, then left without a word.

"Can't say I saw him eat. Poor boy." Nef poked his friend in the shoulder and lifted him up by the collar of his tunic. He was out cold.

"That damn fool." Rel smiled then downed her new drink.

"I should get going, I need to check on Varden before I turn in for the night. I'll walk Kol home as well. Seems he needs the help."

"Sounds like a plan. I can almost feel Dee's stare ploughing into his back."

"Hey, Rhenhardt, let's go." Nef gave Kol a hard shake, still holding onto his clothes. The boy started, then awoke with a sway.

"Ey, ey. No pushin'." He waved a tired hand in the air.

"C'mon, big guy. Time to go home." Nef lifted the drunk from his chair and wrapped one arm around him.

"Home? Home, you say? Weeeeee."

Rel nodded to them as they left, finished her drink then left the tavern herself. She had to meet with Corduvan to see how his training had progressed.

Before long, the Plain's Master was sitting on a wooden crate in the rear of the strider's longhouse, with Corduvan before her, standing in a small sandpit that the striders used to spar. He held his new weapon with awkward pride, the hilt in two hands and the chain, with the blade, resting on the ground.

"Alright, let's see what you've come up with." Rel crossed her arms.

"Yes, ma'am."

He swung the hilt around wide like he was swinging a staff. The chain and blade lifted from the ground and began to give way to a broad, circular cleave. Corduvan realized he wouldn't be able to stop the blade safely, and began to turn with the chain. Effectively turning himself into a top, slowing down his turn — and the chain — until it settled back into the sand.

Rel raised an eyebrow as moonlight struck through the clouds. *Was it almost Moon's Peak already?*

"That's it?"

"Um, yes. I haven't much time to practise lately."

"Well, it is certainly ..." she struggled for the right words, then found them: "Something, I suppose. How about this, try one hand on the hilt, and another on the chain. It might give you more control." The roll of twine unravelled in her mind even more.

A glimpse of realization flashed in Corduvan's eye. "Of course, ma'am. I'll be sure to try that as soon as I can. I'm uh ..." He looked to the ground. "I'm sorry I don't have any more to show you. Tonight was a waste of your time."

"Nonsense, my friend. Not a waste of my time at all! Helping soldiers grow and learn is all part of my job. Now, see to it that you learn how to use that weapon." She had wanted to call it a toy. "If I deem you a threat to our own, I will have it confiscated, are we clear?"

Shock spread across his face. "Yes, ma'am. As clear as the skies over the Endless Plains."

"Good. But if you do learn how to use that thing, I have a feeling you could save quite a few lives. Keep practising, and please, make damn sure you put time aside for it. If I hear the same sorry excuse you gave me tonight, by Gwendall's Blade, I'll keep you in the prisons, guarding you-know-who."

"Yes, ma'am. I will, no need to worry." He quickly nodded.

"Good, you're dismissed. Head home, or to wherever it is you need to be, just don't be here if someone else comes poking about. You're only allowed here because I am. Now go." She gave an upward nod away from the training yard.

Corduvan nodded, picked up the length of chain from his weapon, and scurried away. Rel grinned to herself as she looked to the skies. A clear night, the stars and moon were out in all their clandestine glory. It was time for a good night's rest, and to hold Ashlin in her arms once more.

#

Most of the night in the Strider's Respite was a blur. Kol woke inexplicably in his bed around Moon's Peak. He had broken out in a cold sweat, adrenaline surging through his veins. In his dreams, he heard the laughter of children and the screaming of soldiers.

That was all he could remember: a senseless nightmare that had felt all too real. He usually had nightmares when he was drinking though, so he chalked this up to one of the same. But something about those screams and something about the laughter shook him deeper than he could imagine. Something was wrong, and he wasn't sure he wanted to know what.

The laughing had seemed like a whisper, delivered to him from across the room, on the wind. He sat up in his bed, sweat pouring from his hair. Someone had changed him, he was naked, no longer in his uniform. It was probably Nef: he was always looking out for him.

Kol winced, his head pounded, he had drunk too much, and even though he could remember little more than the plump bottom on the dwarven server, he walked out to his window and looked up to the night sky above him. The moon hung in the air, like a pale coin against the backdrop of a glittering ocean, streaks of red glanced across the vista. It was beautiful, and Kol found himself wondering who else was looking up at the moon at this exact moment. By Esmirla, maybe the dwarf was looking at it right now. He grinned at the thought, if only she were here with him. He would like that. No, he would love that.

Chapter 11

The loud rattling of Kol's door woke him with a start. A heavy fist shook off the wood and reverberated through the house and into his mind. His head felt as if it had been split open with an axe, the light of the early morning sun penetrated his window and seared his eyes like a hot iron. His mouth felt like he had been chewing on cotton, and his eyes even felt rough, like sand, when he blinked.

"Kol!" a familiar voice called, rattling his brain, "Kol, wake up!"

The young strider groaned as he sat up in bed, placing his feet over the sides and leaning forward. "What?!" he yelled back, he winced as his head pounded with the word.

"We've been summoned, get your ass out here!"

The voice was Nef, and the tone in his words screamed urgency. Kol quickly rose, hurriedly put on his cloak and weapons, slung the flat quiver of arrows over his shoulder and did the same with his short bow. He stomped out the door of his house to find Nef leaning against it, his arms crossed, and a look of disapproval on his face.

"Took you long enough," he said flatly.

The words screeched as they reached his ears, he tried his best to ignore them. "Sorry, had a bit too much to drink last night." He raised a palm of one hand to his temple.

Nef shook his head. "I was able to count to seventy during that time. You'd be dead if someone was attacking you. You need to be faster." Nef left the comfort of the wall and waved to Kol to follow before breaking into a light jog.

"Why the rush?" Kol asked, his head throbbing with every step.

"Bronwin has called a meeting of the striders: Thregs were spotted before sunrise."

"In the plains?"

"In the plains."

Sarcasm filled his reply. "Lovely."

They strode through the sprawling town and arrived by the great willow tree at its core. Bronwin stood with Saffron at his side, rows of striders stood in front of him. Almost all of their number. One man, however, sat against the longhouse wall, hand clutched against his side, his face twisted in pain.

Kol and Nef found their places to the left and right of Rel, respectively. They stood at attention as Bronwin towered over them, staring through the Plain's Striders. The Pale Bull looked to the Plain's Master, who responded with a nod.

"Striders!" the voice boomed and echoed as if a landslide. Birds swarmed out of trees, and rats scurried back to their holes. "Thregs have been sighted in your precious Plains once again!" He paused for a moment as the striders looked at him with interest. "It is by your own fault, and by your own hands that these monsters have managed to fester this close to the Halo!"

Those words caused a stir in the square, he blamed the striders for the Thregs' arrival, as if they hadn't tried to prevent it. How could you prevent an enemy from arriving when you had no idea, how or *where* they arrived from?

"It is because of this failure in your duty that I am sending out my own men to quell this nuisance!" He cast his gaze over the crowd again. "And as punishment, if any of my men should fall, an equal number of striders shall face lashings in equal measure to lives lost!"

Silence rolled through the crowd. Even Saffron, standing behind the Bull, stood in awe, his mouth slightly ajar, his eyes glassed with fear. He couldn't be serious: punishing striders if his own men fell?

Bronwin stood with his gaze stern and set, like a marble statue. "You will be given recourse, by your own knowledge. Teach my men the secrets of the Endless Plains, teach them how to survive, for if my men fall, it will not be to Thregs, but to the elements of Esmirla herself! Failure to teach my men will result in the punishment of your own. Bear that in mind striders, for if you do not, blood will be spilled."

Saffron, still behind the Bull, gathered his wits noticeably and raised his gaze to the men and women of the Plain's Striders. "You heard the man," he said with a feeble boom compared to Bronwin's baritone cascade. "We will begin tutoring his men at once on how to survive in the plains. Show them our ways of keeping trails covered, and our lives bountiful whilst at the whims of Esmirla!"

The striders elected to keep things simple, Rel, Nef and Kol made a sequence of informational speeches to Bronwin's men not too long after: how to make suitable sleeping arrangements in the fields, and how to scatter the remains. They also went over reliable watering holes and wildlife locales that the men could use to stay fed and hydrated. Of course, some of the striders would be going with them as guides, but the more the soldiers knew, the less likely it would be that any of them would perish. Rel had pointed out what tracks and signs to look for when away from the usual groups of wildlife, to aid in their hunts. By the end of it all, the three striders were confident that the information they had provided would be sufficient to keep Bronwin's men alive.

Through the briefing, however, Bronwin was nowhere to be seen. He had vanished from sight, which none of them thought was possible.

#

Standing at the edge of the Valley, Bronwin stood with the swamp at his back. He had been surveying the area for a possible forward fortification. The swamplands opened up from a narrow passage between sloping rock walls that worked their way up mountains on either side. These slopes were covered in dirt, mud and grime, but were otherwise sturdy. An eight-metre tall wooden wall, with a gate, built across this narrow opening would provide a good first line of defence against any Thregs wandering closer to Plainsview.

He turned to Algrenon. "Send word to our builders. I want a standard wall built here, to here." He pointed from one side to the other. "Am I clear?"

"As clear as the skies above the Endless Plains, sir."

The Pale Bull raised an eyebrow. "When did you start spouting *that?*"

"Sorry, sir. Something the striders like to say. I'll get word to the builders right away." He turned from the Shield of Northwood and moved back towards Plainsview, two other men in tow.

"You five," Bronwin waved some more of his men over. "Spread out and sweep the rest of the valley. If you see any Thregs, fall back. I'll send for reinforcements and we'll engage."

The soldiers nodded in confirmation, then moved into the valley before them. They paced through the grass in a large sweep. Bronwin watched with a small sense of pride. They knew what it meant to fight Thregs, to watch them tear your family apart. It was how he chose his men. Every engagement Bronwin had with his enemy, he would look for the people they had hurt the most. These soldiers, who had their families ripped from their hands, then torn apart in front of them, made the best fighters against any Threg. They were fierce, had nothing to lose, craved vengeance, and seethed hatred towards the creatures. This made them compliant, and loyal to Bronwin and his cause. Casualties were a given but the Pale Bull's soldiers had much fewer casualty rates than that of any other unit in the land.

The majority of soldiers looked at him like he was a madman sending waves of troops to their deaths. Occasionally this had been true, he had to admit, but why would he sacrifice his best chances at winning a battle, when they were best used later in the fight? Why roll the dice unless you had a good chance of them being in your favour? That was the Pale Bull's method: gamble only when you had the best possible chance at success. You couldn't win all the time, he knew that, but he played smart whenever he could, and his men grew and learned because of this.

Eventually, the need to send other men to their deaths wouldn't be needed, his own men would be the first and last line of defence against the Thregs, an unstoppable force, trained through combat. He would save countless lives in the long run, and that made the sacrifices worth it.

Much time had passed, and Bronwin's scouts returned to him well past Sun's Peak. They reported nothing; the Valley looked to be clear, and the

Thregs were nowhere in sight. Algrenon had returned with builders in tow, who had promptly started clear-cutting trees and building the wall they would use as a frontline in the event of Thregs advancing into the Valley.

#

Corduvan stood in the training grounds of the strider longhouse once more, swinging his foreign weapon through the air. He had a surprising amount of control, using one hand on the hilt and another on the chain. He still lacked much skill, and though Rel would certainly not have him in the field with this weapon anytime soon, she could see him as useful with it in due time.

Since Bronwin and his men had arrived, Rel sought out Corduvan on a nearly nightly basis, wanting to pick up the pace of his training; she had even managed to talk Saffron into switching around the guardsman's patrols so he could have more time to practise. That was paying off: the weapon swayed and swung with more accuracy and purpose than it had before. But more often than not, it would still flail and swing in a nonsensical motion as the eager man lost control.

"Agh!"

The cry came out quickly and snapped Rel out of her thoughts. She looked over to Corduvan and saw him with the chain of his weapon wrapped around his leg. He tried to lift it to untangle his leg, and instead, ended up pulling himself down and into the dirt. He sputtered and spat as he ate the earth below him. He sat up and untangled himself, looking defeated.

"You are improving, Corduvan," the Plain's Master said. "We'll meet again after the morrow. Keep up the work, and I won't have to take your weapon from you." She winked at him and gave him an encouraging smile.

His mood lifted somewhat at this, his eyes showing a glimmer of hope. "Yes, ma'am," he said, rising to his feet. "I appreciate this. Truly."

"Good. I'm having a good time with this myself, truth be told. Now go, get some rest, things are about to get a lot busier around here."

Corduvan nodded and hurried out of the courtyard, Rel walked over to a nearby stack of crates and sat down, leaning into them. She closed her eyes for a moment and watched as the stillness of night settled all around her. The wind ceased as clouds covered the night sky, insects fell silent and even the noise of the town seemed to fade away. A low rumble of thunder rolled through the darkness. She smiled to herself. It was peaceful, nothing but night and the booming thunder around her.

Rain began to fall in a soft patter, dotting the sand and dirt of the training square with moisture. She watched as the darkened spots became more frequent until finally, a steady rain fell and swept through the world, washing away the events of the day. Rel closed her eyes again and raised her face to the sky. She felt the rain wash down her body and soak into her clothes.

Ashlin hated the rain, but Rel loved everything about it. It gave life, cleanliness, and peace. She had lain on her own rooftop often during rainfall, letting it run over and through her, cleansing her thoughts.

Tomorrow, she thought, would be the first time Bronwin made his move against the Thregs. The scout who had come back wounded had lost his ranging partner to the savages. They had found one camp, only three Thregs present. They thought it had been two until the third swept up and drove a dagger into the survivors' side. They tried to fight back, to run, but to no avail. A wooden arrow, tipped with bone, had punched through the back of the other strider's skull and pushed her eye out through the exit wound. The retelling had been grizzly, and the wounded man wept through much of it.

His wound though, Rel worried, was heavily infected. The weapon he had been stabbed with hadn't been clean, he had said. And it had taken him the better half of a day to make it back to Plainsview. After being stabbed with a sharpened bone, and walking through that damnable swamp, it had gotten infected and festered quickly. Pus and dying flesh permeated the opening. His likelihood of surviving didn't look good, the magister had said the infection spread incredibly quickly and had already infected the man's blood. Soon it would be in his bones, and then he would fall prey to his illness. On the morrow, the magister would use a combination of Dead Man's Root and healing magic to ease the strider's suffering as he began his journey to the Soul Spire.

She opened her eyes and found the rain had stopped, the sky clear and the thunder gone. How long had she closed her eyes for? Did she fall asleep? She looked for the moon. It was past its Peak. Ashlin would be worried.

A quick stroll through Plainsview brought Rel back home. The town itself smelled of the earthiness that only rainfall could bring. The Plain's Master loved that smell, it always left her with a feeling that she was connected to the world. She couldn't explain it all too well, but it was something she felt and knew to be true.

Opening the door to her home, Rel stripped naked, lit a fire in the hearth and left her wet uniform on the floor to dry. Ashlin was already in bed, sleeping the night away. Rel peaked into the bedroom and saw her familiar figure under the sheets. She crawled in next to her and wrapped her arms around the smaller woman.

"You're wet," Ashlin said emphatically.

Rel raised an unseen eyebrow. "That's your fault." she chided back.

"Oh-hoh really now?" Ashlin rolled over, and in the darkness, looked into Rel's eyes.

The Plain's Master giggled coyly, and grabbed her lover's hand, guiding it between her legs. "See?"

Ashlin gently rubbed, and slipped her finger inside, kissing Rel deeply the entire time. "I love you." they both said.

They made love once again, taking in each other's beings in a tangling, and entwining bliss. They loved each other, they were one, and nobody — not even a Threg — could take that away from them. Anyone who tried would fail, and lose their lives in the process. Rel and Ashlin were two lovers at the edge of the world, living their lives as happily as they dared.

Chapter 12

Roth and Vera Highfold sat at the opposite end of the dining room table from Alistair; Varen and Maryam were along either side, opposite each other. It was comical to the Arch General how such a large table was utilized for such a small family. Cullen, as usual, was not present for their family gatherings, but this was no matter to them anymore, the Highfolds had grown accustomed to his absences.

Varen was wearing the High Priest's robes, blue, embroidered with gold, whilst Maryam had gone for a more modest approach: a simple dark blue dress over a white shirt and tights. The king, his father, had gone for his ceremonial green doublet, crown perched atop his bald head. Vera matched him in a dress of the same green embroidered with golden vines. The family emanated royalty, even Alistair had decided upon wearing a cardinal red doublet, with slight golden inlays depicting vines across the chest.

Servers spread into the room, placing steaks, corn, and chicken in front of them on the dark wood of the table. Varen motioned for everyone to bow their heads as the servers left the room, then spoke a prayer:

"By Daylen, Esmirla, Gwendall, and Jo-een: the Council of Four. For each of your duties, for each of your skills, your actions; for this world we live, this food we eat, and this kingdom we rule. We thank you."

The Highfolds lifted their heads, opening their eyes. The family of five reached for their utensils and began cutting into their meals. Alistair cut off a chunk of the steak sitting in front of him and popped it into his mouth. He chewed, tasting the black pepper that crusted its outer layer, filling his senses with tingling spice.

"So, Brother," Varen said. "I hear your pet Bull has begun making waves in Plainsview, and he has only been there a couple of days."

The Arch General swallowed, and noticed his father's watchful eye on him. "Yes, he has. He has forces moving out this day to face a small group of Thregs. A spraven arrived early this morning bearing the news." He placed another piece of steak into his mouth.

"Our dear brother has been keeping you well informed then?" Varen asked, biting a carrot off of his fork.

"You would claim Bronwin doesn't inform me himself?"

"That brute?" the High Priest said with his mouthful. He swallowed. "I'd be shocked if he remembered to write any sort of report. You know how he is, so involved in his work, you're lucky to hear from him once per moon."

He was right, it was usually Algrenon that kept Alistair informed, and that was infrequent at best. He did rely on Cullen to keep up to date with Bronwin's doings.

"You speak true." the Arch General agreed. "How fares your expedition in Wreath's Burrow? They arrived yesterday, did they not?"

"Aye, they did. I received the spraven last night. Though I haven't heard anything since. With luck, I'll know something before the moon's turn. The officer you sent seems a bit of a buffoon, I admit."

Alistair nodded as he swallowed another piece of meat. "Aye, I've heard as much. But he came highly recommended by some of our officers, and seeing how your expedition shouldn't see any opposition, he seemed fitting for the job."

Varen chuckled and nodded to himself, chewing a small piece of chicken. "Fair point," he said with a grin, dabbing at his chin with a cloth.

"The two things you boys have going on, have forced me to pull some favours from the north you know?" Maryam looked at them, scolding. "You know, had you given me a little more time," She swirled her fork in the air in front of her. "Oh say, a fortnight, I would have been able to get the coin ready for you quite easily, but noooo, you had to move without patience, force me to collect an early tax from the gold mines. You two are lucky I know what I'm doing." She pointed her fork at them, a small piece of chicken dangling off the prongs. She raised an eyebrow and popped it into her mouth.

"We owe you quite a bit," Alistair said earnestly. "Your efforts have not gone unnoticed."

"Indeed," Varen said, before taking a sip of wine. "We will repay you when the timing allows."

Maryam smiled to herself, seeming satisfied with her brothers' grovelling. All the while, the king and queen remained silent, watching the exchange.

Finally, after clearing his throat and placing down his tankard, Roth Highfold broke the silence: "We're trusting you three to keep this country safe. Are you certain you are up to the task?"

The siblings all looked at each other, a slight pang of worry in their eyes. Alistair, being the eldest, spoke on their behalf: "Yes Father, of course. Varen is simply investigating a rumour in the west, while I'm dealing with small groups of Thregs in the east, the country is in no danger. What urges you to ask such a loaded question?"

"Your haste begs the question." his mother answered, her gaze cool. "You act without planning, assembling expeditions and sending out soldiers without preparation. It is costly, for both the treasury and for your men."

Varen and Alistair exchanged a worried look. "You are ... correct, Mother." the Arch General admitted, his head bowed. "You have our apologies."

Varen nodded.

Their father swallowed a mouthful of wine. "And why did you boys act with such haste?" his tone was accusing, not inquiring, he didn't seem to care for their reasoning, he wanted them to realize how brash they had been.

Varen spoke first. "The rumours I had heard Father: if they are true-"

"*If* they are true Varen. *If.*" The king laid down his utensils, patience leaving his voice. "Tell me, how much research did you put into these rumours, before spending the country's coin and sending a near hundred men?"

"Father, I could not spare the time to delve too deep, else Wixen spies uncover the secrets of our magics instead."

"And if this proves to be nothing more than a ruse, perhaps even perpetrated by these Wixen spies, it leaves us without men and without coin. Our kingdom is barely turning a profit through trade, Varen; we can hardly afford these baseless expeditions. For your sake, you had better hope something positive comes of this venture."

"Yes, Father, sorry Father," Varen silently went back to his meal, poking meekly at a carrot.

"And you, Alistair," Roth said, his gaze of iron now resting on his eldest son. "What of your reason for haste? I understand the Plain's Warden requested aid, but to send Bronwin and his platoon, at such short notice, looked to be overzealous."

The Arch General could feel his sister's gaze on him from the side, adding more tension to the situation. "Father, Saffron was worried, perplexed, and incessant that aid be sent his way. You know how he can be: he wouldn't take common soldiers as a sign of aid, he would take it as an insult. He is not a patient man, I had to-"

"You let that man, that Squid of a man, take advantage of you."

Alistair was dumbfounded, his mouth dry. His father was right, and he hadn't even realized it until this moment, he already knew what his father was about to say, the scolding he would, himself, have given one of his officers.

"You let a man of lesser station and power, pull resources and men out from a Central City, with no repercussions. You let this man cost your family, and your country, coin. You even gave him a titled warrior, which, I may add, runs a much higher wage than that of nearly any other soldier in the kingdom. You are the damned Arch General!" The king's fists came down onto the wood rattling his plate. "You hold more control over our military than any other man! And yet, you let this old, red-faced ranger push you over and take what he wants, without you even realizing it." his father huffed. "You may be my children, but you must stop acting like children. Be the men you are claiming to be. Be calm, collected, and firm in your duties." He looked to Varen. "Do your research before delegating resources," then said to Alistair, "and show your inferiors that that is what they are: *inferior.* The sooner you two understand these concepts, the sooner you'll find yourself ready to take the throne. Am I clear, boys?"

The way his father said 'boys' left Alistair with boiling blood, he was no longer a child, how dare his father treat him as such. But, he pushed away his pride and acknowledged his father's scolding. "Yes sir, it won't happen again. By Gwendall's Blade, I promise you this."

"And by Daylen, I promise you the same." Varen looked over to his older brother with a look of disappointment, Alistair nodded.

Meanwhile, Maryam sat with a smug look on her face, her mood screaming 'I told you so.' Roth noticed this and gave her a reprimanding scowl. She quickly cleared her throat and then looked back to her meal, pretending it hadn't happened.

"Father?" Alistair asked, hoping to redirect the mood of the meal.

The king allowed the redirection, resuming his meal as he had prior. "Yes?"

"How fares negotiations with the Wixen, are we still working on acquiring some of their sword masters for training our troops?"

His father nodded as he put his wine to rest on the table. "Yes yes, we are working avidly to try and persuade them to let us use their sword masters. But you know how stubborn they can be, they aren't giving us much wiggle room for haggling. I am reluctant to give them what they wish."

"What are they asking for?" Varen asked.

"In exchange for five of their sword masters, the Wixen are requesting an embassy here in Valen, staffed with only their men, and free entry into the country for any of their citizens, as long as they hold the proper paperwork from their king."

"That … is rather steep," Maryam admitted. "It could give them immense political power, and the threat of staging a coup to overthrow us would be ever-present."

"Our thoughts exactly," Vera admitted. "They're playing at something, and at this point, we're almost willing to give up. But alas, it is something we will strive to achieve. Wixen swordsmen are the best in the world. If Valenfaar's military could acquire their knowledge, we could expand our lands considerably, even tame the Endless Plains of its outcasts and bandits. We would be secure, and there would be little threat of rebellion with such well-trained soldiers around every corner."

The whole family nodded in agreement. The Valen military was strong, both in number and in skill, but the rebellion all those cycles ago had proved to them that even peasants and settlers could pose a threat. And Wixen swordsmen, though not as great in number as Valen swordsmen, could slay five times what a common soldier could. Valenfaar needed their knowledge if they were to push out beyond the Halo and start establishing the Valen empire.

"With luck, Father," Varen spoke, "if these rumours my men are checking prove true, perhaps we could use newly found information in exchange for the secrets of their swordsmen?"

"Perhaps," Roth Highfold agreed while cutting at some veal. "Time will tell. We are awaiting word from them regarding our previous offer. We need to take this one step at a time and read between all their words. They are master politicians after all."

"So are you, Father," Maryam complimented, "I speak for all three of us. We have faith you will succeed. You haven't failed the country yet."

Alistair rolled his eyes. His sister resorted to flattery more often than he cared for, she was her father's favourite, it was abundantly clear. She was talented with her duties, yet it felt as if there was something else between his sister and father that cemented such a close relationship. Alistair didn't really care what it was, but the favouritism did bother him on some, inane, childish level. He pushed the feelings aside and took another bite of his steak.

Chapter 13

It had been a half fortnight since Bronwin had sent his men into the Endless Plains to take on the camp of Thregs. He hadn't gone with them, he trusted Algrenon could handle it. That man had seen nearly as many Thregs as the Pale Bull had, and he commanded the loyalty of those that followed him without effort.

Bronwin had always liked Algrenon: he was a good soldier, and a decent man, not afraid to do what needed to be done, and never questioned the orders he was given. He saw the reasoning behind everything, and followed Bronwin without question, always dedicating his all at every turn.

Half a fortnight had been more than enough for them to return. Yet, here he stood, atop the skeleton of an eight-metre-tall wall without its gate, built at the edge of a swamp, mosquitoes making him itch at his neck. He was a warrior of legend, and yet, he found himself losing a battle against insects that had no disregard for the man they were so relentlessly attacking.

Beside him, much to his chagrin, was the scholar. A mouse-faced Wixen man who went by the name of Varden. Ever since the Bull had arrived, the scholar had been practically glued to his side. If the man had been Valen, he would have snapped his neck for interfering with military operations. He was Wixen however, and if the Highfolds wanted those sword masters, he had to keep the wretch alive.

Varden broke the silence. "Tell me, Bronwin: do you worry for your men?" he pulled out a small leather-bound notebook and a piece of charcoal from his robes.

"No."

"And why would that be so?" he scribbled into his book.

"My men are talented. They will succeed."

"And if there are casualties? You can't possibly expect a flawless deployment every time."

"Casualties teach the survivors to be more prepared, to learn and grow stronger. A casualty is a lesson, not a burden."

"Interesting," he scribbled faster, then closed the notebook. "May I ask a small favour of you?"

The soldier turned, looked down at the scholar, and raised a behemoth eyebrow. "You request a favour of me? I've done you nothing but favours since I've arrived."

"True. You have answered my questions, kept me company, and the like-"

Kept you company? Bronwin thought. *You forced yourself into my company.*

"But this request could be important to my studies, and will more than likely, allow me back to my country far sooner than you may think."

That caught his attention, being rid of this foreigner would be far more favourable if he were gone sooner rather than later. "Fine," he agreed. "What is it?"

"Well, normally I would do this myself. But seeing how your men have not returned yet, and there is the possibility of Thregs roaming around, I request of you, an escort."

"Why?"

"Take a look, just inside the swamp there, do you see that strange colouration?" the scholar raised a skinny finger and pointed behind them.

Bronwin turned. "Yes."

"That, my large friend, is a shadewood tree. And I wish to study it. Would you do me the honours?"

Reluctantly, Bronwin agreed, he would escort the scholar with a small troop. It would do him some good to get off the wall for a while.

They were walking through the swamp not long after, insects buzzing all around, prompting many curses from the soldiers. The scholar, however, seemed perfectly content. Even happier in the muck and thicker air.

"Just over here," he said, stepping over a rotting log. "Not far now."

The Wixen stepped mere metres in front of the six soldiers. One of them, an archer, tripped and nearly landed headlong into the mud.

"Gwendall's Cock!" he cursed, "Why are we escorting this guy anyway?"

"Back in line, Soldier," the Pale Bull barked.

The soldier fell silent.

"Ah, it's beautiful!" Varden hurried over to the base of the black trunk and stared up into the white leaves. "You weren't here two days ago were you?" he said to the tree. "So where did you come from?" the scholar reached into his robe, withdrawing his notebook.

Bronwin watched in annoyance as the scholar sketched the tree. Though he found this pointless, he had to admit that the sketch looked rather good. It wasn't a life-like re-creation, but it was far superior to what most men and women were capable of.

"Box perimeter. Now," he said to his soldiers.

"Yessir," they said in chorus, then spread out, each taking the corner of an imaginary box, with the fifth man standing upon the opposite side of the tree as his commander.

"Bronwin, this is fascinating," the Wixen had placed a palm on the bark of the tree. "Its bark is astoundingly soft. I wonder ..." he trailed off, reaching into his robe he pulled out a small knife. He poked it through the bark, then halted. "But the wood is so hard! I've never seen anything like it." he scribbled into his notebook once more, leaving his blade in the tree.

Bronwin huffed, then turned away, letting his thoughts drown out the incessant blabbering of his unwelcome guest. He surveyed the thick foliage around them, watching the thicket for any signs of movement. If he found anything, it would either be men, or Thregs. They hadn't fully scouted the swamp prior to starting the wall. There could have been stragglers laying within.

Then, echoing through the nature around him, he heard a branch snap over the blabbering of the man behind him.

"Scholar. Silence."

The Wixen grew quiet, then stood next to him, his eyes also searching the foliage.

Bronwin knocked his gauntleted fist against his breastplate twice: a signal. His men heard this, drew their weapons and hefted their shields, spying the terrain for what had caused the alarm. The Pale Bull pulled the flanged mace from his waist and lifted his shield on his left arm. They readied themselves, spreading their feet farther apart, bracing for an unseen foe.

Another branch snapped, then another, followed by the splashing of water. Someone was coming. Bronwin knocked his mace against his shield gently, sending out a quiet 'ting' to his men. They all turned to match where his gaze had gone. The swamp road, ten metres in front of them, just on the other side of a small row of trees, shadows moved slowly, unbalanced, short. Too small to be Thregs. The shadows ceased their movements, and the sound of metal on leather rang.

"Who goes there?!" a voice called. "Show yourselves or be killed!"

Bronwin grinned to himself. "You fucking fool!" he boomed, "You'll be the ones dead!"

But what stepped through the treeline shocked him, and left his mouth dry.

#

His wrists were raw, his mouth dry and his head pounding. He could hardly feel his feet. It was a blur, all of it. Otheer remembered much and nothing. Algrenon had set up a perimeter around the Threg camp, with the help of the Plain's Striders, and launched their attack. Otheer himself remembered bursting from the tall grass, his hands awash with his magical winds. He had thrust his hands in front of him, sending a gust of invisible power towards one of the monsters, just as he had done a hundred times before. The Threg had been knocked off balance, losing its weapon, while two other men leapt into the fray, carving the beast to pieces.

He remembered watching the striders as they involved themselves, acrobatically side-stepping blows from one of the three remaining Thregs, letting Bronwin's men cleave away at the thick hide. It had all gone so well, no fatalities, and no injuries. The four Thregs had fallen easily, almost too easily. Otheer had spent the last six cycles with Bronwin, after the man saved his village from an encampment of the horrors. The mage had quickly requested entry into the Pale Bull's unit as a form of repayment, thankfully, the warrior had agreed to his request, saying that a mage would be of great help on the battlefield.

Then everything had gone black, and he remembered nothing. The assault felt as if it had been days ago. Otheer had no idea if that wasn't accurate. Whether it was a moon ago, or a fortnight, he could not guess. But now, he knew exactly where he was. Though he couldn't figure out what had happened that led him to be where he was, he knew that the Thregs had taken him captive. The rope around his knees and wrists felt as if it were made of hair, not twine, it was too soft.

The mage struggled to crane his head, to look at his legs, and sure enough, the ropes binding his legs together were not ropes at all. But hair. And worst off, he recognized the hair, the blond and brown mix of a friend. It was Keetlyn's, one of the soldiers who had fought with him however long ago. The mage shuddered. He tried to summon a tempest in his bound arms but couldn't. He would need to bide his time before he made his escape, regain his strength.

He couldn't see much. He was placed on the ground, facing what he assumed to be a tent. Otheer tried to think nothing of it. By Daylen, he just wanted to remember what had happened, where his friends were. Keetlyn was likely dead, or so he hoped. The thought of his friend, laying on the ground, scalped and alive sent shivers down his spine.

Otheer's jaw was sore and felt slightly out of place. He twisted and, using what little strength he had, pushed his face at an odd angle into the dirt. His lower jaw popped and snapped back into place. He nearly screamed but managed to stifle it to a pained groan.

What he heard next silenced him immediately. Footsteps, heavy footsteps, somewhere behind him, followed by a sharp pain as a blade pierced his right leg and lodged itself in his bones. He breathed hard, then screamed as he was pulled through the dirt by the thing in his leg. Only one thought rang through his mind during the ordeal, *why* had the Thregs taken him prisoner? They had *never* taken anyone prisoner, not in all of recorded history.

What would happen to him, Otheer couldn't be certain, no one could be certain. He supposed that like everything, time would tell. He could only hope that if what he discovered was not to his liking that time would take him shortly after as to avoid prolonging his role of a Threg prisoner. Goosebumps curled down his back as he realized that the only guarantee he faced, would be that he would never see home again.

#

Bronwin chewed his lip and felt a mixture of anger and sadness well up within him as Algrenon told him everything that had happened. The hunt against the Thregs had gone off without a hitch, the beasts slain with ease with nobody injured or killed. Until that is, their ambush had been ambushed. Nearly two dozen Thregs had amassed from the grass, somehow unseen by the forces that had assailed their comrades.

Algrenon had given the order for retreat, immediately realizing the day was lost. But it had been too late. In a matter of heartbeats, four of their men were cut down and savaged, the two Plain's Striders included. Otheer, their mage had been lost. This upset him, Otheer was their only mage. It was rare for his kind to enlist with the Sovereign Guard, most of them preferred church business.

Only Algrenon and three others had survived. In no small part due to the odd occurrence that the Thregs had chosen not to pursue. The Pale Bull was told that they seemed content and left the survivors to their own devices.

None of it made sense: the Thregs had never been spotted in any larger number than a dozen, nor had they ever ambushed Sovereign troops, or let their enemies escape. Though he had this feeling before, he was certain that the Thregs he faced now, were not of the same mind as those in the past.

Behind him, Varden had ignored the conversation and went back to the shadewood tree, blathering on and on about one thing and the next. Constantly fascinated by the workings of a useless tree.

Now, Bronwin realized, he knew what he would have to do. He gave the order, and they all began to move back towards Plainsview. Algrenon with his survivors in tow, and Varden with the small complement of guards that escorted him.

"If I require these men again, Bronwin, may I bring them with me?"

"Why?" he asked flatly.

"To continue my studies on that tree. It really is fascinating, and besides, the sooner I figure out its secrets, the sooner you have leave of my company, remember?"

Bronwin snorted, then agreed. "Fine. Take these five as your personal guard. If they have any problems with this, send for Algrenon."

"Thank you, sir. Thank you." The scholar bowed his head slightly as the groans of his escort broke the air.

It wasn't long before they had arrived back in Plainsview, the sun only moving slightly in the sky. The longhouse the Plain's Striders called home loomed before them in the centre of town. Bronwin reached forward, ducked his head and pushed through the door, his men following. Not that he cared, but the scholar had disappeared shortly after they entered the town.

The Pale Bull pushed through one door and the next, much to the protest of many striders. Finally, the door to Saffron's personal office opened, revealing the Squid inside, sitting behind his oaken desk, looking as boiled as a frog.

"Ah, Bronwin," he said. "To what do I owe the pleasure?"

"Stow your shit, Squid. We have a problem."

The Plain's Warden looked over the men in the room, as if seeing them for the first time, his expression was one of concern. "Where are the rest of your men? And mine?"

"Dead," Algrenon said flatly.

The men of the Sovereign Guard explained the situation and told Saffron what they had to do next. A ranging, three of the striders' best. Not to engage, not to trap, only to observe from afar. Using the Halo has their vantage point.

The Squid reluctantly agreed. "Alright. I'll send for Rel and her Hands, have them out first thing in the morning. It's nearly sundown as is."

Bronwin nodded. He would have preferred them sent out *now* but he supposed they would need time to prepare. He needed any information on the plains he could get, and with the natural vantage point that the Halo provided, it would be the perfect opportunity to gain something worthwhile.

He turned to Algrenon. "Take your group and put them on leave for now. I'm putting you in charge of the wall as of the morrow. Now go, do what you will for the rest of the day."

"Yes, sir." the officer bowed his head, then left the room with his soldiers.

"You realize, Bull, that if I lose my three best due to your wants, you will not have the striders' cooperation." The Plain's Warden's eyes bore a look of anger, it would have caused a weaker man to stumble backwards. But not the Shield of Northwood, he stood, matched the gaze, and grinned. "Is that a threat, Saffron?"

"Threat or promise. Take your pick."

The Pale Bull leaned forward, resting his hands on the warden's desk, then whispered: "Then it'll be your head I use as a club, to break the spines of the rest."

#

The small house he had been given had not upset Varden. In fact, he was rather pleased with the arrangement. It was a single room, but that was fine. He only needed a bed and a desk anyway. He had left Ajwix with plenty of coin to keep him fed, and to buy whatever equipment he would need. He wasn't a rich man, but he was well enough off that he could afford more luxuries than most. He would be fine for the time being, but he couldn't stay forever.

He sat hunched over the small wooden desk in the corner of his one-room shack. Looking over the notes he had taken earlier in the day. The shadewood tree: a tree with a black trunk, and white leaves. Upon closer inspection, Varden had found the tree to have incredibly soft bark, both in density and in feeling. It had resembled that of felt, like some robes or gowns used by the wealthy. Yet when the bark had been pierced, the wood underneath was nearly as hard as stone, prompting the Wixen to apply a great deal of strength to his dagger to set it into the trunk.

That was all he really had time for though, before Algrenon and his group of survivors had emerged from the treeline. He wanted to study further, but he resented the fact his first day of study had been cut short. He took another look over the notes and realized something. He had made no mention of sap. Not every tree had sap, he knew this, but that wouldn't stop him from checking again. He was a scholar, after all, he had to explore every avenue available to him.

"Guess I'm going shopping then," he said to himself as he reached for his satchel. He slung it over his shoulder then walked out into the sprawling town of Plainsview before him.

The town was practically a city, there was no hiding that. Though it lacked the large walls and stone architecture that the Valens were so well known for and opted for a more modest, wooden approach, it was still impressive in scale.

There weren't many homeless either: a few beggars here and there, but that was it. Varden always tried to leave them something when he passed by, a bronze coin or two, an apple, whatever he had on hand. But really, that had only happened maybe four times since his arrival. The town was rather efficient, most men and women working away at their day-to-day lives, pulling in what coin they could, and staying off the streets. They reminded him of Ajwix and that made him smile.

"Ah, finally," the scholar pushed open the door to a small wooden shop he had spied the day prior.

"Evenin,'" the broad man behind the counter greeted. "Almost nightfall, 'bout to close shop. What can I get for ya?"

"You're a carpenter, correct?"

The man nodded with an affirming grunt.

"Oh good. Tell me, are you able to make a tree tap for me?"

"A tree tap? Fer what?"

"Sap. Have you made them before?"

"Course I have. What you need it for?"

"Well, I wish to study a tree's sap."

"Which tree?"

"A shadewood tree." the scholar smiled.

With a raised eyebrow, the carpenter shrugged. "Alright, I'll make er up for ya. But you might want to see a blacksmith after, I've heard the wood on those things can be mighty tough, might be you need a steel punch to make your opening."

Varden nodded. "Yes yes, I will see the blacksmith when I have the tap. How soon can you have it ready?"

"Well," the carpenter said with some thought. "Yer in luck. Orders have been slow of late. I'll have it ready by Sun's Peak tomorrow."

"Perfect. Thank you. And here, for your troubles." the Wixen left one gold coin, and one silver coin on the countertop, the carpenter looked at them with wide eyes.

"This is too much!"

"But it is not, my friend. What you see as a simple tap, I see as a way of sealing my future! You do not realize how important this little device could be to my research." the scholar turned to leave. "Now if you'll excuse me, I can start to see some stars in the sky, and I really should be heading in for the night. I shall see you at Sun's Peak. Take care!"

#

The tavern was busy that night, and Rel wasn't too happy about it. There were rumours, strange rumours, and not just about the Thregs in the Endless Plains. Something to the west, something no one really knew how to explain. The Plain's Master, Nef and Kol, had been summoned for duty on the morrow, and so decided to grab a drink before they journeyed onto the stony cliffs of the Halo. But the drinks had inadvertently given more cause for alarm than for relaxation.

The rumours told of towns — loved ones housed within — going quiet: the usual letters and the spravens carrying them hadn't been appearing for nearly seven days. Of the villages affected, one stood out to her: Farnwood. It had been where Olenna and her lover Atlas had gone.

The dwarven server brought three tankards over and set them down on the table. Rel thought she caught her wink at Kol before leaving.

"You two seem to be getting along well," Nef said, his eye as watchful as ever.

Kol blushed, his cheeks turning a rosy red. "You could say that," he said, fiddling with his drink. "Had a picnic after Sun's Peak." he grinned widely.

"You should take her up on the Halo when we get back," Rel said before taking a sip of her mead. "The stars look amazing from up there." she put her tankard down with a dull thud.

Kol's eyes lit up. "That-that is a great idea, Rel! I think I'll do that." he was visibly excited.

"So, what's her name?" Nef asked with a sly grin.

"Steena," Kol said sheepishly. "Steena Wardly ... It's a gorgeous name."

"It really is," Rel said, smiling warmly. She had never seen Kol that way, he seemed smitten, and by a dwarven tavern maid at that! How sweet. "You two will make a cute couple."

Kol blushed again. "You think so?"

"Think so?" Nef interrupted, "I know so!" he raised his drink. "Now, here! To Kol's newfound love!" he spoke loudly, letting Steena herself hear the proclamation.

Rel noticed as the tavern maid and Kol made eye contact, and shared an embarrassed grin. Rel raised her tankard. "For love!"

The embarrassed strider finally raised his drink but didn't say anything. The tankards thudded together before they downed their drinks. They shared a laugh, and Nef gave Kol a good firm slap on the back.

"Proud of you. You make sure you take good care of her." he flashed him a smile. "And your drinks are on me tonight!"

Chapter 14

The morning came quickly and the briefing came quicker. It was time for Rel, Nef and Kol to head up and onto the mountains known as the Halo. Where they were to keep watch, from the edge, for five days. Rel looked to her Right and Left Hands. They were ready to go, ready to climb the stone that surrounded their country.

They marched into the Valley with confidence in their step, eventually passing the wall Bronwin had built on the far side of the swamp. They found the path they were looking for off to their left, buried beneath the foliage. They walked the path for the better half of the day, hardly speaking as they went, focusing on their feet with each step, and wracking their brains on what they might end up finding when they reached the summit.

If Rel remembered correctly, there would be a small cave further ahead that they could camp inside for the night. The Valley began to fall away below them, and the swamp resembled little more than a weedy puddle. She stopped for a moment, and let the sheer scale of the world envelop her. She was so small; she was important and would do important things, she was given her title for good reason. But on the whole scope of *everything,* there would be people that she couldn't even begin to imagine, doing things that seemed impossible to her. It was humbling and gave Rel a sense of freedom that she had seldom felt before.

"Hey, you done sightseeing or are you coming?" Nef was looking down at her from further up the trail. "It'll take us another five days, at least, to get to where we need to. And it's only going to get colder."

#

It was Sun's Peak and Varden marched his way into the carpenter's shop he had visited the night before. The carpenter was there, as expected, fiddling with some saw. He turned to face the scholar, then with a look of realization, disappeared into another room. He emerged with a small wooden tool in his hand. A simple tap: a tube of wood with a spout angled downwards at one end.

The carpenter handed it over. "'Ere you are. Should be good to go."

Varden took the tool in his hands and looked it over closely. It wasn't nearly as good as what the Wixen carpenters could produce. But he supposed it would suit his purposes.

"Yes yes, this will do. Thank you. Now, could you point me in the way of the blacksmith?"

"Of course: 'ead east fer two streets, then 'ead down the street with a butcher on the corner. Third building on yer left. You can see the smoke from 'is forge."

"Thank you," Varden left the shop and hurried off in the indicated direction. As he did so, he flipped the tap in his hands, observing it closely. He immediately regretted the sum he had paid for it. But it was too late now, he had already paid, and he would look a fool to try and change what had already been given. Stuffing the tap in his pouch Varden looked for the butcher's shop and the smokestack that would mark the next piece of his path.

Before long, he had found the blacksmith, and much to his luck, the man already had a steel punch made for him. The carpenter had sought him out the previous night and told the smith that Varden would be along. Apparently, the Wixen's generosity had paid off.

He needed his guards now, his studies demanded it of him. If he were to wed and carry on his family name, for anything less, he would disappoint a thousand generations of ancestry.

Varden reached the small barracks near the eastern gate, his guards milling about.

"Alright, gentlemen, let's go. We have studies to conduct!" He thrust a finger into the air excitedly, his satchel pouncing as he stepped.

The soldiers rolled their eyes, but didn't object, they retrieved their things and followed as their duty demanded. They left Plainsview through the Valley Gate towards the swamp. Varden looked at the muck and insects with excitement, a proud grin on display.

As they walked, the Wixen scanned the trees for the familiar black and white of the shadewood. Eventually, he found it: jutting out from the water like a beacon. He couldn't wait to get his hands on the marvellous creation to see what secrets he could unlock.

The great black trunk stood out as a symbol of what his future could be, and all it would be. The scholar knelt in the water and waved over a soldier. When he arrived, Varden handed him his satchel.

"Why am I holding this?" The man was visibly annoyed.

"I don't want my notes or tools to get wet." Varden replied, eyeing the trunk, "Can you reach in and look for a wooden tube-esque tool?"

"Esque?"

"Tube-like, my boy, tube-like."

He reached his hand into the satchel and felt around. "If that's what you mean, why didn't you just say that the first time?"

"Well I did, but I used a word with which you were not familiar. My apologies. I've become accustomed to being in the company of fellow scholars."

The soldier huffed, then pulled out the tree tap Varden had been seeking. "This it?"

The Wixen looked up, a look of glee in his small eyes. "Yes, thank you! Can you find me a steel rod in there as well? Careful though, it has a pointy end."

"A pointy end?"

"Yes, like your sword my boy. Don't stick yourself with it."

"Alright, here it is." The guard held out his hand, a foot-long steel rod was held therein.

"Thank you. May I borrow your dagger for a moment? I seem to have forgotten something."

The soldier sighed heavily and handed the scholar his blade. "If Bronwin hadn't put me here, I would have killed you by now, you realize that right?"

"Noted. Now please be quiet, I must focus." Varden lifted the steel punch towards a spot on the trunk, and using the hilt of the dagger, pounded it into the trunk. It was difficult, more so than any tree he had ever worked with. The wood was as hard as stone, but steel was harder. He drove the punch in slowly until he was satisfied. He handed the dagger back to the soldier and yanked the punch free.

"The tap now please?"

The man grunted as he handed him the tap in exchange for the punch.

"Thank you," Varden hefted the tap in his hand and slid it into the opening. It fit perfectly. "Can you find a vial for me?" He reached his hand out expectantly.

A short moment of shuffling and the soldier handed it to him without a word.

Pulling on a piece of string from his robe, Varden tied it and fashioned a sling for the vial to sit in. Lifting it towards the tool, he tied the container onto the wood, with the lip of the tap angled into the opening of the container.

"Perfect!" The scholar stood, and waved his guardsmen forward, he held out an arm for his satchel which was placed there shortly after. "Thank you, Guardsman. Take this for your trouble," The Wixen fished inside his robe and pulled out a silver coin. "A bonus for your services."

The guard took the coin eagerly, placing it into his pocket. "Thank you." He seemed to be holding back tears, as the man sniffled Varden heard him say. "I might be able to get my little girl something sweet for tonight because of you. Thank you."

Varden grinned, hiding a pang of sorrow for the man.

#

Rel, Nef, and Kol had arrived at the height of the Halo the previous night. They had climbed for four days, through the wind, snow and cold of the mountain range. They had discarded their cloaks for heavy fur made from Valen bears. Wrapping themselves in their cloaks, they stumbled out of the small cave they had used as a camp the night before, their fire now nothing more than smouldering coals. The wind buffeted them as the final gusts of a blizzard swept across the mountaintops.

"The blizzard looks to be clearing up, Rel!" Kol called back to her. The dark brown of his cloak became more visible by the second.

"Nef!" she called behind her. "Did you hear that?!" The wind nearly drowned out their cries.

"Scarcely, but yes!"

Scarcely? Where did he learn that?

Rel couldn't see her friend behind her, but she knew he would be following the sound of her voice, and her footsteps in the snow.

By Esmirla it was cold, the winds nearly cut through the cloak with every step she took, threatening to sink into her bones. She couldn't wait to begin their descent.

Kol had stopped moving up, he only looked out into whatever it was Rel couldn't see.

"Kol!" she called, "What is it?"

"I'm at the edge Rel, but I can't see shit! We'll need to wait for the snow to clear some more!"

"Alright!" she replied. "Let's head back to the camp then, keep warm in the meantime!"

Kol turned and began moving back, Nef arrived shortly after.

"Are we heading back?" he asked.

"Yes, only for the moment."

Kol interjected. "The snow is still falling too heavily for us to see past the edge."

"But I just got here!" Nef grinned. "Alright fine, we'll go back."

They arrived in their small hovel of a camp and ignited the coals of the fire. Striders kept small camps all throughout the Halo, offering protection for themselves whenever a patrol would range upwards.

"I don't get it," Kol broke the silence. "Why send us all the way up here, I can't even feel my toes! If they need eyes on the plains, why not just send us into the plains?"

Nef snickered. "You really can be a fool sometimes, you know that?"

Rel grinned. "They sent us up here because we've already lost too many in the plains. And besides, Saffron wants to us to survey as much of the plains as possible, easiest done from up here, isn't it?"

Her Left Hand agreed with an unamused snort.

"We know you don't like these rangings, Kol," Nef said, looking at his friend. "It's no secret. If you'd rather work the longhouse, just say so."

Rel opened her eyes widely at Nef's bluntness.

"What?" her Right Hand said, noticing her expression. "It's not like you haven't noticed it either. I just don't get it."

"Get what?" Kol asked behind an angry gaze.

"Why you continue to do the rangings. Just tell Saff you'd rather help in town. We always need more hands there."

"I-I don't know."

"No, you do know."

Rel tried to cut in: "Nef, don't."

"No Rel," he shot back, "I will. I'm tired of his melancholy every time we leave town!" He looked back to Kol. "You do know. Is it that little dwarven girl back in town?"

Silence.

"It is, isn't it? You don't want her to see you as some servant to the striders. You want her to see you as a warrior, her protector, is that it?"

"Fuck off, Nef."

"That is it, isn't it? You want to look big and strong, right? Well, let me tell you something." He leaned in closer. "We'd rather see you live a happy and mundane life rather than a miserable, exciting one. Being big and strong is all well and good, but if she only loves you for your strength, you've picked the wrong woman. Now make up your mind, I'm sick of seeing you looking like you've sipped at piss every time we go out into the plains. It's going to get somebody killed."

Kol stood up, frustration and anguish contorting his face, and left the camp without a word. He strode out into the dissipating snowstorm, sunlight starting to stream in through the clouds.

"That wasn't necessary, Nef," Rel said, looking at her friend accusingly. "He didn't deserve that."

"No. He didn't. But he needed it. You've seen it too. It's only a matter of time until he gets careless and gets someone, or himself, killed."

"You didn't need to be such an ass. By Esmirla, Nef, learn some compassion."

"I was plenty compassionate, Rel. Did you not hear what I said about Steena? Was I wrong?"

"No, you weren't, but you could've gone about it better." she stood, and left the camp, looking to catch up with Kol.

She found him, standing at the edge of the Halo, frozen in the new sunlight. Staring out into the golden sea below them.

Nef arrived close behind her. The three of them stared into the Endless Plains. Even from here, they could never have seen the end of the grasslands, it was so vast, so wild, and so unknown to even them.

There was something wrong with the plains. On the horizon, what they had expected to see as blue sky clashing with golden grass, they saw blackness. A thousand spires of smoke reaching into the sky, an artificial cloud cover: an army.

Tents covered the fields in a pink that washed out the gold of the plains. The Thregs had amassed an army, thousands upon thousands in strength. The camps looked as endless as the plains themselves.

"By Gwendall's Blade," Nef gasped, "there's bloody thousands of them."

"What-what do you think they're doing?" Kol asked.

"What do you think?" Rel stepped forward. "That's an invasion."

#

Standing in the small sandpit near his house, Corduvan stood ready with his weapon. The hilt held in one hand, the chain in the other, he eyed the target dummies around him with a nervous eye. He was supposed to have met with Rel, but she had been on duty, so he took it upon himself to keep up with his training on his own. He had with him a much more important person watching his performance. Someone who held infinitely more sway over him than Rel, the Pale Bull, and even the Highfolds. On this night, his son watched him. Only five cycles old, his brown eyes were filled with excitement at seeing his father use a weapon no one else had.

Corduvan did a small warm-up with the weapon, spinning the chain-linked blade over his head in several circles before moving his hand further up the chain and spinning it beside him. His forearms let go of the cold they once held and warmed to the feel of training.

"What are you doing?" his son asked curiously, "Are you pretending to beat up the monsters?"

Corduvan smiled at his son's insistence. "No no, my boy. I'm only warming up right now."

"Warming ... up?"

He chuckled. "Yes son, making sure I don't hurt my muscles when I do something hard."

"Oh, I get it. I think ..." the boy trailed off.

Corduvan spun the weapon a few more times over his head, to his left, and to his right, before slowing the chain and sliding his hand up, holding it just before the blade.

"Are you ready, Brinn?"

"Ready for what, dad?"

"To see me beat up the monsters! To keep you safe."

"Yes, Daddy, oh yes, I'm ready!" The boy bounced on his bottom.

Corduvan stood, a look of determination taking hold of him. He stood in the middle of the sandpit, dummies spread about him in a circle. Plenty of opportunities to experiment. He knew already that this Wixen blade would be useless in close quarters, so he only trained at range. He would never be caught on the battlefield without his sword anyway, so to him, this mattered little, a simple switch of blade at the right moment, and he would be ready for any situation.

Corduvan slid his grip down the chain, letting the blade hang just above the ground. He began to spin the weapon upwards, letting momentum carry it up, over, and behind him where it swept down to finish the arc. He let it spin a couple of times, then, on the third rise of the blade, he released it, letting the point travel through the air, like a thrown knife. It struck the first target dummy. Not in the heart, where he wanted it, but in the gut. A decent hit, but not a kill.

"Whoa!" Brinn gasped, his shining eyes illuminated with awe.

With a tug, Corduvan yanked the blade free, and slid his hand up the chain, recovering the spin he had established. He moved the spin back over his head, and as the weapon began to circle to the right, he launched the chain forward. This time he hit his target, a slash across the throat.

Perfect, He thought. *A kill!*

"Did you mean to do that, Daddy?" Brinn asked, unsure of what the strike was supposed to have done.

Corduvan didn't answer, instead, he continued the spin, then lashed out at another dummy, striking it in the leg. The slash travelled far lower than he would have liked, hitting just above the ankle.

He continued spinning the weapon and striking out with various ranged stabs and slashes, his aim was getting better, but he only hit half of the shots he tried to take. A cut across the chest turned into a gouged-out eye for one dummy. Corduvan cursed with this, as he hadn't intended for a kill. But Brinn lit up with excitement, knowing full well what a blade to the eye would do to a monster. This made the soldier smile, his son's laughter and joy could cheer the spirits out of a man sentenced to death.

Corduvan's eyes opened: he was supposed to be on prison duty, guarding the top floor.

"Brinn!" he called, pulling in the chain, "Time to go home!"

"Awww," he said with a frown and his own version of a pouty lip. "But why? You didn't beat up all the monsters." his tone grew quieter with each word.

"I beat up enough to keep us safe tonight. I'll get the rest later." Corduvan holstered his weapon, and picked up his son, putting him on his shoulders. "Now, I need to go protect more people right now. And I need you to protect your mother. Can you do that for me, Brinn?"

The little boy nodded his head, with a thin smile.

Moments passed and Corduvan opened the door for his son, the little boy walked into the house, turned to his father and waved. "Bye-bye, Daddy, I love you."

"I love you too, son. Now go. Keep your mother safe. I'll be back before you know it."

Brinn didn't fully understand the situation with his mother, she had a sickness in her head. She couldn't remember many things anymore, a lot of the time forgetting that Corduvan was her husband, it pained him to have to remind her of this nearly every day. But the way her eyes lit up whenever she realized it was true, nearly made him cry each time. She forgot simple things, like where the hearth was, *what* a hearth was, where the front door was, and even how to speak some days. But one thing always stayed in her mind, a beacon of hope for her, and that was Brinn. Their little boy was the only thing she held on to, no matter how her mind fared, she always had Brinn, she always knew he was hers, and that she was his. The little boy who, as of the moment, was single-handedly making her life worth living. A tear rolled down

Corduvan's cheek as he marched into the prison, he wiped it away and nodded to the guard located just inside.

"Top floor today, Corduvan?"

"As sure as Daylen," he replied with a nod. "Everyone behaving themselves up there?"

"Far as I can tell!"

Corduvan smiled, then ascended the steps. He nodded to each guard as he passed, ignored the chiding from the prisoners, and found his way to the top floor. He walked to the far end of the hall, and stood watch, his hand on the hilt of his sword, his makeshift weapon tucked away and wrapped into his belt.

"OI!" a gruff voice called, "You dere! What's yer name?"

Corduvan turned to the man known as Dry Eyes. He rolled his eyes. The man was an utter joke, a criminal, but a joke. Corduvan was there the day he was arrested, but even he didn't truly understand what had happened. Confusion, a horse — stuck in a compromising position — and a woman with a broken back. One thing was certain, however, and that was that this man, this Dry Eyes, was the one responsible.

"What's it to you?" he replied.

"Just wonderin. Gonna have to tell ma boys who to look fer once they bust me outta here."

"Your boys?"

"Heh," The bandit laughed, before sending a glob of spit to the floor. "Ma boys'll be here, that I can tell you fer certain!"

"How many boys you got comin for ya?"

"At least two," he said confidently.

"Two?"

"Aye, maybe three. Could even be ..." he trailed off. "What's aftah three?"

"Four?"

"Ah yes, whatevahs aftah four. Your little Sovereign fellows ain't gonna know what slashed 'em! I'll be in Ajwix by the next moon I thinks!"

Corduvan rolled his eyes and ignored the rest of the blathering. It was like this every single night, every damn night. 'Killed dozens of hundreds. I did. Warlord I was.' and the always famous, 'I was a Highfold once you know! Ruled with a stone fist!'

Corduvan couldn't wait for home, to put his head to rest, and see what the next day had in store for him. Hopefully, he would have market duty, he always liked market duty.

Chapter 15

Many cycles ago ...

Sitting in the small sandpit, a freakishly large boy dragged his fingers through the grains. He drew a small city and a small band of stick figures holding spears just beside it. At the age of six, Bronwin had an eager fascination with the military, how all the soldiers worked, what they wore, and how they fought with one another. They were heroes, the men who kept him and his family safe from the scary things that lurked in the wilderness beyond the small hamlet of Northwood.

Scary green things that hid away in bushes and shadows, very tall, very skinny scary things. It was one of these monsters that had killed Bronwin's older brother when he was only a baby, not even old enough to remember anything. No matter how hard he tried to stretch his memory back to those times, he couldn't remember. He wanted to remember, wanted to see his brother in his head because even at the age of six, he knew he'd never be able to see more of his brother than the old wooden plaque placed where he had been buried.

Bronwin traced his finger in the sand on the other side of the soldiers. He drew even taller stick figures, then with the fine edge of his fingernail, gave them long, sickly, strands of hair. They were the scary things. Only having seen them once or twice, they haunted him, he would never forget what they looked like.

Quickly, Bronwin dragged his finger through the men with spears, severing them just above the legs, and did the same to one of the monsters. He drew in the sand an even bigger stick figure, much taller than the others that he had just killed. It stood with shield and mace. A swipe of the hand and all the monsters were gone. Leaving only the one tall stick figure alone to defend the city behind him.

Bronwin smiled to himself. He wanted to be that man: a protector, a saviour, to hold the title of Shield. A title that only men who dedicated much of their Sovereign career to a particular city or village would be given. He wanted to look at each and every person, and feel loved, welcomed, and trusted. He wanted to help them, to make sure they all felt safe. He smiled sadly and thought about his father going off to the Big City, to be a guard, to be a hero, a real hero. Bronwin missed him.

"Keep your mother safe while I'm gone, my boy," he had told him. "Can you do that for me?"

"Yes." he had replied eagerly.

The memory was so clear to him, the passing of trust and responsibility from his father to him was a momentous occasion. It was the first time in his life that had ever happened to him. And he was only six! Not even some of the older kids could say they had to protect their mothers.

A rock slammed into his forehead and cast him to the ground. As he lay in the sand, he looked at the rock. No bigger than the palm of a boy's hand. He winced and held his own palm to the pain on his head. He pressed hard, but it didn't help. He had felt this pain before, when he hit his head off a table, trying to duck down underneath to get the bowl he accidentally spilt at dinner. His parents had chuckled at him, but now he heard awful laughter.

He sat up, frowning, and turned to where the rock had come from. A group of boys stood not far away. Pointing and laughing.

"Did you see that?! I got him!" a boy with flabby cheeks and messy brown hair cheered between laughs, "I got him!"

Another boy, clean, not a blemish on his face, and with sand-coloured hair laughed along. "He's a hard target to miss, Saff! Look at the size of that freak!"

Saffron: no more than eight cycles older than Bronwin, and already an absolute fiend of a child. He wanted to be a soldier too. An archer, he said, wanted to shoot things. Kill things that couldn't hit him back.

Coward. Bronwin thought. *When I'm older, I'm going to beat you up, and there won't be anything you can do to stop me.*

For the most part, he thought that would be true: he was already the size of Saffron, and he wasn't fourteen. The boys started to walk closer, Saffron with another rock in his hand larger than the last.

"Hey! Tallboy! Yeah you, you freak!" The bully spat to the side, causing one of his friends to stutter his step in avoidance. "Catch!"

The second rock soared through the air between them. Bronwin raised a hand to try and catch it. It glanced off his fingers, cutting him with one sharp edge. He yelped, and put the finger to his mouth, sucking on it.

"You big fucking baby!" Saffron called, standing still, "You'll never be a soldier! Never! You can't even catch a rock! Come on, guys. Let's leave this freak alone." The bully turned, his friends laughing as they followed.

Bronwin waited until they were gone before he let himself cry. His tears dropped into the sand beneath him, darkening the walls of the drawn city, and the head of the stick figure that was supposed to be him. He cried and cried until the sun began to set and he could no longer see his drawings through the wet sand.

"Bronwin!" a soft voice called, "Bronwin, there you are!"

It was his mother, and she sounded relieved to have found him.

"You should have been home ages ago my dear, are you-" she stopped talking when she saw his tears, the bruise on his forehead, and the scabbed cut on his finger. "Oh, Bronwin. What happened, my love?" She knelt in the sand next to him, and pulled him close, pulling his head to her heart.

He could hear his mother's heart beating, that familiar rhythm like a drum that always made him feel at ease. It was faster today though, he wasn't sure why.

He tried to tell his mother what had happened. "It-it-it-it," he tried to say between sobs.

"Was it that mean boy, Saffron?"

He nodded.

"Oh, my sweet," She pulled him in tighter, kissing the crown of his head. "One day everything will work out. When you are older. I just know it …" she trailed off for a moment as if lost in thought, before coming back to the situation at hand. "Now then," she said cheerfully. "I have some venison cooking at home, black pepper and honey. Would you like some? It's your favourite."

Bronwin looked up to see her smiling face. So calming, so serene, his perfect mother. Her green eyes showed so much love, worry, and pride that the boy couldn't help but start to feel better. He nodded, a little more energetically than he had last time. Black pepper and honey venison was something he sometimes dreamed about. He always ate everything on his plate, and he always got dessert afterwards too. He couldn't wait, the sobbing of the day was behind him.

"Can we race home?" he asked hopefully.

"Only if you promise to let me win this time!" his mother said smiling.

"I am not promising anything!"

"Well alright, fine. We can race. On *my* go this time okay? No cheating." She tapped him on the nose with her finger, then stood, she lifted the skirt of her dress above her feet.

Bronwin stood up next to her, already his head at chest height on his mother.

"Ready?" she asked.

The boy nodded.

"Go!"

Bronwin took off in a dead sprint in the direction of home, his mother trying her hardest to catch up. He leapt over a small log and continued to a small river. No time to slow down, he could hear his mother's footsteps growing louder behind him. He quickly looked around and saw no way across. In a single leap, and with a loud giggle, his mother was across. She looked over her shoulder, grinning widely.

Taking a few steps back, the boy readied himself and exploded forward, using his own legs to cross the gap. He landed on the other side but stumbled for a moment before regaining his balance. Bronwin began to gain on his mother, but she had already reached their home. Leaning against the wood she coughed loudly into her hands, looked at them, then wiped them off at her sides. She swallowed hard, then looked at her son.

"You almost won!" she said excitedly. "Do you know why you didn't though?"

Bronwin thought for a moment, then remembered one of the lessons she had taught him two cycles ago:

You are different from the other kids, Bronwin. Don't be afraid to use that to your advantage. You're bigger and stronger, and that's okay. They might make fun of you, but do what you know you can do better than they can, and they'll listen to you eventually.

"I didn't use my big legs properly?"

His mother grinned proudly. "That's right, remember, do what you know you can do better than anyone else. Right?"

"Right!" he said confidently. "Next time, I'm going to win!"

"I sure hope so. I certainly hope so." She kissed him on the forehead.

That night they ate their venison, the boy cleaning off his plate faster than any child his age had the right to, and they had dessert: a collection of berries in a frothy, cool cream. They sat next to the hearth and the mother told stories to him about his father. The things he would be learning in the Big City, and what he might look like when he came back home to Northwood.

"He'll be a bit bigger, Bronwin, bigger than the last time you saw him. He'll be so strong that he could save the whole village by himself! So strong in fact, that he could cut down a tree in only six swings of an axe."

Bronwin nearly dropped his bowl. "Whoa, really?!"

His mother laughed. "Well, maybe, I guess we'll have to ask him to show us when we see him won't we?"

"When will that be?" he asked innocently, his eyes glittering.

Bronwin's mother frowned. "I-I don't know," she stammered, looking lost. "But now is a time for sleep, wouldn't you say?"

"Well ... okay," He cast his eyes down. "I guess so."

Bronwin was tucked under his blankets, his mother sitting next to him, her hand on his chest. "You sleep well now my-" She coughed into her hand, frowned, then wiped it on her dress. "You sleep well now, my dear," she said with a grin. "And remember, tomorrow brings you one day closer to seeing your father, and one day closer to growing up."

"I know. I hope you have good dreams," he said. "Really good dreams. Of Father, and, and, fruit!"

Bronwin's mother laughed. "You too Bronwin, I hope you do too. Now go. Sleep, and put your head to rest, and may the Veil Strider grant you safe passage through your mind, and bring you back to the world of the waking as the sun rises in the sky." She kissed him on the forehead. "I love you."

"I love you too!" he rolled onto his side as he closed his eyes. The Veil Strider guided him through the worlds that his mind created as he slept.

Chapter 16

Present-day ...

They had taken four days to climb the mountain path, and it only took them three to get down. Climbing down was easier than climbing up, and it was much easier when you had the motivation of an invading army approaching your home.

All three striders had arrived at the longhouse in Plainsview exhausted and out of breath. They were quickly escorted into Saffron's office, which already had a prized guest awaiting them: Bronwin, the Pale Bull and Shield of Northwood.

Saffron looked up from his desk at the tired rangers. He stood with a sense of urgency when he saw their condition. Bronwin however, stood a little straighter as he watched them with a look of benign amusement.

"What's wrong?" the Plain's Warden said alarmed. "What's happened?"

"Sir," Rel regained her composure. "We have information from the Halo. And it's not good."

"What is it, Plain's Master?" Saffron said, stepping out from behind his desk. "What have you learned?"

She cut straight to the chase. "It's the Thregs, sir. They have an invasion force in the plains."

Silence, then a low grumble slowly growing louder, until finally, Bronwin exploded into laughter. His booming voice nearly shaking the very walls they stood within.

"An invasion force? Of *Thregs?!*" he roared, "Surely you jest?"

Rel looked at him, lightning dancing in her eyes, and took a step forward. "I do not jest when it comes to military matters, *Bull*. You would take care to remember that."

Bronwin's grin left his face. He took a step forward in return and glared down at her. "And just who the fuck are you, to talk to me like that?"

"I'm the woman with the information *you* need to save this town and this country. Should you want to know what I know, I suggest you start to show some respect to the striders, or you'll have to pull this information off my dead lips."

"Don't tempt me," the Bull growled, his voice like gravel.

"You two, that is *enough!*" Saffron stepped between them and gave Rel a small push back.

The Plain's Warden turned sternly towards his Right Hand. "Rel, you will tell us what you know, that is an order."

She crossed her arms. "And as for Alistair's Pet, here?"

"I said that is an *order* Plain's Master."

Rel took a deep breath in, and slowly let it out, calming herself. "There is an invasion force in the Endless Plains. When we left, it was about a half a fortnight's ride away. They could be closer by now."

"What is their number?" Saffron asked.

"If I were to guess, around 50,000. But that was only from what we could see. There could be more en route. We can't know for certain."

Nef and Kol shifted uneasily at the mention of more Thregs where they could not be seen. Saffron shifted too, but not Bronwin, as much as Rel would have loved to see the man look uneasy, he stood firmer, his face that of a hardened soldier, ready to wage war.

The Plain's Warden finally cleared his throat, breaking the silence. "Are you sure of this, Plain's Master?"

"As sure as Gwendall's Blade was sharp, sir."

"Well ..." he trailed off, then turned to the Shield of Northwood. "What do you need of me and my striders?"

The reply came without delay. "The prisoners."

"What?" Saffron was baffled.

"We're going to conscript them. If they survive, they'll have their crimes cleared, and they will be given freedom, back into Valenfaar. If they die, then they die. Their sentence will have been served."

"There's only 200 prisoners here Bronwin. That's not nearly enough to-"

"I shall also write to Alistair to request more troops and conscripts from Sun Spire. Send me a scribe at once, and a runner, I need Algrenon."

Nef stepped forward. "I'll deliver the message to Algrenon, sir."

Bronwin turned his behemoth head to face the man. "So, one of you *do* know how to play nicely with others?" he looked at Rel as he said this. "Good. Deliver my message at once."

"Yes sir." Nef turned on his heel and, at a jog, left the room.

"As for me, sir?" Rel asked, "What would you have me do?"

Saffron stepped forward, his posture now straighter than it had been moments before, he wore the look of a commander.

"Rally the striders. As quickly as you can. Get their gear in top shape as fast as possible, then begin to organize short-range patrols in the plains. No further than five kilometres out from the edge of the Valley. Am I clear?"

"As clear as the skies above the Endless Plains."

"Excellent, and Kol?"

The young boy turned to face his superior, a hint of lamentation underlying his gaze.

"You are to aid Rel in whatever she needs until you are ordered otherwise. Am I clear?"

"Yessir," there was hesitation in his voice, something was worrying him.

"Alright. You two are dismissed. Go now, and get everyone prepared."

Rel and Kol left the room. Kol struggling to keep up with Rel's determined strides.

"Are-are we really going through with this?"

"What do you mean?" Rel snapped back.

"Defending against this invasion, with *him* as our officer? This is going to be a mess Rel, we-we've lost already, I can feel it."

"As much as I dislike him it is our duty to defend Valenfaar, whether he is our commanding officer or not. You and I will stand our ground until our last breath. We do not leave each other behind."

Then, much to Rel's surprise, the young strider sounded firm and confident. "Yes ma'am."

He had his mind made up, she knew, and she knew he had chosen correctly.

#

"Are you certain that is what you heard?" Varden jotted down the soldier's words into his journal.

"Um, yes?" The man seemed confused. "That's what I heard. Yes," he reaffirmed. "A camp of Thregs had shown up that day. I'm positive now."

"Alright, alright, that's good. Thank you, uhh-"

"Corduvan."

"Ah yes, Corduvan. Thank you. Your words will aid my research into these beasts." Varden closed his journal and began to turn away, but stopped as the soldier began to speak again.

"I thought you were studying those trees?"

Looking over his shoulder, the Wixen matched eyes with the Valen. "They are the focal point of my research, yes. But as a scholar, I do enjoy studying ... other things, from time to time. A sort of break, if you will."

Corduvan scratched his head. "Well okay then. Take care?"

"Take care, Corduvan, and do be careful."

Varden walked away quickly and began to sift through his thoughts as he went. Thregs were appearing at random in the plains, in no particular pattern he could ascertain. The striders themselves were tight-lipped about the whole thing, something about not wanting to spread worry or some such. So, being the brilliant man he was, and knowing how people worked, he knew that rumours would spread. A strider would tell a family member, or a trusted guardsman, and the rumours would spread from there, like a virus.

To try and avoid the imminent dilution of the proverbial waters, Varden had decided to speak to the Sovereign Guard soldiers stationed on guard duty. Always making sure to ask three or four soldiers at a time on whether the days the Thregs appeared had been accurate or not. It was near impossible to make an accurate assumption with inaccurate information, but thankfully, most of the stories lined up, with the occasional error, like whether the Threg camps had arrived during dawn or late morning.

From what Varden could see, there was no pattern. They arrived randomly, without cause, and rather fast, and then were killed just as quickly by Bronwin's men. How stubborn those men were, Varden would have to turn to the Veil Strider herself to get any answers from them. He huffed and sighed. Did no one understand the fact that his research was important? Not only to him but to his future family as well?

Much of that day had been filled with the usual hustle and bustle of Plainsview but it was mixed with a strange sense of duty and foreboding: guardsmen and striders alike were being called out of the woodwork. Being summoned for some purpose that was unknown to them. To Varden, he already felt he knew the answer. Something to do with the Thregs, it really was the only logical choice, as it was the only oddity, in recent memory, able to cause this much of a response.

As Varden paced the town, wandering from guardsman to guardsman, he noticed prisoners were being escorted to some unknown location. One gruff-looking man, whose eyes were extraordinarily red, voiced several objections to his treatment from his handlers.

"Oi! Don't you touch me dere! How dare you? Do you know who I am?" The man blinked and looked through squinted eyes at the soldier pushing him around. "Well?"

"Well, what?" the guard had asked in return, defiantly.

"Don't you know who I am?!" The prisoner was angry, frustrated, and a little embarrassed.

The guardsman smirked, then chuckled to himself. "Oh, believe me, Dry Eyes. We all know exactly who you are. Now go!" He gave a hard push and forced the prisoner down the road.

Varden smirked as he watched Dry Eyes try and find his way down the road. Blinking like he had a gust of wind in his face, and squinting as if he had no reprieve from the sun's blinding light.

Gradually the sun began to set, and the stars began to shine in the sky, small licks of white candlelight, hovering high above Valenfaar. The previous night, Varden had observed something remarkable: he saw stars, a deep red, streaking across the night sky, east to west. This hadn't been the first case of this since his arrival, it had happened numerous times, and each time he recorded the day on which he saw them. It was, to him, a sort of side project, a natural phenomenon to take himself away from his primary study of the shadewood tree.

Returning to his temporary home, Varden placed his notes on Threg sightings down on his desk. Then undressed. Naked, he lit a candle and drew the blinds. Sitting down at his desk, he lit another candle, looked at his notes and began to try and make sense of the sightings.

Much of the night slipped by, and the scholar let out a heavy sigh, he was getting nowhere. None of it made sense. He pushed his research on the Thregs aside and pulled over his notes regarding the stars that had moved across the sky. Something to keep his mind working, stopping him from reaching a dead-end, always progressing. As he looked at the days he had written down, his eyes grew wide with realization.

"May the Veil Strider carry me endlessly!" he said agasp, his eyes darted back and forth between the collections of notes. "Well, I'll be damned." he sat back in his chair, a smile on his face.

Chapter 17

Rel stood in the training square of the Plain's Striders, Nef and Kol at her side. Rows of their troops stood before them. The cascade of chatter echoed through the night air, carrying off into the distance.

Clearing her throat, she roared: "Striders!"

The rangers fell silent, their postures straightened with their gazes locked on the Plain's Master.

"On the morrow, how we operate will shift dramatically: our rangings will be cut shorter. Many of you may have heard by now, that an army of Thregs is stationed within the Endless Plains. We estimate them to be 700 kilometres out, with the potential for rapid movement. From now on, until we have more information, all patrols will be kept to patrolling within five to ten kilometres out from the Valley mouth. Should any patrols venture further, you are on your own and will be beyond the help of both the Plain's Striders and the Sovereign Guard. Is that clear?"

A quick, synchronized nod.

"Now," Rel continued, "for the sake of simplicity, all patrols, groupings and schedules will remain the same, but all ranges will be kept within the distance mentioned. Understood?"

Another quick nod.

"Though the Pale Bull is our commander. Your orders will come directly from myself, or Saffron. Should a Sovereign soldier try to command strider forces in the field, you are well within your rights to disobey them if you deem it appropriate. Should you disobey orders from myself or the Plain's Warden, you will be tried for treason. We will *not* accept less than full cooperation from all of you for the duration of this campaign. If we fail, the country could be in danger. Do your jobs, and do them well, millions of lives depend on us." Rel stomped her foot in a salute, and the Plain's Striders mimicked the gesture. A resounding thud echoed as the soldiers dropped their feet.

"Best of luck, striders. Dismissed."

As the swath of rangers moved away from their gathering and back to their homes and stations, the sound of a single set of hurried footsteps stood out above the rest. Rel turned to find a man with pale skin, and dark hair waving a piece of parchment in the air before him.

"Nef! Nef!" he called.

Nef turned to face the man bewildered. "Varden?"

"Yes, yes, it's me!" he stopped short of the striders, out of breath. "Who's in charge? They need to see this."

"I'll be the judge of that," Rel said, stepping forward. "What is it?"

"It's the Thregs. I think I know how to predict their movements."

"Oh?"

#

Kol struggled to keep pace alongside Rel and Nef. The Wixen had described his findings so fast that he had trouble making any sense of the words. Now, with Rel's determination guiding them, they marched through the longhouse.

It was nearly Moon's Peak, and Kol needed to be meeting with Steena. He looked around frantically. He couldn't miss his rendezvous with her. He had been looking forward to it for days. Never in all his life did he think he would fall for a dwarf, but when he looked into her eyes, he couldn't help but feel a rush of life flow through him, like his body was revitalized by her presence.

"Um, Rel?" he asked nervously, "Permission to be relieved?"

Without turning to look at him, she answered flatly: "For what reason?" Her gaze held firm ahead of them as they passed through another room.

He lied. "Illness, ma'am."

"You are ill?" she rebutted, a hint of concern creeping through.

"Yes, ma'am. Not terribly so, but another night's rest should have me in fighting shape."

The Plain's Master chewed her lip before giving her answer. "Permission granted. I expect to see you at first light, am I clear?" This time she turned to look at him.

"As clear as the skies above the Endless Plains."

A curt nod. "Good, now go."

Kol turned on his heel to leave the weaving mess of halls and rooms that comprised the longhouse. He was careful to watch his pace: if he moved too quickly, he would be caught in his lie.

It had felt like days but Kol had finally broken away from the longhouse and began making his way towards the Strider's Respite. Steena would be waiting for him. They were to gaze at the stars, to take in the natural beauties of the unknown world that seemed to thrive and glow above them.

Plainsview was nearly empty, the only people who meandered through the streets were soldiers, tavern workers, and whores. Not a single Plain's Strider was in sight, they were either already at home resting for their patrols on the morrow, or already heading into the plains to begin their work.

"Ah, a young little strider, eh?" a sultry voice called out from an alleyway, "Tell me Little One, what could I do for you tonight? You look stressed, let me help you with a little ..." she hissed. "Release!"

A dark figure stepped out from behind the nearby shop, a whore in a torn blue rag walked out, her left breast hanging freely, her legs scabby and bruised. Kol blinked in the dim light, he had seen her correctly. Only wearing two rags, one to cover her right breast — and part of her left — and another to cover her womanhood, which was almost peeking out from beneath.

"You want to help me? Go back to where I can't see you. I have a woman waiting for me," he spoke much more bluntly than usual, he didn't care to deal with her kind, not tonight.

"You're loss, Little One." the voice trailed off as the woman melded back into the shadows.

Kol arrived at the tavern, his Little Love standing out front, looking to either side of the street. When she saw the strider, her eyes lit up and nearly began glowing in the dark.

"Kol!" she called, running over, her arms outstretched.

A large grin spread on his face as he embraced her. "Are you ready to go?" he asked excitedly, "I know the perfect spot."

"Yes, yes, I'm ready. Let's go now!"

Kol grinned again, thoughtful and caring. "Let's go, my love. We have a sky to watch."

#

Saffron sat in his chair, eyebrow raised at the scholar before him.

"You think lights in the sky are telling the Thregs when to advance?"

"In a manner of speaking, yes." the Wixen replied, spreading his sheets of parchment along the warden's desk. "You see, I've been passively studying rumours of Threg movements, and they all, and I mean *all* of them seem to be reported within a day or two of a star shower!"

"A day or two?" Saffron asked, "How can you be sure of that?"

Rel watched as Varden sighed and tried to describe it for a second time. She felt sorry for the foreigner: Saffron was stressed, with little sleep, and directly under the thumb of the Pale Bull. Who, Rel reminded herself, was also present in the room, a sceptical look on his face.

"The days are estimates as I cannot get a consistent answer from more than one person! One soldier says one day, and two other soldiers say another! Unless you have a better idea of how to track their movements, this is our best strategy. Do you not agree, Plain's Master?"

The scholar turned to Rel, and she nodded in reply. "His idea does show some logic, sir. It couldn't hurt to keep an eye on the sky and try to match it with reports from our striders."

Saffron sighed heavily, his eyes bloodshot. "Fine, fine. Varden, I cannot spread my striders much thinner, if you want constant reports on the skies, you'll have to keep an eye on them yourself. Otherwise, our reports on the star showers will be sporadic and you will have to live with that." He looked at his Right Hand. "And Rel?"

"Sir?"

"You are to pass any reports regarding Threg movements to Varden here for collaboration, is that clear?"

She nodded.

"Good. Now Varden," Saffron turned back to the scholar. "I'll assign you a mix guard duty of Sovereign Guard and conscripts to escort you during your studies, to give Bronwin's men time to prepare for the enemy, they'll keep you safe."

"Yes, of course, thank you, Warden." Varden looked out the window behind Saffron. "And would you look at that! We might get to test my theory sooner, rather than later!"

Red streaks of starlight began to mar the sky, east to west, arrows of an unknown goddess. Varden grinned as he scribbled back into his parchment.

#

He watched as Steena's eyes lit up with the red glow of the streaking stars. Kol grinned inwardly to himself as he felt his heart flutter and his blood rush.

By Gwendall's Blade, she's beautiful. He thought, lost in her wondrous gaze.

"They're so beautiful, Kol!" she gasped, pointing, "Whoa! Did you see that one?!" She looked over towards him and caught his gaze. "Hey, you're not even watching!"

Kol grinned and chuckled to himself. "No, no I'm not."

"And why not? Are striders forbidden to look at the stars or something?"

"No, of course not. I have my eye on something even better." He leaned in and gave her a kiss, she returned the gesture with passion, her cheeks welling up as she blushed in the moonlight. To Kol, it felt as if their heartbeats had synchronized, as if this moment was perfect for the two of them, and that no one else could ever experience something so wonderful.

They pulled away from the kiss, and Steena looked at him with wonder. "Kol, can I ask you something?"

"Of course."

"What do you plan on doing? I mean, I've heard rumours about Thregs, and …"

He placed a finger to her lips. "No need to worry, my dear. We'll be leaving, and I have a plan, something that will pay our way out of this town and into the safety of the Central Cities. I'll work as an assistant for a noble family once we arrive. Everything will be fine."

"What do you mean? You're leaving?"

"And I want you to come with me."

"Wh-why are you leaving? You're a Plain's Strider!"

Kol shook his head. "I know, but the plains aren't where I want to be, I can't stand it out there, it all feels … wrong. Will you come with me?" He held both her hands in his.

"Of course, I will. I just worry. How will you pay for us to travel to a Central City?"

"I have another half a fortnight of rangings before our carriage arrives outside the gates, to take us west. I have some things hidden in the plains, and I plan on grabbing them while I am out. I've kept a stash we can use to pay for whatever we may need."

"You what?"

"I know, it seems mad. But I knew I'd have to leave one day, and I've been checking on it when I get the chance to make sure everything is alright. We'll be okay, but nobody can know about this, not even Rel. Alright?"

"Okay …" she said, trailing off. It had been a lot of information to take in all at once. Within half a fortnight they would be leaving to restart their lives.

"Now, let's enjoy this night while we can. Who knows what the skies will look like in the Central Cities." Kol wrapped his arm around her and pulled her in close, her head resting on his shoulder.

#

Ashlin stood with her arms crossed, her lips pursed, unamused. "You are doing *what?!*"

Rel stood, feeling defeated. "We're going to war against the Thregs." Her shoulders slumped.

"Rel, you can't be serious, you really expect me to let you go out there, knowing what those things can do?!"

The Plain's Master took a step closer. "Sweetheart, I know you're worried, but I have no choice, I swore an-"

"An oath!" Ashlin cried, "Yes I know you swore that gods forsaken oath, and I hate it! I hate it! I hate it, even more, every time you step out of those gates. I don't want to lose you, Rel. I love you."

"And I love you. One day I will die-"

Ashlin pulled away, a tear rolling down her cheek.

"And when I do," Rel continued, "I promise you it will not be by one of those monsters. When I die, I'll be thinking of only you, while I lay on my back in old age, feeling happiness at all the memories we made in our life together, and looking forward to the ones we'll make in the Soul Spire."

Ashlin smiled faintly at the words. "I love you," she said. "Forever and always."

"And always and forever." Rel continued.

"No matter what." Ashlin looked up and kissed Rel deeply. As she pulled away she giggled. "Do you remember the first time we ever said that?"

Rel grinned widely. "Yes, yes I do. I seem to remember you thinking it was quite silly at the time."

Ashlin blushed, the red in her cheeks clashing with her blue eyes in the light of their hearth's fire. "It was something I said by *accident* Rel, I thought I was a fool."

"And what did I say?"

"You thought it was adorable, and refused to let me stop saying it. We were outside the walls at the time, you brought me partway up the Halo to see the stars." She held her lover closely. "That's the first night we made love."

"It was," Rel said caringly. "And I'll never forget that night, no matter what."

"No matter what," Ashlin repeated, "now, shall we have a late supper before you go and fulfil all those damned oaths tomorrow?"

"You did remember the pepper this time right?" Rel looked into the pot of stew with a raised eyebrow.

"Jo-een take me!" Ashlin cursed as she rifled through the cupboard.

"When in Gwendall's Name are you ever going to remember the damn pepper?"

"Probably the day the world ends," Ashlin said with a laugh. "Let's add it now, shall we?"

"Better late than never, you rhenhardt."

"Oh, hey now, that's unfair."

#

Shortly after Moon's Peak, Bronwin found himself sitting in the small home he had been assigned. He sat on the side of his bed, armour laden on the floor, with shield and mace propped up beside the door.

So the Thregs have an army, He thought. *Who would have figured?*

He rose from the bed and walked over to his window to look out at the night before him. His home didn't have much of a view, a small garden, then a little further, the walls of Plainsview, but he could at least see the night sky clearly. He would need to keep a close eye on that now, as any sign of a streaking star could be a sign of enemy movements. Did he really believe the scholar on his findings? He didn't. But until a better explanation came up, he would play along.

He began to prepare himself mentally for what he would be doing on the morrow. The prisoners would be equipped and assigned squads. Algrenon would be mixing them in with the Sovereign troops at their disposal. Before long, however, Alistair will have sent reinforcements. Wall guards, volunteers, conscripts, whoever could hold a weapon or don armour. No doubt there would be mercenaries in the mix, soldiers loyal to coin and little else. Whatever Sun Spire could do without.

Walking back over to his bed, the Pale Bull put his head down and closed his eyes. It was that night, that he dreamt of a strange weeping on the wind, smiles as wide as the walls of Valen themselves, and children; children dominated his dreams. They were murdering families, warriors, and priests alike. Nobody was left untouched.

Chapter 18

The halls of the Highfold Keep echoed loudly with each step Alistair took. His gold and red armour reflected the late after-morning light that shone through the windows. His sister struggled to keep step next to him.

"Alistair, please, slow down," Maryam voiced with concern, "Why the rush?"

The Arch General took note of his pace and slowed it to something more acceptable. "My apologies. I have tidings from Plainsview, *urgent* tidings."

"That is why you beckoned me, is it not?"

"Indeed, it is so."

"Well?" she asked, annoyed, "I had to postpone lunch with Father because of this. What do you need?"

"Coin, and lots of it."

The young woman's eyes widened. "Alistair, we only just recovered from the troops you *just* sent, what could you possibly need more coin for?"

"Mercenaries."

"What?"

Alistair spoke quietly as they walked, checking his tone to ensure no prying ears could make out his words. "An army of Thregs has been spotted in The Endless Plains, Maryam. They estimate it to be 50,000 strong. I'm sending what men I can from Sun Spire, but I can't send everyone, else risk the chance of raiding from local bandits. I'm sending what I can from the allocated budget, but I need *more* coin to get more help. I'll end up leaving Sun Spire with a skeleton crew."

His sister recoiled at the information. "Alistair, are you certain?"

"I am," he confirmed, "the sightings came from Rel herself, the Plain's Master."

"Alright," His sister bit her lip. "I might be able to allocate some resources from our Foreign Envoy budget, enough for possibly a few companies of mercenaries, so long as you choose wisely, and don't spend too frivolously."

"The Foreign Envoy budget? Won't Father be furious with you?"

"Possibly," she admitted. "But with an army of 50,000 Thregs, I doubt we will be doing much foreign work until the situation is dealt with. Worry not,

Valenfaar: The Crimson Plains

dear Brother, I will soothe our good father."

"Good is a rather strong word," he said with a snort.

"Hey now, he gives you a hard time, I know, but he still loves you. You do know that, right?"

The Arch General stopped, his red cloak settling behind him, turning to his sister he locked eyes with her. "Oftentimes I doubt it. Now I must go, I need to speak with my generals."

They hugged before departing. It didn't take long, as with Alistair's quickened pace, he found himself in the war room, standing over the carving of Valenfaar with a large red circle around Plainsview. Two of his generals walked through the door not long after him, they stood, hands clasped behind their backs, and waited to be addressed.

"At ease, gentlemen," the Highfold commanded, "no need for undue stress or discourse. Please relax, we have much work to do."

"Yes, sir," they said in chorus.

The first general was double Alistair's age at the mark of fifty. He was a man of average height, but with a chest built like a brick. His grey hair was trimmed short, nearly bald. The man's armour was a dark metal, standard steel painted a slate grey, with dark green outlining each segment of his plate. Theofold Lethwell had taught Alistair almost everything he knew about how to lead, tactics, and troop movements, if someone were to counsel him on who to send to Plainsview, it would be him.

The second man, about ten cycles the former's junior, stood tall, his hair beginning to turn a silvery grey. Wylandt Fedd stood in a neatly kept officer's uniform, the collar buttoned up close to the base of the neck. The uniform itself was a deep royal green, with gold lining. The jacket hung ever so slightly below the waist where a pair of crisp straight green pants covered the rest of his body. This man had taught him everything he knew about swordplay, duelling, and the psychology of soldiers on a battlefield. If someone knew what groups could fight well, it would be him.

"Gentlemen, we have a situation in Plainsview. I trust you read the missives I sent you?"

They nodded.

"Good, so you now know that we have a rather ... large problem on our hands. That invasion force is going to be a headache for us. Wylandt, I need to know which groups of soldiers you feel are best to send to Plainsview — ideally from Sun Spire — but we can pull from other Central Cities if we need to."

"Sir," the man said with an air of confidence. "We can send the fourth through twelfth battalions to Plainsview for reinforcement, leaving behind the Wall Guard to watch over the city. It's a lot of men, around 3000. So they may have to camp outside town, just past the western gate, in the fields here." He pointed to the map on the table.

Alistair nodded. "Alright. It doesn't come close to what the Thregs have, but I suppose it could buy the rest of our troops more time."

"Indeed, sir. We can pull a large number of troops from Moreen as well. Bandit activity seems to have completely halted in the area, so we should be able to hold the city with a basic garrison of 20,000, instead of the usual thirty."

Alistair nodded. They were outnumbered, and Thregs were classically more fearsome than any man. Their best hope would be a bottleneck in the Valley. Even so, the odds still weren't great. Maybe Alistair could requisition the Sword of Magus from his brother? No, Varen had them deployed elsewhere.

Gwendall's Cock. he cursed internally.

"Sir?" Theofold asked through the silence.

Alistair started. "Yes, yes, that will have to suffice for now. Can we pull any troops from the North or South?"

Both generals shook their heads. "No, sir," Theofold confirmed, "The south is being plagued by a sickness of some sort, their men are needed to maintain security and order for the time being. And as for the north ..." He trailed off. "We haven't had an arms treaty with the Arvelians for nearly a dozen cycles. We'd have to send an envoy to parlay if we wished for their aid. And by the time an agreement would be met, it would more than likely be too late. We'd have either repelled the attackers or have fallen back."

Alistair nodded slowly. *It will have to do.*

"Wylandt?" Alistair asked, looking over his shoulder to the door of his war room. It was left open a crack: a sign.

"Yes, sir?"

"Send Bronwin a spraven, tell him of the numbers we are sending his way. And tell him to prepare the Valley for a defensive war. He'll need all the time he can use to get things ready."

"Yes, sir."

"Good, then go."

The general turned on his heel and left the war room, shutting the door tightly behind him.

"Theofold?"

"Yes, sir?"

"Go see my sister, and begin preparations to send troops to the Pale Bull. The sooner the better. Do you know which mercenary company you wish to hire as aid to our forces?"

"I do, sir."

"Who?"

"The Anvil's Hammer. They are led by a man named Velamir. He's a bit full of himself and can be difficult to work with, but his men are a solid group; good with a sword, if not with a conversation."

"Good, get everything ready and sent out as quickly as possible. That is an order. Dismissed."

Theofold, mimicking the gesture from Wylandt, turned on his heel and began to leave. Alistair noticed the war room door was left ajar again even though Wylandt had shut it tightly behind him.

The Arch General stood tall and crossed his arms. "You know Brother, it wouldn't kill you to leave the door closed when you enter?"

Cullen's voice filled the air around him, both physical and imaginary in its presence. "Now that wouldn't be much fun, would it?" a chuckle shook Alistair's mind.

"And to what do I owe the pleasure?" Alistair asked with a grin.

A hard silence drifted on the air. "Events are in motion Brother," the Spymaster said. "I've seen some interesting things, both in the east and in the west."

Alistair raised an eyebrow. "What have you seen in the west?"

"I'm not entirely sure. Smoke, but lacking fire, screaming but lacking voices. And … songs, but lacking music or rhythm. I shall keep an eye on the Sword of Magus as they are heading in that direction. I suspect they'll discover something on their travels."

Nodding, Alistair leaned against his war table. "And the east?"

"Thregs, and lots of them. They hold the Endless Plains hostage. I have witnessed many Wixen and other envoys alike being cut down by the dozens. Hundreds being taken … as livestock."

"Livestock? Not prisoners?"

"No. The Thregs do take prisoners, though they are rare. They need bodies for tools and weapons, we are but game to them, just as deer or elk are to us. Have you not read on the Thregs?"

"Yes, of course, I have. This knowledge is not new to me, though I was not aware of how little numbers they took as prisoners." Alistair chewed his lip. "Have you noticed any trends with their prisoners?"

"I have."

"And?"

"The truth is rather disturbing Brother. We will need to tell Varen when the time is appropriate."

"Why not now?" Alistair didn't like keeping secrets from his brother. He knew Varen, and he could be a vindictive bastard when he is left out of the loop. If Cullen thought it concerned the High Priest, then surely it had to do with mages. He huffed mentally, he would need to trust the Spymaster's judgement as he had always done.

"His attention is required in the west, if we share the information I am about to provide you, he may recall and head eastward. This is not needed."

"Okay, so, what have you found?"

#

Otheer squirmed as he leaned against the bone cage. His leg, the one they had dragged him by all those days ago, had begun to rot. He hadn't a clue as to how long he had been the Thregs captive. He was still tied up with Keetlyn's hair. The blonde and black streaks soaked through with mud, blood and pus.

He had hoped Keetlyn was killed before he had been scalped, but after Otheer had gained consciousness for the tenth or twelfth time, he had witnessed his friend: Keetlyn was laying in the dirt, alive, but catatonic. The flesh from his scalped head was muddied and stained with dirt, maggots chewing on the rotten flesh. His friend didn't move, he didn't make a sound, he just lay there, eyes glassy, his chest falling gently with his breath.

Otheer didn't know how many days ago that had been. It could have been one, it could have been ten. He had no way to know. He was fed rotten food, kept barely hydrated, and oftentimes beaten to the point of blacking out. They had never bludgeoned his head though, leaving his mind mostly intact.

There had only been a few handfuls of prisoners that Otheer was able to notice. Mages, all of them, their robes dirty and bloodied, their bodies broken, rotting and bruised, but kept alive. Each night one would be dragged away, never to return. This he had expected, executions — most likely for the sake of cruelty — seemed to be a regular occurrence in the Threg camps.

Struggling to sit up, the mage fought against dizziness and nausea to straighten his posture. He had dislocated his shoulders days ago from his bindings, and they were swollen to the point of rigidness. Grunting, he wiggled his way up, then grimaced at the throbbing in his body. He had lost feeling in his wounded leg.

The haziness in his vision cleared for a few short moments, letting Otheer take in his surroundings. The Thregs were on the move, moving their tents, gutting bodies, and slaughtering animals. Otheer had recognized this behaviour, each time they moved, they left nothing but blood and decaying bodies behind. Day by day, the golden grass of the Endless Plains was being painted a deathly red, and the speed at which they moved seemed to increase each time.

Wet, heavy footsteps sounded behind him. He tried to crane his head around to face whoever was approaching, but he couldn't. His body fought him with every ounce of strength he had left. The door to his cage opened, and a Threg stood before him. The beast squatted down in front of him, a dagger of bone in its hand.

The beast before him looked at the mage with big, wandering eyes. Its vertical nostrils flaring with excitement and fetid breath. The Threg smiled, revealing rows of large, inhuman teeth, browned and rotting. It leaned in, and opened its mouth wider, revealing the fibrous black tongue housed within. It dragged the wet filaments along his face, groaning with pleasure as it did so. Otheer wanted to shudder, but he couldn't. He tried to summon up another tempest to set himself free, or to force the creature to kill him, but he could feel the winds evaporate shortly after they began to brew. He was already dead, they just hadn't killed him yet.

The Threg's head snapped down and looked at the man's leg. Its face showed what could only be puzzlement. As the beast looked over the rotting leg, he hefted the bone dagger up and dropped it above the dying flesh. The strength of the blow was so intense that Otheer could feel the blade break and splinter the bone within. Then a sharp tug, and another blast of pain, the creature tore the leg free and threw it out of the cage. Otheer didn't scream, he didn't even flinch, the small reserves of energy he had left wouldn't let him have the pleasure.

He could feel the blood running from his stump and it was calming to him. He liked it and found himself relishing the sensation, as it was so different to what he had been experiencing since being taken captive. It was cooling, calming.

The Threg who had given him the pleasure hoisted the mage's broken body over its shoulder and began to carry him out of the cage. From over seven feet in the air, Otheer could hardly keep the world from spinning around him. His vision blurred and rotated as if he were being cast into the raging currents of a river. If he hadn't felt the blood rushing to his head, and out his stump, he wouldn't have been able to tell which direction was up. He faded to blackness.

A hard slap to the face startled him awake and Otheer found himself kneeling — somewhat — in front of a strange-looking Threg. Its hair was long and bedraggled, thin and oily — like that of any other Threg — but he wore a bone chest piece.

Why was this Threg wearing armour? What type of importance did he hold within their ranks, and why was he brought before it? All these questions plagued Otheer's mind as he watched the creature's pupils dilate with pleasure. Its breathing began to quicken, and the nostrils along the side of its nose began to flare and breathe wildly, almost like a wild boar preparing for an attack. This look did not hold malice or anger. Only pleasure and eagerness.

The beast stepped forward, the mud squishing beneath its long, finger-like toes. The mage tried to look around with his peripheral vision.

Another footstep.

He could see the bodies of other mages, the ones he had seen pulled away from their cages — another footstep — their necks were slashed so deep the heads were nearly cleaved away. Another faster footstep squished into the mud.

The mage's bodies were grey, lifeless, a look of pain and weariness clouded over their dead eyes.

Two more rushed footsteps. The Threg's eyes were wide with joy. Nearby Thregs began to crowd around.

That's when Otheer realized it, why was it muddy? It hadn't rained, not as far as he knew. He tried to watch as the next foot came closer to him — only a few more until the monster was there — and watched as a thick fluid spread between the creature's toes: blood. It was blood, the entirety of the camp had been muddied with the blood of man. So much blood. Otheer could feel the life in his body waver, his stump pouring his own essence into the mixture.

The Threg stood before him now, its gaze cast over him with a perverse pleasure. The Threg reached down with a large hand and gripped the top of Otheer's skull. Its fingers nearly reached around the entirety of his head. Nails dug into the mage's cheeks, as he felt the Threg grab a hold of ... something.

Otheer screamed for the first time he could ever remember. He felt the tempest within him flare to life as the creature pulled at the invisible force inside his body. The winds flowed up from his chest and into his head, flaring out his mouth and nose with a rush of warmth. His arcana, his magic, the force that he had learned to use for nearly his entire life was being ripped from his body.

He screamed and flailed as much as his body would allow, a surprising amount of strength permeating from its depths. The Threg raked its nails upwards, scratching Otheer's face as he felt his magic being torn from him. His body was a flame of pain, the winds of his arcana pushing and pulling, trying to stay contained within him. A strange green glow began to swirl around the Threg as Otheer's magic permeated itself in the space surrounding them. The swirls of green wind flowing into the pores of the beast.

The mage felt his body grow limp and grey as the final portion of his arcana left his body and flooded into the monster in front of him. As Otheer fell to the ground, he felt a rough blade pierce the flesh of his neck, it pushed hard and dug deep. He felt cartilage pop and rip as blood rushed from the wound. Then, blackness enveloped him as the Soul Spire had received another Valen life.

Chapter 19

Bronwin stood tall over his men, and even taller over the Plain's Striders. Four days since the last star shower and the Thregs had been spotted closer to the Halo than before. So far, Varden's theories had proven correct. The Pale Bull resented to agree with him: he found that anytime the scholar opened his mouth, Bronwin felt the overwhelming need to drive a metal spike through his own ears to halt the blabbering.

Three days ago, he had received a parchment from Alistair and his generals. Troops were being moved to Plainsview to help with fortifications. The numbers they were sending weren't promising, he wanted more. They had already braced the wall past the swamp with steel and stone two days after the report came through, but it still wasn't finished.

Even now, as the Pale Bull looked over its construction, he could feel the weight of his assignment pushing down on him. And he *relished* it. This was his chance to punch a hole so large through the Thregs, that the scaled bastards would be reeling for dozens of cycles to come. He would funnel them into the Valley and crush them with the strength of his men. 50,000 Thregs was a lot, but the Sovereign Guard wouldn't back down from the fight, so long as he and Algrenon — and regrettably, Saffron — kept their troops circulating consistently, they would be able to pull through this with an easy victory.

The addition of prisoner conscripts to his forces allowed Bronwin to keep security running through Valen's Passage. It also allowed him to keep the scholar protected while studying the shadewood tree in the swamp.

#

"All I'm sayin," the prisoner repeated, "is that we just ain't sure *how* many dozens of hundreds of people I've slaughtered." He puffed his chest out proudly, the surrounding prisoners and guardsmen rolling their eyes.

Varden knelt in the swamp, pulling the vial off the tap he had left in the shadewood tree many days ago. "Do you even recall how many a dozen is?" he sighed with frustration, as he looked over the glass.

"Do I even what?" Dry Eyes replied.

"Recall," Varden said annoyed, putting a cork onto the instrument, sealing it tight.

"I uh ... Hmph," The prisoner fell silent.

Varden rolled his eyes as he stood up in the muck. He held the vial before him, eyeing its contents intently. It had taken a very long time, but each day Varden came to expect the shadewood tree, he had found a little more sap pooling in the bottom of the vial. The substance was a white watery fluid; the same shade of white as the tree's leaves. There seemed to be very little sap in the shadewood tree. The vial had been "full" for days and hadn't gathered another drop. That was strange, only a single vial of sap, and even then, the glass vessel was only slightly more than half full. Any other tree would have given him more.

Varden looked at it quizzically, then placed it in his pouch. He would study it later when he didn't have a blathering idiot following him around.

"Alright, gentlemen," the Wixen announced, "my studies here for the day are concluded. Shall we move further down the valley to see Bronwin?"

One of the Sovereign men nodded, then waved for everyone else in the group to follow. Varden trailed near the back of the group, the conscripts were in the centre, flanked by soldiers at either side.

Valen's Passage proved to be little challenge for them. The workers moving supplies from Plainsview to the defensive site had stomped down the ground, creating a wider roadway than there had been before. Much of the landscape had already begun to be altered and machined into obstacles easily overcome. The paths themselves were cleared of any vines and plant life, some trees had been cut back to allow room for wagons and larger building supplies.

If there was one thing Varden recognized, it was mastery. As much of a brute and a killer this Pale Bull was, he was most certainly a legend in the highest degree. Everywhere the man had stepped caused Varden to be impressed at how men followed him, how he always knew what needed to be done next. The scholar could only wait in anticipation to see how he would fight. If he was as fierce a warrior as he was a commander, he would be granted the title of "Master" if he ever arrived in Ajwix.

#

The strider's longhouse had been bustling with activity the last few days, Rel and Saffron had been busy assigning patrols and going over the changes to their regular rangings for a second time.

"How does everything look?" Rel asked, looking over a small map on his desk. On it, there were several small arrows drawn showing where the striders were patrolling. Further out from the passage mouth, at the five and ten-kilometre mark were two large, horizontal red lines, marking the range they were to patrol. The plains were vast, an ocean of grass. Five to ten kilometres was a pittance of an operational area, only a fraction of what the striders were used to.

Saffron sighed. "Everything looks as good as we can get it, Rel. Until we have those fresh forces. I think this is the best we can muster." The warden leaned back in his chair, his face awash with anxiety. "Rel, I need you at the construction site, helping Bronwin oversee this wall of his."

Rel went to object, but her mentor raised a hand.

"I know how you feel about him, by Gwendall's Blade, I'm convinced we *all* feel the same. But he is our commander in this campaign, and his orders are law. You know that as well as I do, Plain's Master."

She tightened her gaze and straightened her posture. "Yessir, of course. I shall perform my duty to the best of my abilities."

Saffron gave a resigned sigh. "At ease, Rel." He leaned forward on the table, looking annoyed, his hair hanging in long messy dregs.

"Sir, If I may?"

The Plain's Warden looked up, his boiled skin damp with sweat. "Of course, Rel."

"Would you do me the honour of joining me? It might be good for you to get a break from all this," She waved a hand at the mess of parchment and maps on his desk. "And let the others see you in the field for a change."

Her mentor sat back in his chair and thought for a moment. He grinned. It was something Rel was not used to seeing. It was a nice fatherly grin that spoke about how he cared for those under his command.

"I think I might do that," he said proudly. "Let me get my things, then we'll depart."

Rel nodded and returned a grin of her own. Saffron left the room for a few long moments then returned in uniform. Shortsword and long knife at his waist, short bow on his back. It looked odd to her. He had gained a lot of weight and looked a little out of place in full strider garb, but there was an air of authority to it all, an air of inspiration.

"You look, erm..."

"Don't lie to me, I can already tell this uniform is too damn small."

They both laughed. It was true: the clothes sat tightly around his not-so-newly formed girth.

"Ah well," Saffron said with a chuckle. "Shall we head out to see our friend?"

Rel clenched her teeth, then nodded. "Yessir. Lead the way."

The two figureheads marched out of the longhouse and into the town of Plainsview with an air of authority, a commanding presence for anyone who could see them.

They walked in silence, the Valley Gate opening for them wordlessly. Even Valen's Passage felt as if it bowed down to the two striders as they moved.

It had taken a while for the two commanders to arrive at the wall. Workers toiled, carrying logs, wooden planks, stone, and metal struts from wagons to the wall's frame. It looked to be nearly done.

Standing amongst a group of soldiers, Bronwin towered over them, a mountain among hills.

"Bronwin!" Saffron called, spittle glistening in the air, "How fares the project?"

The Pale Bull stiffened, then turned to face the Plain's Warden. "Everything is going according to plan. We should have it done within the next three days. As long as your people make an attempt to keep our resources flowing."

"Plainsview will provide to the best of its ability," Saffron said with a respectful nod, moving towards the soldier.

Rel watched with curiosity, as the two exchanged passive-aggressive words.

Bronwin snorted. "And if the 'best of their ability' isn't good enough?"

"It will be," the Warden said flatly. "Or we'll all perish much sooner than expected."

"I should hope so, Squid. If I need to bail you out again ..." he trailed off, a smirk on his face. "Well, let's just say I may end up getting distracted in the heat of battle."

Rel's blood began to boil, the audacity of the madman had her ready to reach for her blade.

"Are you threatening the Plain's Warden?" Saffron asked, his eyes blazing with fury.

"It's not a threat, Squid, merely a warning. A lot can go wrong during battle, especially when Thregs are involved." He shrugged. "I wished to let you know that I can't promise your safety once they come marching through that valley mouth." He hefted his flanged mace and pointed it towards the east. "It's only a matter of time now, old man."

Saffron said nothing.

Rel took a breath in, and began to speak, but was cut off by hurried shouts behind her.

"Plain's Master! Plain's Master!" a strider called, sprinting towards them from the wall.

Rel turned to face the three scouts and jogged over to them. "What is it?"

The one who had been calling for her answered, out of breath. "We-" they breathed heavily, "we bring news from the Halo, ma'am," they coughed, "of the Thregs."

A voice sounded from behind the Plain's Master, it was Saffron. "What is it, Rel?"

"Sir," the tired strider said, trying to straighten her posture. "The Thregs are moving; coming closer to the valley mouth."

"How far out?" this was Bronwin, having taken an interest in the conversation.

"About 500 kilometres out, by our best guess, sir. They move quickly, but not consistently."

Saffron sucked on his lip audibly. "Five days ago we guessed they would be here within half a fortnight. We've been scrambling to meet that deadline. They seem to be moving slower than anticipated."

"You do know why that is, do you not?" a pompous voice called from nearby.

It was Varden, sitting with his back against a tree, his cloak and trousers soaked from the waist down. He was scribbling in his notebook.

The Plain's Warden turned to face the Wixen. "Do enlighten me, Scholar."

"You really should take my theories far more seriously." He snapped his journal closed, tucked it into his pack, and stood. Brushing off his robe, he waved a hand. His troop of guards moved with him. "Do you not recall what I said five days ago, the night of the star shower?"

Looks of dumbfounded confusion settled relentlessly among the faces of the striders. Even the Pale Bull himself looked like an outsider.

"May the Veil Strider lose you," Varden cursed, "I told you stubborn, bloody Valens, that the Thregs could be moving in relation to those pretty red streaks you see in the sky." He pointed up into the air mockingly.

Saffron's eyes opened with a hint of realization. "Yes, I do recall this. It was only a theory, however, a rather far-fetched one at that."

"Maybe so, but it was the only theory we had at the time ... and still is." Varden turned to the strider who had delivered the report. "When did the Thregs begin to move?"

The woman looked to Rel nervously, who gave an affirming nod. "You may tell him."

"Um, four days ago."

"And when did we see the star shower, my dear Plain's Warden?"

"Five days ago," Saffron confirmed, "it could be just-"

"No, it could not be just a coincidence. Pardon my bluntness. Every report of Threg movement has been following one of these celestial events. It would take a fool to think it equates to something else!"

Bronwin opened his mouth to speak but was cut off by a gruff voice.

"Those words dere, what do dey mean?" One of Varden's guards approached. "Now, don't get me wrong, imma smart man and all, but dem words, I don't think I've ever heard of em before!"

Varden sighed loudly and rolled his eyes so hard, Rel thought they would spin all the way around. "You dolt ... would you be silent for more than *two small moments?!*"

"Whaz that word mean?"

"Which one?" the scholar refuted, "Small? Well if you would let me crack open your skull I could-"

"Nah, not dat one. Dolt. Whaz that one mean?"

"It means-"

"Can I take a guess?"

"No, no you may-"

"It means imma handsome man, dunnit?"

Varden's body trembled, he looked as if he wanted to collapse. "Yes, why not. Sure. Okay. It means you're handsome!"

Rel and the rest of their circle stood in awe at the conscript's stupidity. She could feel the small tug of a grin on her lips, but she fought it off and went to push on with the previous conversation. "Bronwin, I believe you were going to say something?"

"Yes. Scholar, you are certain these Thregs move after a star shower?"

"I have no reason not to believe that," he said affirmingly. "Everything I have observed so far points to this being fact. Unless there is something I have missed."

"Why would they be moving like that?" Rel asked, "Why not advance quickly, push through us before we can prepare?"

Varden bit his lip and thought for a moment. "I am not certain. I imagine only the Thregs themselves actually understand their reasoning. If we were to capture one we might-"

Bronwin roared a laugh. "Taking a Threg captive is useless, Scholar! The things can't speak our tongue! How do you suggest we interrogate them?"

"There are ways, my dear Bull. There are ways. If you do happen across an opportunity to take one of them alive, please take it. I would love to study them. What we could learn could prove invaluable to our war effort."

Bronwin grunted. "No promises."

"I wouldn't expect any. A battlefield is no place to make promises. But please do try, if you're so inclined."

"We'll see what we can do for you, Varden. Thank you for all your help." Rel made eye contact with Saffron and shared a nod.

"A pleasure, Plain's Master. A pleasure to be sure."

The conscript from earlier spoke up, looking at the Pale Bull. "You a mighty large lad there, you are. How did they get ya to be so big?"

Bronwin raised an eyebrow. "They?"

"The gods. I ain't evah seen a man big as you. How did dey do it?"

The Shield of Northwood refused to answer, he only grunted and went to turn away.

The man called after him, swatting at a fly. "And why do dey call you dah Pale Bull anyway? Is it that fancy trinket dangling there?"

Rel watched as he pointed to a pale dagger hanging off of Bronwin's uniform. She hadn't noticed it before, she wasn't sure how, it didn't have a sheath, and glistened with the colour of clean ivory. The Bull refused to acknowledge the question and began calling out orders to his men.

Chapter 20

Many Cycles Ago ...

Soon, Bronwin thought to himself, *Soon I'll be rid of Saffron and his rhenhardts, and soon I'll be enlisted in the Sovereign Guard.*

The boy had told himself this day after day. For each morning, the impending feeling of crawling out of his bed to face the day grew heavier and heavier in his chest and mind. He was large, but he was kinder than most too. But why was it that Saffron and his friends had decided he deserved their ire? Why did they throw stones at him so relentlessly all through his childhood? Why did they shove his face into the mud whenever he tried to cross a field?

He kicked at a small stone on the roadway and continued. He was fifteen cycles old, and taller than every person in Northwood. Many even wagered he would be taller than any man in Valenfaar. That much had yet to be proven untrue, not a single man, soldier, nor baker or blacksmith would stand even close to his height. Not even sixteen, and he already rose well past six and a half feet tall. Many priests and magisters that had come through town had wagered that he would stand more than seven feet tall at the apex of his growth.

Most of all, Bronwin wanted this to not be true, to be a lie, or a fabrication, something that the others were saying just to vex him, to chide him even. But he continued to grow and continued to hate himself for it. He knew it was silly, it wasn't his fault he was so tall, it wasn't anybody's fault. But he felt that if he could somehow shrink to normal size, then the rest of the children in the village would leave him alone. He was strong, and he was smart, and he was kind, he tried his best to be the person his mother would have wanted him to be. But he was different, and so he was made a target. They called him the Threg of Northwood because of his height. Which was better than being called that because of his looks.

He continued to kick the stone as he walked somberly towards the cemetery. The town priest waved to him, he waved back and gave a short nod. Biting back at the tears he felt welling up, he swallowed hard. Even two cycles later, this day was difficult for him, he guessed it would always be so. Regardless, he continued to kick at the stone until he found himself at the rocky wall that marked the edge of the cemetery.

Leaving his kicking stone behind, Bronwin sauntered into the small field of tombstones. 300 lay buried in the cemetery, with another 500 on the other side of the village. His brother was buried in this graveyard, as was his father. The man his mother promised would come home one day, who would come home a soldier, a man of power and bravery. Someone who would defend their homes and country until his dying breath.

Bronwin was told that this had happened five cycles prior, that his father was trying to save a small village near the Central Cities from Thregs. Only, his duty as a soldier ended as quickly as it began, the spear of a Threg, rammed through his chest had seen to that. There was some kind of sick humour in it: both his older brother, and father, killed by Thregs, half a country apart.

Nine cycles ago, his mother had begun showing signs of Grey Lung. He hadn't noticed it at the time and only thought his mother was coughing from the race they had had. But no, as the days turned into fortnights, and the fortnights turned into moons, and the moons turned into cycles: his mother's condition had worsened beyond belief. Weight loss, pale skin, red eyes, coughing blood, spells of dizziness, and unconsciousness.

The priests and magisters did what they could for her, but Grey Lung was so rare in Valenfaar that their efforts had failed. She died in her bed, in severe pain, and now she lay buried, next to her husband and son.

Bronwin found the gravestones and knelt in front of them, he rested his forehead against the middle stone; his father's. He reached out to either side and placed a hand on both his brother's and mother's tombstones. He closed his eyes and felt his tears drop into the grass before him.

Though we were not born in this country, He thought to himself, in prayer, *And though we left Ajwix behind in search of a better life,* His lip began to quiver, *I vow to protect the people of this country to the best of my ability. To be a true Wixen Master. To be a protector, a shield among a sea of swords. And though the Veil Strider carries you all to a new world, a new life, a new body, know that everything I do will be in your name, in my name, and for all those that would need our help.*

We are Wixen, we are the Zucanas of Northwood, and I shall carry this name with pride and honour. May the Veil Strider grant you all safe passage through your mind, and bring you back to the world of the waking as the sun rises in the sky, and as the moon sets on the horizon.

May the Veil Strider bring us together once more, in a time far from now, where the winds cease to blow, and the seas fail to pull, where the moon and sun halt in the sky, and when the stars fade out. Granting us the Veil: where we shall be together to witness the creation of a new world, in the wake of the Strider, that which will guide us into an eternity of deathless existence, a world where the Veil and reality are one, where we *are one, and where we shall find peace. We are the Zucanas and we are Wixen.*

Bronwin swallowed hard and raised his head from the tombstone. The prayer was something his mother had taught him when he was old enough to understand what death meant to the Wixen people. It wasn't an end, it was the soul of a person moving to another plane of existence, where they would grow and learn, and bring themselves closer into the true holds of the Veil, when they were truly a Wixen Master, in every sense of the word.

He pulled his arms back to his sides. "I love you all."

Rising to his feet, Bronwin stepped away from the stones, held his head high and marched out of the graveyard, and back the way he came. A thick sheet of grey moved across the sky, slowly at first, but gaining momentum with every gust of wind. Before long, a gentle pattering of rain covered the world around him. The rain wasn't heavy; it left a peaceful pittering sound with every drop.

The road began to build with mud and grime, the brown mess layering the bottom of the boy's sheepskin shoes. He grimaced at the feeling of mud between his toes but continued on. Then there was laughter, followed by the familiar feeling of a stone forming in his stomach. Bronwin recognized the laughter: Saffron and his friends.

Cautiously, he stepped towards the sound of the older boys and peered around a small tree. He could see the group, three of them, teasing Saffron.

"Oh c'mon Saff!" one called, "You say you want to be a Plain's Strider? And you're scared of that?!" The boy pointed somewhere out of sight.

Saffron shook his head, his thick hair wet with rain. "No! I don't see what the point in this is!" He looked flustered, annoyed, and — truth be told — scared.

This piqued Bronwin's interest as he watched on. What could have Saffron, of all people, scared?

The teasing and chiding continued, before Saffron finally agreed to do whatever it was his friends were telling him to do. He stepped away and crawled through a fence into a muddy patch of land. The boys whooped and hollered towards something out of sight.

Then Bronwin's eyes opened wide, he realized where they were now, he had been so lost in thought that he hadn't even realized where he had been walking.

A huff of air could be heard, followed by the sound of hooves. A gigantic bull sauntered out from its pen, its fur a pale grey-brown, its horns the size of a shortsword's blade. It looked to Saffron with eyes of malice, as if wondering who the fool entering its home dared to think they were.

The bull charged.

The boys at the sidelines whooped and hollered some more, edging the beast on, throwing stones to enrage it even further. Bronwin took off in a jog towards them.

"Well if it isn't the Threg of Northwood!" one of them called, tossing a rock towards Bronwin. He missed.

"What is he doing?!" Bronwin called, his voice a hammer in the rain, "Why is he in there?!"

Another boy turned. "He's putting his valens where his mouth is! Proving he has what it takes to be a Plain's Strider!" The bully crossed his arms and looked up at Bronwin, his eyes reeking of hatred.

"That thing'll kill him!"

"Then he won't be good enough." the second boy followed with a snort.

"That's not for you to judge." Bronwin watched as Saffron's nimble figure sidestepped the bull's charge.

All three boys cheered.

"Atta boy, Saff!"

"Lucky step, you rhenhardt!"

"Betchya can't do that again!"

Again, Bronwin stared as Saffron sidestepped charge after charge. The boy was growing tired; the bull wasn't. Its energy was fuelled purely by the rage that it felt due to a stranger's presence in its home.

One slow step and Saffron was tossed into the air, the creature's snout lifting him up like a toy. The horns hadn't found a mark, thankfully, and he landed heavily in the mud, winded and out of breath.

The three boys on the sidelines cheered and jeered.

"Looks like your luck is running out, Saff!"

"Oh, c'mon, that didn't look too bad!"

"What are ya, four?! Get back up!"

Bronwin felt a twitch in his legs, something telling him to move forward. But he held off, the fear of what the other boys would say or do to him outweighed his want to help. He watched as Saffron tried to get back to his feet, only to be bludgeoned by the bull once more. He was tossed backwards, sliding through the mud from the force of the blow.

"Aren't you going to do something?!" Bronwin asked the boys, "It's going to kill him!"

"If you're so worried," one of them replied with a scoff, "Why don't you do something about it? Besides, we don't like Saff that much anyway, and we doubt you do too."

Bronwin hefted up a large rock and climbed through the fence. He stepped foot in the bullpen and walked forward, the animal was charging once more at Saffron in the mud.

"Oh, look at this. The Threg is actually going to do something? I betcha he's all fat under there, not a pound of muscle on em, the freak."

Laughter erupted through the rainfall. Bronwin brought his arm back, then launched the stone with all his might. It struck the bull in the neck, slowing it to a trot. It turned away from Saffron. Its eyes glowed with newfound hatred. The beast brought its head down and began to charge.

Bronwin stood, his stance wide, arms outstretched and watched as the bovine horror stampeded through the pen. Mud sprayed with every step, the sound of its hooves growing louder and ever closer. Huffs of air could be heard as the creature heaved angry breaths, its eyes flashing with the lightning of hatred. As if to say: "Get away from my home. You do not belong here."

Step by step, heartbeat by heartbeat, the two behemoths grew closer, the bull closing the gap with pure speed and power. Bronwin counted the heartbeats, then sidestepped and quickly turned to face his foe.

"Get outta here Saff!" he called, "Go, get out!"

The sound of hurried footsteps and wheezing behind him were the only acknowledgements Bronwin had time to receive. By the time he realized Saffron was back on his feet, the bull had already charged a second time. Again, he sidestepped and narrowly avoided the blow. This continued on, again and again, each time growing more tiresome than the last.

Bronwin had barely avoided the previous charge, having to cast himself into a roll to get enough distance, he wiped mud off his brow and made eye contact with the bull. It was between him and the fence line now. The boys on the other side watched in mute amazement. If Bronwin tried to run for the fenceline, he would be caught and gored on the bull's horns. But he could feel it in his legs that he didn't have the energy to toss himself around anymore. He had one more idea, and by the Veil Strider was it a stupid one.

The bull began to charge, stomping through the muck, its eyes screaming death, its hide slick with rain, but aching for blood.

His mother's words rang in his ears, from nine cycles ago: "Do what you know you can do better than anyone else."

He nodded to himself, to his mother, and fixed his gaze on the bull, matching the blood lust. He wasn't a fast boy. But with his size, he was strong.

Do what you know you can do better than anyone else.

He grinned. *Better than anyone else,* He repeated in his mind, *Even better than you.*

Bronwin raised his arms and reached out as the bull closed in, he grabbed its horns and braced himself. The sheer force of the charge met with the sheer strength and posture of the boy resulted in a near stalemate. Bronwin's posture didn't falter, he was pushed through the mud, leaving tracks from his massive feet as the bull continued to push. His arms hadn't given way. Bronwin breathed in deeply, then, in one heave, twisted the horns, forcing the bull to the side, and with a push, forced its head into the mud.

The creature regained its footing and shook the mud from its snout. Its eyes were nearly glowing in the greyness of the rainy day. Its breaths huffed louder and louder with every passing moment before it charged again. Bronwin braced himself and grabbed onto the horns, letting himself be pushed through the mud, and again, he twisted to the side and cast the bull to the ground.

A third charge, and again the beast met with Bronwin's full strength. The boy's arms could keep this up for as long as the bull could. But this time, when Bronwin attempted to twist the horns, the bull resisted and adjusted its footing. It continued to push him towards the fence. If Bronwin got to that point, he would break through and topple, leaving himself at the mercy of his foe. He couldn't allow that. Not now, not ever.

He began to squeeze, he squeezed as tight as he possibly could, and began to twist his right hand with all his might. The fence was getting closer, he knew that, he could almost feel it. But he could also feel the pure strength he held coursing through his veins. He squeezed ever tighter and began to twist his hand more. He felt it: a crack, a splinter, a caving of structure. The horn he held began to give way. The boy screamed in anger as he snapped the horn off the bull's skull.

The creature roared in pain as it continued to push, Bronwin leaned in towards the broken horn, and using it as a weapon, began to plunge the tip of the ivory into the animal's neck. Over and over he drove it into the beast's flesh. Blood poured from the wound and covered his hands. He continued to stab, the mud becoming stained. As blow after blow landed, Bronwin felt the bull's strength waver and fade. He screamed again and broke free the other horn. He took the head of the creature in his gut, nearly knocking the air from him, but as this happened, he drove both bone daggers into either side of his foe's neck, and as he had done before, twisted the beast, and cast it aside, into the mud.

The bull writhed in pain, before succumbing to its wounds. It lay at the fence, at the base of the bullies' feet. They looked up at the exhausted Bronwin, blood smeared on his hands and face, horns in each hand. They were in awe. Wordlessly they stared, mouths agape.

"B-Bronwin?" Saffron asked nervously, "A-are you okay?"

The Pale Bull gritted his teeth, he couldn't believe he had just killed a bull with his bare hands. "*Get out of here, now,*" he seethed, "*Go! Leave me be!*"

The boys did so. It hadn't taken long, but eventually, word got around Northwood of what Bronwin had done. That was when they had started calling him the Pale Bull, and that was when he finally gained respect from his peers. Within a cycle of that day, Bronwin had joined the Sovereign Guard and had the horns of the bull carved into a proper dagger and an ale horn.

It had gone largely unspoken, but there would always be respect between both Bronwin and Saffron. He had saved his life after all, and in return, Saffron had never once spoken against the Pale Bull, he had always come to his aid, regardless of his personal feelings, a way to try and repay the debt that he would now owe for the rest of his life.

Chapter 21

Present Day ...

It had only been a day since the order to watch the stars was given, and Kol was trapped out in the wilderness of Valen's Passage, staring upwards at the dark sky he had once loved to search. But now — now that he had to watch the stars for the sake of duty — he found himself dreading it. This was the second night in a row he had been placed on star-gazing duty, and he was ready for a star to shoot straight through his skull.

It was almost time for him to go into the plains and grab his stash; when he returned he would take Steena away from the warzone that would be Plainsview, and take her to the Central Cities where they would be safe and could live in comfort. He would have to create a new name and profession for himself. If word travelled to any kind of high-ranking Sovereign soldier about who he really was, Kol would be tried for desertion and beheaded without a second thought. And Steena would be given up to the streets, stripped of all their belongings and left to fend for herself.

Now he sat against a large tree, he didn't know what kind and he didn't care either. He was already out of the job mentally, now he just needed to make it happen in the physical sense.

He let out a loud sigh and looked back to the skies, nothing. There was nothing that night: not a single star in the sky began its streak across the blackness. He watched the moon, as it hovered iridescently in the air, a puppet held by unseen strings in the darkness.

Kol sat and watched the sky for some time before another strider relieved him of his post.

"Hey," the man whispered in the dark, pale moonlight awash on his face, "your watch is over. You head back to town, get some ale, and some rest." He patted Kol on the shoulder, like an older brother, then gestured his head towards Plainsview.

"Alright, thanks," Kol replied, "Some ale sounds pretty good right now."

"Take care, my friend."

The two shared a quick nod as Kol stood and began his walk back to town.

It hadn't taken long, or at least it hadn't felt long. He was, admittedly, zoned out thinking about his soon-to-be-freedom in the world, and all the happiness it would bring him.

The Valley Gate to Plainsview opened before him with a low creak, and he let the torchlight of the town light the way ahead of him. He paced into the local tavern, Steena wasn't working, she was at home getting her things ready for their departure.

Walking over to a random table that stood bare in the middle of the room he took a seat. A server wandered over his way with his usual mug of ale. Kol thanked him, then sat and began to eavesdrop on the conversations around him.

"So," he heard one soldier say, "you hear from that sweet cousin of yours back in the Capital?"

His friend snorted in affirmation. "Oh yeah. I've heard from her, that's for sure."

"And?"

Even though Kol couldn't see them, he could almost feel the rise of an eyebrow.

"Some limp-dicked prick bit her fucking ear off not too long ago."

There was the sound of a tankard landing heavily on a table.

"You want some help finding the fool when we head back?"

There was no reply, but the sound of sadistic laughter told the strider all he wanted to know.

Kol's ears perked up as he tried to chime in on another conversation. He managed to hone in on the voice of a woman, a whore presumably, though he couldn't be certain.

"A spraven came from Sun Spire not long ago," she said, her voice failing to keep silent. "Someone said it held a message of mercenaries coming to town. A whole lot of 'em too."

"Really?" an exasperated man replied.

"Aye," she said, and Kol could imagine her wide-eyed nod. "Good fighters too, not some ragtag group looking for a few valens."

"You know what they're called?"

"No, I wasn't able to find that out. People talk, but they've been less loose-lipped than usual nowadays. Can't get anything good out of anyone! 'specially with that Pale Bull strutting around like he owns the place."

The strider snorted to himself, and upon finishing his ale, rose from his chair while placing a couple of copper valens on the table before walking away, deciding that this night would be the night he went out for his stash. Why wait? He and Steena would be ready to leave in the morning.

#

Sitting in his study, Varden stared closely at the shadewood sap before him.

Valenfaar: The Crimson Plains

The vial lay on his desk with the milky substance resting within. He chewed his lip, pondering the implications of drinking the sap. Normally, he would have another scholar or physician nearby in case it proved to be hazardous. But it was past Moon's Peak, and he was alone, his troop of guards, off doing whatever it was they did to keep themselves busy.

He shrugged and reached for the vial, popped open the cork, and sniffed at the contents. It smelled ... flat, as if nothing were there. He took a deeper sniff: nothing. He curled his lip and studied the vile once more. Was he really going to go through with this?

Without thinking any further, he placed the vial up to his lips and tossed his head back. The sap had no taste, if Varden could compare it to anything, he would compare it to water. As it flowed down his throat, he felt it evaporate and fill his body in a strange mist, not unlike inhaling steam or incense. Then there was nothing: no sensation, no strange high, no gut-wrenching pains or numbness.

The scholar put the vile down with a frown. "Well, that was disappointing." A few short heartbeats passed. "I was hoping for-"

All of his senses left him momentarily, taking presence in some other place. A blur of light, sounds, smells, and feelings swirled not just around him, but through him. He began to hallucinate, something that seemed real, not fake or supernatural like the high from most narcotics. Something that he knew, at his core, was unequivocally *real*.

He stood atop the defensive wall, and down below witnessed as Bronwin hefted his mace and took his first steps towards an attacking force of Thregs. But as quickly as this had occurred, it disappeared. The Wixen was back in his study, naked, fully coherent of what was around him.

He sat back in his chair, eyes wide in bewilderment. "May the Veil Strider carry me," he gasped. Varden knew already what he had seen, a memory that was not his.

Chapter 22

The defensive wall at the edge of the swamp was finally finished. It stretched from one side of Valen's Passage to the other, wood and stone reinforced with iron and steel. It stood shy of fifty meters tall, with small ballistae mounted securely on top, and a reinforced gate allowing the transfer of troops to and from the mouth of the passage. Archers lined the battlements, baskets of arrows placed next to them for easy access. Striders would be patrolling from five kilometres in the plains, straight to the wall. Nothing would be coming down the passage without anyone knowing. Granted, Bronwin could see the plains from his perch, but he still preferred to have scouts further out. One could never be too careful.

"Sir, how does everything look?"

Algrenon stepped up next to him and looked out over the entryway to Valen's Passage.

"Everything seems to be in order," the Pale Bull said flatly. "Well done."

"Thank you, sir," Algrenon beamed. "Any word on Threg movements?"

Bronwin shook his head. "Nothing yet. Though I expect that to change shortly. Those star showers have been more frequent, the striders are keeping a close eye on them for us."

Algrenon nodded. "Do you really think we stand a chance against them?"

The commander shrugged. "We've killed plenty of them before. Why should this be any different?"

The Pale Bull's lieutenant went to voice something but decided against it, and instead, gave a nod of his head.

"Algrenon?"

"Yes, sir?"

"Fetch Saffron, I wish to speak with him."

"Of course," Algrenon paused as if debating to say something, averted his gaze, then turned on his heel and left. Leaving whatever thought he had unspoken between the two of them.

Bronwin pondered this for but a moment, but no longer. Had his lieutenant spoken his mind, it might have caused a rift of some kind between them. The Shield of Northwood would not like that, he needed his Right Hand to be dependable, to have faith in him, any chance of fucking that up was not worth the hassle.

#

Corduvan and Rel met during the day for a change, as most — if not all — of the striders were out on patrol, the two of them could freely use the training courtyard without any hindrance to others around them.

"So, you've been practising?" the Plain's Master asked incredulously.

"Yes ma'am, almost every night."

"Alright," Rel said, taking a seat on a nearby crate and crossing her arms, she grinned. "Show me."

Once again, Corduvan stood in the centre of a circle of training dummies. The hilt of the weapon he possessed sat snuggly in his belt. From where she was sitting, Rel could tell that Corduvan had decided fastening the handle to his garb would be better for control of the blade. The Plain's Master watched as he took the chain in both hands, and let the blade dangle before him.

He began to spin the weapon in a backwards circle, it picked up speed, then shot forward in a flash, embedding itself in the chest of a target dummy. A quick tug and the blade was out. She watched as he slid the chain through his hands, keeping the blade's path as straight as possible before bringing it back into a spin. He turned, keeping the momentum moving, then allowed the chain some slack on the upswing, the blade shot forward and up, cutting across the face of another dummy.

She was impressed, the Sovereign soldier had clearly been training. The blade clattered to the ground for a moment before it was pulled back into his hands. This time he swung it around in a large horizontal arc, again giving the chain some slack, the blade slung outwards and slashed across a third dummy, cutting into its throat.

Corduvan pulled the chain back and holstered the weapon, he looked to Rel with a look of curiosity.

The Plain's Master smiled wide and stepped towards him. "Well done, Soldier! You have my blessings."

"Thank you ma-"

Rel held up a hand. "Don't thank me. Keep practising, and don't kill any of us out there, alright?"

He nodded. "Yes, ma'am, of course." A grin pulled at his lips.

"Good, now get out of here, go back to your home, or patrol, or whatever else it is you need to be doing. I have a feeling things are going to be getting interesting."

Corduvan walked out of the training yard. Rel stood by her lonesome and looked at the dummies around her. They would all have been killed, surely. But she couldn't help but worry about how that weapon could be used for defence. If someone got in close to Corduvan, he would be done for. A chain that thin wouldn't block a blade. But the weapon was Wixen-made, it wouldn't be cheap steel, or cheaply tempered either. She supposed there was a chance the tool had some surprises waiting for her.

A familiar voice called out to her. "Hey! You off for today or what?!" Nef was approaching from the longhouse. "You aren't going to start telling me that the Plain's Master is taking time away from duties with a Threg army on the horizon are you?"

Rel chuckled. "No, of course not. I was doing an evaluation. Heading back to the passage now actually. Care to join me?"

He shrugged playfully. "Well, I suppose so. I am needed there …" He looked at the sun and noticed it was near Sun's Peak. "Earlier this morning?"

They both laughed. "Well let's hurry then shall we?" Rel winked.
"Plain's Master Rel, are you challenging me to a race?"

Before she could answer, she was in a sprint towards the Valley Gate. "First one to the gate wins!"

"Esmirla's Cunt," Nef swore under his breath and took off in a sprint behind his friend.

The two striders exploded from the training yard swift of feet, not a sound made between the two of them. The dirt roads of Plainsview quickly opened up before them. Townsfolk running their day-to-day errands darted out of the way.

Rel immediately took to the rooftops. Using the small lead she had on Nef, she shimmied up the side of a shop and began to run along its sloped roof. She rose to the top and let the downward slope on the opposite side carry her momentum, at the precipice she leapt and found herself on the flat roof of another building. Continuing her sprint, the Plain's Master took long, fast strides from rooftop to rooftop, only stopping for fleeting moments to spy Nef working his way through the crowded streets below. She saw him leap over a small cart of linens.

Rel launched into another sprint. Their finish line came into view, looming at the edge of the city. The Valley Gate, the doorway to Valen's Passage. As she leapt over a small alleyway, Rel took another look for Nef in the thinning crowd. Much to her surprise, he had taken the lead, having pushed his way through the city with remarkable speed.

"Oh, you have gotten faster, haven't you?" She smirked to herself and picked up her pace. Sliding down another sloped roof, the Plain's Master landed on the dirt road with a roll and exploded forwards once more. Nef ran no more than ten feet in front of her, but it made little difference, she was taller and lighter. She quickly closed the distance and caught up to her friend. Rel watched her footfall and timed her next move well. With a subtle adjustment to her step, she brought her foot down onto the back of Nef's boot.

"What are yo-" he was cut off by a scramble of footwork, then a mouthful of dirt as he fell.

The Plain's Master laughed and ran to the wall, she could hear muffled curses and obscenities behind her. She had won, though just barely. But Esmirla be damned if she were to lose to her Right Hand. Nef needed something to work towards, if she didn't beat him to the punch regularly — and with grace — how would he ever be expected to replace her when she inevitably took over Saffron's role as Plain's Warden.

"You cheated," Nef said as he approached, brushing dust off from his uniform and spitting dirt to the side.

Rel tilted her head to one side innocently. "There were rules?"

A frustrated sputter. "Well, fine. I guess we didn't lay out any, but next time," He pointed a finger and wagged it up and down. "Next time we will."

They grinned widely at each other, and the Plain's Master shrugged. "Maybe we will, maybe we won't!"

Their laughing was cut off by the urgent cries of a familiar voice. Not far away, Varden ran, his troop of guards struggling to keep pace in their armour.

"Plain's Master!" he called, "Plain's Master, I bring urgent news from my studies!"

Rel and Nef exchanged a cautious glance before she stepped forward. "Breathe, Scholar. What is it, what news do you bring?" The joviality evaporated, she was back on duty.

"I have been researching the shadewood tree, ma'am. I have discovered ... something."

"What is it?"

"You won't believe me, but ... it gives a vision of the future." Varden did not smile, he looked worried.

"The future?" Nef said, stepping beside Rel. "Are you telling us that you're some kind of prophet now?"

"No, not at all Nef, I am no prophet, but the power that manifests itself within a shadewood tree plays the part quite well."

"Slow down," Rel interjected, holding up her hand. "What do you mean it 'gives visions'?"

"Ah yes, of course. My apologies for jumping ahead. You see, I found a shadewood tree in the swamp not long after my arrival here, before Bronwin's men went missing. I tapped the tree to collect and study its sap. It was strange, I only received a small amount, not even enough for a-"

"Get to the point."

"Apologies. I drank the sap I obtained, and I saw ... something."

Nef raised an eyebrow. "Are you telling me that shadewood sap manifests as a narcotic?"

A glimmer of joy exposed itself in Varden. "I see you are keeping with your practice Nef, well done! But no. That is not it. I have dabbled with hallucinogens in the past, this was no hallucination. It felt as if I were reliving a memory, if only for a few heartbeats. But somehow, I knew this memory had not happened yet, as the circumstances to allow it have not come to pass."

"Let's say I believe you," Rel said. "What did you see?"

The scholar looked her in the eyes, passion and honesty filling the air between them. "I saw Bronwin taking his first steps towards the Threg army, and the Thregs were winning."

#

The trader's convoy was little more than scorched wood, meat, and hair by the time he had arrived. A careful boot stepped over the loose remains of what was once a face, the flesh beginning to rot and decay.

Around the wanderer, the grass was burnt, carts overturned, and horses gutted where they lay. Smoke lingered out from the carcasses of the carriages, their wares burned to ash, left smouldering under the midday sun of the Endless Plains. Kneeling, he picked up the hilt of a small dagger and weighed it in his hand. Perfectly balanced from blade to hilt, with delicate engravings etched into the metal.

Wixen. he thought, *A Wixen convoy.*

The carnage gave all the evidence he needed: the convoy was travelling from Ajwix to Valenfaar, but they met the Thregs first and were promptly massacred.

The dagger dropped back to the ground as he stepped over a body, then another, and another, each one missing a limb, and several locks of hair. The heads were left raw and bloodied where the hair had been torn free.

There were a handful of bodies in the midst of the butchery, but not enough for a full caravan with guard detail. Where were the rest?

Circling another smouldering cart, he found his answer: a pile of bodies, many missing several body parts, flies circling them. The mask he wore blocked out most of the smell. The viscera he had been following, though vile, would have caused even him to vomit had he caught the scents in their true form.

Kneeling in front of the mass grave, he reached out a gloved hand and lifted the head of a dead guard. To his surprise, it broke off at the neck with a wet squelch. The wound was not clean, it looked like the soldier had been sawed through with a rusty blade.

He tossed it behind him and peered through the viscera once more. Nothing of note, nothing important. He had looked through what remained of the cargo, what little the Thregs hadn't taken. All that had been left were several articles of clothing, the occasional dagger, and a shield or two. All the food had been taken, as well as the majority of weapons.

"Hmph," he said to himself. "Another convoy ripped to pieces. By Daylen, this isn't good." Stepping nimbly away from the aftermath and into the tall grass of the Endless Plains, the traveller looked in the direction of Valenfaar, and much to his chagrin he saw first-hand what changes the Thregs had made to the area.

The once golden grass of the plains had been dyed crimson. Like a painter had dragged a massive brush over their masterpiece, smearing the beauty it once held for the sake of violence and carnage. Slowly but surely, as the Thregs advanced towards his home country, they would be creating the Crimson Plains, a place of death and gore, where only one species could thrive.

Cullen ... A faint whisper called from deep inside his mind, yet great in distance. *Cullen* ....

Cullen's head snapped up to attention and listened once more.

You are needed elsewhere, Cullen. I suggest you heed this call with haste.

"Why is it always me who has to deal with these issues? Why can't someone else do it for a change?"

Chapter 23

The reports his scouts brought in from the west held Alistair Highfold in shock. Dozens of villages had ... something happen to them. He wasn't sure what, but he needed to send a detachment of troops to investigate as soon as possible.

The Arch General paced over to the window of the war room and let the white light of the sun bathe him in his armour. He sighed and looked out to the city. Valen, these people and everything they knew were his to protect. The Thregs in the east were a problem, one that required almost all of his attention, but now there were reports of ... things in the west, and he began to worry if he had the troops to deal with both issues simultaneously.

Turning slowly, Alistair moved his way back to the map placed in the centre of the table, he leaned forward, grabbed a quill and dipped it in red ink. He made a circle around the town of Plainsview. That would be problem A, if he could at least find out what was going on out west he could hopefully send out a mercenary company to deal with it, which he had designated as problem B for the time being.

He looked to the edge of his desk where a sealed scroll sat, it had come for Varen. He reached out, grabbed the parchment and paced to the one door that led to the throne room. Alistair knocked on the door; it opened to reveal a royal guard.

"Yes, sire?"

"Here," Alistair held out the scroll. "Bring this to my father, tell him it's for Varen. They should be meeting shortly."

The guard took the letter. "Yes, of course, sire," The door closed.

Walking back to the war room table, Alistair looked at his map; a large number of troops had been moved from the city of Moreen and began making their way east. This left the Central City short-handed, but they still had a sizeable defensive force. The troops they had and the walls of their Central City would be enough to deter any attack.

He looked to where Sun Spire sat: the Anvil's Hammer had left the city and would be arriving in Plainsview within the next few days to support the Pale Bull. He chewed his lip and began to feel the sensation of stress rushing into his body. Alistair was a well-trained general, but he had never dealt with such issues in his lifetime. Skirmishes here and there, small rebellions, sure, he had seen those and quelled them easily. But an invading army of monstrosities, and the disappearance of, at least, hundreds of peasants at the same time? This was a first for him, both in theory and in practice, and he was beginning to feel it.

Maybe if I borrowed the Sword and sent them out east as well ...

The sound of a door opening broke that train of thought. How long had he been staring at his map? Had his brother already arrived?

Without turning, Alistair could hear Varen's familiar footsteps on the marble floor.

"Good day, Brother," the High Priest's voice came as a shock.

Startled, Alistair looked up from the map towards his younger brother. "Ah Varen, good to see you. I'm glad you could make it." stepping forward, he reached out a hand. His brother took the grip and shook firmly, each with a finger extended.

"It's my pleasure. What did you need?"

"The Sword of Magus, I need them in Plainsview, there's something odd going on. I'd like Jo-een to take a look."

Varen looked dismayed, then shook his head. "No can do. They're already deployed to the southwest, to Wreath's Burrow. Surely you've heard about the events out that way?"

The memory slapped the Arch General like an open hand. "Shit. You're right." he paused as his mind recalled previous events. "My apologies, I did know. The situation out east has me pulling out my hair. Saffron and Bronwin are asking for more men than I can afford to send their way. We need to keep the Outlier Cities protected, or we lose out on food."

"A difficult budget to balance," his younger brother looked at the map, his eyes drawn to the encircled Plainsview. "What is the situation out that way anyhow?"

Alistair held in a sigh. "Thregs, and a lot of them." He paused. "I'll figure it out though. Sorry to have bothered you."

The High Priest grinned slightly. "Nonsense, you never bother me, Brother." He placed a hand on the golden pauldrons of Alistair's armour.

"Liar," The older Highfold returned the grin. "Now then, how does it go out west? Jo-een turn up anything?"

Varen appeared to withdraw for a moment before speaking. "Not sure yet. Still waiting to hear back. But word is, some of your scouts have found some odd things."

"Aye, close to a dozen towns abandoned. Not a single soul in sight. Nearly a dozen bodies in each one."

The High Priest looked startled, but with realization hidden beneath. "A dozen towns? Abandoned? By Daylen ..." He paused for a moment. "Did I tell you they have an Aegis soldier with them?"

"Aegis?" Alistair combed his memories. "Garridan, I'm guessing?"

Varen chuckled. "You're good. How'd you know?"

"He seems like the kind of man for that duty."

"Not far wrong there. Though he didn't have much choice. He saw something worrying in Wreath's Burrow, hence the Sword being deployed." His younger brother paused, realizing something. "You know all of this already, are you sure you're alright?"

The Arch General felt blood rush to his face out of embarrassment. "Yes, you're right. Just stressed. I have towns begging for protection, strange shit going on in the west, and now, Daylen knows how many Thregs to the east. I'm having trouble distributing the men."

"Don't worry about the west. My men will deal with that. Use whatever you can to make your life easier."

That sounded good, one less problem to worry about for the moment. Varen was capable, and so were his men.

"Thanks, Varen. I owe you." He looked back to the war room table and remembered the scroll that had been sitting there. He turned back to his little brother. "Did Father give you the scroll that came?"

"Aye he did, I have it here." The High Priest retrieved the parchment from the folds of his robe and broke the seal. The mage quickly scanned the message before an expression of anger and frustration bloomed.

"I know that look. What is it?"

"That fucking Covenant again. They're spreading their wings, and much faster than we agreed on." The priest looked over the letter again. "They've already spread to close to a dozen towns in the last moon, all in the name of their God of Death. Sacrifices have increased to six deaths every fortnight instead of the usual three every moon. That's quadruple what they used to do, and that's in each village, it's a wonder they have any followers left, they're slaughtering people!"

"Fucking fanatics." Alistair agreed.

"Knew I should have put an end to them when we first got elected. But no, Jo-een talked me out of it, that bloody fool."

Sitting against the war room table, Alistair relished in his brother's anger. There was something humorous about it. "So what are you going to do about it?"

His brother seethed. "Bloody animals. I'm going to Mordum, I need to speak with Fenrich; he's broken our agreement. They agreed to keep their influence low, to keep the sacrifices at a minimum, and in return, I would leave them be. For a while anyway."

"Did they know about the 'awhile' part of that deal?"

His brother wore a grin of malice. "What do you think?"

"I'm going to go with a 'no'." Shaking his head, Alistair pushed further. "You're pretty adamant about these guys, eh?"

Anger danced through Varen's eyes. "With Daylen as my witness, I'll quell this little cult of theirs. You know how long I've been pining for this, you don't kill for religion, not unless it's in the name of Daylen. Even those bastards at the Church of Clouds and Gwendall's Forge will be praising Daylen by this time next cycle."

So Varen wanted a religious crusade run through the country?

"You worry me sometimes, Little Brother."

The High Priest laughed. "You have no need to worry, I'll be just fine."

Alistair realized his question had never been answered. "So I ask again," Alistair said. "What are you going to do about Mordum and the Covenant?"

His brother had already begun to head back to the throne room, looking over his shoulder he said. "I'm going to fill my coffers with their blood." Varen paused. "Before I forget, do you know where our brother is?"

Alistair refocused his gaze. "Cullen? Somewhere to the southwest, I think. Why?"

"Can you get in contact with him?"

"I mean, it's not easy, but I can definitely try."

"Thank you, if you do get word to him, have him meet me in Mordum in ten days' time. I may need his help."

"That's a bastard of a hike for ten days. Mordum is out to the east!"

"Our brother has always had a knack for travelling. He'll do just fine."

And with that, the High Priest opened the war room door and disappeared behind it.

As one door closed, the opposite one opened, but with nobody to follow it.

"Ah, Cullen, how long have you been listening?"

Again, the voice boomed from every corner of the room. "I'm always listening, there is little I do not already know. I will meet with our brother in Mordum, and I will take into account his mental state. He seems to be working against the country's best wishes."

Alistair nodded thoughtfully. "Thank you, Cullen."

"You may also wish to hurry your efforts in the east, the Thregs have begun to move once more. You do not have long before they lash out in Valen's Passage. I have seen this, and more."

"How do you-" The opened door slammed closed.

#

Rel stomped through the longhouse in search of Kol. No one had seen him for days, he had seemingly up and disappeared one night after his watch. Another strider had relieved Kol of his duty that night and saw him head back to Plainsview. After a morning of asking around, a couple of other denizens that frequented the Strider's Respite had told her that they had seen him that night. He had sat down, taken a drink, and then left.

Opening the door to Saffron's office, the Plain's Master looked to the Plain's Warden. "Sir, Kol is missing. Requesting permission to form a search party."

He looked up at her, concern danced through his eyes briefly, before a tone of absolute resolution set upon him. "I can't let you do that, Rel." He looked back down to his tomes.

"Sir?"

"I am saddened to hear our strider has gone missing, especially one so close to you. But we just don't have the manpower to mount a search at this time, the Thregs draw closer and will be in the passage within a fortnight."

"Sir, all I need is-"

The Plain's Warden held up an open hand as he put down his quill. "Plain's Master," he said. "You have my answer already. And if I may ask, where would you even begin to search? The plains, the town, or more inward towards Sun Spire? Do you know which way this young man went? Do you even know if he's alive?"

Rel swallowed hard. She hadn't the faintest clue where he went. He up and vanished after the tavern, and it wouldn't have been hard for a strider of Kol's standing to blend in with his environment.

"No sir. Not a clue," she admitted.

"Then my answer is final. Unless we come across something solid to work with; you are to resume your usual duties. Kol will be considered missing in action until proven otherwise. Do I make myself clear?"

Blood rushed into Rel's face, she was embarrassed. She bit her tongue. "As clear as the skies above the Endless Plains. Sir."

"Good," Saffron returned to his writings. "Was there anything else?" he asked without raising his gaze.

"No sir, that is all."

"Then you are free to go. Head to the defensive wall when you have the chance. We need as many talented soldiers out there as possible."

"Yes, sir," Rel turned on her heel and left the office.

Where had Kol gone? She hadn't the faintest clue and had failed to gather useful information from the townspeople. She had looked for Steena at the tavern, even asked around for her. But no one knew where she was, or where she would have gone. The girl wasn't one for strolling through town, she often worked, went home and only left for errands or work. By Gwendall, none of the tavern workers even knew where in town she lived, not even Deeanne.

It wasn't long before Rel was in her own home, rifling through her things. Ashlin stood in the doorway behind her, her blue eyes filled with concern.

"Rel, what is it?"

"Kol's missing. No one knows where he could have gone."

"Did you try-"

"The tavern?" Rel interrupted, "Yes, he was seen there. And no, I can't seem to find the dwarf either."

Ashlin stood in silence for a moment. "You know Kol hated being a strider. Maybe he and the dwarf left? Start something new without the stress of formally breaking ties?"

Rel turned and looked at her lover. "Ashlin, that would be desertion. He would be tried and executed for such an offence. Even he isn't stupid enough to do that."

"He hated being a strider, and he loves that dwarf. Both hatred and love are very powerful motivators, Rel. You know that." Ashlin walked forward and placed her hands on Rel's shoulders, she leaned in. "He'll turn up, I'm sure of it. And knowing you, you'll accept him back with open arms and keep him from facing trial on his own." She leaned in closer and gave her a kiss. "Now, shouldn't you be at that damned wall?"

The Plain's Master sat in silence for a moment, absorbing the theories that had been shared. Had Kol left the Striders? Why didn't he say anything, surely he could've left under more legal means. It would have taken more time but-

"Rel? Are you there? Shouldn't you be leaving?"

Shaking her head and snapping back into reality, she matched eyes with Ashlin. "Yes, you're right."

#

Varden reached into his pack and grasped the item he had been searching for: his tap. He crouched in the swamplands before the shadewood tree once more. He looked over the tree and placed the tap lower than he had previously, hoping to get a trace amount of sap. Hopefully, by placing the tap slightly lower on the trunk, he would be able to accrue a couple more drops from the tree. It was a long shot, but without another shadewood to test ...

"Why in the Soul Spire are we back here?" a gruff came from behind.

The scholar felt a pang of stress and annoyance as Dry Eyes spoke, he felt it every time the conscript flapped his lips. It was like listening to a child whine and drone. Incessant, never-ending. Though even Varden had to give children credit where they deserved it: they were able to hold a coherent thought.

"We are back here, my dear Dry Eyes, to hopefully further my study of this tree. And as you are part of my entourage, you are required to be here as well."

"My bloody shoes are soaked right through! I'm gonna get da Rot!"

Varden rolled his eyes as he rose to face him. "Do you have any open sores on your feet?"

"Do I 'ave what?"

"Scratches, wounds, blisters, warts?"

"Ah. Uh, no, I don't think."

You never think. the scholar thought.

"Then you won't get the Rot."

"I won't?"

"No," The Wixen turned back to the tree and made another hole before sliding in the tap. After slipping another vial under the opening of the small device, he stood, brushed his hands off and turned to his men.

"Alright. Let's head back to the wall, shall we?"

Varden had realized, upon arriving at the wall, he was the last person of any import to be there. Bronwin stood atop the wall with Rel, Nef, and Saffron in attendance. They seemed to be speaking hurriedly amongst themselves. Varden strolled his way to the rightmost stairs and ordered his men to stay behind and rest.

Step after step the scholar climbed, all the while thinking about how he had gotten himself stuck in Plainsview. And why didn't he just leave the border town and move inward towards the Central Cities? He supposed the fact that he had already found a shadewood tree was reason enough to loiter, but there was also something about this incoming threat that had him curious. He wanted to see it, and he wanted to see how it would play out. To witness the first Valen defence of an invasion would be a notable achievement in his scholarly career. It could aid the Wixen armies if they ever chose to attack, but most of all, he would be the only living Wixen to have observed such a feat. It was a meaningful fallback if his study of the shadewood tree fell flat.

Varden approached the group with a welcoming smile. "You four seem rather vexed, or am I mistaken?"

Rel turned to face him, while Nef, Saffron and Bronwin remained deep in conversation.

"Ah, Varden," Rel said, a look of concern soured her normally good looks. "Strider matters, nothing of your concern."

The Wixen held up a hand in understanding. "Say no more, my dear Plain's Master. If it is none of my concern, then I shall not worry."

A commotion, sounds of yelling and worry behind them, towards the swamp. Rel and Nef turned their heads. Varden looked to his men at the base of the stairs: they rose to their feet, hands on the hilts of their weapons.

Good. Dry Eyes fumbled, nearly fell but finally placed his hand on his own weapon, mimicking the others.

A child came running from the swamps, oddly proportioned and looked to nearly waddle in her haste. "What an odd-looking-"

"Rel!" the child had called, with a voice too mature for someone of their stature, "Rel! It's Kol!"

The Plain's Master launched herself back down the wall to the grassy floor beneath, Nef hot on her heels. Varden worked his way down behind them, letting his mind wander. When he reached the bottom his men circled around. They moved towards the child.

Upon closer inspection, it wasn't a child at all: it was a dwarf; a woman. The scholar thought he recalled seeing her around the tavern a few times before, though he couldn't be sure.

"Steena," he heard Rel say calmly. "Steena what is it? Where is Kol?"

The dwarf looked as if she had been crying, panic settling like stone. She had been worried for days, even Varden could see that.

"He-he-he," she stammered, "I don't know." She shook her head, tears streaming. "He-"

The Plain's Master knelt in front of her. "Steena, breathe. Take a breath, take all the time you need. Where is Kol? Bronwin ... wants to put him on trial for desertion. Myself and Saffron are trying to stop that from happening."

Steena looked perplexed, then shook her head. "No, he didn't desert. At least ... not yet."

"What? What are you saying?"

The tavern maid took a few more deep breaths, then caught her composure. "We were going to leave together. He was planning to desert, but ... he never came back."

"Never came back? Where did he go?" Nef had said this, stepping forward and crouching down next to Rel.

"It was around half a fortnight ago, Rel ... He went into the plains to get something: his stash, he called it. It was supposed to pay our way to the Central Cities."

"He went to the plains?!" Rel and Nef looked at each other with worry. "Why didn't you tell us sooner?"

Steena's breathing was panicked. "I-I was scared I'd be arrested, interrogated." She looked past Rel's shoulder at Bronwin. "I heard you were looking for him, so I came to find you ... you were always so good to him." She dabbed at the tears rolling down her cheeks.

So Rel's Left Hand went into the plains, did he? the Scholar thought, *He's as good as dead.*

Chapter 24

Atop the wall, Bronwin looked over the fields before him, wondering when the grass would be bloodied and ruined.

"Bronwin!" a voice beckoned behind him, "Bronwin!"

The Pale Bull turned and cast his gaze downwards. Algrenon stood, waving one arm towards him. "Bronwin!"

"What is it?"

"Our scouts are ready, shall I have them advance?"

Chewing his lip, Bronwin thought about the Thregs, they were getting closer, but as of previous reports, it should be safe for his men to move.

"Do it," he said flatly, letting the boom of his voice carry his orders.

His officer nodded, then waved to the group of striders behind him. Beneath, the Shield of Northwood could feel the gate of the wall open and then close. He looked back to where he had before, watching the striders as they jogged down the passage, and ultimately, out of sight against the Endless Plains.

"Algrenon!" he boomed without turning.

"Sir?!"

"Prepare the men. I want everyone ready for battle by nightfall. I expect they'll be here on the morrow. And send a runner to the scholar, we'll need his men as well."

No answer. It meant he was already on the move. And hopefully, the Anvil's Hammer would arrive this day as well. The more troops he had, the better.

#

After leaving the longhouse, Nef looked at the willow tree in the centre of town. There seemed to be a commotion below the branches. A group of civilians had assembled around ... something. He moved forward to the precipice of the gathering. Step by step, man, woman, and child began to move and shuffle, clearing the way for him.

He had reached what everyone was gawking at: it was a group of men, around fifty in number. Their armour shone with ridiculous polish, the image of a blacksmith's anvil and hammer emblazoned on their chest plates. At the forefront of the group stood a man with fair skin. His hair was a golden blond, and ridiculously straight. He looked like the hero out of a little girl's story. His eyes were bright blue, he had a chiselled jaw and a smile that looked more pretentious than it was toothy. His teeth were perfectly straight and nearly glowed with white light.

"Ah! A strider, excellent!" he said, his voice clear and well-practised. "Tell me, my friend, where do you request the Anvil's Hammer?" He reached out a hand.

Nef stepped forward and took the hand, extending his index finger out in typical Valen fashion. The two men shook.

"The name is Nef, you're Anvil's Hammer?"

"That we are. You know who I am already."

"I do?" The strider raised an eyebrow as they released their grip.

The soldier grinned pompously. "I am Velamir, Captain of the Anvil's Hammer."

Nef nodded slowly. "Right ... Well, Velamir." He nearly shuddered at the name. "If you'll come with me, I'll take you to the Pale Bull, he'll wish to see you."

"Ready yourself to be in awe, Nef." Velamir grinned widely.

"And why is that?" They pushed through the crowd and began making their way towards the Valley Gate.

"Today you will get to witness the reunion of two legendary warriors! The Pale Bull, and myself! It has been cycles since I've seen the man. I expect he'll be enthralled to see me."

The strider lifted his eyebrow. "Odd, he hasn't mentioned you before."

"Oh?" Velamir frowned. "No cause for alarm, he probably doesn't know we're coming."

Oh, he knows, Nef thought. *He just doesn't give a shit.*

"Maybe," he replied, "we'll see soon enough." Nef could feel himself becoming more and more vexed in the mercenary's presence. Was vexed the word he was looking for? He could have sworn he heard Varden use it.

#

"I'm working on it Rel, but it's not looking good for your Left Hand. The boy has vanished, and now you tell me that he planned on deserting? Whether or not he's been captured by the Thregs doesn't change his fate. You realize this, right?"

Saffron looked to Rel with genuine concern, his eyes bloodshot and red, a sign of fatigue and worry.

"Yes Saff, I realize that, but we shouldn't discount the possibility he might have changed his mind. A deserter isn't a deserter until they've left, are they?"

The Plain's Warden looked at her like a father. "Rel, regardless of whether or not he left, he went off his station without a word. Even if he does come back from the plains, Bronwin will want him tried for desertion. The boy is condemned by his decisions."

Awash with frustration she snapped. "Saffron, we can at least give him a chance in the trial. We can come up with something."

"You want me, or your fellow striders, to lie to the Valenfaar Arch General after being sworn in under the oath of the Council? Surely you jest."

"No, Saff, I don't jest. Does Bronwin know what we know?"

The warden shook his head. "No, he doesn't. Neither he nor anyone close to him heard what Steena said. Speaking of the girl, how is she?"

She sighed deeply and shook her head ruefully. "Steena ... She's doing alright. She just needs time. She wants to know we're doing what we can to find him."

"Which isn't much," Saffron said, defeated, as he began to pace. "The Thregs are advancing closer and closer each night. And we've restricted our scouting outside the passage for fear we'll lose more troops. Esmirla's Rains, Rel. Who knows how far the boy went into the plains for his stash? If we find him, it'll be because he was smart enough to avoid the Thregs and come back home. Not due to our efforts."

He was right, he was always right, and with an invading army on their doorstep she knew things looked slim for her Left Hand. She hoped that his skills as a strider would carry him through whatever he was involved with now.

"You don't have to lie Saffron, but please, let me. If we get a trial for Kol, let me speak in his defence, let me propose his innocence to Alistair. It's only fair, he's my Left Hand, and therefore my responsibility."

"And what of me Rel? What of your Plain's Warden? Are you too selfish to see that as Plain's Master, you are *my* Right Hand?!" He was growing angry. "Should Alistair see through your lies and deceit, in the unlikely event of a trial, he'll look to me to explain not just Kol's errors and broken oaths, but he will ask me to look at yours as well!"

"Saffron, I-"

"No Rel, don't speak any further. You are fond of the boy, I realize that. But do not risk yourself, your Plain's Warden, or your fellow striders in defence of one fool boy's actions! We don't even know if we'll survive the coming attack, let alone if the boy survived and even receives a trial!"

"Saffron, please. He's alive, I know it."

"How, Rel? How do you know?" He turned to her, fury lashing out of his eyes.

"I just ... I know him, he's my Left. He's alive. And until I've heard what he has to say, I will not assume his trial is over."

The Plain's Warden smirked, then chuckled with amusement. "You're as stubborn as the Bull, you know that, Rel? If any of us are making it out of this, it'll be you two. But do not think that makes my anger misplaced or unfounded. You are talented, and I value you, both as a person and a strider. But if you dare lie to the Arch General, do not doubt my loyalty to the country, I *will* call you a liar. You do understand that, do you not?"

"Yes, Saffron, I do. I hope that it does not come to that. I apologize for upsetting you."

"I too hope the same, my friend. I do." He leaned against his desk and looked back to Rel, the familiar fatherly look flashed back into his eyes, like the turning of a page. "I accept your apology, it does not seem difficult to anger me recently. Bronwin is pushing for all sorts of resources that we simply cannot provide. And Alistair is stretched thin for reinforcements as is. The Anvil's Hammer arrived today, and small squads of troops have been coming in nearly every other day. But I fear it is not enough. And there's also the matter of- no, never mind."

He looked sad, his eyes were watery.

"What is it, Saff, what else is there?" Rel stepped forward and put a hand on his shoulder. "You seem sad, what's wrong?"

"It's my family, Rel."

"Your family?"

"Yes, my brother and nephews. I haven't heard from them in a moon. It has me concerned, they usually write to me on the fortnight."

"I'm sure they're alright. Where do they live?"

"It's a small farming village, very small. Farnwood. It's out west, closer to Moreen than Valen."

"I'm sure they are faring fine, continue to wait for word. I'm certain you'll hear back soon. The farming season is busy this time of cycle, I'm sure they have their hands full and they'll write you soon." Rel smiled reassuringly, it wasn't much, but she could see it helped a bit.

"Thank you, Rel. I hope your words ring true. I'll hold out hope for a little longer. They're the only family I have left, I don't know what I'd do without them."

#

Varden had spent his time, whilst waiting for more sap, studying the soldiers around the defensive wall. It was enlightening to see the kinds of patterns and mannerisms that each group of men had adopted during their service. The men that hailed from the western half of the country seemed to stand a little taller. Whether this was due to confidence or some other reason, remained to be seen.

Then there were the ones from the east, their accents surprisingly different from person to person. Varden assumed that this occurred due to the number of foreigners that passed through the eastern edge of the country whilst making their way towards the Central Cities.

It wasn't long before he could hear the muffled sounds of marching. Looking to the swamp, Varden watched as Nef emerged from the dank underbrush, a magnificent-looking man in tow, with a reasonably sized group of men behind them. Around half a hundred, if he were to guess.

The man who accompanied Nef looked to be the leader. His posture, mannerisms, and the way he spoke gave way to all of this. He stood tall, proud and nearly standoffish, his tone firm and commanding. But what caught Varden off guard, was the way his armour glinted, nearly mirror-like. The way his hair was groomed to fall straight down past his shoulders, the golden yellow clashing with the near chrome of his armour looked ridiculous. He looked as if he were to perform for a child's party, not fight Thregs.

The scholar waved to his guards as he got up to make his way over towards their guest. Bronwin, for a man of his size, snuck up on him.

"Our guest does not concern you, Scholar."

Varden started but kept his gaze forward. "On the contrary, my big friend. Everything that happens here is of concern to me. I am a scholar, and though this is not my primary means of study, if I can be the first person to record the event moving forward, I may make my mastership regardless of the shadewood trees."

"He does not concern you."

"And why is that? Is he not someone of note, someone of worth?"

Bronwin snorted in amusement. "No, he isn't." The Bull lengthened his stride and met with Nef before Varden. They exchanged hushed words before the pretty-boy-soldier interrupted.

"Ah, Bronwin, my friend!"

Nef stepped to the side allowing the Pale Bull to stare down at their guest, his gaze flat and uncaring.

"What are you doing here?" he growled.

"I am here to help you with your little problem."

The Pale Bull raised an eyebrow. "You, help?"

"Of course! I always help my friends when the-"

"I am not your friend."

The pretty boy took a step back, offended, a look of over-exaggerated hurt on his face. "Oh, Bronwin, you ail me! How could yo-"

The Bull took a step forward and jabbed a sausage-sized finger into the smaller man's chest plate. "You are not my friend, you are not my ally. You and your sorry unit of men do not deserve to have been paid from the Arch General's pockets. You should be putting yourselves on display on a stage in Sun Spire, not preparing to fight Thregs in Valen's Passage! Do you not remember the last time we met?"

"I seem to recall you helped my unit in a small scrap a few cycles back."

Bronwin bellowed a laugh. "Help, *you?!* Bah! Your pretty little head was on a bandit chopping block when Algrenon came through with our first wave of troops. Your men were being lit ablaze before I brought up the rear with my wave! And let me ask you, Velamir." he spat as he said the name. "You're men managed to cut down, what? Half a dozen bandits? Now tell me, how many do you recall *us* slaying?"

Velamir stuttered, then sputtered. "I, uh, I-"

"The full camp. Close to two dozen, in a matter of moments." Silence filled the air between them. "So I ask you once more, *boy.* You think you can help *me?!*"

The confidence of the young captain wavered before a false sense of security took hold, he stood straighter but began to shake in his armour. "Yes. We, of the Anvil's Hammer, are here to aid you in whatever way you see fit. Where will you have us?"

Bronwin smirked. "That was almost spoken like a real soldier. Your men will man the wall and aid with the construction of spike barricades at the outer line. Is that clear?"

"Yes, of course."

The captain turned to his men. "Alright! You heard the man, man the wall, aid with the spike barricades! Find an officer and proceed from there. Move out!"

Velamir turned back to Bronwin, gave him a respectful nod and began to move with his men. The Pale Bull seized him by the shoulder.

"Not you," he said. "You're not going with them."

The mercenary looked up with a flash of worry. "What would you have me do?"

"You?" Bronwin smirked. "You're going to clean the Shit Pits."

The soldier shrugged away the mammoth hand and stomped angrily in the direction of the Shit Pits, whether he knew it or not. Without a glance, the Pale Bull left and resumed his duties, coordinating soldiers and aiding with the construction of barricades for the outer line.

"Well, that was ..." Nef said.

"Amusing?" Varden finished. "Enthralling?"

"Yes," The strider nodded. "Enthralling, indeed." He smiled widely, gave Varden a firm pat on the shoulder and disappeared back into the swamp.

"He's one mean fucker, ain't he?" Dry Eyes said from behind. "Makin a man like that work the Shit Pits? Damn shame that ..."

The scholar turned to Dry Eyes. "You can't be serious? You approve of that man?"

The bandit shrugged. "If a man can look that good, and be a soldier. He has gotta be good, eh?"

Varden rolled his eyes as he shook his head. "You're brain dead. Absolutely brain dead. I sometimes wonder how you get up in the morning every day. Tell me, when you awaken, do you need to think about whether you want to blink, or breathe first? Because you clearly cannot do both."

The bandit cocked his head to one side, confusion and vacancy filling his stare.

"I think you used too many words, sir." another soldier remarked to a chorus of laughter. Dry Eyes looked hurt, but the vacancy was still there, trying to make sense of the slander Varden had just thrown his way.

Sounds of shouting from the gate bounced through the Valley. The Wixen turned to see the wooden gates of the defensive wall opening. Limping through were two striders, one carried by the other, blood staining the dull yellow uniforms.

"Bronwin!" Algrenon called from atop the wall, "Bronwin, the striders have returned!"

The Pale Bull jogged over, Varden not far away.

"What is it?" the warrior asked, "Where is your third?"

"Dead, sir," one strider panted as she placed her comrade on the ground, "It's the Thregs, sir. They're at the mouth of the passage. We hardly made it back alive."

"How many?"

The woman shook her head, tears streaming down her cheeks. "Too many," she huffed, "I didn't have time to count, we ran as soon as they attacked."

"Algrenon! Get the barricades out and begin forming defensive lines! Sound the horn!"

#

A throbbing head, an aching back, and the groaning of a stomach long without food. Rolling over the muddy pit he had called prison for the better part of ... how long? He wasn't sure. He could hardly recall where he was. What he assumed to have been the past few days, could have been moons or cycles. The delirium and haziness of it all had Kol wondering where he was, for how long, and why. The strider recalled a force-feeding of some kind earlier, but whether it was that day or the first time he had gained consciousness, he wasn't sure.

Kol sat up and shook his head, trying to rid himself of the dizziness he felt. It didn't help much, instead, the motion racked his brain. He stopped and brought a hand up to his temple.

"Esmirla's Cunt ..." he groaned

Looking up, the swirling shapes he saw began to give way to more coherent figures: around him was a cage of bone and he sat in a pool of red mud. Plenty of similar cages surrounded his own, all with either groaning people, or dead ones. Even a few children hung from ropes tied to the top of the structures.

He searched his foggy memory for the slightest hint as to what had happened. As he did so, he moved his jaw from side to side, felt a slight crunch, then began to cough. Shards of teeth flew from his mouth as if they were shrapnel and a fresh blast of pain forced him into awareness.

He was captured, and captured by the Thregs no less. He remembered now: the large patch of Deadman's Root that he had found was to be his ticket out of Plainsview and into a life in the Central Cities. He wanted to sell it off in batches, and there was enough in that patch to have paved them a way straight to Moreen if he saw fit: the Root could fetch a higher price the further from the plains he travelled.

He had nearly made it to his patch of Root too when a Threg leapt out from the grass and ... that was all he remembered of that night. The memories came to his mind as if molasses on a cold winter morning. Slowly, he remembered his first glimpse of consciousness, a violent clubbing, then ... nothingness once more. This memory came again and again, on different days, in different cages and at different times.

He looked around bleary-eyed and watched as a Threg walked over to a small piece of peppered meat. The creature reached out for it and grabbed hold with a large hand. Kol felt nausea rising as the "pepper" began to disperse and fly away in a swarm. The beast took a large bite out of the meat and groaned with approval.

A more urgent thought took hold of him: where was he? How close to the Halo were they? And was it too late to save Steena? He searched the sky to find that it was near Sun's Peak. As he craned his head, the mass of rock that was Valenfaar's Halo stood before him, a monolith to the natural world. They were at the base of it. He recognized this part of the mountains, he had been here hundreds of times before. They were a few kilometres out from the mouth of Valen's Passage.

In the distance, a horn began to sound.

Chapter 25

The busy streets of Valen were something Alistair disliked. It troubled him and his honour guard as they travelled. He attempted to petition his family to establish a series of tunnels beneath the city so that he and his family could move out of the public eye. The project was deemed too grand and too expensive. And every time the Arch General walked the streets he was reminded of that.

Walks through the city were a pleasant distraction from his constant stresses as Arch General; a moon ago, the position was simple: keep fresh troops in supply, and rotate them out when needed, attack the occasional bandit camp, or send the Pale Bull to take down a Threg encampment. But now, he had cities and troops vanishing in the west for reasons that Varen kept to himself, and an invasion in the east.

A commotion on the streets in front of his honour guard caught his attention. A preacher for the Covenant of Souls Abnegation, his brother's most loathed religious competitor. Whatever this woman was saying had upset some of the populace.

Alistair motioned with his hand: the honour guard formed up in front of him, clearing a passage through the busy streets towards the preacher. The two guards at the forefront broke away, allowing for Alistair to greet the woman.

"Arch General!" the woman called. Madness sank into her voice.

"What's the problem?" The Arch General crossed his arms and gave the woman a flat stare.

Madness kept her gaze. "Well!" she crowed, "I am offering the fools of Valen salvation from chaos! Can't a woman speak freely!?" Her head was craned to the side, not unlike a dog hearing some faraway sound.

"You are allowed to speak freely, yes. Of that, there is no doubt. Though you seem to be upsetting some of my people."

A man began to curse at the woman and shout. "You useless wretch! Go back to your cultists! Lunatic!"

Alistair turned to the man as the crowd backed away, giving the prince and his men space. "You, sir. What is your name?"

The commoner looked at Alistair with wide eyes of realization. "Matthew, sire. My name is Matthew," he said meekly.

"Come here."

Matthew did so.

"What was this woman saying to have offended you and these other people so horribly?" Alistair crossed his arms and looked to the city dweller with authority.

"Well, sire. She was speaking of the rumours that have been arising of late! Strange voices and songs in the west, and invaders in the east!"

"Yes! The rumours have been told, and they have been told true!" the hag cried again, her voice cracking, "Our Covenant will offer you peace and freedom! You are too foolish to see that it is the only option!" she cackled to herself.

Alistair ignored the woman. "Yes, I have heard these rumours. Yet they are largely unfounded. There have been oddities in the west, but my brother has that taken care of. And there have been reports of invaders to the east, but that is merely no more than a skirmish, which I am handling myself. But that is not what has upset you, is it?"

Matthew shook his head. "No."

"Then what has she said, regarding these rumours, that would have you so vexed?"

The man thought for a moment, gathering his thoughts. He looked to the woman, who looked back to him, raving unspoken words.

Matthew ignored her maddening eyes. "She tells us Daylen, Esmirla and Gwendall have forsaken us! That magic, nature, and war itself have all been turned on the Valen people! She preaches that the only god left for us is the god of death, Jo-een! She says that if the rumours are true, then we're all dead already and that if we are to sacrifice ourselves now, that we'll gain favour with the god and spend the afterlife like kings instead of souls cast to the depths of the Soul Spire!" He breathed heavily.

Alistair turned to her, a flatness in his face. "Is he speaking the truth?"

"Oh yes! Oh, yes he speaks true, young Highfold! Gwendall's Blade will remove our heads, Esmirla's Cunt will gobble up your cocks, and Daylen's Magic will smite us all from the Soul Spire! Jo-een offers you, me, and all of you-" She raised her arms out to either side and did a small twirl from where she was standing. "An opportunity to save yourself these ailments and flourish like kings in the Soul Spire!" her cackle echoed off the stone walls of the surrounding buildings.

The Highfold held up a hand to silence, then spoke, firmness in his tone. "So you did say these things?"

The woman nodded quickly with a toothy grin, amusement behind her eyes. It wasn't until now that Alistair realized the crowd had fallen silent, only the bustling down the street could be heard like an echo on the wind.

He nodded. "You should consider yourself fortunate, for it seems Daylen has not forsaken you yet. Had my brother heard these words of yours, you would be silenced. You would have lost your freedom to preach."

The preacher gave an over-exaggerated shrug.

"However, as I am not my brother, nor am I in any position to make any claims on religious authority, my options here are limited."

"Cast her out!" Matthew yelled.

"Cast out the witch!" a woman called from the crowd.

"Skin her alive!" roared another voice.

The Highfold ignored these calls for punishment. "Now, though my options are limited, you have caused a disturbance in my fair city, which I am sworn to protect. With this, I can do something. I could have you tried and sentenced for disturbing the peace, which is a full cycle in the Highfold Dungeons, or if I pushed my case enough, I could label you as a martyr and a terrorist, and the result of that trial would be execution. Are you aware of this?"

"Oh aware I am, Princely General!"

Alistair held up a hand again.

"Do not speak. Listen." He stepped closer to her and leaned into her ear. He could smell and taste her body odour. "Fortunately for you, I am walking through these streets as a distraction from my duties," he whispered, "I will arrest you for harassment and have you sentenced to a full moon in the dungeons. Should I encounter you again in these streets, your following sentence will be much more severe." He inhaled deeply. "Now, under no circumstances will I ever, Gwendall guide me, ever sentence you to death. You will not earn that freedom with me."

She crowed with laughter as two of Alistair's guards grabbed her by the wrists. "You Princely General, you Princely *Fool!* You cannot keep me from death! You can't keep any of these people from death!" she roared with madness and laughter as she was dragged through the streets.

The crowd still stood around him, silently watching. He turned to the people, casting his gaze like a wave over them. "Go! Be about your business! She will trouble you no longer!"

The crowd dissipated, and Alistair's remaining guards pulled themselves back into the protective formation they had held. Turning to look at the sun, Alistair realized it was nearly dusk. Even with his honour guard, they wouldn't stand a chance once the cutthroats and robbers made their way into the darkened streets. As tight a hold as Alistair and the City Guard had over the criminals of the city, they would always be outnumbered.

He quickened his steps, he was to meet with Cullen promptly.

Night fell through the Highfold keep as Alistair moved through the halls.

"Brother!" a voice called from behind him, "Brother!"

He stopped and looked over his shoulder. Maryam came jogging towards him, a parchment in her hand.

"What is it, Sister?"

She looked displeased with him. "Do you have any idea how much money you are costing the kingdom with your little defence in the east?" She looked down at the parchment. "Lumber, stone, steel, food, convoys, weapons, mercenaries, conscripts, armour, shields, blacksmiths, payroll, engineers, the list goes on! You have cost us a fortune, and for what? A few more Thregs than you expected? Need I mention that our infrastructure is seemingly failing in the west for reasons unknown to me? And our darling brother refuses to enlighten me regarding the situation!" She huffed and placed a foot down, looking at him like a mother scolding her young.

The Arch General shook his head. "War is expensive, dear Sister. I apologize for the cost this has taken on the kingdom. But there are far greater numbers in the plains than we had anticipated. I need every man I can get."

"How many could there be? 100? 500? 1000?"

He looked at her flatly. "50,000, and those are but estimates. Surely I do not need to tell you how much damage to our infrastructure 50,000 Thregs could inflict on our country?"

She started and stepped back. "50,000?!" A hand rose to her chest. "Are you certain?"

He nodded solemnly. "They are but scout estimates, there could be more, there could be less."

"I had no idea, Alistair. I can see why you have spared no expense, I apologize for my haste in being so critical."

The Arch General smiled at his sister apologetically and placed his gauntleted hands on her shoulders. "You should not apologize, Maryam. I should have let you know about how dire the situation had become. The blame falls to me, how were you to know?"

"Thank you," She grinned and looked down at her feet.

"No need to thank me." He patted her on the shoulder. "Now, I should get to the war room, I am late to meet with Cullen.

"Take care Alistair, are we still going to sup on the morrow?"

"Yes, of course," He grinned and turned away. "I shall see you then!"

The door to the war room was left ajar; not a good sign. Alistair held his breath and stepped in, the door slamming shut behind him.

"You are late." the room itself seemed to say.

"I am sorry, Cullen. Our sist-"

"Yes, I heard. You've been spending too much coin for her liking."

"How did yo-"

"Onto our meeting. My attention is required elsewhere, or ... will be required elsewhere I suspect."

Alistair found himself stumbling over what he was about to say, how did Cullen hear his conversation? Where in Gwendall's Blade was he required? He found his words. "Yes, of course. What is it you wished to share with me? And why not send a spraven when you have such an urgent agenda?"

"Spraven's are too slow. My word is faster."

Alistair blinked at the bluntness of his words, *Spraven's too slow? What in Daylen's name?*

"Thregs have made it to Valen's Passage. They may have already besieged the outer wall as we speak."

The Arch General snapped to attention, the questions he held previously falling away from his mind. "When? When did they get to the passage?"

"They arrived shortly after Sun's Peak. I have seen them in their numbers."

"Are we ready for the defence?"

"Of that, I am not certain, I had to turn my attention elsewhere shortly after. The Bull had assembled a formidable defence. If the outermost wall falls or has fallen, it will be a costly battle for the Thregs."

"Gwendall's Cock ..." Alistair cursed under his breath. The door to the war room opened and promptly shut. The conversation was over.

Though the potential fallout of an already collapsed defensive perimeter flooded his mind, Alistair couldn't help but wonder: *how had Cullen travelled halfway across the country in half a day?*

Chapter 26

Thousands of Valenfaar's Sovereign Guard stood on duty to face the coming onslaught, ahead of them — with the setting sun serving as a grim reminder of the task at hand — the Thregs had assembled. Their tall, gangling frames stood as tall as the Pale Bull himself, rows upon rows stretching out into the passage and the plains themselves.

Bronwin's forward scouting force hadn't returned. As such, he hadn't a clue of how much of the opposition stood before him. It could have been hundreds, or it could have been thousands. In the comings and goings of his troops and the constant spectacle of battle prep, there would be no way to come to an accurate estimation until the enemy had closed the gap. The Pale Bull looked to his side and gave Rel a firm nod. She returned the gesture and left his side, descending to ground level with the rest of her forces.

Behind the wall, the Plain's Striders had assembled. They were not to operate on the frontlines, as much as Bronwin would have preferred this, they were to move through the battle after it had begun, daggers in a crowd, offering aid and protection where the more heavily armoured, and encumbered soldiers would need it.

In front of the wall stood 10,000 Sovereign troops, his own men a dozen rows from the front, with the conscript forces at the front lines.

He turned to an officer at the top of the wall and gave him a nod. The man shouted down to another officer in the field below, and in turn, he too shouted to an officer further up the line. Small, individual shouts echoed down the rows of soldiers until finally, one final, barely audible cry went out. On this command, several units of men moved spiked barricades in front of their formations, shields and spearmen in behind.

There it was, a two-kilometre wide passage blocked off with spikes and spears, 10,000 men, and a short defensive wall adorned with archers and ballistae: their defence against the Thregs. He hoped it would be enough, and he hoped the fresh troops arriving in the morning would be enough to strengthen the resolve of the men already in the field.

The Bull looked to his left and nodded to another officer, he cried out, and the archers nocked their arrows, and ballistae were loaded. All they had to do now, was wait.

"Do you think your forces will be enough?" Varden asked, walking up next to him.

Bronwin grunted as he nodded.

"You have 10,000 Sovereign men down there, correct?"

"That is right."

"2000 conscripts. Who, I may add, are promised freedom if they serve the nation?"

"Yes."

"And less than 200 Plain's Striders? They are rather nimble, and very adept with their weapons, but do you think those will do against Thregs?"

"They'll have to."

Varden chuckled.

Bronwin turned to look at the scholar. "What is so funny?"

The Wixen shook his head as he grinned. "Your positivity! I find it amusing."

"How so?"

"You have 10,000 men and women, most of them haven't seen a Threg in their entire lives. A small portion of them, your men, have had experience. You have 2000 conscripts on the front lines, who may very well run at the first horn, chancing trial over battle, and a compliment of striders who may or may not be effective. You do realize how ragtag this seems, do you not?"

"You have not witnessed Valen people fight, have you? We will hold our ground."

Varden smirked. "And you have not witnessed the Wixen fight. One of our swordsmen is worth ten of yours, at the least. Or so I'm told."

"Your swordsmen are talented," Bronwin agreed, "But we are fighting for our homes. That pushes many to fight that much harder. Even the conscripts know this. And besides, where could they run? I've placed them between my men and the Thregs for a reason, no matter where they decide to flee, they'll be cut down."

"You have ordered this of your men?"

"Of course. Desertion is punishable by death. They turn tail, they lose their life. They know this."

The scholar chuckled again. "I look forward to chronicling this, assuming we survive."

"We'll survive."

Much to his surprise, even in the distance, he could see the Thregs were kept into surprisingly neat lines. Normally a Threg camp or patrol would be held in chaotic formations, not military ones. Yet before them, stood an unknown number of the beasts in formation. It wasn't nearly as clean as a Valen formation, but it wasn't as crude as he would have liked it to be. Then, the mass in the distance began to shuffle: they were advancing.

The sound of a horn startled Nef into alertness. He was tired, dreadfully so. He had hardly slept in days. The thoughts and anxiety of an impending invasion had kept him up most nights, and on the nights he did sleep, he was restless, tossing and turning, nightmares plaguing the few moments of sleep he would attain. And yet, as adrenaline began to flood his veins, knowing a fight was about to be had, he felt awake, alive, and ready to topple a mountain.

Rel had finished her speech, but he had tuned most of it out. Something about protecting their country, home and people. A rehash of any motivational speech one could read from a tome. It made little difference to him, he didn't need the speech, he would do his duty to the best of his ability, regardless of what lay beyond the wall. He couldn't help but feel like something was missing, the Left to his Right: Kol. Up and out, gone into the plains and simply vanished. No scouts reported seeing him since his departure, nor had they seen any traces of him in the plains thereafter.

Kol was a talented strider, he hated his duty but he at least took it seriously enough to be a ghost in the grass. With any luck, he was alive and stuck behind enemy lines. Maybe, just maybe, he would be the only one to survive this whole mess. Nef smirked at that idea: desertion, punishable by death, yet Kol might just outlive those who would put him to trial.

A second horn sounded: the Thregs were attacking. The air grew still, not even a bird dared chirp; the tension was so thick that you could lodge an arrow in it. The striders waited in silence to hear the sounds of battle from beyond their sight. A call went out: the archers atop the defensive structure raised their weapons, ballistae raised to match. Their arrows sharpened to the point of ridiculousness in preparation for the thick hide of the Thregs. They fired.

#

Varden watched as the barrage of arrows and bolts rose into the air, streaking towards the onslaught sprinting towards them. There was a visible shuffling in the conscript lines as they held their shields and spears. Then it occurred to him: Dry Eyes was somewhere down there, about to face the might of the Threg army head-on. The simpleton, though useless of mind, hadn't the chance to show the scholar his skill with a blade. Perhaps the once-bandit would survive this yet, though Varden had his doubts.

Soldiers craned their necks as they watched the arrows fly; they impacted into the Threg lines dropping several foes. Ballista bolts drove the attackers off their feet and pinned them to the dirt. Many of the beasts continued to pour forth, the projectiles jutting from their flesh, faces, and bodies. A few more moments passed and the horde of monstrosities threw themselves onto the spiked barricades. Even from his perch, Varden could see the conscripts thrusting spears as ferociously as they could. Roars of anger and terror followed every move.

The Thregs continued to toss themselves onto the barricades, as the ones in the rear stepped atop the corpses of their brethren. All too quickly they had climbed up and over the barricades and began thrashing towards the men trying to fend them off.

Though the Thregs began to cut away, slowly, at the front-most line, they were still making progress, the conscripts were struggling with all their might to push back the attackers.

"Your conscripts appear to be falling."

"That was their purpose," Bronwin said as another volley of projectiles careened overhead. He looked to an officer at the base of the wall and nodded.

The officer returned the nod and began to call out down the rows. Until finally it reached the frontlines. A row of soldiers, behind the conscripts, fell back, creating a divide between their forces and the criminals. A select few men moved to the opening and began to pierce barrels, letting their contents spill onto the grass. When they were finished, the soldiers moved back even further.

A call went out from atop the wall, and the archers lit their arrows ablaze.

"You're sacrificing the conscripts?!" Varden gasped.

Bronwin nodded. "It is necessary."

The scholar shook his head. "They may be prisoners, but they are still living people, are they not?"

The question was left unanswered. The lit arrows flew, some landed amongst the Thregs, others amongst the conscripts, but the majority of them landed in the oil that had been strewn about the grass. It ignited as black smoke began to flood the air, creating a wall of death behind the prisoners.

It wasn't long before the carnage had been washed out by a wall of flames, the onslaught from the Thregs hidden away from prying eyes. The line of soldiers stationed behind the carnage cleared more space, then waited, swords and shields ready to meet their foes.

Varden could see the nervous shuffling of the soldiers bracing themselves to meet their enemy. No amount of bandit detail, patrols or training could have prepared them for a full-scale invasion from the Thregs. And how could it? The Valen people had never known Thregs to work in large numbers, even Varden struggled to recall some faint rumour in a Wixen library book about Thregs working with some form of cohesion. Unless he could recall for certain, the scholar would hold his tongue.

#

Rows upon rows of soldiers stood in front of Corduvan, he held his sword at the ready and felt the familiar weight of his Wixen weapon around his waist. The wall of flame had to have been no more than 200 meters in front of him, the sounds of battle reaching out from beyond the crackling. Screams, grunts, metal on metal and even the occasional bellow of a non-human, a Threg. It would seem the conscripts were faring better than many would have given them credit for.

Then, a body emerged through the flames, arms flailing wildly: a man. His weapons were gone, his leather armour cast in flames. He didn't scream, for how could he? The fire would be burning the very air he would be using to fuel his cries. Another body flung itself from the fire, rolling on the ground in front of them. Even from here, Corduvan could see the uncomfortable shuffling of the men in front of him. Then another body, and another, and another, until finally, swaths of conscripts erupted from the wall of death, their arms flailing in silent resentment.

Something rolled out of the fire at impossible speeds, wrapped in a swath of flames. It rolled, bounced and smashed into the front row of soldiers, eviscerating their armour and impaling those it landed on. It was one of the spiked barricades; it had been thrown.

Another barricade rocketed out from the unknown and cut through even more of the Sovereign Guard. Men raised their shields in anxious protest, hoping to protect themselves from the wooden fixtures. All along the line cries went out as their own defences were used against them, until finally, a mass of Thregs burst forth, their scaled skin burning in the fading sunlight.

The Sovereign Guard charged, eager to meet their prey in the small opening they had created. If not for the rush of adrenaline and the push of the men behind him, Corduvan would have been too scared to move. Yet he found himself in a sprint, clad in armour, ready to cut down a creature much larger than he.

The first row smashed into the Thregs forward assault. Weapons rang against shields and tore against flesh. The Sovereign Guard worked carefully, trying to position themselves as best as they could. Corduvan knew, from tales told in taverns, the spacing would open up significantly as portions of the Valen lines fell, or made progress into the Threg lines. The ebb and flow of battle would change from two waves clashing, into the push and pull of currents, some moving one way, others moving the another. This would be where the chaos would start: when units of men and women would mesh with that of their foes, and where an opponent could be coming not only from the front, but also from the side, rear, or Gwendall forbid ... below.

More screaming, roaring and the ringing of steel permeated the air. He could feel the tension rising within him, wanting to lash out to rid himself of the feeling, but if he did that now, he would be wasting his energy. No more than 100 meters from the front now, his feet continued to press onwards. The Thregs standing tall over his fellow Valen soldiers, their vertical nostrils flaring and pulsing in anger, their tongues, like bundles of fibre splayed and flailed as they cut down man after man.

Corduvan watched as one creature took the head of a hatchet into its side. It didn't even flinch, the soldier carrying the weapon tried to pull away, but the skin was too thick and held firmly onto the weapon. The Threg grinned a toothy grin and drove a sword of bone through its attacker's chest. The body was cast aside as the beast moved to the next man.

Fifty meters from the front. He hadn't noticed it before, but the smell of sweat and blood began to fill the air mixed with the stench of piss and shit. Men often spoke of battle and how you could smell the fear around you. Fear did not have a smell, not on this day, fear never had a smell, he concluded. These were the delusions of a mind intoxicated on battle. If fear did have a smell, it smelled of blood and sweat, it smelled of a battlefield.

A woman, no more than ten meters in front of him was cut down, other soldiers moved out of the way of the Threg who had performed the act, leaving only Corduvan to face it. He raised his shield and locked eyes with the creature. It swung its weapon.

#

Rel stood before the wooden gate of the defensive wall as it opened. The lumbering machination didn't creak, it was too new for that. But would it survive the day? Only time would be able to answer that question.

The order had gone out: the striders were to head into the battlefield, which had now been raging for longer than would have seemed possible, the neat rows of soldiers had dissipated into swarms of squads, working on their own for survival. The striders would move out, blurs on the field and aid any squads which would need them. Their goal was not to kill, but to impede, impair and distract. But if a few Thregs fell to their blades, that would not be seen as a problem.

"Striders!" Bronwin called from atop his perch, "Go!"

With a look of sheer determination and a stern nod, Rel waved her hand forward as dozens of striders wove their way into the battlefield beyond the gate. Rel and Nef brought up the rear, making sure no cowards remained back. Much to her relief, there were none. Though the battle had turned into a myriad of chaos there were hundreds of Valen troops remaining at the base of the wall: a final line of defence to keep the structure from falling.

Rel wove through the lines of soldiers and quickly lost sight of Nef. This was expected and she hoped to see him at the battle's conclusion, either there, or in the Soul Spire.

The Plain's Master broke free from the neat rows of soldiers and into the tides of war. Groups of two or three men swung at Thregs with reckless abandon, panic filling their eyes with every slash. Two or three men to a single foe, their sheer size and thick skin proving as big an obstacle as a fully armoured cavalry troop. But they weren't unstoppable. The Pale Bull had cut down hundreds of the creatures during his cycles of service, and even she had killed a Threg before. But these men had never fought them; a winnable scenario, but lacking the proper battlefield experience to be efficient, ultimately resorting to panic and wild swings.

Rel locked her gaze onto a pair of Thregs moving towards a group of five soldiers. She unsheathed her blades and moved in a dead sprint, her feet silent on the grass, she shot past the soldiers and garnered the eager gaze of the creatures in front of her. She was much smaller than they were and much faster. The first creature swung, a sword of steel. A quick sidestep out of the way, and she launched herself forward, raking one blade along the Threg's side, and another along its thigh. The monster howled in frustration as she ducked a swing from its ally, lashing out with the tip of her long knife she drove it deep into the Threg's hip, and with a yank and twist, pulled the blade free.

Now, with the two Thregs turned to face her, the five soldiers she had passed leapt into combat, driving their blades into the rear of their foes. They were like wolves to a deer, driving their weapons mercilessly into the invaders. The two Thregs fell as dark blood seeped from their wounds and soaked into the grass of Valen's Passage.

Rel smirked, and found her next target.

#

Nef strode through the battle with strength and purpose in every step. His blades dripped with Threg blood. He hadn't killed a single one, but he had managed to slash and hack away at them for Sovereign troops. He looked to his right and watched as another strider ducked a blow from a rusted mace. The man swung his blades wildly at his target, only to find himself kicked onto his back by a Threg he hadn't yet taken notice of. Nef could almost feel the crunch of bone from where he stood as the man's chest was crushed beneath a scaled foot.

Turning his attention forward, Nef rode another wave of adrenaline, a Threg was swinging at a single soldier; the woman ducked and weaved, only bringing up her shield when absolutely necessary. Before the strider could get close enough to engage, a blade attached to a chain launched itself out from the chaos and buried itself deep into the Threg's arm. The creature howled, its frayed black tongue splayed towards the sky. The blade was pulled back, just in time for the first soldier to drive her sword up and into the beast's neck. The Threg twitched, then fell dead.

Nef stood in wonderment at what he had just seen. Then a soldier, one of the town's guards came out from the bloody battle and offered the woman a pat on the back. The guard looked up, and locked eyes with Nef.

"Sir," He saluted quickly, not wanting to tempt the relative silence they had for too long. "My apologies, didn't mean to steal your trophy."

Nef waved away the comment. "No trophies to be won here, Guardsman. Well done. What is your name?"

"Corduvan, sir."

"Good work, Corduvan. See to it you make it out of here alive."

"Yes, sir," He nodded, turned towards a scream, and jogged off back into the fray, chained blade hanging from his hand.

Nef grinned to himself. The smile quickly dropped as he saw a flash of movement out the corner of his vision. He instinctually ducked. A rusty sword sailed directly where his head had been a moment ago. A quick shift of weight and the strider leapt back, clearing himself some distance and giving him room to think.

He found the long knife in his left hand beginning to tremble. Taking a deep breath, Nef tightened his grip and stepped towards his attacker. The Threg swung three well-practised swings with its weapon; the strider weaved and twisted away from each cut using only as much movement as was necessary. During a fourth, diagonal swing, Nef sidestepped and brought the blade of his sword into the creature's wrist. The Threg grunted, dropped its sword and rose its hand into a vicious backhanded slap.

The blow caught the strider across the right side of his face, sending him reeling and stumbling away, he landed on all fours. The metallic taste of blood welled in his mouth. He spat, and once more, out of the corner of his eye, he saw movement. Weapons still in hand, Nef pushed himself into a roll and dodged the stomp of the Threg's foot. Lashing out with his long knife, Nef cut into the thick hide of his attacker and watched as blood hardly seeped from the wound.

He cursed, and rolled again, clearing himself some distance. He rose to his feet and found the freak moving towards him. The hand he had cut hung loosely at the wrist. The skin wasn't cut too deep, but Nef could tell he had broken the wrist. The creature seemed not to notice the injury in its leg. It held no weapon, yet the angry pulsing of its nostrils told Nef that it was short-tempered, and didn't care whether or not it held a blade: it would kill the strider if it could.

Nef made the first move and went in for the attack. The Threg threw a surprisingly straight punch. Nef cocked his head to the side and managed to avoid the impact, then sidestepped and raked the creature's ribs with his sword. He could feel the skin begin to peel back at the blow, but it wasn't deep.

He turned and locked eyes with the Threg, the monstrosity stepped towards him, and in a glimpse of horror and gore, grabbed a hold of its injured hand, and began to pull. The crunch of bone and the tearing of flesh stunned Nef as he watched the creature remove its injured appendage.

"Esmirla's Cunt ..." Nef cursed under his breath. He shook himself back to alertness and moved in.

The Threg responded by throwing their own hand at him. It sailed wide and landed somewhere out of sight, followed by another backhanded slap, had the hand been attached it would have made contact, but knowing the now shorter arm span of his attacker, Nef decided it was redundant to avoid the blow: that was when he realized his mistake.

Though the hand remained dismembered, and though no physical blow came, the strider found his eyes awash in a spray of blood. His eyes stung from the thick fluid and drove him to subvert his attack. Instead of raising a blade in offence, he raised a hand in protection, violently wiping his sleeve at his eyes in hopes of restoring his vision.

Nef hardly had the time to fix his predicament when he felt the mammoth impact of a foot into his back. He felt his body bend and pop at the blow, forcing him to the ground, winded and blind. He rolled onto his back, to see the blur of the Threg standing above him. He couldn't breathe, he could hardly see and he was tired, so very tired. He had pulled countless patrols the past moon and had hardly slept when he was off duty. The adrenaline washed away as he braced himself for the impact. Even with blurred vision, Nef could see his attacker held another weapon in its hand; it swung.

#

From atop the defensive wall, Bronwin could see the menagerie of the chaos below. The fight was being won by the Sovereign forces. Though it would not be a clear-cut victory. The conscripts were considered annihilated, trapped between a wall of Thregs, and a wall of fire. Very few of them would have survived.

The Pale Bull's men had the Thregs outnumbered, and that would be the reason for their victory. He could see the striders flowing through the combat, streams of water around stones in a riverbed, they hacked and cut, cleaved and dodged as the Sovereign troops cut into their distracted foes.

Velamir's men had been doing surprisingly well. He could see their ridiculously polished armour still glinting beneath the dirt, sweat and blood that had marred it. They had lost a few men but still, they held. Even the pretty boy captain of the mercenaries showed surprising grace with a blade, it flowed almost as peacefully as the man's hair did.

Bronwin's men were dominating the battlefield, their losses looked minimal and their kill count seemed higher than that of the rest of the army. Scores of Threg bodies began to pile up before them. They knew where to aim; they were experienced. Even though Threg skin was thick, and their muscles strong, their bones were weak. Aiming for joints, and fighting with blunt weapons were the promise to success. Blunt weapons didn't need to pierce the skin to be effective, they just needed to hit.

A familiar voice sounded from beside him. "A rather pyrrhic victory this will be, no?"

The Pale Bull nodded in response to the scholar's question.

"And if they send another attack?"

"Then we'll fight them off too."

"Will you? Your men will be tired, and your numbers much smaller than what you had this morn."

"More men are coming daily from Sun Spire and the Central Cities. We will reinforce. The men that survive today, will know how to better fight in their next battle."

Varden raised an eyebrow. "Oh? The Thregs have more than a few troops out in those plains." He pointed with a finger. "How many men do you hope to have to outnumber that force?"

"Enough."

The Wixen laughed. "You are a fool, Bull. This isn't a small skirmish against a camp. This is a war, an army versus an army. You can't possibly hope to win with intimidation alone, can you?"

Bronwin snorted. The Wixen knew nothing of Thregs, at the first sign of a greater force, the creatures ran, knowing they'd been bested. They were more animalistic than they were smart. He knew that to beat the Thregs, you had to play the game of bears, look bigger, look meaner, and you would win. It had worked time and time again with his own troops. It would work here.

The Pale Bull watched as a strider, a woman, wove through the battle cutting at legs and arms as she passed, working her way up to a Threg. The beast wore a leather chest piece, and a spaulder made of bone on its right arm. The creature's hair was in the typical oily dregs, as it roared its splayed tongue at the woman. In its hand, it held a gleaming steel sword. Wixen.

The strider swung a feint, then anticipated an attack, she sidestepped. The Threg didn't flinch, didn't attack, but stepped with her and reached a hand out, grabbing her by the throat. A moment later, the Thregs blade was plunged into the side of the strider's skull. The body was cast aside like trash as another strider swept in for the distraction. The man fouled up his attack and panicked. His shoulder twitched, then sprung to life as the short sword went into motion.

The armoured Threg rose its own sword a moment sooner and severed the strider's limb at the forearm. The hand, and blade it was holding, disappeared into the battleground, soon followed by his head.

The armoured Threg cut and cleaved its way through the Sovereign men expertly. It parried, dodged and countered with practised ease. Bronwin smiled and called Saffron from further down the wall.

"Saffron!" he beckoned, catching the man's attention, "You have command of the defence until I return!"

"And where might you be going?!" the Squid yelled back.

The Shield of Northwood didn't answer, instead, he hefted his flanged mace from the loop on his belt and worked his way down to ground level. The wooden stairs creaked and groaned under the weight of Bronwin and his armour. He could see Saffron watching him from the corner of his eye, a look of bewilderment in his eyes.

A few moments later the gate of the defensive wall opened. The defensive line of soldiers separated, allowing their commander passage. As the Pale Bull stepped further into the battle, he found himself more at peace than he did while on the wall. With every step, he could feel his breathing slow, more methodical, less laboured. The adrenaline flooded his body and lent him the strength and control that only it could provide him. He stood far taller than that of his men, he matched a Threg's height with ease and matched their strength as well.

One of the horrors approached with eagerness and swung a rusty sword. It bounced harmlessly off the Bull's shield. Bronwin responded in kind, his own weapon, shattering its chest. A spray of blood poured forth from the Threg's maw, as it fell lifelessly to the dirt.

Another Threg, having witnessed the swatting of its kin, took up the mantle of assault. It stepped forward with a spear in hand and thrust forward.

The Pale Bull effortlessly twisted and avoided the strike as he thrust his own shield into the shaft of the weapon, causing it to travel wide and away from him. One swing and Bronwin's mace shattered the monster's arm, a second, and it destroyed the Threg's shoulder blade. It collapsed.

A third Threg turned and ran: it had seen its better. Bronwin smirked and continued towards his intended target.

The Pale Bull watched as the talented Threg cut and cleaved his way through soldier after soldier. Sovereign Guard after Sovereign Guard approached the beast, moving to flank, ambush, and attack their target. Yet every attempt was met with practised fighting, countering, feinting and footwork. The Threg parried and cut down foe after foe leaving a trail of bodies in its wake. Bronwin watched as the beast slapped a Sovereign spear aside, then plunged its blade through its attacker's neck. The Threg locked eyes with Bronwin and grinned a wide, yellow-toothed grin.

The Pale Bull maintained a calm persona and moved closer. The Threg moved in kind. The space between warrior and monster grew ever closer. Other Thregs avoided the conflict to allow the fight to happen, to see their superior come out the victor. A show of power, skill, and force.

It would seem, the Shield of Northwood thought to himself, *That you bastards do have some semblance of honour. Hope you don't mind if I shit on it.*

#

From atop the wall, Varden watched as the Pale Bull made his way closer to the battle-hardened Threg. He watched as the maelstrom of combat swirled around the two behemoths, both Thregs and men falling alike. The Plain's Striders worked wonders on the lumbering beasts, allowing the Sovereign Guard to cut them down with relative ease.

Though Bronwin maintained a confident air, even the scholar knew that the warrior had to have noticed the same thing he had. That the likelihood of another battle working out in their favour would be small if nigh on impossible. A contingency plan would be best, perhaps evacuating the town and falling back to the Central City of Sun Spire.

Turning his attention back to the battle at hand, Varden continued to keep an eye on the Pale Bull, and in a brief moment, his mind swirled with realization. He blinked, shook his head then refocused. The sight he gazed at now, he had gazed into before. Bronwin stood, battle-ready with a foe in a near-matching pose before him, battle and blood swirling as if a typhoon. It was the vision the shadewood sap had bestowed upon him, a memory that was not yet a memory, nor his. In the vision, he had seen it from the battlefield itself, a disembodiment of some kind. Whereas now, he glimpsed it from the top of a wall.

The Wixen looked to where he would have been standing had he been in the very spot his vision had foretold, and yet, there was nothing there, not even a drop of blood, it looked completely pristine, untouched from the battle.

There was no pause for talk, no time to size up one another in a dramatic fashion. There was no human element to the initial encounter, man and Threg immediately launched into their duel. Bronwin led with the more aggressive swing of his mace. The Threg in turn twisted and stepped away, letting the blow miss. It countered, swinging its own weapon skillfully towards the Pale Bull.

The commander reacted with the raise of his shield. It absorbed the blow, then with a thrust, went for a blunt strike with the barrier itself. The Threg saw the attempt and stepped away, causing Bronwin to overstep and stumble forward. He reacted masterfully and used the sudden burst of forward momentum to regain his footing and launch himself into a charge. He pulled back, as if to swing, but didn't.

The Threg flinched to block an attack, as Bronwin pushed his shield forward. The blow landed hard into the beast, causing it to recoil back. Its ribs looked malformed, the blow broke more than a couple. It howled, fibrous tongue flailing in the air. Fixing a hard stare on Bronwin, it advanced.

The Pale Bull swung his mace, only to have it slapped aside by the Threg's sword. The creature countered and raked its blade along the side of the man's armour. It didn't look to have pierced the thick plate, and Bronwin's footwork kept it from doing little more damage than a scratch. He looked to be smiling, then turned and lashed out with a punch from his shield.

The blow connected with the side of the Threg's head and sent it recoiling back. Bronwin followed and lifted the bottom tip of his kite shield, smashing the point into his opponent's jaw. Blood flew from the creature's mouth and Bronwin dropped the head of his flanged mace into its shoulder blade, then its head. The Threg's body warped around the blows as its bones broke and its skin split. Its skull sunken in and malformed, more a bowl than a cradle for its brain.

The Threg fell lifeless to the ground. This distracted and disturbed its nearby allies. They moved with hesitance at each of their foes, allowing their smaller counterparts to cut them down with much less effort than they had previously. Eventually, the Thregs began to falter and turn away from the Sovereign Guard in droves, leaping back through the wall of flames — now much smaller than it had been before — and towards the mouth of Valen's Passage, back to the Endless Plains. It would seem that, for now, the battle was won.

Chapter 27

Roth and Vera Highfold stood before their eldest son expectantly. Alistair stood before them in the throne room, his head bowed as his scarlet cloak draped the dark marbled floor behind him.

"You bring word from Plainsview?" the king asked with authority.

Alistair looked at him. "Yes, Father. Bronwin has successfully fended off the first wave of invaders. The country is safe, for now."

"And what of our casualties, how did we fare?" his mother asked with growing urgency.

The Arch General hesitated for a moment: he didn't know yet. "We are unsure of the exact number of casualties."

"What are the estimates?"

Alistair swallowed hard, the numbers weren't good. "We estimate 2000 conscripts killed in battle and another 3000 Sovereign troops." He bowed his head lower.

His father took a step forward. "And the enemy? What size force did they attack with, and how many were slain?"

"We believe there were no more than 2000 Thregs, estimates put the survivors at 500." he braced himself.

"So you're telling us," his father said sternly, a hand rising to his forehead. "That we lost 5000 men and women to kill only 1500 of the enemy?"

"2000 of those men and women were conscripts, sir. They were used as fodder by the Pale Bull, they were never intended to survive, most of them had never held a weapon in their lives. They were criminals." he spoke quickly, keeping his head low. The numbers were staggering, and not in their favour.

"Regardless of this fact, my son," the queen said. "That would still put our military losses at a two-to-one ratio. 3000 of ours, for 1500 of theirs. How many Thregs are in the plains?"

"Our scouts put estimates at 50,000, though this number is now slightly reduced."

"And your forces were last placed at 10,000," Roth said annoyed. "And now *that* number is significantly reduced."

Though Alistair wasn't looking at his father, he could feel the king's gaze tearing through him. "We have more men moving to Plainsview with every passing day. We will refortify, reinforce, and adjust our strategies for the next wave."

His mother spoke with a modicum of patience. "Be sure that you do. For if another wave attacks and we suffer similar casualties, we will be forced to order a tactical retreat to Sun Spire. Is that clear?"

"Yes, Mother."

"You may rise." Roth finally said.

Alistair did so, his knees thankful for the release.

"You are free to go about your business. We have a new treaty to broker with the Northern Tribes that requires our attention."

Both Roth and Vera turned and began to head towards the rear of the throne room. As Alistair turned to walk back to the adjacent war room, he felt the familiar touch of his mother's hand on his shoulder. He turned to face her.

"Mother?"

She embraced him, and as she did, spoke softly into his ear. "I know you are stressed, Alistair. You are dealing with a difficult situation. That is not lost on me, nor your father. We know you are doing everything you can to keep our people safe, and we are sorry we cannot help you any further. Our expertise lay in politics, and treaties, not in war and battle. You have been well-trained, and I am certain that you will do what is best. Just remember, you can't win every battle. Men will die, battles will be lost, and some will hold you accountable for that. But that's inevitable, you are the Arch General, and we are so proud of you."

She pulled back and cupped his cheek in her hand. She smiled lovingly at him, then turned sharply before he could reply. Alistair caught himself in a sort of morose grin as he watched after her. She had always been his biggest supporter and the most loving person towards him in his family. His father had always preferred his sister, and Varen always preferred people from outside the family, such as that man-child, Jo-een Tolshin. While Cullen had always been the more independent of the four siblings, never sitting still for more than a few moments.

Alistair, however, had his mother, the lovely Vera Highfold, once Vera Hrenclaven. He knew he was fortunate, but the duties he was forced to perform for his country kept him feeling as if he was the more unfortunate of his family: having to manage the life and death of nearly countless men and women.

He had generals helping him, and guard captains in each city working on a more local level, but ultimately, whatever happened to each and every Sovereign soul would fall to him and his actions or inactions. But that was the way of his life, a constant and never-ending ball of stress that would continue to roll until he was either dead or until he left office. And since his parents were healthy, it was looking like the former would prove the more correct.

Walking calmly, keeping his head held high, the Arch General moved towards the door of the war room and pushed it open. As he closed the door behind him, he heard the door on the opposite side of the room close at the same moment.

"Cullen, I hope?"

A voice rang out. "Who else do you know that could muster up my way of conversing with you, dear Brother?"

Alistair chuckled, much to his own surprise. "No one. But if you can do it-"

The Spymaster cut him off. "Then someone else can. Very true."

"Yes, then someone else can." The older Highfold let out a deep sigh and leaned against the wall, crossing his arms, he leaned his head back and began to speak. "Tell me, what news do you bring to me, this day?"

"I come with news of Plainsview, Wreath's Burrow, and Farnwood. If you are so inclined."

Alistair leaned forward, his attention fixated on the room and the voice that emanated from it. "You could say I am inclined, yes."

"Excellent," his brother's voice said. "In regards to Farnwood, the town has been scorched and cleansed by our dear brother's Right Hand. As has been the anomaly in Wreath's Burrow. Both towns are deemed clear of any threat."

"He scorched the towns? Why?" He paused for no more than an instant. "No, ignore that. That is for our brother and his Sword to handle. Not for me, I have enough on my plate. What of Plainsview?"

"The town holds, as does the passage. As you are well aware. You are also aware of the number of losses both sides have endured. The Thregs maintain a sizeable force in the plains and will move when they see fit. The Pale Bull will not hold the passage again. This, I can assure you. I would advise ordering him to fall back to Plainsview, leave traps and an ambush within the passage."

Alistair nodded as he chewed his lip. "Not a bad idea. Should the Thregs begin an assault, it would be best if we evacuated the town. I don't want innocents caught in the battle."

"Yes, of course. I will keep a close eye on this particular matter. Things are progressing outside of my influence in the west, but I can at least aid where I can with the Pale Bull."

This caught the Arch General's attention. His aid? Cullen had never offered aid before, outside of providing information. "What do you-" The door slammed open and closed again before he could finish.

#

Rel strode through the rows of injured and dying soldiers as they lay behind the defensive wall. Hundreds, if not thousands were left beaten and bloodied by the end of the battle two days prior. They had won, but it did not bode well for future engagements. The Thregs had been beaten back, but they had taken out a swath of the Sovereign forces.

She knelt next to a wounded woman and looked at the man treating her. "How is she?"

He shook his head gently but didn't speak a word. He didn't even make eye contact.

The Plain's Master clenched her jaw, wiped away some sweat from the wounded soldier's forehead, then rose to resume her path.

It wasn't long before she came across Nef, a small bandage wrapped around his head.

"Glad to see you're finally up and about," Rel said with a grin. "You almost had me worried."

Nef grinned sheepishly. "You'd have a lot more to worry about if that guard hadn't saved my ass."

"You know ..." Rel remarked with the playful raise of an eyebrow, "You never did tell me what happened to you out there. You were a little out of it."

A chuckle rolled lazily from her friend's mouth as he sat down on a nearby log. "Well, my fight with that Threg didn't exactly go as planned. Damn thing ripped its own hand off. He knocked me to the ground, found a weapon and was ready to cleave me in two. Then, all of a sudden I hear the sound of a chain. The next thing I know, the Threg slumps over next to me, and that man, Corduvan, is helping me up. That damn guardsman with the ridiculous weapon actually saved my ass. Can you believe it?"

Rel grinned widely, it would seem the scorn and attention she had given Corduvan had paid off.

"Oh, by Gwendall's Blade, I can believe it. He's a good man." Rel looked around for a moment. "Speaking of which, have you seen him?"

"It's been two days, Rel. And I've only been back on my feet since this morning. I haven't had much chance to see *anybody*. But I'm sure he's around."

"Thanks. We'll catch up a little more later, right now, I need to finish my pass, and you need some rest." She flashed him a caring smile.

"Alright. I'll be here if you need me."

Rel turned and continued her march into the rows of wounded. Plenty were dying by the hour, either due to infection or blood loss. It wasn't easy walking through the lines of dying troops, but she knew it was important for her to do so. She was someone with a position of power.

It hadn't been long on her walk before she stumbled upon Saffron and Varden speaking with the Bull. The two smaller men looked visibly distraught.

"You can't be serious, Bronwin. You can't be. This is absurd." Saffron was shaking his head ruefully. "That will never work."

"What won't work?" Rel asked as she approached, hands on her hips.

The scholar turned to face her, worry flashing through him. "It would seem that our friend here is a little more bull-headed than his title would imply."

The Plain's Master raised an eyebrow. "Oh?"

"He ..." Saffron sighed rubbing his temples, "He wishes to attack the Thregs, in the plains, once our troops are rested. It's a fool's gambit."

Bronwin said nothing. He only stared in Rel's direction, looking to see her reaction.

There were a few long moments of silence before she spoke her mind. "That will never work. Even if we could push them back, our losses would be catastrophic." She turned to the Bull and matched his gaze. "Surely you jest?

You can't be considering this."

Bronwin snorted.

"Bronwin, please," Varden interrupted, "Please see reason. Our losses far outweighed that of their own in our last engagement. It would be suicide to launch an offensive against an army of that scale. Even if you had the advantage with numbers it-"

"Enough!" the Shield of Northwood roared, "I will *not* be questioned by the likes of you three. You forget who is in charge. The decision is mine, and mine alone. We will show the Thregs that we are not to be trifled with and that the Sovereign Guard is more than capable of matching them in a fight."

"How can you possibly expect this to work?" Saffron took a step forward, a bead of sweat running down his cheek.

"The same way we won the last battle. We kill their strongest warriors, and the rest will retreat."

"Okay," Rel cut in. "Even if we do happen to find their best fighters, how many will we lose weeding them out? How many will we lose if they don't retreat? And what if they don't retreat? There are too many things that we do not know yet, Bronwin. Our best chances at surviving this are to mount a defence, not the opposite."

"If you continue to question my authority in these matters, I will have the two of you tried for treason, and you Scholar, I will have deported from our country, and into the hands of the Thregs. I am your commander, and you will follow my orders to the letter, is that clear?" Bronwin looked at all three of them.

A silent tension grew thick and humid. The three concerned denizens looked at one another, uncertain. Finally, Bronwin let out another snort, and turned to leave, as he stepped away, Rel took a deep breath.

"No," her heart fluttered.

The Pale Bull stopped and glanced over his shoulder. "I beg your pardon, Plain's Master?"

"No. I will not blindly follow orders while you sacrifice our men and women in some pointless battle!"

Bronwin turned, met Rel with an obsidian gaze and stepped towards her. He glowered at her, face turning red with rage. "You dare disobey *my* orders, strider?"

"I dare not follow orders that would see me, my striders, and my country sacrificed."

"You would dare commit treason?"

"It's no more treasonous than what you propose, Bull." She spat at his feet.

Bronwin raised a behemoth, armoured hand and swung his open palm towards her.

Rel jumped back, avoiding the blow, and unsheathed her long knife. The Shield of Northwood responded in kind, pulling his mace out of the ring it so casually sat. He moved in towards her, readying his weapon.

"Stop this, both of you!" Saffron bellowed, stepping between them, arms outstretched to either side.

"She dares to commit treason! I'll have her head!"

"No! You will not, Bronwin!" Saffron roared, "Not without a trial."

The Pale Bull calmed slightly and hung his mace back through the ring he had pulled it from.

Turning to Rel, Saffron looked at her with fury. "Stand down, strider," he said through clenched teeth.

Rel did as she was ordered, sheathing her long knife and fixing her posture.

"She will be tried for treason, Squid."

"No, no she won't," the Plain's Warden said defiantly. "She is not of the Sovereign Guard and does not answer to you for disobeying orders. She is a strider, and she will answer to me. I will see that she receives her just punishment and no less."

Bronwin looked to have a new shade of red painting his features. He kept his eyes locked with Saffron as he growled. "So be it, Squid. But someone will answer to the Sovereign Guard for her behaviour."

Saffron gestured for Rel to follow. He spoke to the Pale Bull as he turned. "Be certain to let me know when you find out who that will be."

Laughter roared from behind them as they left. "You really haven't a clue do you, Squid?" The Bull chuckled. "She may not be of the Sovereign Guard, but if I remember correctly, Alistair is your superior, just as he is mine. In turn, *you* will answer for her behaviour. *You* will be tried for treason."

Rel and Saffron stopped dead in their tracks. The Plain's Master looked to her superior, tears threatening to well in her eyes. "Saffron, no, you ca-"

"I can, Rel," he muttered with sombre reflection, "And I will ... It is my duty." Saffron turned to face Bronwin. "So be it. We will see this trial through after I have dealt with my Plain's Master."

"That we will." he replied, "I'm looking forward to this."

#

Varden stood aghast at what he had witnessed. Though he was not native to the country, he had grown rather fond of the few denizens he had met. Rel and Saffron were well-put-together individuals and as far as he was concerned, they hadn't deserved the scorn nor wrath of the Pale Bull.

Today's words and actions gave the scholar reason to doubt what he had said about the Pale Bull prior. He was beginning to doubt that the man would have achieved mastery in Ajwix. The man was as much a brute as he was a respected warrior, he couldn't help but wonder what circumstances had led Bronwin to this manner of behaviour, and whether or not he was naturally born to be the way he was.

With a quick shake of his head, he brought his attention back to the scene around him. Wounded soldiers, sick and dying, lay scattered through what had once been a green field. That's when his eyes spotted it: a shadewood tree amongst the edge of the swamp. It looked to be an ash tree, yet ... shadewood.

How curious, the last tree Varden had inspected had been similar in appearance to an oak. Intriguing. The scholar felt for his satchel, he could feel the small iron rod and his tap through the fabric.

He made his way towards the swamp, but couldn't help the feeling that he was forgetting something. He checked his robes and satchel again, but everything was there.

"By the Veil Strider, what have I forgotten?" he said to himself.

Varden stood bewildered. He never forgot anything. What did he lose? His eyes opened with realization as the answer struck him: his guards.

He turned to look side to side for the familiar faces of his guardsmen, he quickly picked one of them out, laying in a small cot. The Wixen approached the wounded man.

"Well, my friend. I'd certainly say you've seen better days," he said with a slight frown. "It pains me to see you this way."

The soldier laughed. "Bah! You should've seen me on my wedding night, I looked far worse!" he sputtered with an injured cough.

Varden started. "I had no idea you were married!"

The soldier chuckled again, but it turned to a groan of pain as he held his bandaged side. "Not married anymore, the bitch left me for a bandit! That poor man. That day was the happiest of my life, you know?"

Even the scholar couldn't help but chuckle. Though he was not married, he had often heard of the trials and tribulations that could become a constant part of one's life during the union.

"May I ask you something?" Varden asked.

"Of course," He began to cough again.

"Do you happen to know where the rest of our group is? I've been having a troublesome time finding them."

The guard looked saddened. "They're all dead, sir. I was the only one who held breath until the battle's end."

Varden sighed. It probably sounded as if he was agitated instead of saddened. But he was heartbroken. The men that had been following him around for a couple of fortnights were gone, out of his life. Them, and all the stories they held, told, or would make, were gone, never to be heard or written down by another soul again.

"All of them?"

The soldier nodded ruefully. "Aye. Looks like it's just you and me. Well, once I get back on my feet." He coughed again.

The scholar nodded. "It would seem that way. I doubt Bronwin is willing to replenish our numbers."

A noisy voice rose from behind them, a rough voice, a stupid voice. Followed by alarming calls from the other soldiers.

"By Gwendall's Blade, you're alive?!" a perplexed archer yelled.

"Esmirla's Cunt!" another exasperated.

"Of course, I'm still alive! Tougher than anything out there I am! Ya shoulda seen em, runnin with their tongues flappin like a toddler's!" the voice roared with laughter. But everyone around the words stared in disbelief.

Varden stood beside the cot and made his way over towards the commotion. What he was thinking, he couldn't believe. But as he pushed through a line of soldiers, the sight of Dry Eyes set his mind straight.

The conscript stood in his ragged leather armour, scorch marks marring every inch of his clothing. Blood streaked across his face, and above it all, his telltale red eyes gleamed through the soot. Dry Eyes had survived.

"By the Veil Strider," the scholar gasped.

Dry Eyes turned to face the Wixen. "Well look who we 'ave 'ere! If it ain't the Wixen himself! How much fightin you see?"

Varden cast his eyes over the conscript, taking in his burnt and torn clothes, the dirty scuff marks on his bare skin, and the deep brown of his eyes. They were rimmed with red. Had he been crying? The scholar decided to keep things jovial and not press the emotions of his guard.

"Well my friend, I clearly didn't see nearly as much fighting as you did. How do you fare? It's been two days since the battle."

The bandit seemed to stutter at this line of questioning: "I-uh. I did good!" he finally said with confidence. "I did better than any other fighter out there, I did! You shoulda seen em; the Thregs I mean. Ran with their tails ... erm, tongues, between their legs they did! Aw, it was glorious! I musta slain hundreds of 'em!"

Varden nodded, not believing a word that was said, but he played along. "Well fought, friend." the scholar cringed at the use of the phrase. "But that does not explain your absence for the past two days, where have you been?"

The man rocked back and forth on his feet slightly. "Well, I was chasin 'em out!"

A couple of soldiers nearby laughed.

"You were what?" Varden asked, with shock lining his face, "Please tell me you jest?"

"I am many things, Scholar," he said with a booming voice. "But a liar is not one!"

The Wixen nodded, biting his tongue at what the simpleton said. "Well, since your back. Would you mind escorting me a little ways towards the swamp?"

Dry Eyes sputtered and spat as he tried to assemble anything close to a phrase together. "You want me to *what*? Have I not done enough to earn meself a little break?"

"I am asking you to do your duty, *conscript*." he argued, "Do you wish me to speak with Bronwin or Algrenon of this disobedience?"

The bandit's eyes lit up with fear. "NO! No, you don't 'ave to do that! I'll see you there, safe and sound, I will!" He placed his hands on his hips and puffed out his burnt chest in a display of attempted heroism. It looked to Varden that he was wincing from pain as he saw some pink skin flake off as the bandit puffed out his chest.

"Right. Come this way, would you kindly." Varden led the way, Dry Eyes following close behind.

The two men walked in tandem with each other, around cots filled with the wounded, over bodies wrapped in cloth and around small campfires being used to cook their food, boil their tea, or cauterize their wounds.

Then, at the edge of the swamp, stood the shadewood tree Varden had spotted.

"Huh, another one of these, eh? What makes 'em so special?"

Varden sighed at the question. "No one has truly been able to study them, my simple colleague. So, I intend to do just that. I want to understand how these phenomena of nature work."

"How the ... what, of nature?"

"Never you mind, Dry Eyes, never you mind, these things are for me to worry about. You just keep me safe, will you?"

"But of course! If there's one thing I'm good at in this world, it's keeping you alive!"

"Is that so?"

"You isn't dead, is you?"

Varden had to chuckle, he certainly wasn't wrong, for he certainly was still alive.

Before long, the two men had arrived at the base of the shadewood tree, this one, much to Varden's relief, was not located in knee-high swamp water, it rested on solid, trustworthy, disease-free, ground.

"You just, keep watch for me, will you? I doubt anything wild, or otherwise, would attempt to attack us here, but you can never be too certain."

A gruff grunt and a sharp nod out of the corner of Varden's vision told him that Dry Eyes understood. Good. The scholar pulled out his metal tap and hammered it home into the bark with the hilt of his own dagger. He reached into his satchel, flopped his hand around, and found the small vial he had been looking for. It had been cleaned since he last used it, and he inspected it once more with a critical eye. The last thing he wanted was to contaminate this new test with a previous test's sap.

He reached up and hung the vial off the tap as he had done previously, now all that was left to do was-

A gush of sap flowed from the tap and into the vial. Some of the white fluid spilt and fell to the ground. Then, just as suddenly as it had started, the flow of sap was over. The vial was full to the brim.

"By the Veil Strider ..." Varden muttered to himself, careful not to let Dry Eyes hear. He grabbed the vial, sealed it with a cork and retrieved the tap once more from the shadewood tree's trunk. He placed his tools back into his satchel and called for Dry Eyes to follow back to the defensive wall.

"Done 'ere already?"

"Yes, that we are."

"We gonna be comin back here every day like the last one?"

"No, my friend, no we will not. Maybe once more, but that will be all."

"Huh, why is that?"
Varden smiled. "In all honesty, Dry Eyes, I've no idea."

Chapter 28

The confines of Saffron's office had never felt so constricting. Not in all her life had Rel felt so claustrophobic in the presence of her mentor. She looked upon his usually red face and found it redder than it ever had been before. His eyes burned with fury, but not hatred, not even disappointment. Just anger.

"You do realize, Plain's Master, that my head will be on the chopping block for your temper tantrum yesterday, do you not?!"

The wood of the longhouse seemed to vibrate with every word the Plain's Warden roared, his voice cracked and boomed as if thunder shattering crisp night air. Rel faltered at every syllable, every word. She had never seen him so furious. Could she blame him though? For her rash actions, she consigned him to death. Had she not so blatantly stood in opposition to the Pale Bull, she would not have doomed Saffron to the gallows.

"Saffron, I-I." she stammered, "I didn't think, I was too-"

"Oh, believe me, Plain's Master," his voice dropped to a growl. "I do realize you were not thinking, we all realized you were not thinking."

"Saffron, I'm-"

"Sorry?" he finished for her, "Save your sorries for the battles that are on your doorstep."

He pulled out a sheet of parchment from a drawer on his desk and reached for his quill. He began to scribble onto the sheet in a flurry. "Do you understand why I am so furious with you, Rel? Do you, past all your arrogance, see why you have vexed me so harshly?"

Rel's heart fluttered with fear. She tried to spit her words out but found herself sputtering. Wanting nothing more than to vacate her words from her mind she nearly blurted out her next statement. But, much to her relief, she was able to refrain from the outburst and pulled her tone to that of a calmer one. "Because I've doomed you to execution..."

That she had done; doomed her only father figure to death. The man who looked after her nearly her whole life after moving to Plainsview, and in a single outburst of tired, fatigued emotion, she had molested that relationship as if she cared nothing for him. It was no wonder Saffron was furious.

The Plain's Warden chuckled morosely. "I do not fear death, Rel. In a way, I look forward to it, I am convinced my brother and his family have perished, I still have not heard a word from them. I might get to see them again ..." he trailed off. "But no, you have not vexed me for sending me to the chopping block. You have vexed me because I now have to designate my replacement. And in doing so, I put the one person I love, more than the plains, in direct danger."

Rel's eyes opened wide, her gaze locked onto the parchment on his desk top. She could almost make out what the document was, but with no certainty.

Saffron stood up, and with a fatherly gaze walked over to Rel. He placed his hands on her shoulders and looked into her eyes. "I apologize for my outburst. It was wrong of me. But, with what you had done yesterday, you have forced me to delegate my replacement. The notice is there, on my desk." He gestured with his head towards the document. "I'll be notifying Alistair Highfold with all haste that you will be the Plain's Warden."

Rel's breath stopped in her throat, she felt as if he was choking her. She wasn't ready, she needed more time.

"You are more than ready, Rel. You have already surpassed where I was as a Plain's Master. You will do the Plain's Striders proud. But ... you're now going to be directly in Bronwin's sights. He will see you as a threat, and he is your superior. After today, you answer to the Sovereign Guard, no longer to me. Is that clear?"

She nodded.

"Good," he chuckled sadly. "You know, I'll be watching you from the Soul Spire. You always were a daughter to me." He grinned slightly, a pang of pain in his eyes. "I should be going, I need to send this letter to Valen with all haste." He turned, grabbed the parchment from his desk, sealed it with hot wax, and reached for the door. "And before I go, Rel. This office is now yours. Enjoy it. The walls ... they do a good job of listening to one's problems when no one else is around. It will help, I promise you." He opened the door and stepped through, looking over his shoulder he locked eyes with a stunned Rel. "I'll see you in the morning, Plain's Warden."

As the door closed, the new Plain's Warden fell to her knees and wept.

#

A dark blur, an ever-present haze, and the sharp pangs of hunger rocked Kol awake from his restless sleep. He could feel his body being pushed and pulled, manoeuvred like a sack of meat through the mud. A stick scratched against his cheek, but he didn't care. He could feel little more than the splitting of his skin as it raked his flesh. It didn't hurt, not anymore, it just simply was, and would be, neither painful, nor pleasurable, but another fact of his situation.

Kol lay on his back blinking wearily as something dripped onto his cheek. He grimaced at the thick fluid, then gasped as a large swath of it cascaded onto him. He sputtered and sat up, awake and wiping at his face. As his vision cleared, he realized the Thregs had dumped congealed blood on him in an attempt to make him stir. And it worked, he nearly jumped to his feet at the realization, but his broken body kept him firmly grounded.

He jerked and spasmed awkwardly but found himself unable to move more than a few inches. Attempting to arch his back, he broke into a sputtering cough, the foreign blood rose into the air and softly fell onto the strider's chest. A thick scaled hand grabbed Kol by the shoulder and rolled him over, firmly held the collar of his torn uniform and hoisted him to his feet. The strider attempted to hold his footing, but couldn't; the tendons in his legs had been cut and he could hardly stand. He would have no other choice than to be content with being dragged through the mud.

It hadn't taken long, or had it? Kol couldn't be sure, between the blurred hazes of vision and the blackouts, he hadn't been sure if he had been dragged for moments or for days. Ultimately, it didn't matter all too much, the Thregs kept him just enough alive to be of use for one reason or another. For what reason that was, he wasn't all too certain, though he imagined that he would one day find out.

More time passed. The blurred light of the sun didn't seem to have moved, but he couldn't be sure. Finally, the dragging stopped, the mud settled around him, and he was dropped onto his knees, his body a shattered and wounded mess. He sagged into the mud, arms hanging loose.

Another hand reached down and grabbed his jaw. Kol thought he could feel a tooth or two move as the Threg manoeuvred his mouth open. The strider sputtered awake as a wash of cold, clean water filled his senses. He hadn't tasted something so clean, so right, since he was captured. He coughed, jerked, and spasmed, as he tried to gorge himself, but as quickly as it was there, it was gone again. Kol opened his eyes wide in search of the water, or even the skin it came from, but all he saw was a circle of Thregs standing around him. The shock and joy of the water cleared his blurred vision.

Before him stood a large group of Threg soldiers, these ones stood apart from the others, well-armed and armoured with weapons more than likely stolen from the traders that had been killed in the plains. In the centre of the group stood another Threg, slightly taller than the others, not more muscular, and bearing no armour, or even a loincloth. He, Kol could plainly see, stood bare to the world, the only piece of equipment he bore was a large two-handed great axe, a lock of blonde-brown hair hung from the pommel, attached with sinew and flesh.

Kol shivered. He was looking at what he could only guess was the leader of the army, the one assaulting his homeland, and the one who would be in charge of his life. Another Threg in modest leather armour stood next to the leader, a staff in one hand with a human skull hanging via its spine from the top, blood, hair and flesh stuck to the bone: a recent sacrifice.

The Threg with the staff took a step forward and held an open palm towards their hostage, Kol felt his body writhe with energy and vitality, in a matter of moments, he felt as if he had rested and slept for days on end. The aches in his muscles receded, the severed tendons in his legs felt renewed, and his memory soon began to come back to him. He had been with the Thregs for nearly a fortnight, the horrid meals and rotten meat he had been fed on a daily basis nearly made him gag as their flavours flashed through him, but the sensation he currently felt kept those feelings of nausea and repulse away.

Kol went to rise up but was halted by the magical Threg, a quick stiffening of the creature's hand caused Kol's body to tighten. It wasn't uncomfortable. It was like a mother holding her child, a simple message: *Don't, you aren't ready for that step.*

It told the strider all he needed to know, his body hadn't actually been healed, just stimulated in a way to make him feel renewed. The naked Threg took a step forward, blade in hand, and a gaze of care in his vile eyes. As the beast took his steps closer and closer to Kol, he heard the mage behind him speak a single word, telling Kol who was standing in front of him.

The word came through harsh and guttural, the fibrous tongue struggling to articulate the word: "Threg."

This creature before him, this abomination to his country was known as Threg. Their Highfold.

Threg took two more behemoth steps forward and knelt in front of the strider. It grinned widely at the small man in front of him. Opening its mouth, Threg dragged the bundle of hollow tubes that was his tongue along Kol's cheek.

The ranger wanted to shiver, but the magic holding him kept him feeling calm and confident. He found it exhilarating that he could match this beast's gaze without feeling a shred of fear in his body. He had never felt so strong in his life. As that thought crossed his mind, the mage lowered his hand and Kol felt every ounce of strength he had vanish from within him. His vision blurred, his breathing became more laboured and his thoughts began to swim away from anything resembling consciousness.

He could hear a series of small rapid grunts, something akin to laughter. Then, as quickly as it had left him, he felt the strength return. The strider gasped for air, his lungs filling with oxygen as fast as they could. He felt his heart rate strengthen with every pump, and he was aware once more of what surrounded him.

The creature standing before him, the one he now knew as Threg, pointed to a crude drawing in the mud. Kol knew immediately what it was: Valen's Passage. He could easily see the mouth of the passage, and the lines that marked where the Pale Bull's defensive wall stood. Threg began to draw several arrows coming from the direction of the plains, and towards the defensive wall, he then looked to Kol with a tilt of his head.

Threg began to dot the mud from the plains, indicating how many troops he commanded in preparation for the invasion. Then pointed back to the wall, and gave Kol a gaze of uncertainty.

The strider began to shake his head, he wouldn't tell Threg how many soldiers they had stationed there, he couldn't, that would be treason.

As quickly as Kol shook his head, the strength he felt left him once more.

The mage visibly flexed his hand, forcing the strider's muscles taut, sending pain and aches rolling through his body. Kol tried to cough but found his throat too tight to vacate air, he choked, tried to cough again but began to spasm uncontrollably as his chest and lungs began to contract and expand unnaturally.

In a blink and a wash of relief, the strength returned to his body and a breath of air rushed into Kol's body. He felt whole again: no more pain, no more choking, his muscles felt renewed for the third time within a few short, yet agonizing, moments.

Again Threg looked to the strider and pointed to the lines in the mud. Again, Kol shook his head. Once more, pain screamed through him as his body convulsed, seized and faltered. He began to choke, he felt nauseated but couldn't vomit and he felt his bowels evacuate something that ran down his legs. He shook again, before losing consciousness.

Chapter 29

Alistair Highfold sat not in his war room, but in his private study adjoined to his quarters within the Highfold Keep. He sat over an oaken desk, staring annoyingly at the papers and maps in front of him. The door to his study slowly opened with a creak, then slammed shut, causing the Arch General to jump and nearly knock over the candle he was using for light.

"By Daylen! You're awfully loud for a man who's not even here, you know that?"

A disembodied voice echoed through the chambers, emanating from everywhere.

"Now is not the time for jokes, Brother. I have witnessed the size of the Threg army in the plains."

Alistair looked up from his desk and focused on an empty spot in the air, imagining the silhouette his brother might have produced if he were present.

"And how have you witnessed this, I thought you were in the west?"

"I can be wherever I please, sooner than you can even comprehend. I witnessed their army from the Halo."

Valenfaar's military leader sat back in his chair with an air of impatience. "And what is it that you saw? What is the size of their force?"

Cullen's voice came through flat and serious. "The previous estimates were correct: their forces number around 50,000. They will take Plainsview and breach our borders. You need to order an evacuation of the town and begin fortifying it to slow down their troops. Pull back a significant force to inform and aid Sun Spire for when the Thregs reach their walls."

After Cullen spoke, silence lay thick within the room. Alistair's throat had gone dry, he hadn't noticed until he attempted to speak with a frog-like croak. He cleared his voice. "Are you still near Plainsview?"

"Yes, I can be there before sundown."

"Good," Alistair rose to his feet, a slight sway in his stature, his body felt weak, numb and not his own. "Tell Bronwin to abandon the defensive wall, lay traps during his exit, then fortify Plainsview to the best of his ability. Evacuate, fortify, and trap. Those are his orders. Tell him to move what troops he can to Sun Spire, as per your suggestion, ideally the wounded and the conscripts, they'll hopefully have time to rest and recover before the Thregs arrive at the Central City."

The door to Alistair's study opened and slammed shut once more.

"By Daylen ..." He began to rock on his heels but caught his footing before falling back into his chair. He needed his generals.

# #

Looking over the injured men and women of the Sovereign Guard, Bronwin wanted to feel some semblance of grief for them, for their families, or for their children — if they had any — but he could not. This was the very job; no, duty, they had agreed to. He almost felt bad for the conscripts, but a quick reminder that they were mostly — if not all — criminals, had the Pale Bull back to his logical frame of mind: they could either die by the noose, headsman's axe, or by combat. He was happy that they at least had the opportunity to die whilst doing some good.

The sun was nearing the horizon opposite the plains, the shadows grew longer as they stretched into Valen's Passage and beyond the small defensive wall that had held back the Threg's first advance. Bronwin grinned, to think that they had won the battle. Casualties had occurred, but that was a result of every conflict.

If the Thregs attacked next, they would know even further pain as the men and women of the Sovereign Guard drove them back into the plains from which they came, painting the landscape with the blood of both man and Threg. A victory that would be sung for many cycles to come. Until sunrise the next day, however, the Pale Bull would keep most of his soldiers on guard shifts, keeping a rotation of fresh eyes on watch at all times.

Bronwin began to move his way through the wounded and dying, listening to their laboured breathing, groans, and moans of pain. This was the Sovereign Song of Victory, the ability to moan, groan and breathe told them all they had survived, that their enemy had not the chance to utter forth such sounds, that they could no longer affect the world in one of the ways that could matter most: influence, the ability to influence the very air with their words, sounds, and thoughts. The Sovereign Song of Victory was one of life, and one of very little musical enjoyment. The message was clear, they had won, they were breathing, and the enemy was not.

Arriving at the stairs to the defensive wall, the Pale Bull was joined by Algrenon. They began to climb.

"Sir," he said, nearly out of breath. "My apologies, but we've spotted someone coming down the passage. Human. Your orders?"

Bronwin raised an eyebrow. A man had come down the passage? "Do we know who they are?"

"No, sir. We do not."

"Let them approach the gate. I will see them myself."

Algrenon nodded without a word, then moved back down the stairs.

It wasn't long before the Bull had found himself at the top of the wall, gazing down and over the edge into the carnage that had littered the passage below. The Sovereign Guard had done a good job at cleaning the bodies out of the area and moving them away, and still, a few skeleton crews remained to continue the work through the night. Not far off, however, Bronwin could see his guest.

Judging by the build, it was a man, average height and musculature, with nimbleness and agility in every step. He paced over bodies, around weapons and on shields, each footfall was calculated and always landed where he wanted them to. He wore a black cloak, mask, gloves, pants, trousers, and boots, allowing him ample movement, but very little — if any — protection.

"Cullen," the Pale Bull muttered to himself, "to what do I owe the pleasure?" He squinted suspiciously at the Highfold making his way through the darkening valley.

"Algrenon!" Bronwin boomed, "Open the gates for our guest, and bring him up here yourself."

The creek of the heavy wooden doors was all the answer the commander needed. He watched as the Highfold walked stoically towards the wall, and then out of sight, presumably through the gate.

Why would Cullen Highfold be here? He would have his answer soon. Bronwin let his thoughts trail off for a few fleeting moments before he heard the sound of footsteps behind him. He only heard one set, and this threw him off as he turned to see both Algrenon and Cullen.

The Highfold looked even smaller than he remembered. "Cullen," Bronwin said solemnly, giving the man a welcoming nod. "I apologize for the messy yard."

Cullen didn't react.

"Worry yourself not, Bull. The state of the passage is an unfortunate necessity in the defence of our country. You have done well in your first engagement. You have my praise." Cullen's blue eyes searched the commander for something, though Bronwin wasn't sure what.

"Thank you, sir. The Sovereign Guard have done well, and will continue to do so during the next attack."

The Highfold walked to the ledge of the wall and looked out into the passage, Bronwin turned to match his gaze. It was getting darker now, the trees, gore and mountains began to turn a sullen blue as the sun set behind them.

"You say that, Bull. Yet, you do not realize the gravity of the situation you face. The Thregs have far more in number than you realize. This is information that has been presented to you, yet you ignore it. Why?" The smaller man didn't bother to face the commander, he didn't care for an answer.

The Shield of Northwood stood, staring into the mouth of the passage. Somehow, the words uttered by the mysterious Cullen struck home with him more than those written by the Arch General. Something about this elusive agent told Bronwin he held an unfathomable amount of knowledge as if he were not a man, but something more.

The Pale Bull shook his head and resumed the conversation. "What are my orders?" he finally asked.

There was no delay, no sign of emotion from the Highfold, his reply came quickly as if it had been an arrow previously nocked, ready to be loosed. Cullen had already known what Bronwin would say.

"You are to retreat to and fortify Plainsview with all haste. Pull men back to Sun Spire and prepare a defence there. Evacuate the town, trap the very wall we stand atop and attempt to lay small ambushes within the swamp. This comes from Alistair himself, with the exception of the final detail, that is my idea. But regardless, it would be in your best interest, do you not agree, Bull?"

A rush of air forced from Bronwin's nose was the only answer he wished to give, but remembering the fact that he was standing in the presence of royalty, Bronwin swallowed his pride. "Yes sir, I shall see to it that it is done. We will hold Plainsview from the Thregs."

Cullen chuckled to himself. "You will not hold Plainsview, Bull. This is known by all but you. Plainsview will fall, and you may well fall with it. But the sacrifice of yourself and your men will not be in vain. You will buy the time needed for the Sovereign Guard to hold the line at Sun Spire from the Thregs. This will be assured." the Highfold quickly turned around, black cloak twisting as he stepped.

A few short, quiet steps behind the Pale Bull, and the man stopped making a sound. Bronwin turned to see the royal and found nothing. Puzzled, he walked over to the opposite edge of the defensive wall and peered over the ledge. There was nothing, he hadn't jumped, simply vanished. Catching the eye of Algrenon down below he called out to the officer.

"Algrenon!" his voice roared. "Did you see where our guest went?"

"Sir?" he replied with a raised eyebrow, "I thought he was with you, was he not?"

Frustrated, the commander decided it best to leave that mystery unsolved for now.

"Nevermind. A discussion for another time. We have preparations to make: evacuate the defensive wall, lay traps and begin moving what wounded we can to Sun Spire. Whatever men and women we have who can still fight are to begin fortifying Plainsview for an attack. Is that clear?"

"Sir, I thought we-"

"Is that clear, Soldier?" Bronwin cut him off. "Or do I need to find someone with a better sense of authority?"

"N-no sir," Algrenon stammered, "It shall be done," he turned to some nearby officers and soldiers and began barking out orders. It wasn't long before all the men and women in the passage were on the move. The wounded were carried out on stretchers, groaning and complaining as they were vacated. The sad souls had no idea how long of a trip they had ahead of them. By the time they were able to wield a sword again, they'd be atop the walls of Sun Spire to face the Threg horde once more. And should Plainsview fall,

Bronwin was more than determined to make it out alive.

Chapter 30

Five days, five gruelling days of escorting the wounded and dying away from the defensive wall. Five days of learning the ins and outs of her new position. Rel hadn't seen much of Saffron since the day of her so-called promotion. Had it been out of anger, depression, anxiousness or otherwise, she wasn't sure.

Word, however, had already begun to spread among the Plain's Striders about their new Plain's Warden, and rumours had begun to spread that their former warden would be put in front of the headsman.

Nef had come to congratulate her and tried to pull her out of the longhouse and to the Respite for a round of drinks. Though the reasons for her promotion were macabre and carried an air of bitterness to them, the promotion was a good thing for her in the long run. Rel was determined to be a great Plain's Warden, she had wanted it her entire life and had devoted more than one sleepless night to the meticulous thoughts and plannings that would see her excel at her newfound post.

Even Ashlin had tried to congratulate her with a round of her usual sexual encouragement. Rel had turned her down. The idea that she had forced Saffron's handover and future punishment plagued her mind like an illness, tainting the very things she had wanted for so long. Every moment she stood in the longhouse, and every moment she thought of herself as a strider, she felt guilt and bitterness. Bitterness towards herself, but more towards the Pale Bull.

Rel bit back a curse and threw the wooden cup on her desk against the wall. A splash of wine covered the wooden panelling as the vessel bounced along the floor. Leaning forward, the Plain's Warden placed her forehead in her palms and breathed deeply, trying to regain her composure. She needed to be calm, she needed to be composed. She and Saffron had been summoned by the Bull for Sun's Peak.

A knock on the door jolted her attention forward.

"Enter," she spoke, surprising herself with the calmness in her voice.

Corduvan entered.

"Plain's Warden," he spoke with an affirming nod, "All the wounded are evacuated from the wall. Traps are in place and the fortifications of Plainsview are ahead of schedule."

Rel nodded. "Thank you, Corduvan. Have you already told Bronwin?" She made sure to use the Bull's name, else have her ire pronounced further with the use of the more derogatory 'Bull' she so often preferred.

"Yes ma'am. Word comes from himself and Algrenon. He also wishes to remind you of his summonings at Sun's Peak."

"Thank you, Corduvan. I haven't forgotten. I'll be there."

"Yes ma'am," He looked at her for a moment, as if to say something.

"If there is nothing else, Guardsman, you are dismissed."

He paused and hesitated for a moment before nodding his head. "Of course. Send a runner should you need anything." He turned and closed the door behind him.

"By Daylen ..." Rel cursed to herself. Nothing felt right, nothing felt good. At best, Saffron would be declared a traitor and cast out of Valenfaar, at worst: today would be his last. It was all up to the Bull.

Not a moment passed by that didn't have Rel's heart pounding both in her head and her chest. The headache she felt pulled at her thoughts and wrapped her mind with pain. Her shoulders were tensed to the point that an arrow would bounce off had she been shot. The morning passed by achingly as the sun rose higher into the sky.

Finally, Rel stood and looked out the window of her office: it was just about Sun's Peak. Biting back a curse, she donned her cloak from the top of her desk. It was heavy, soaked with sweat and tears, yet she fastened it anyway.

Walking out of the longhouse, Rel's skull throbbed with every step, her eyes burned from her sobbing. Throat dry, she attempted to swallow and winced in pain. Everything felt like a haze around her. The town she had called home for so long looked to be washed in a tone of yellow-orange. Her vision felt tunnelled like she couldn't see out of her peripherals. She could if she focused, but a moment of searing pain stretching from eye to mind told her that idea was not a good one.

The dirt flattened underfoot, some mud made sucking sounds as she stepped through it. Soldiers on stretchers were carried away, groaning and moaning, townsmen and women were loading up wagons, saddlebags, packs, rucksacks and whatever else they could fill with their things as the Sovereign Guard guided them from their homes. Rel wasn't sure when, but at some point, this town would be a warzone. Dirt would be layered with armour and flesh, weapons would stick from the soil where merchants once stood. The townsfolk would be gone, hopefully, and only soldiers would remain, broken and battered, scared but unwavering.

How did she know this? She didn't. But after seeing how the Thregs fought at the mouth of the passage, she knew — regardless of what the Bull thought — that Plainsview was lost. They needed the support and walls of Sun Spire, and that was something they did not, and could not, have here. They were trapped with wounded and tired soldiers, wooden fortifications, and meagre troops filtering in from the Central Cities. The troops had begun to trickle in, a squad or two every few days. Something about an issue to the west and keeping more in reserves for reasons not known to the Plain's Warden.

The town square was quiet. Bronwin and Algrenon stood, side by side on the other end of the court.

"Where's the old man?" Bronwin's voice echoed.

Rel shrugged. But made no reply, otherwise.

"You'd do well to show respect today, Warden." Algrenon spat in Rel's direction.

The Plain's Warden didn't care, she was too tired, too stressed. Deprived of emotion she sighed and closed her eyes, tilting her head to the ground. She would have nodded off standing there, had a rough hand not clasped her on the shoulder.

"I'm right here," Saffron said towards the Bull. Then quietly to Rel: "I'm right here, Rel."

A small pittance of energy returned upon hearing Saffron say her name. She grinned wearily and looked at him. "It's great to see you."

The former warden looked rough, his eyes sunken with dark circles underneath. He looked as if he hadn't shaved since they last met, his hair was matted and oily. He looked like he had been on a drunken bender in the streets. He was sober now, the confident look in his eyes told her as much, and his posture didn't carry the sway of a drunken man.

One thing that stood out as odd was his uniform. He wore a traditional Plain's Strider's uniform, neatly kept but slightly faded. His old uniform, the one they had chuckled at as he donned it many days ago.

Bronwin boomed from across the square, "Good of you to join us, Squid!" he spat. "Let's get this over with already, we have a town to fortify."

Bronwin and Algrenon began to make their way forward, Rel and Saffron did the same, whispering to one another as they stepped.

"Where have you been?" Rel asked.

"Soul searching," came the reply. "Nothing for you to worry about, Rel. I kept out of trouble."

She nodded. "So what do we do?"

"We listen. We might not like what he has to say, but we listen. Once he has spoken, we work from there."

"Doesn't seem like much of a plan." she returned.

"What would you have us do? Kill them? No. We can't plan a response until we know the approach. You know this, Rel, just as well as I do. This might not end well for either of us. Keep that in mind." Saffron swallowed hard as if he already knew what was to happen.

The four warriors met, face to face.

Saffron spoke first. "Say what you will, Bronwin."

"Former Plain's Warden Saffron," the Bull spoke, "Your former Plain's Master, Rel, has committed an act of treason against a commander of the Sovereign Guard and her people. The punishment for this is death." Bronwin looked to the former Plain's Master. "What say, you?"

Rel cleared her throat. "I committed no such act. My words and actions were in the interest of the soldiers of the Sovereign Guard and that of

Valenfaar. To risk their lives pointlessly would be treason." She matched his gaze and hoped there was a fire in hers.

The Pale Bull snorted. "You were of the Plain's Striders, and therefore I cannot pass judgement onto you." He looked at Saffron. "As you so accurately reminded me. Saffron, what say, you?"

"The actions of the Plain's Master were not fueled by thought, but by tired emotion. She was not in a steady place of mind, and therefore should not be tried as such. The battle took tolls on everybody, even yourself. Many of us are not in our right minds. She should be given rest not-"

"Enough," Bronwin cut in, "Your Plain's Master is highly regarded. Algrenon, did you see tiredness, or exhaustion during her outburst."

"No. I saw fury and anger. She knew exactly what she was doing. If I didn't know better, I'd almost say she had it planned ahead of time."

Rel hadn't noticed at first, but Varden stood at the edge of the town square, watching. Waiting. Was he going to say something? She hoped he would.

"Saffron," Bronwin stepped forward. "As Plain's Warden, and follower of the Arch General of the Sovereign Guard, you are to take upon you the punishment that would be given to your disciple. You are aware of this, are you not?"

Saffron swallowed hard and nodded. "If only you would consider-"

"I will consider no other course of action, Squid. She dared to attack a commander of the Guard. Unless anyone comes forward with evidence to prove her mental state as abnormal, a life will be had for her crimes, and if I can't take hers, yours will more than make up for that."

Rel looked back to Varden out of the corner of his eye. The Wixen was hesitating.

The Pale Bull turned. "Algrenon, would you kindly?"

Algrenon stepped forward as Varden opened his mouth to speak, but no words came, only the sound of steel punching through flesh: a dagger into Saffron's heart.

"This has been a long time coming, Squid." the killer muttered through clenched teeth, a grin on his face.

Rel's body exploded with adrenaline. Her skin prickled at the air as she watched her mentor crumple to the ground. She screamed and dropped to her knees above him. She didn't think it was possible, but she sobbed and the tears flowed freely.

Rel cradled Saffron's head in her arms as she rocked on her knees. Everyone averted their gaze, Varden stepped back in astonishment and the Plain's Striders looked to Bronwin with a mix of anger, confusion and fear. What were they to do? What would Rel command of them?

Nef came running from the crowd and dropped next to her.

"No!" he cried, "No, no, no, no, no!"

"It happened, Nef." Rel spoke between heavy breaths, "And it's my fault." her voice cracked. "I pulled a blade on the Bull, and Saffron answered for my crimes."

"You did what?!" Nef's mouth hung open.

"I killed him, Nef." she squeaked, "I killed Saffron." Rel gritted her teeth. "And I'll kill *him* too." she looked at Bronwin as he and Algrenon left. "Will you help me? Nef, will you help me?" the warden looked up at him with fire in her eyes. "You, me and Corduvan. We'll take that man's head and save lives." she rocked with Saffron one more time before falling into silent contemplation: she would kill the Bull.

#

Nausea began to fade, Varden had moved from the square quickly after Saffron's execution. He wasn't usually one to grow weak over the sight of blood or bodies. He had witnessed the battle in the passage without issue. Yet, this trial, no; this murder, had him queasy. He wanted to say something, to step forward in defence of the striders, but he had already known that Bronwin would have cast his voice aside, followed quickly with the scholar's body shortly thereafter. No, silence had been his best choice, regardless of the knots in his stomach.

He turned into an alleyway and sat in the dirt, his back against a wooden wall, breathing heavily. The nausea faded as he reasoned with himself, and surfaced once more when he thought of Rel, rocking on her knees over the body of her mentor. He had caught a glance from her during the stand-off as if pleading him to say something. But what would he say? It wouldn't have made a difference. Inhaling sharply through his nose, Varden held his breath for a few moments before exhaling slowly, then repeated the process until his nausea had finally faded for good.

What would he do next? He wished to remain in Plainsview, to witness the critical defence of the country's borders. Yet, he was not sure if he would be welcome, or if he would survive to tell the tale. Reaching into his satchel, Varden removed his notebook from inside and opened it to its most recent entry. Perhaps Past-Varden could shed some light on the predicament for him.

He began reading through the Wixen language, letting the words linger in his mind. Nothing stayed with him for nearly long enough as he kept finding his gaze drawn to the bottom edge of the pages. They were soaked, why were they soaked?

Flipping the pages, moving further into the past, Varden found his answer and felt ridiculous for not realizing it sooner. The pages had been this way for days, it had happened whilst he extracted sap from the most recent shadewood tree in the swamp.

"Varden, you fool," he remarked silently to himself. His eyes opened with realization. "Varden, you damnable fool! May the Veil Strider leave you stranded!"

The shadewood tree would, perhaps, shed some light on the situation. Varden reached into his satchel once more and felt the familiar cool, smooth glass of the vial. He pulled it out and looked at the milky sap with eagerness.

He could feel himself beginning to salivate at the thought of drinking it once more. That was odd: he didn't recall a flavour the first time he had consumed the fluid, nor could he recall an after-taste. All he could remember was the hallucination he had experienced: Bronwin, standing against the Thregs in the passage.

Curious, he thought. *Addiction, to the hallucination? Questions for later.*

The scholar opened the vial, placed it to his lips and threw back his head. His vision whirled into that of a small home. A woman toiling away over a hearth, making a soup or a stew. She was adding pepper to it. Her hair flowed golden-yellow, or blonde — it was hard to tell — but her eyes shone a bright blue. Her angular face was grinning as if she had finally achieved something with the dish. There was a loud knock on the door, more of an angry pounding than a knock. The woman's eyes opened wide as the door shook and a voice boomed through the room. He couldn't make it out.

The vision vanished and Varen was back in the alleyway. Again he witnessed a memory: one that was yet to happen, and one that was not his. What was the shadewood tree trying to show him? He would need more sap.

The Wixen jumped to his feet and began to search out Dry Eyes. He needed more sap, and he needed it sooner rather than later. Both instances of his consumption of the shadewood sap, Varden realized, had shown him images, memories, or foretellings of bloody events. Though it was still far too early to draw any conclusions. For all he knew, on the next vial, he would see a couple making love for the first time. After his past visions, this would have been a welcome sight indeed. If he were extraordinarily lucky, maybe he would even see two women together.

A grin played at his lips for thinking so boyishly and with the wrong head. Shaking the right one, he pushed the juvenile thoughts aside and embraced the fact that he would likely see more death in future visions.

#

The Strider's Respite fell to a grim silence as Nef walked over and sat at a vacant table. Deeanne brought him a mug of ale and a small plate of bread, then walked away without saying a word. The strider could feel eyes poking and prodding him from a distance, and as much as he wanted to, Nef wouldn't indulge them by meeting the other patron's gazes; he wouldn't let them see his confliction.

Rel, his friend — and mentor — wished to kill Bronwin, the Pale Bull and Shield of Northwood. A legendary hero to the Valen people and one of the chief military minds in the Sovereign Guard. She didn't simply wish to commit treason, she wished to commit murder. A set of crimes that would have not just a person, but their entire family executed for being related. And she had asked him to be involved; asked him to help her enact revenge for Saffron's death.

Nef mourned the man, but he felt resentment towards Rel for acting so rashly, consigning their mentor to death, and for asking him to be involved in her scheme. Bronwin knew damn well what he could have charged her with. He could have had her and Saffron for treason and had Ashlin and everyone else they loved killed. But no, he chose mercy and tried only Saffron, which only required one life to be taken, as he had no family nearby or people with which he schemed.

It was clear to Nef that Rel had overlooked this mercy, and instead, fixated on the death of her mentor. He couldn't blame her though, not completely, even if he wanted to. He had a decision to make, and he didn't find any option palatable: he could go along with Rel's plan and help her kill Bronwin, mark himself a traitor, commit treason and get killed for his friend's recklessness. He could do nothing, and stay out of it completely, more than likely taking the mantle of Plain's Warden in the future, but at the loss of his closest friend, the guilt that would follow him would last a lifetime.

Nef sipped at his ale, swallowed, then took a bite of his bread. The dryness of the food caused him to pause for a moment: stale. He swallowed hard and took another sip.

Or ... he thought to himself, letting the word linger in his mind. No, he couldn't: that would guarantee Rel's death and that of Ashlin. The same would happen if she acted against Bronwin anyway. He searched his mind for more clarity, letting the chaos of Sun's Peak sort itself out in his mind.

Corduvan, Rel has grown fond of him. He realized. *If Corduvan gets involved in this too, his family will be killed. His little boy ...* Nef took a larger swig of ale and swallowed hard. First thing was first, he would try to talk Rel out of her plan before any more blood could be shed.

Nef reached into his pocket, grabbed a few copper Valens and placed them on the table. He stood to leave, then turned and reached back, returning a single Valen back to his pocket. No way was he paying for stale bread.

Chapter 31

Scout detail: Corduvan couldn't believe it. Bronwin and his pet officer, Algrenon, had assigned him scouting duty at the outer edge of the swamp.

"Keep an eye on the wall," they had told him, "report back, if anything happens."

"Gwendall's Blood," he swore to himself. He wasn't a Plain's Strider, nor a scout, he was a town guard. Sitting, up to his waist in swamp water by the order of a brutish man, was by far one of the low points of his career. He would have preferred to keep an eye on Dry Eyes. Despite all that, he would do his duty and sit in stinking water watching a wall that had been trapped to the loins.

Corduvan wasn't alone, but part of him wished he was, two more Sovereign Guardsmen had joined him. He didn't know one of the fellows, but he knew the other: the Captain of the Anvil's Hammer and all-around pain in the ass, Velamir. The pretty boy made a note of keeping his hair up in a bun to keep it dry.

"Hey," The unknown guardsmen crept up through the water. "What's that?" He pointed through some branches at a silhouette atop the wall. Pacing back and forth, the hooded figure looked to be judging something. The figure walked along, peering over one side, then the other, looking along the length of the wall, then back down either side of it. They shook their head more often than they nodded. Corduvan watched curiously.

"Should we report this?" the soldier asked, not taking his eyes off the silhouette.

"No," Corduvan replied flatly, "They're only inspecting the wall. If they tamper, then we'll report."

"Okay ... who do you think they are?"

"No clue. But they know the wall is rigged, otherwise, they wouldn't be alive right now. They're either very smart or have been keeping an eye on things."

"Or both."

"Or both." Corduvan agreed with a nod.

Suddenly, the scouting detail didn't seem too bad. The arrival of this hooded figure definitely made things more interesting.

"Oh, gross, what was that?!" a boyish voice cried, "Something brushed my knee!"

Corduvan whipped his head around, glaring at Velamir. "Would you keep it down?!" he whispered harshly, "We're supposed to be hidden!"

The mercenary huffed, "Well, I never asked to be here. This murky water is tarnishing my armour.

"Oh, boo hoo." the other man mocked, "Grow up."

"I beg your pardon?" Velamir snapped, rising to his feet. "Do you know who you're talking to?!"

"I'd rather I didn't." The soldier turned to look back towards the wall, puzzled. "They're gone."

"What?" Corduvan too, looked to the wall, peering through branches and leaves. "Where in Gwendall's Blade did they go?"

"No idea."

Velamir crouched down into the muddy waters again. "Where did *who* go?"

"Thank you for finally joining us, kid." The townsman rolled his eyes.

"What do you mean? I've been here the whole time?" The mercenary looked confused.

"Nevermind," Corduvan peered closely at the wall, the figure was gone, but the sound of heavy footfall could be heard, and barely felt through the swampy earth beneath their feet.

#

The wall had been assembled haphazardly. Cullen was shocked it had stood for its inaugural battle against the Thregs. But then again, none of the Thregs had actually made it to the wall. The Highfold had been wandering the top of the structure, looking at the makeshift machinations that were supposed to have rigged it to explode upon any kind of tampering. Though it was crude, Cullen reckoned it would kill off a few Thregs when they got here. Knowing the monstrosities, they would charge at the wall expecting resistance, once they were through, it would blow, cleaving through their first few rows of troops.

Looking at it again, the explosives used would create a large amount of black smoke and likely set fire to much of the local flora. Perhaps it was to be more of a signal flare than a trap? He couldn't know for certain. What he did know, however, was that there was another meteor shower the previous night. Red streaks, arcing from east to west. The Thregs would spring the trap this day.

There had been three men watching Cullen as he paced the defensive wall, he knew this before he had even entered the Valley. Even the common person's arcana can be a warning signal, to those capable of seeing it. They had been distracted, giving Cullen enough time to leap off the outer edge of the wall and into the former battleground. The Highfold marched along the leftover viscera and wondered about what kind of fear the average soldier had felt going up against the Thregs.

He had watched the battle from afar, from partway up the valley walls. Cullen had witnessed the sacrifice of the conscripts, and he had even witnessed the man known as Dry Eyes and his miraculous survival. The bandit had hidden beneath the corpses of his comrades, curled into a ball and wailing. Until he was stepped on and summarily knocked unconscious.

Cullen watched his step as he traversed over a Threg's severed hand. The skin around the wrist had been torn as if a sheet of fabric. The Highfold turned his head up to the sky, inhaled for a short breath and immediately sidestepped a Threg's wild sword. The creature had been watching from the outskirts of the battleground since Cullen had arrived and had done a decent job hiding among the bodies of its comrades.

Another swing, horizontal, and Cullen leapt back avoiding the blow by a hair's width. The moment his feet touched the ground, he launched himself forward, the twisted blade of his crystalline daggers glinting in the sunlight, a faint black smoke twirled within. Thrusting his arms forward, Cullen buried the daggers into the Threg's chest, pulled them out and side-stepped a groping hand. Again, the man plunged his daggers into the side of the creature, pulled them out and leapt back. He landed gracefully in the grass.

Cullen stood, relaxed and calculated as he watched the Threg. The creature ran one hand over the wound in its side and looked up at him growling.

In a blink, and a flash of black smoke Cullen was in the air, daggers poised. He let the momentum of his manoeuvre mixed with gravity and his own strength fuel his strike. The Threg craned its head up to match its foe. As Cullen came through the air he thrust the daggers towards his enemy. One burst through an eye and planted itself deeply into the Threg's skull. The other drove through the mass of black tubules that was a Threg's tongue and lodged itself into the creature's throat.

The Threg fell back as Cullen rode the body down like a winged beast. They landed with a low thud. Cullen removed his daggers, and the blood flowed off the transparent blades as if water off glass. Again, he leapt back as two more swords swung in place of where he had just been standing. More Thregs, they had been circling the prior fight, only moving in when they witnessed the Highfold vanish, then reappear in a puff of black smoke.

Again, the moment Cullen's feet hit the ground, he launched himself forward to his fore-most foe. The creature braced itself, but to no avail. Another puff of smoke and Cullen was gone, only to reappear behind the rear Threg, one dagger planted in the back of its skull, the other sailing through the air to puncture and drive through the neck of the Highfold's final opponent.

The second body hit the ground as Cullen appeared atop the defensive wall, daggers back in their sleeves. At the mouth of the passage, he could see the approach of the Threg army. They were going to breach Valenfaar.

It didn't take long for Cullen to reach them, he moved through the brush quickly and came up behind the man known as Corduvan.

"You boys should head back to town." his voice cut clearly through the silence.

The men jumped and turned as the mercenary captain, Velamir, brandished his blade.

"Who in Gwendall's Name are you?" he asked, moving a lock of hair away from his face.

"Put your weapon away," Cullen said. "It will do you no good."

Velamir took a step forward, pointing the tip of his sword towards the Highfold. A hand appeared on his shoulder and held him back.

"That's Cullen Highfold," Corduvan said, stepping forward. "Was that you on the wall?"

Velamir lowered his blade as Cullen disregarded him. "Yes, that was I. The Threg army is just beyond it. They'll trigger the wall shortly." He looked beyond the structure and pillars of smoke began to reach into the sky. "Go back to Plainsview. Inform Bronwin, he'll know what to do. We've spoken previously."

"Yessir," Corduvan didn't hesitate, waved his men forward and moved back towards the Outlier City.

"Was that really Cullen?" the Highfold could hear the other men asking.

Cullen sat in their place, comfortable, legs crossed as he watched the wall in their stead. It took the Thregs far longer to get to the structure than he had anticipated. Could it be that they were moving cautiously after being driven back the first time? Perhaps. Though Thregs had never shown that much tact in the past. But, and he quickly rebutted himself, they had also never operated in the capacity of an army before, and that was clearly something they were more than capable of doing.

Then, it began to happen. The door in the centre of the wall began to shake and convulse. Slowly, at first. Then faster and with more strength; they were trying to breach it. The sound of wood on wood could also be heard as Thregs began to deploy ladders. Had some not appeared atop the wall, Cullen never would have thought they would use ladders, let alone construct them.

More and more Thregs began to line the structure, peering cautiously into the field before them, for signs of ambush or traps. Thankfully, Bronwin and his men had done a surprisingly good job at trapping the wall; most explosives were placed within the structure, where permitted.

Before long, more than fifty Thregs lined the fortification, and Cullen could only guess as to the hundreds just beyond it, and thousands more further still. The explosives had been placed inside the wall, with several more deposits stored just underneath the ground beyond, with one or two bodies covering the disturbed topsoil. The explosives wouldn't provide the biggest or deadliest bang, but it would be enough to wound, disturb, and possibly kill a few Thregs.

The Highfold began to wonder if the Thregs had some form of morale. They ran after one of their best warriors was bested. But he doubted it. They may have been more sophisticated than anyone had given them credit for, but they were still savages. The few he had fought, felt merciless and almost careless. They didn't care if they were injured, they only wanted to succeed.

Regardless, the morale-deprivation tactic of hidden explosives was worth the effort, at the very least for the sake of research.

Thregs began to climb down the wall, taking stairs, handholds, and some just jumping to the ground below. One of the beasts must have hit one of Bronwin's triggers. A small string, that if pulled, would cause a flint to spark along some stone, placed next to oil-soaked rags, igniting the explosive and fat-filled barrels. The deadly cascade began from the northern side of the wall, working its way south. Explosives detonated in a fiery cacophony. Thregs were scattered to each of the cardinal directions, and everywhere in between. Barrels of fat burst amidst the explosions splashing fire and death outwards. The wall continued to detonate, as did the ground beyond it.

Thregs roared from the passage as fire engulfed their allies. The sound and shock waves shook the vegetation surrounding Cullen. Leaves were blasted back, branches were torn from trees and smouldering viscera littered the ground. The final explosion rocked the very earth Cullen crouched upon as fire and smoke belched into the sky.

The defensive wall of the passage was no more. Smouldering remains of bodies and wood were all that remained. The barrels that had been filled with fat and grease coated the passage with a deadly fire, cutting off the Thregs from the remainder of Valenfaar for a time. The smoke curling into the air would provide Plainsview all the proof they needed that their trap had been sprung, and even though they had bought themselves more time, they still didn't have much left before death knocked at their door.

Cullen rose from his crouch, adjusted his mask and disappeared.

#

Rel turned to look east, towards the Endless Plains, in an attempt to see what had captivated the town's gaze.

No, she thought, *It's too soon. They weren't supposed to have gotten to the wall for another two days.* Or so she had hoped.

Smoke billowed out on the horizon. Not close, but closer than she would have liked. If they were lucky, the grease fires would buy them a couple of days time to finish preparations. The Plain's Warden immediately moved to the longhouse to summon her striders. People crowded in the town square, some murmured, others screamed and shuddered whilst children looked on in a mixture of bewilderment and worry. Rel pushed her way through.

Soldiers rushed towards the eastern wall of Plainsview, to aid in the fortifications. The striders, however, had other plans that would have them on the other side of the wall. It was an old defensive strategy that Saffron and Alistair had come up with long ago. Every strider knew of it. But due to the nature of the swamp beyond Plainsview, they needed to finalize it.

It hadn't taken long for Rel to reach the rear courtyard of the longhouse, and it hadn't taken very long for all of the striders, or what was left of them, to make it there too.

The Plain's Warden stood atop a wooden crate and let her voice carry to the dwindled number of men and women she had left under her command.

"Plain's Striders!" she called, "Anvil's Hammer!" The mercenary band had been summoned at the request of Bronwin, to aid them. "The Thregs are upon our doorstep! This day they have sprung our trap at the very site where we pushed them back nearly a fortnight ago. And they wish to move against our homes, our friends and our families."

She paused, to make sure her words were understood. She caught Nef's gaze from the small crowd and nodded to him. He didn't return the gesture. Averting her gaze, Rel continued her speech.

"They threaten each and every one of us, those we love, and even the very ale we drink!" Several men in the crowd raised their fists, with a few of the women. "We wish to have lovers to fuck after a hard day's work, do we not!?"

Cheering.

"We wish to wash the blood from our souls away with tankards of ale, do we not?!"

More cheers.

"We wish to sleep in our beds, play with our children and watch them grow old, do we not?!"

A chorus of strength bellowed through the courtyard.

Rel smiled at the striders, and even at the Anvil's Hammer. "If we are to fuck, drink, and raise our children, then we need to strike brutally against an even more brutal enemy. The Thregs wish to take away our wants, no, our rights, to fuck, drink, and grow old. Well, what is it we wish to do to them?" What came forth was an eruption of unintelligible words; different answers varying from killing, slaughtering, maiming, beheading, and the like.

"Good!" Rel roared as the crowd quieted, "We shall do all of those things, but first, we need to make sure we are prepared, so they cannot do the same to us." She paused, waiting for the echo of her voice to subside. "Between us and our enemies lies a swamp, as you all know. Each and every one of us have come to know those muddy waters intimately as we have traversed them daily while fulfilling our duty to our country!" She looked around the crowd. "Starting immediately we are to move into the swamp, once again, in preparation for an ambush. We are all familiar with the plan in which I speak, but just in case some of you have taken a blow to the head," she said with a grin. "Allow me to refresh your memory."

Looking again at the faces of her striders, Rel could see through the new vigour that they were tired, exhausted even. Many of them still ached from the battle at the wall, and even more were still bruised. They weren't even close to being able to fight at full capacity. But they didn't have much choice. Anvil's Hammer looked a little worse for wear but still seemed capable, despite their captain's ridiculous sense of style.

Everyone grew silent, there were a couple of grins from Rel's comment, but the reality of the situation settled throughout the crowd. They were going to be standing toe-to-toe with the Threg again. The monstrosities that tore their friends and family from life and limb would be in front of them, ready to repeat the process with even more ferocity than they had before.

The Plain's Warden cleared her throat and then laid out the plan for everyone. It was an old plan, meant to demoralize and create disorder among an invading enemy party. The striders were to move into the swamp the day prior to the Thregs' assumed advance and hide in the trees. It was a simple ambush. When the Thregs approached and were stationed squarely in the centre of the swamp, striders were to rain arrows onto them. When they ran out of arrows, detachments of Sovereign Guard would enter the area and engage the threat. The striders, at this point, would move from the safety of the trees and onto the rear of the battlefield to cut off any retreat from the enemy and encircle them. As the striders were already surrounding the Thregs, the majority of them would find getting to the rear an easy task, with a small portion joining in the fray with the Sovereign Guard towards the front of the enemy formation.

"Any questions?" Rel asked, eyes studying the group for any sign of uncertainty.

Velamir moved a lock of hair from his eyes, then locked eyes with the Plain's Warden. "Who, from the Guard, will be aiding the Anvil's Hammer?"

"You will be joined by a group of fifty soldiers led by our own Corduvan. I have already relayed the plan to him, and Bronwin has assembled the rest of the men."

"Fifty men?" Velamir inquired, "We alone lost twenty in the last engagement, which leaves the Hammer at thirty men. You have 125 striders here, at best. That puts us at just over 200 fighters. How are we supposed to stop the army? We'll be slaughtered."

Rel looked to Velamir with a gaze of appreciation and respect. It was good to see he, at least, pretended to care about the country and its troops, not just himself.

"We are not to be engaging the entire army," she said. "We are to prevent their scouting parties from reporting back to their main force. We already know they sent small groupings ahead of their army. They've been doing it since the beginning of this invasion; they want to avoid as much loss of life as possible."

Velamir looked relieved, but also incredulous. "You can't be serious? Thregs concerned with loss of life? Those brutes aren't capable of such compassion."

"Compassion? No," Rel shook her head. "They seek to conquer, and they can't do that without soldiers. I believe they care less about losing life and more about losing conquest." She paused again, then continued her thought. "If we kill their scouting parties, they lose life that could contribute to conquest, and without the information those scouts could provide, they'll need to either send out more scouts to find out what happened or commit to a blind advance. Either way, it puts us into a better position than before, no matter how slight."

Velamir nodded. "The Anvil's Hammer is yours to command, Plain's

Warden."

#

Corduvan had finished relaying the plan to his troops for the ambush and began to make his way back to the town gate to help with further fortifications. He needed rest, but he wanted his wife and Brinn to have even a small chance of coming back to Plainsview in the future. He couldn't stop working, there were too many jobs to be done.

Holding a wooden spike at the top of the wall, the townsman watched as a soldier hammered it into place with repeated whacks from a mallet. They locked eyes and Corduvan could see the fear and hesitation in the man's eyes. As if he were saying: "This isn't going to be enough, is it?"

Corduvan nodded reassuringly to the man, not letting him know that his real reply would have been: "It'll have to be."

A light tap on his shoulder and Corduvan turned around and saw Rel standing behind him.

"Plain's Warden! A pleasure to see you, what can I -"

Rel cut him off. "Corduvan, please. Call me Rel."

She looked tired, *very* tired.

"Alright," He looked back at the soldier, who was tying in the spike with some rope. The man gave Corduvan a nod.

Standing now, the townsman turned to face the Plain's Warden. "Alright," he said. "What can I do for you, Rel?"

"We can't talk here," she said with haste. "Come with me."

It took longer than Corduvan would have thought to arrive in Rel's office at the longhouse. But, the twists and turns, and double backs she had taken to get there nearly tripled the length of their journey. She had said it was to keep any of Bronwin's lackeys from following them or to make their job as hard as possible. Corduvan hadn't seen anybody following them, but alas, she did have far better senses for those things than he did, they were — in part — one of the many reasons she was Plain's Warden.

Rel paced her office floor and offered Corduvan a seat. He took it, afraid he might not rise from the chair again due to fatigue.

"Can I trust you, Corduvan?"

He was slightly startled at this question. "Yes, of course, Rel. You've shown me great kindness and proven yourself to be a great leader with the betterment of Valenfaar in your heart. You can trust me."

Rel chuckled. "You speak kind words. But you do not yet know what I wish to entrust to you yet, do you?"

"No ma'am. I do not."

There was a deep and slow inhale behind him. Corduvan turned to see Rel trembling. She cleared her throat, then spoke. "When the Thregs arrive at Plainsview. I plan to kill Bronwin during battle."

Silence didn't just fall upon the room, it seemed to have invaded it. Nothing could have changed that. Even a screaming child would have fallen mute in the sudden cold. Corduvan's skin bristled with anxiety. He had just said she could trust him unconditionally, and then she tells him that she wishes to kill the Shield of Northwood. It was insane.

One word breached the silence, a juvenile word, but a word nonetheless: "Why?"

What Rel said next came pouring out of her like water out of a bucket. "He is a reckless, thoughtless brute with no care for human life or those he claims to defend. His end goals are victory over the enemy, no matter the cost of lives. He throws scores of good men and women at a problem until he overwhelms them with blood and bodies. He claims to protect Valenfaar, but he sacrifices those he vouches to save at every opportunity. How can we claim to be saving the country when a large portion of our people are all lying dead on the ground? They may be soldiers, but they are also farmers and fishermen, hunters, fathers, and mothers. What happens when no one is left to teach others how to farm, how to fish, and how to hunt when there is no one left to father a child or give birth to one? The country will crumble!" She stopped to breathe.

Corduvan stood, turned to her and placed a hand on her shoulder. "Rel, you can't be-"

"Serious?" She cut him off. "Of course I'm serious. You saw how many men and women he threw at the Thregs in our first engagement. Sure, we won. But the cost was far too great. And that was only a portion of the Threg's army. How many more will he throw at their primary force before they are driven back?"

"Too many." Corduvan found himself agreeing.

"Alistair is also pulling as many forces as he can to the west, and we have no idea why. We're stuck with limited numbers, a man who will sacrifice most, if not all, of those numbers, and an invading army that is proving smarter than we ever gave them credit for. Under the guidance of Bronwin, we will fail and Valenfaar will fall to the Thregs. He needs to die so that someone else can take over."

"Who? You?"

"No. I'll be executed for treason. I'll take Ashlin and vanish until it is safe to return." She shook her head. "We'll try to put Nef in charge, he's next-in-line for Plain's Warden."

Corduvan's tired mind was now more awake than it had been in days, working through all the information quickly. "Shouldn't someone of the Sovereign Guard take charge?"

Rel's head snapped up and locked eyes with him. "No one in the Sovereign Guard is of high enough rank to take command over such an important defensive operation. Leadership would fall to the next highest-ranking official, the Plain's Warden; until such a time Alistair can appoint and send somebody new to take over."

He nodded and chewed his upper lip in thought. "If I agree to this. *If* I do not wish to be executed, nor do I wish to vanish."

"You won't have to. You'll be seen as innocent. I'll be the one to drive the blade, all I need you to do is keep him distracted when I get closer. Call out to him units that need help, point out Thregs that might pose a threat. Anything will do, do your job a little too well, and you'll be more than okay."

Corduvan couldn't believe it. "I don't know, Rel. I can't help you leave, you know that."

"I do."

"Does Nef know about this already?"

Rel nodded. "Yes, he does. Though I haven't told him that it would be him taking over the operation. He'll do great as Plain's Warden, but he'll need to be forced into the position."

#

The next day Nef had received word that it was time for them to move into the swamp and get ready to lay their ambush. Trudging through the mud he made it beside Rel. He couldn't believe she wanted to kill Bronwin, commit treason and put the entirety of Valenfaar at risk. The Pale Bull's methods could be brutal, harsh even, but there was no denying that they provided results. He had yet to lose a battle against the Thregs. Loss of life was great, but the lives saved were greater. Alistair had placed him there for a reason, and Nef was not a person to doubt a smart man's reasoning. Rel, however, was too stubborn and too steadfast in her beliefs to accept that maybe, just maybe, an idea she didn't like was the best possible course of action.

"Rel," he finally said between sloshing steps. "You can't kill Bronwin. It's insane. He's our best chance at defending Valenfaar. You don't have to like that, but it's the truth. He wouldn't be here if Alistair, Daylen, and Gwendall didn't have a plan." He was calm and collected. He knew Rel wouldn't give him a second glance if he spoke out of temper.

"Leave the gods out of this," Rel said. "You, nor I, have any proof that they have a plan here. For all we know, it could have been Gwendall himself sending the Thregs after us with those damned star showers. You're right, Alistair did put him here for a reason. But I think that reasoning, while logical, is flawed. There are people better suited for the task."

"And who might that be, Rel? You?"

"No. Not me, Nef."

"Then who?"

"That remains to be seen, I think. All in due time my friend." The Plain's Warden moved forward at a faster pace, the conversation was over.

Nef cursed under his breath and continued to trudge through the muddy waters. The air was thick and filled with the dank smell of mud and wet wood. Soon, he imagined, it would be filled with the scents of battle. His skin prickled at the thought of it.

Mosquitoes swarmed around him, he batted and swatted at them as much as he could. It helped little. He began to sweat. It was warm in the swamp, and humid, and trudging through the waters made the trek harder than usual. Normally, they'd have taken the pathway through the swamp, but Rel didn't want to leave any footprints. So they were going through knee-deep waters towards the ambush point.

Velamir and his men had stopped some distance back, by a few patches of black spindly plants. That was where they would wait.

It wouldn't be far now: striders were already climbing into trees and getting into position. Feet scrambled on bark and hands clasped at branches. Sticks and twigs fell to the water with quiet splashes. Nef and Rel made their way to what would be considered the rear of the ambush zone and began to climb. Something caught Nef's attention out of the corner of his eye.

"Hey Rel, was that here last time we came through?" He released one hand from the tree and pointed at a shadewood tree off to their right. It looked like an ash tree, but with white leaves and a black trunk.

Chapter 32

Night had come and gone in the swamp quickly. It was difficult to find a chance to sleep, or even nap. But the following day seemed to scream their way like an angry spraven. Rel tried to imagine how Velamir and his men felt trying to sleep on the ground. Sleeping in knee-deep swamp water seemed to be a drowning hazard. But she had faith they would be fine.

The sun reached into the sky and filtered light in through the treetops. There were no birds chirping at the sun, no frogs croaking in the waters, nothing but an eerie silence. The sound of mismatched marching came from the direction of the old wall: the Thregs. Rel swapped an affirming look with Nef as they pressed themselves into the trees. Feet planted on branches. A quick look around confirmed that the other striders were following suit. In mere moments, over 100 striders were invisible to anything standing on the swamp floor.

Moments crept by like days as the marching grew louder and louder. Eventually, the grunting breaths of Thregs broke the placid silence, like sand against a window. They plodded their way along the road in a jumbled formation. They peered through the swamp, up into the trees and down into the water. They moved further and further, closer to the heart of the ambush.

With every step, Rel's heart quickened, she had her bow drawn and an arrow nocked, ready to fly. Rel and Nef both emerged from their positions at the same instant and loosed their arrows. Both shots landed in the backs of their targets, causing the Thregs to growl and snap viciously at the space around them.

More arrows flew, sailing out from the trees like mosquitoes, poking and prodding at the thick skins of the Thregs. Then a body fell: a strider. Then another, and another. They began to fall like autumn leaves.

Rel watched in stunned horror as the barks of some trees began to twist and writhe. Turning from their usual browns and greys, into the dark green of the Thregs. The bark at her side began to warp, revealing an eye and flared vertical nostrils. The Threg reached out for her, long fingers trying to grasp her throat. Rel screamed and drove the arrow she held into the creature's mouth. The black spindles of its tongue lashed out in defiance. Quickly, the Plain's Warden drew her long knife and brought the tip up and into the creature's chin. Its body careened to the murky waters below, where it joined the Plain's Striders.

She looked to Nef, and to her relief, found him safe. There hadn't been a Threg waiting for him. Velamir's men, and Corduvans, had already run into the battle and were clashing blades with the invaders. Behind them, where they had lain sleeping most of the night, the black plants that sprouted from the water began to move. They breached the surface and continued to extend, revealing their roots to be the vile heads of the enemy: they had been waiting for them the whole night.

"Corduvan!" Rel cried, "Velamir! Behind you!"

Corduvan couldn't hear her, he continued to lash out with his weapon just the same. Velamir had heard her words and turned, ordering the Anvil's Hammer to focus on guarding their rear.

"Hammer! To our rear, we've been flanked! *Move!*" his last order thundered through the Sovereign lines.

The ambush had backfired; what few striders didn't have Thregs in the trees with them were watching in horror as the monstrosities jumped from one branch to the next, working their way closer. They fired arrows and clashed blades in vain attempts of survival. One by one, the striders were brought down to their final number.

Rel turned as the branch she stood on shook, threatening her balance. A Threg was there, walking carefully towards her. The Plain's Warden roared and launched herself at the beast. Tossing her bow aside she pulled out blades and slammed them into the horror's chest.

#

Nef watched in astonishment as Rel ran her blades through her foe. He also tossed aside his bow before climbing down. The waters began to change from a muddy swirl, into a red-brown mix of gore. Running over to Rel he found she was okay. Shaken up, but otherwise fine.

"Rel, we need to fall back. We've lost."

The Plain's Warden stood straighter. "I know. Find Corduvan and Velamir, we fall back to Plainsview." She looked at him, fury dancing like lightning in her eyes. "Now! I'll meet you there!"

She went to run, but Nef reached out and grabbed her shoulder. "Where are you going?!"

"Someone needs to tell Bronwin what has happened. Do you see anyone else here capable of doing it? It's either you or I, Nef. The rest are dead."

The reality of that slammed into him like a mace; arrows weren't falling from the trees. Striders were in the water, floating morbidly along the battlefield. His stomach twisted. Was he really one of the last Plain's Striders?

Nef found his voice. "Fine, you go. I'll get the others out of here."

Rel hadn't said a word, she turned and began to weave through the carnage.

Nef also took off without a word, blades at the ready. He broke away to his right and began to snake between soldiers and Thregs alike, looking for the captains. He slashed at legs and the backs, forcing the enemy to kneel or turn, giving the Sovereign soldiers the opportunities they needed to fell their foes. The battle was going poorly: their men were surrounded, facing almost double the number they had planned, and without the aid of the Plain's Striders.

A Threg exposed its leg to Nef as he passed. He lashed out with his sword and watched the Threg drop to its knee as a blade breached its skull. Up ahead, Nef saw Corduvan, twirling around his weapon and lashing it out at the soft spots on his foes. The new Plain's Master watched as the small dagger-like blade careened through the air and landed in the eye of the enemy. The monster convulsed, growled and then collapsed.

Nef took his chance: sheathing his long knife, he reached out and grabbed Corduvan by the shoulder. "Corduvan! We retreat, now!" he hadn't meant to yell, but the clash of blades and smashing of shields around him didn't give Nef any alternative.

Corduvan appeared not to see him, nor hear him. The Plain's Master shook him hard. "Corduvan! The battle is lost, pull back!"

The townsman shook himself awake, locked eyes with Nef and gave a slow nod. "Fall back!" he cried, his senses returning, "Fall back to Plainsview! To Plainsview!"

Men and women looked around, confused, then understood. Several were cut down in those briefest of moments, but the rest began to work back towards the Anvil's Hammer and Velamir.

Nef turned again and began to head that way himself. Looking for the mercenary captain, he continued his hit-and-run tactics. Finally, in a small clearing ahead, Velamir fought and cut at his foes. The normally shiny armour was stained red and brown, his long locks of hair matted, drenched in sweat, mud and blood, both human and Threg. He was a mess, but his eyes blazed with fury as he cut away at the thick skin of his attackers. One movement after the other, the blade careened and twisted as if it were a bird in flight. Velamir swatted with the flat of his blade and cleaved with its edge.

As the Plain's Master approached he watched as the mercenary deflected a Threg blade off his shield, and followed up with a slash of his own. He cut deep into the Threg's chest but did not kill, his blade stuck in the hide. Velamir pulled his other arm back and lashed out with a punch from the brim of his shield. It landed with a low thud on the enemy's abdomen, sending it back and freeing the blade. The captain pulled his weapon back again, and with surprising accuracy planted it in the cut he had made. It did not stick, he pulled back again and drove the tip through the Threg's chest, killing it.

Velamir ripped his blade out of the corpse then looked to Nef and gave him an understanding nod. "Fall back!" he cried out, "Fall back to Plainsview! Fall back!"

The men and women of the Anvil's Hammer brought their shields together and began to push back against the Thregs, once the Sovereign Guard had joined their line, they stabbed and fought to create an opening. But it wasn't working.

"Gwendall guide my blade," Nef muttered as he sheathed both his weapons and ran towards the shield wall. His feet were swift, his movement light and his body agile. The Plain's Master spotted the unknowing soldier who would aid him in his gambit. In a quick one-two step, Nef planted his first foot on their lower back and his second on her shoulder. He launched himself over the Threg line.

He turned with a snarl and drew his blades. Once more he brought the edges of his long knife and shortsword across the legs of his foes, causing them to drop. A shield bashed the Threg's face in and it fell back, stunned. Nef reached out with his weapons and slashed in a quick three-cut combo at another's spine. It convulsed, turned and then fell from a blade within the shield wall. A third perished, then a fourth, and a fifth. The opening was being created, one body at a time.

The Plain's Master had been spotted: two Thregs broke away from their dead, opening the gap further, and moved towards him. Much to his surprise, Nef was smiling and moving *towards* his enemies. The first Threg swung a mallet and missed as the strider twisted out of the way and drove the tip of his sword into the monster's arm. He pulled it out and cut at the opening. The arm fell away as Nef's long knife screamed upward into the Threg's chest.

The second took a swing with its axe. Nef moved in a circle, placing the first Threg between himself and the other, the axe landed solidly in his puppet's back. He continued in a circular motion removing his long knife from the corpse. Two slashes to the chest, and three more to the legs brought it down. Nef never stopped his circle and arrived behind Threg number two. He grinned widely as he shoved the tips of his blades into the creature's spine. It fell to the ground, lifeless.

The gap was large enough now that soldiers began to make their escape towards Plainsview. Velamir and Corduvan came running out, waving for their soldiers to follow.

Nef slowly walked away from the carnage, letting the escaped troops flood past him, he would wait until the final soldiers had made it out of the ambush, then follow from behind. Thankfully it hadn't taken long. Looking over his shoulder, the Plain's Master watched as the last few soldiers were struck down, blades in their backs. He picked his pace up to a jog and followed along with the rest, the Thregs staring after them.

#

Atop the Valley Wall, Bronwin watched as a stream of Sovereign Guard stumbled and limped their way towards Plainsview. The town opened its gate to them, offering them the safety of civilization for them to lick their wounds. Soldier after soldier came through as Rel shook her head next to him.

"Your striders ate it big, eh?" he grumbled.

"It was a trap. They knew we were coming and what we were doing ..." the warden trailed off. "They killed all of us ... except ..." Rel's eyes snapped up in relief to find Nef walking his way towards Plainsview, a soldier under his arm.

"Except you and your little friend, it would seem." Bronwin wouldn't admit it to Rel, but he knew the loss of the Plain's Striders would be a problem. Though they weren't Sovereign Guard, they had proven themselves useful in a fight and would have been a boon in the days to come.

A thick silence fell between the two of them. The realization set into both their minds. Though Bronwin would wager the reality settling in his mind was far more grounded than the one settling within his counterparts. The loss of the Plain's Striders gave rise to more than one issue. The immediate problem would be the loss of support for the Sovereign Guard in defending Plainsview. They were good shock troops: great at causing chaos in enemy lines and opening ways for the more armoured troops to clear the field.

The long-term problem, however, left Valenfaar without the external scouts it needed to keep watch over the Endless Plains and the convoys that would come through. Raiding would increase and loss of trade with Ajwix would damage the country in ways that were beyond his problem. But this was his campaign, the fault would ultimately fall on him and Rel. Could he shift more of the blame to Rel? Maybe. But at the moment, he wasn't sure how he could push that agenda. How he could get her out of his way? Eventually, he would have what he needed.

Soldiers limped in, beaten and bloody. Looks of pain adorned their faces as if they were ill-gotten heirlooms. Men and women were weeping as the gate's door closed, sealing off the passage from Plainsview. Bronwin and Rel traversed the wall with steady and slow footfalls. He noticed that the warden's steps were heavy. She was hunched over, like someone who had carried hay bales every day for the past moon. If she didn't find a way to recoup herself soon, his problem of dealing with her might sort itself out on the battlefield: she would be cut down easier than he would care to admit.

Velamir approached, the soft soil padding his feet. "We took heavy casualties, sir." The mercenary glanced at Rel briefly, then looked away. "They were waiting for us, hiding in the trees and the water. It was a massacre." He paused, lost in thought. "It was a *fake* scouting party," he added.

Velamir looked back to Rel, exhausted anger in his eyes. "How did they know we'd be there?!" he bellowed, "No one was supposed to know of that plan but your striders, and us! Who sold us out?!"

The Plain's Warden stood, her skin caked with cracked mud. She showed no emotion. "No one ... not a single person has left town unaccounted for ..." she trailed off, pondering something, then brought her attention back to the conversation. "No one could have told the Thregs our plan. The town has been under tight guard for a long time. Since before you got here Velamir. I'm not sure what-"

"Plain's Warden!" a voice called.

There was a second voice from the wall. "Ready your bows!"

"We think you might want to see this." the first voice called again. His tone worried.

Bronwin looked at Rel as she let out a burdened sigh. She took in a deep breath, raised her shoulders and fixed her posture, then began the ascent up the wall. Bronwin was close behind. If whatever this was concerned her, it concerned him.

Rel had cleared the final steps more than a few moments before Bronwin had. He was in no rush to get back to the top, his armour was beginning to feel heavier with every step.

It didn't take much longer, but Bronwin passed the final step with a heavy thud and looked towards where Rel had been standing. She leaned on the wooden battlement of the wall, shock and awe emblazoned on her face. Her jaw hung ajar, and her eyes looked to bulge from her skull. Her skin, normally so full of colour, looked pale and grey. She trembled and a word fell off her lips, though Bronwin couldn't make out what that word might have been, it seemed deeply personal.

He stood beside her, keeping his posture professional. What he saw, he would admit, surprised him, and he was rarely surprised. There was no way the Thregs could have surprised him the way they just had. The number of times he had fought them in battle had shown them to be tribal savages. What stood before him showed they had some logistical capacity, some form of reasoning and mercy. No, not mercy. Upon another look, he realized that nothing merciful had happened to the person standing before them in the passage. Mercy would have been death.

Chapter 33

Rel tried to push the words — the name — out of her mouth. But couldn't find the strength. Her throat had gone dry when Kol had been released from the grip of a Threg and pushed towards the gate. The boy, her friend, stood there wavering, staring ahead at the ground in front of him. Terror haunted his gaze. He had seen what happened in the swamp, the bodies of his fellow striders floating in the water. Even from here, she could see that his hair was patchy and growing in clumps, his skin yellowed and face gaunt. He looked skinny, his strider's uniform — what was left of it — hung off him as if it were a grain sack.

She summoned an ounce of strength. "Open the gate," she ordered coolly and through cracked lips.

"No," Bronwin's order superseded her own. "It could be a trap. They could be waiting in the swamp for us to open the gate. Send a squad into the passage, just to the tree line, then we'll retrieve the strider."

Rel felt anger rise in her. But, for once, she couldn't disagree with his assessment. If the Thregs were smart enough to take a prisoner ... a realization erupted: the Thregs knew of the strider's plan in the swamp. The only way they could have known that was if a strider had told them. Rel looked back to Kol with pained eyes threatening tears.

What did they do to you, sweet Kol? What did they do to you, for you to sacrifice so many lives?

Below her, with a creak and a shudder, the gate within the wall opened and a squad of Sovereign Guard left its safety while the doors closed behind them. Weapons drawn, they moved slowly towards the haggard strider kneeling in the passage.

The soldiers approached, then passed Kol without a second glance, their eyes locked on the treeline before them, keeping watch for any disturbance that might alert them to a Threg.

"How interesting ..." a soft voice came from beside her.

Rel flinched. "Varden, you startled me."

"A pleasure as always, Plain's Warden. My apologies, I didn't mean to startle you." The Wixen never turned to look at her, he kept his gaze transfixed on the strider below. "I believe I know the source of your information leak,

Rel."

"Yes," she agreed, biting back tears. "I wish it were not true. By Gwendall's Blade, I wish it so."

"Making a wish over a dead man's sword will not change the truth, Plain's Warden. Only sufficient, believable lies can do that." Varden paused. "I do wonder if he will tell lies when he is dragged through those doors."

Shaking her head, Rel defended her Left Hand. "He won't. He'll be honest."

"And you can say this with certainty?" Varden pressed. "He's been gone for fifteen days. In the hands of the Thregs. There has never been a Threg prisoner documented in both of our countries' histories. We never thought they were smart enough to have basic tactics. Yet today, they show us otherwise. They keep prisoners, they question and torture them. The latter part of that is an assumption, yes, but looking at your boy-"

"Man." Rel corrected through clenched teeth.

"My apologies, looking at your man down there, we can say it's a rather safe assumption, can we not?"

The Plain's Warden nodded her head reluctantly.

"They've also shown us they know how to use information to plan devastating ambushes prior to their hostile's arrival. Though I will not mention that any further for the time, I imagine it has taken quite a toll on you."

"Thank you," Rel said, her voice cracking with fatigue and anger, she cleared her throat. "What are you getting at?"

"What I'm 'getting at', Rel. Is that to us, what we thought we knew about the Thregs, is all wrong. We are, in essence, dealing with a completely new foe. One we don't know. You say Kol will tell the truth, but that is based on your knowledge of him prior to being captive for more than a fortnight. While your hope is admirable, I can't help but wonder how fifteen days as a Threg prisoner could change a b-" he caught himself. "How that could change a man. He might not be able to speak of his own volition anymore."

"Are you saying they took his tongue?" Rel looked to the scholar.

"Yes and no." Varden's eyes searched the tree line. "They could have taken his tongue. Absolutely, that is a possibility. But the thing I'm trying to infer, Rel," He turned to look at her, sympathy in his calculating eyes. "Is that he could be broken mentally, not physically. Unable to weave truths because he might not know them from lies. For all we know, we could get him behind these walls and he will babble like a madman. He could tell truths, he could tell lies — whether intentional or not — or he could babble."

They both looked back to Kol and watched as two soldiers picked him off the ground. The strider's head hung low, his chin almost touching his chest. Legs dangled behind him as he was dragged through the grass. Several soldiers continued to search along the tree line for signs of the enemy. But they had found nothing and would continue to find nothing, no matter how long they searched.

"He'll tell us the truth," Rel said finally. Feeling her own certainty reinvigorate her.

Varden chuckled. "You know, Rel. Despite everything I just said: I'm inclined to agree with you." The scholar grinned thinly. "Call me an optimist if you will."

Rel turned, travelling back to the soil below. Her footsteps pounded rhythmically as she moved. Step after step she descended, breath quickening. She loved Kol like a little brother, or perhaps even a son. She hadn't watched him grow up, but she had watched him mature, speak for hours about Steena, and even gave him advice on how to approach her. As Rel descended another step she looked up, and perhaps by chance or perhaps by fate, Steena was standing there looking at the open gate with tears streaming down her face.

The Plain's Warden took a deep breath as she landed on solid ground. She found Steena's eyes and gave a respectful nod, sending the message: "Everything will be alright. I need to talk to him first though. I'm sorry."

Steena returned the nod telling the Plain's Warden that she understood. Rel flashed a sympathetic and thankful grin. The poor girl must have been going through so much.

Kol was finally brought through the gate. The two guards carrying him stood there as the door closed again, not sure where to take him. Bronwin motioned something just outside of Rel's field of vision, and the men put him down in the dirt. He collapsed onto his knees and sat there, back arched, legs curled beneath him, head hanging low.

Rel looked at Bronwin, he gave her a nod. She was thankful for that and would make sure to let him know after she had spoken to Kol. She needed to be brief though, the boy clearly needed rest and medical attention.

Rel could feel her heart pounding in her throat as she approached. He had been missing for so long, and they weren't able to send a single man or woman after him. She was ridden with guilt, happiness, and excitement. It was Kol, it was really him, he had finally come back. The Thregs had released him. But why?

The Plain's Warden pushed back an intrusive thought. No, now was not the time. Questioning could wait, right now, he needed help. Finally, she was looking down at her Left Hand, a caring grin on her face as she dropped down to her knees with him. He was crying. Tears raced down his cheeks, mixing with the dirt and blood and whatever else that clung to his skin. The smell was foul, worse than foul, but Rel didn't care, he was here and he was alive.

She cleared her throat. "Kol," she finally said. "Kol, it's me, Rel. I'm here, you're finally safe."

He began to heave as he collapsed forward, resting his head against her breast. He sobbed and bawled into her uniform, staining it dark with tears. She said nothing as she held him and stroked what was left of his filthy hair. Many guardsmen had gathered around at a respectable distance, Varden was with them, his conscript guard too. Bronwin stood closer, off to Rel's right, watching them for anything out of the ordinary.

The Pale Bull probably didn't know it, but Rel had already had a quick inspection of her friend on the way over. No weapons, no unseemly bulges in his clothes. If he was hiding a weapon he would have a hard time getting to it. She doubted this would be an issue. The Thregs were more sophisticated than any of them had thought, but even still, the Plain's Warden doubted they were capable of brainwashing.

Rel let him cry for as long as he needed to. He cried, and he sobbed, and she could feel her skin beginning to moisten under her tunic from the tears. He began to pull away and started to snort, trying to clear his nose so he could breathe. She placed her hands on his shoulders and gently pushed him back onto his knees.

Once Kol had sat back he slowly brought his gaze up to meet his mentor. Looking into the young man's eyes was difficult. Kol wasn't the man staring back at her that day. He was someone different. He was Kol only in name and uniform. His eyes were sunken and hollow, cold and dead. Both were yellowed and bloodshot, one with burst blood vessels, drowning out the whites of one eye in a wash of red. His small nose was bent like a tree branch in three places, and swollen to more than twice its former size.

He tried to speak but his lips split and began to bleed, the corners of his mouth had been scarred up to his cheeks. The Thregs had cut at his mouth. These scars began to open and bleed as he struggled to find his words.

"Kol. No-" Rel tried to stop him. "Whatever it is can wait, let's get you some rest."

"No." he croaked, a fresh stream of tears rolling down his cheeks. "Rel, I-" he broke off and began to bawl again. But not for long, he regained what composure he could, breathing in sharply through his nose, past all the snot.

"I told them."

Rel recoiled. "What did you tell them?" Her eyes widened as the intrusive thought tried again to invade her mind. "What did you tell them, Kol?" she kept her voice calm and measured.

He cleared his throat. "I told them about the swamp. About the plan."

Rel's eyes opened wide. It was true, he told the Thregs of the ambush, every strider knew of the plan, Kol included: it was part of their training. Tunnel vision fixed itself on her Left Hand's wounded and misshapen face, her hands reaching out for his cheeks. "Kol, we'll talk about this all-"

Before her hands could clasp his skin, Rel watched in astonishment as the shape of Kol's face and head began to warp and morph before her eyes. His face melted and began to shift to a reddening pulpy mess. Kol began to fall as he underwent this transformation. A chunk of metal began to protrude from his face: the head of a flanged mace.

Bronwin's weapon came through hard, fast and brutal, it crushed Kol's skull in one powerful swing. The body fell to the ground dead, unrecognizable. The crowd that had gathered around gasped, Varden staggered back in shock and horrified surprise. Rel froze, eyes wide and glazed over, her mouth trembling open, her hands still reaching out for her friend's cheeks. Her throat was dry, she couldn't speak, couldn't scream or shriek, even though she wanted to. Her body felt a strange rush of both exhaustion and adrenaline. She tingled, burned, chilled, and numbed simultaneously.

"Treason." Bronwin finally said. "Punishable by death. The boy admitted it-" The Pale Bull turned to the crowd. "You all heard it! The Plain's Strider committed treason! By Valen Military Law, treason is punishable by death!"

As Rel watched Kol's blood begin to soak into the soil, she found her voice. It came out hoarse. "He was not your soldier to judge." she croaked.

"What did you say, Plain's Warden?" Bronwin turned and stared down at her. Behind him, Varden raised a hand over his mouth in awe.

"*He was not your soldier to judge.*" She looked up at him defiantly, tired and blazing eyes glaring back at him. "Just as I was not yours to judge-" she began to find her voice. "A Plain's Strider is not yours to judge! A strider is the responsibility of the Plain's Warden, *not* the Sovereign Guard!" Her breathing was furiously quick. "You have overstepped your bounds, Bull."

Bronwin, much to Rel's surprise, stayed calm. She didn't like this, he had prepared himself. He had already entertained Kol's loose lips as a possibility and planned for the outcome.

The Pale Bull took a small breath in. "I have not overstepped my bounds, Warden. I have enacted the only punishment that was feasible."

"It was not your punishment to give."

"No? Rel, I have done you a favour." he kept his voice and expression level. He knew exactly what he was doing.

"Doing me a favour?" Rel stared daggers into his eyes, but only met his hard metallic gaze. Her ferocity wouldn't win here. "And what was that favour?"

"Were there any other possibilities for judgement?"

"What does that-"

"Answer the question-" Bronwin interjected. "Were there any possibilities, other than death?"

Taking a deep breath, Rel thought for a moment. She looked at the dirt beneath her feet, then the crowd. They had all been witnesses to Kol's confession. He was guilty of betraying Valen military secrets to the enemy, a decision that cost all of the striders their lives. Had he kept his mouth shut, and endured the torture, he would have taken the secrets to his grave, and the striders wouldn't be nearly extinct today.

She swallowed hard. "No," she finally said. "There was no other alternative. Not with his confession being public. Death would have been the only solution ... or exile." Rel turned to look at the closed gate, her gaze took her beyond that, to the Endless Plains, where the exiles would have gone. It was the same as death, ruling out the option of exile as a separate punishment. "But exile and death are one and the same now."

"Yes," Bronwin agreed. "You have now admitted that the boy's punishment was death. I made it quick and painless. There was no need to drag out the sentence, no need to patch up a dead man and waste the magister's time, or the village's food and resources."

Rel bit back anger, there would be a time to lash out, a time to go after him.

She inhaled deeply through her nose tasting the sweat and fear in the air. The dank, humid air sat heavy in her lungs; it was hard to breathe. "That is correct. You were wise in your judgement, Bronwin."

The Pale Bull nodded to her, then waved to Algrenon who had been standing with Varden. The man approached Kol's body.

Rel looked his way. "No," she said flatly. "We'll take the body." Nef stepped over too, ridden with sadness and regret. "You took Saffron, we'll take him."

Algrenon looked back to Rel and nodded. "He is your dead then, treat him well, Plain's Warden."

"We will." Nef had said, placing a hand on Rel's shoulder. "We'll see he is sent to the Soul Spire."

#

The whole thing had been barbaric, but even Varden couldn't have denied Bronwin's reasoning. Kol was sentenced to death the moment he made his confession. His very *very* public confession. Had the boy realized there were more than just himself and Rel in the area? Surely he had. Yet he made the confession anyway; had he waited until they were behind closed doors, Rel probably would have worked to keep him safe, to hide his tracks. Then the boy might have at least stood a chance at surviving until the Thregs arrived at the gates of Plainsview.

Perhaps, though, the young strider had wanted death. Veil Strider only knew what the Thregs would have done to him. That, and the guilt of killing the entirety of the striders would be a lot to weigh on a heavy heart. Varden came to the conclusion that Kol wanted death. He might not have welcomed it, but he wanted it, needed it, else he would have taken it himself after he had been treated, or sooner.

The scholar watched as Bronwin, Algrenon and most of the crowd dissipated back to where they had come from. He himself, however, sent Dry Eyes off and made his way towards the striders standing about their friend's corpse.

Nef approached him first, placing a gentle hand on the scholar's chest. "What is it, Varden?"

"I only wish to accompany you two, for a moment, anyway. Not for long. Don't worry." The scholar's eyes were kind and caring.

"Thank you," Nef said after a moment of contemplation and stepped aside.

Varden stepped forward, the strider following him in step, standing over Kol's body was a sight the Wixen was ill-prepared for. Various pieces of skull, meat, brain matter, and tissue littered the ground, clumped into the dirt and soaked into the soil. Much to his surprise, Varden didn't feel nauseous. He found himself crouching down next to Rel, who had collapsed onto her knees sobbing.

Nef stepped around her, crouching on her opposite side. They both put a hand on her shoulders. Rel didn't look up, didn't look around, just knelt and cried. Her tears fell into the soil, mixing with Kol's blood and whatever might have been buried there long ago. They were joined for eternity now, Rel and Kol. Varden realized. His blood and her tears are in the ground for eternity.

Another set of footsteps approached from behind, slow and dragging. Varden looked up to see a very short woman, a dwarf, blubbering as she dragged her feet towards the corpse. The scholar recognized her from the tavern, Steena, he believed her name was. The dwarf came over and collapsed next to them. She began to wail

Some time had passed and the Wixen had done nothing but sit in silence, offering his respect and prayers to Kol and those weeping for him. Finally, Rel had wiped her tears, Steena followed the example of strength soon after and did the same. Nef remained crouched, with that same look of sadness and regret across his face as when he first approached the body. Varden could hazard a guess that Nef was beginning to wish it had been him, and not his friend who was taken by the Thregs. Maybe then, the striders would still exist beyond two over-tired souls.

"Nef," Rel said in a whisper. "We should move him now. Start a pyre behind the longhouse. Steena-" The warden looked up at the dwarf. "You should come too, he'd want you there." her voice cracked.

Steena nodded wordlessly.

"Then it is my time to leave, striders," Varden said whilst standing. "I have no place at this funeral. I wanted you to know that you have the thoughts and prayers of this aspiring master, and he wishes you all well in the days ahead."

"Thank you, Varden." Rel looked up at him with bloodshot eyes. "You are a good man. I wish you well during the battle ahead."

"Save your well wishes for your friends and fellow soldiers. For I do not plan on being here. My time in Plainsview has come to an end, unfortunately. I will begin making my way towards central Valenfaar. I aim to see the city of Valen before the Thregs attempt to make it that far."

Nef stood tall. "Safe travels then, Scholar. And a splendour of knowledge." The two men shared a grin before Varden left the site of the execution.

If he was correct, Varden needed to get out of town fast. As he stepped through the busy streets and stepped over the mud-ridden cobblestone paths, he began to think more and more about the reason why he had decided to leave. The morning of this day, the very day he would be leaving Plainsview he had tapped another shadewood tree, this one had just been towards the outskirts of town. Upon ingestion of the sap, he witnessed Plainsview under siege, once again he had only witnessed a few fleeting moments, but it was enough to see the town was left in utter ruin, men and women fighting with all their hearts.

Two things stood out in that vision that told him to run far. The colour green. Not the same shade as the Thregs, however, but a brighter, hotter green. The second image was that of another shadewood tree: the massive willow tree within the centre of Plainsview had changed: its colours morphed to that of a shadewood, which he had now taken as bad omens, signs of death and sadness. Nothing good was to be found where a shadewood tree would appear. Did he understand the science behind it? No. But now, he would have to make for the Capital and hope for the best.

He would take Dry Eyes; a guard, no matter how inept, would be valuable on the road ahead. He just hoped to the Veil Strider that the simpleton's ravings wouldn't drive him mad before they made it to their destination.

Chapter 34

The pyre had been built with Kol's body atop the mass of wood and thatch. Nef, Rel, Ashlin and Steena stood in silence, looking at their friend in the middle of the strider's courtyard where Rel and Corduvan had trained. They had wrapped the body themselves as the town magister was too busy with the wounded. Rel held the torch in her shaking hand, refusing to light the pyre. Ashlin held her other hand, which helped some, but couldn't quell the anger she felt welling up inside her towards the Pale Bull. That brute of a man had carried out the trial and execution barbarously.

Ashlin gave Rel's hand a squeeze and they looked at one another. Rel released Ashlin's hand and stepped towards Kol. He looked comfortable, peaceful even. Not a worry in the world for him anymore, he was in the Soul Spire. But where in the Soul Spire the gods would have put him, she didn't know. One who would doom so many souls would have to be held accountable. Rel shook her head and quickly banished that thought. How could she think so ill of her friend? The Sovereign Guard never had anyone survive being taken hostage by Thregs for an extended period of time. They had no way of knowing what kinds of torture Kol endured. Would the same have happened if the roles had been reversed? She liked to think not but there was no way to be certain.

Three more steps. Rel was surprised to find herself counting out each footfall in dreaded anticipation for Kol's final farewell.

Two more steps. She could feel her hand shaking even more. She was tired, stressed, broken-hearted and furious. Oh, how she longed to feel her long knife cut into Bronwin's skin.

One more step. Rel began to raise the torch.

"The Endless Plains, our land, our duty," Rel spoke, voice wavering, "Valen's Passage, the door, the Valley."

Nef stepped up beside her and continued the Strider's Endless Range. "We stand to protect, hold fast to defend," they took turns.

"We are the Plain's Striders, the men and women that comb the land."

"To protect those that would fall by the harshest hands."

Ashlin stepped up as Rel continued. "Your ranging is complete, your oath is done."

Steena arrived next to Nef as he recited the next line. "Go free our brother, and leave as one."

"A new duty awaits you in the Soul Spire."

Together they finished: "May you serve, with freedom, and a lively fire."

Rel brought the torch forward and ignited the pyre. Flames leapt up from the base and swallowed Kol's body. Ashlin was holding Rel's hand again, and Rel hardly noticed. Nef stood with his head down, focusing on his bootstraps, perhaps in prayer, and Steena stood beside him, weeping into a small handkerchief. The poor thing looked tired and ragged, she hadn't stopped crying since the execution.

The Plain's Warden squeezed her lover's hand. Ashlin looked at her, blue eyes shining in the light of the fire. How beautiful she was, Rel wanted to kiss and hold her, but now wasn't the time.

"I need to speak with Nef," Rel said. "In private, as the final striders," Ashlin said nothing, only nodded in understanding.

The Plain's Master's head raised a touch at the mention of his name,

Rel released Ashlin's hand and turned to Nef. "Shall we?"

He nodded.

#

Rel's office was a mess, a dimly lit mess. Nef could hardly make sense of anything in the flickering orange glow. It was in disarray: parchments and seals were strewn about as if thrown in anger; a chair was toppled on the floor; ink trickled down one side of her desk with no quill or ink-pot in sight. The mess was new. But when had Rel found the time to come to her office since Kol's passing?

"You been alright, Rel?" Nef finally asked as the warden paced.

"No. I'm not. Thregs will be knocking at our door any day, we have only two striders, the damn Bull just executed our friend; the only person we had who might have known *something* about how the Threg's army operates. Gwendall knows he spent long enough in their camp to have noticed something!"

She huffed and stomped behind her desk, laying her palms flat on the scattered parchments. She looked at Nef with bloodshot eyes. "I'm stressed, I haven't slept, I haven't eaten, and I can hardly keep down water. Nothing makes sense to me right now! You could put me out in the plains, this very moment, and I wouldn't have the slightest idea what to do for the night. So no, I am not okay. By Daylen, Gwendall, Esmirla, and all the others, I am *not* okay." She breathed hard. "All of this while dealing with Bronwin's so-called 'tactics'. You know what his solution is to everything, Nef?"

She didn't wait for him to respond. "Throw more bodies at it! Numbers aren't the only thing that wins battles! They're effective but, eventually, you'll run out. Alistair has stopped sending nearly as many troops to us — which tells me he has other issues — and what he does send are scraps, old men, crippled boys and haggard prisoners! We need to fall back and reinforce Sun Spire, but no, that damn Bull is too damn stubborn! May Gwendall cut him down where he stands!"

Nef stood in a daze at the tirade. "Rel, please. He's our best chance-"

"Best chance?! How is he our best chance? The losses we endured during our first engagement were colossal! We drove them back, but we took the worst of it. The Thregs are supposed to have more, *a lot* more, coming our way. You understand that, right?"

"Yes, of course," He walked forward placing a hand on the desk, opposite his friend. "But I also understand that Bronwin is the foremost Threg expert that Valenfaar has. He's fought them more than any other soldier in the lands. He has something planned, I can feel it. He'll pull through. Alistair wouldn't have sent him here if he thought otherwise. Our Highfolds are smart people, this time around, we need to have some faith in their judgement."

"Have faith in their judgement? I mean no offence, Nef. But Alistair is not here, no matter how sound his judgement is, he cannot possibly understand the entire situation from his war room."

That was a point that Nef couldn't argue. Yes, Alistair was a smart man and a smarter soldier but he would only know what Bronwin reported. Though Nef had faith the Bull had been accurate.

"Rel?" he asked, changing the course of the conversation. "Why is it, do you think, that Alistair hasn't come to Plainsview? You'd think an invading force would be something he'd want to see."

Rel bit her lip and shook her head. "I have no idea. We know *something* else is going on in Valenfaar. There has to be, otherwise, every able-bodied soldier would be arriving and threatening our food stores for the next ten cycles. But now we're getting scraps. Something is pulling his attention away, something that is more urgent than an invading army."

"What do you think it is?"

Again, the warden shook her head. "No clue. But we may not live long enough to find out."

Nef leaned back from the desk, crossed his arms and looked at his old friend. "You think we're going to do that badly in the days ahead, eh?"

"Not in the battle Nef, no. The day after the morrow I make my move against Bronwin." her voice was flat, calm, and cool. She showed none of the anger and panic from moments before. Her gaze was intense, burning with icy fury.

Nef's heart fluttered with the candles flickering in the room. He was worried this would be where their private conversation would lead, betraying not just Bronwin, but Alistair Highfold and the rest of the Sovereign Guard.

"Rel, you can't be-"

"I am serious, Nef," She cut in. "That man needs to die, he can't keep throwing soldiers at the Thregs like he has! Too many will be killed. The best thing we can do for the Sovereign Guard is to kill him and remove him from command. And if we're careful-"

"You would have us commit treason? You know there are only two outcomes for that, right? Death or exile. And right now, exile is looking awfully similar to death, Rel. They'd cast us into the plains where the Thregs would kill us within half a fortnight!"

Rel leaned further over her desk, candlelight burning brightly against her dark skin. Nef could see she was starting to sweat, it beaded on her forehead and threatened to roll down her face and into the candle below.

"We won't get caught. The only witness will be a dead one, Nef. And if his pet Algrenon is with him, we remove him too. Give credit to a scout or one of the conscripts. We could even try to frame that prisoner Varden took with him."

"Rel!" Nef shouted, "Listen to yourself! You're speaking like some kind of criminal. Killing witnesses and framing others. What's happened to you?! What would Ashlin or Saffron say?!"

The Plain's Warden recoiled and the orange glow on her face darkened. What Nef said staggered her, took her off guard. Then it was his turn to recoil, to stagger from the unexpected. There was laughter. Not manic, more nervous. But it was laughter, and it was coming from his mentor.

The laughter subsided as quickly as it started, but Rel's voice betrayed a hint of amusement. "What would Ashlin and Saff think?" she shook her head with a grin. "Ash would start an argument, saying that I can't just kill somebody like that. But she would do little more. Saffron would have removed me from my post and sent me up to the Halo for three moons to scout. Upon my return he would have scolded me, then placed me back into my position believing I'd have learned my lesson. He always was a softie."

"And you loved that about him; how fatherly he was."

"Yes, yes I did, Nef. And Bronwin took him from us too. Even though it was my fault he died ... I couldn't hold my tongue."

"So hold your tongue now, Rel!" Nef leaned forward on the desk again, letting the candle light his face from below. "Why must this man die? He's here to defend our homeland, let the man do his job. Lives will be lost either way, but I will not betray Alistair or the Sovereign Guard because my superior doesn't like one man's tactics!"

"My mind will not change, Nef. I will do what I have to do to save our people." She stood defiantly, arms crossed over her chest. "Do not forget that I am your Plain's Warden."

"And do not forget that I am your Plain's Master, Rel. Not that either of our titles mean much now. But what would you do if you did manage to kill Bronwin? Take command of the defence?"

"No. I don't know. Unless Alistair were to send one of his two puppets out from the Capital. But that isn't likely to happen, I don't think. Those men are too old and lived longer than most. They have my respect, but I don't think they could weather what we are up against."

"And how would you fight the Thregs? What kind of tactics would you use that Bronwin hasn't already? In open combat, he pushes numbers. He's laid traps, which have worked. He's tried an ambush, and that didn't work. What else would you do differently?"

Rel held her breath for a moment, probably in thought. "Had we not been pushed back so far already, I would have used the valley walls to our advantage. Have archers posted, maybe move some troops up and over the Halo to flank the Thregs from behind once engagement began. More traps and ambushes. As we stand now, it would be best if we rigged Plainsview to the top of the Soul Spire with traps, and left. Set up defences at Sun Spire and hold them off there."

Nef snorted. "If we were to move our defence to Sun Spire, the direct command would fall to the City General there, not to you. It would be under her command. And who even knows if the Thregs will hit Sun Spire? They could follow Gwendall's Spear and circumvent the city altogether. They'd be opening their backs to attack, sure. But the Spear isn't easy to navigate, especially for wounded and exhausted soldiers. Even if they did reach the Thregs, they'd be little more than mosquitoes pestering a bear." He leaned forward further. "We need Bronwin, Rel. You don't have to like it, but that's the truth of the matter. He knows Thregs, he's got experience."

"Nobody has experience against an army of them, Nef! He's fought small groups of around a dozen or so. Not thousands!"

The Plain's Master stood up straighter now, his hands still firmly planted on the messy desk. "And what experience do you have against armies?!" he roared, "I'd rather place my life in the hands of a man with little experience instead of a woman with none!"

Rel stepped back, shock betraying itself on her face. Her mouth hung agape before twisting into an angry snarl. "So that's how it is then," she growled, "You'd rather place your life in the hands of that brute instead of the hands of your friend and Plain's Warden. Is that so?"

Even Nef had to take a moment to fully understand what he had just said. He took in a deep breath and exhaled slowly through his nose. Closing his eyes he tilted his head down, then opened them again as he met her gaze, filled with anger and hurt. "I suppose it is, Rel."

"Leave."

He did so.

#

Another sip of ale had Bronwin actually starting to enjoy his downtime. The tavern that night was filled with more soldiers than he had seen before.

With most of the peasants already gone from Plainsview, the few that remained avoided the Respite. They had bigger things to worry about than getting drunk, and the soldiers that were here, the ones that weren't on duty, had big enough worries that they wanted, perhaps needed, to get drunk. The ale horn the Pale Bull normally had hanging around his waist did its job well: keeping his thirst at bay.

Algrenon sat next to him, slammed down his empty mug and wiped his mouth onto his arm. Leaning into Bronwin, he whispered: "You know those striders were having a pyre for that traitor, don't ya? What a bunch of fools. A traitor doesn't deserve a pyre!" Bronwin's Right Hand swayed in his chair.

The Pale Bull chuckled. "It's not something you or I would do. Let those fools have their ceremony, it means nothing. The traitor is dead, as he deserves to be. The striders won't last through the battle, I don't think. They're tired, they're exhausted, and now they're broken. Let the two of them have what they will, for they won't have much more soon."

Algrenon smiled slyly. "I'll drink to that!" He raised someone else's mug to his mouth voraciously, gulping at the drink. He finished with a loud belch and slammed it down in front of the bewildered soldier to who it belonged.

"Hey, that was mine!"

"Aye!" roared Algrenon, "And I'll buy you another!" He waved his hand and the tavern keeper responded with a nod and a wave of her own.

Bronwin took another sip of his horn. He was drinking slowly, for if his scouts reported to him of another star shower, or of approaching Thregs, he didn't want to be fighting with a hazy mind or a hangover.

He noticed the sheepish dwarf serving maid was not present. He supposed she was grieving over her traitorous lover. How could she grieve for a man such as Kol the Plain's Strider? She should have felt anger and disgust in him, not love and worry. Pathetic were the throws of love, something he was happy he never bothered to indulge in. Even if he had wanted to, his job and reputation wouldn't allow it.

Another sip, but when the horn reached his mouth Bronwin was surprised to find it empty. When had he finished it? He was drinking slowly, or so he thought. No matter. He didn't need more. He rested his hand back down on the table and let his mind wander to Rel. The woman was a traitor and if she should survive this defensive campaign he would find ways to see her court marshalled and tried as a traitor. He would see her, and that blue-eyed-bitch of a lover, killed or exiled. A woman had no place in command of such large forces, they could be far too emotional, and Rel's behaviour since he arrived in Plainsview was proof enough of that.

"Bronwin, your horn is dry!" Algrenon roared.

By the Veil Strider, he is loud when he is drunk.

Bronwin's man lifted the mug that was not his and began to fill the horn.

"Hey!" the soldier spoke in protest, "That's mine, you swine!" He reached for the cup but Algrenon just chortled and pulled it away as he poured more into the ale horn.

"I'll buy you another!" Algrenon spoke again. It had quickly become a common term from the man's lips. Bronwin had heard him say it nearly a dozen times since walking into the tavern, and something told him he might hear it another dozen times before the night was done.

The door to the tavern opened and silence fell through the room for a few fleeting moments before folks went back to their chatter. One of the last striders had walked through the door. He looked exhausted, like he hadn't slept

Valenfaar: The Crimson Plains

in half a fortnight. The man looked around and after a third glance of the room, he found the Pale Bull and began to make his way over.

The tavern keeper offered the strider a drink, but he waved his hand, telling the keeper to leave him alone. The woman nodded her head respectfully and went back to the tables that needed to be served. It would be a long night for her, Bronwin guessed, especially with most of her help gone.

It didn't take long, but it took longer than it should have for the strider to make it to the table. "Bronwin," he said, almost out of breath.

From so close, the Pale Bull noticed that the strider stank of body odour and dirt. His hair was slick with sweat and oil, his skin covered in grime.

What was the strider's name? Net? No, that wasn't right. Nel? Nefl? Then it came to Bronwin: *Nef! The boy's name was Nef, yes that was it.*

"Strider," he said. "Did your send-off go well?"

"As well as it could have, sir."

Sir. Bronwin liked that. The boy knew who was in charge.

"But I have something urgent to tell you."

"Oh?" Bronwin looked up and raised an eyebrow. "The Thregs on the move already?" Everyone nearby froze for a moment and listened.

"No, sir, no news on that front." Everyone went back to their discussions and drank. Nef leaned in closer, Bronwin could smell his breath: no alcohol, no Dead Man's Root, the strider was of sober mind. "But I do have something I feel you should be aware of."

The Pale Bull snorted and waved his hand to those sitting at the table. The men, and one woman, looked at him nervously then nodded and moved away, leaving Bronwin and Nef alone.

"Sit," Bronwin motioned to an empty chair.

Nef did so, scooted the chair in and leaned forward on his elbows, hands clasped in front of him. "Thank you. What I have to tell you is important, I believe it to be very important to the success of this defence."

Bronwin took a mouthful of ale from his horn, closing his eyes as he did so. When he was finished he put the horn down, flat on the table, a bit of trickling ale rolled out onto the wood. "Well-" he said impatiently. "Out with it!"

Nef swallowed hard and began to wring out his hands.

Bronwin raised an eyebrow. "You're fidgeting. What is it that you want to tell me?"

"I-it's about Rel, sir."

Bronwin perked up, leaning forward over the table. Had the Strider-Bitch finally snapped? With the way Nef was behaving, surely it wasn't something he *wanted* to tell him but something he *needed* to. "Go on, boy." Bronwin relaxed, it was clear to him that he had already won the strider's loyalty. Why else would he be here?

Nef looked the Pale Bull in the eye for a fleeting moment, then quickly looked down to the table again. "Rel doesn't like how you've been running the defence of Plainsview; the defence of the country."

Bronwin chuckled. It was no secret to him that Rel didn't like the way he operated. But Alistair had put *him* in charge, not her, not Saffron, and certainly not any of the other striders. Besides, he had already won Valenfaar's first bout of open combat with Threg forces. He knew what he was doing, and he knew how to do it.

He cleared his throat. "That is not new information to me. We've been at odds ever since I stepped foot in this town."

"Yes sir, I understand that. But Rel, she-" Nef paused, swallowed hard again.

"She *what?*"

"She plans to kill you, sir. The day after the morrow." He was shaking.

Bronwin's eyebrows shot up in alarm. "Is that so?" He stroked his chin for a moment to help him hide the smile that would have formed on his lips otherwise.

So the bitch has finally snapped, eh? By the Veil Strider, this is good fortune. I can finally get her out of the way.

"So she plans to commit treason and murder, is that right?"

"Aye." Nef's voice wavered.

"And on the day after the morrow? When did you hear that?"

Nef looked Bronwin in the eye, this time he held his gaze. It seemed his strength had come back to him. "She told me tonight. After the pyre." There was a pang of regret behind his eyes.

"Don't be ashamed, boy," Bronwin assured him. If he could've put a hand on the strider's shoulder, he would have, but from across the table, it would have been more awkward than reassuring. "You've done the right thing: you've told your commanding officer of a conspiracy to commit treason. What you have done will save many lives. Now, is there anyone else she might approach with her plan? Anyone else who might help her?"

A glimmer of hope came into Nef's eyes. "Yes, I can think of two people she might tell. You won't kill them, will you? They are good people."

"I won't kill them if I don't have to," Bronwin said with a surprising amount of honesty. "They'll be arrested and sent to Sun Spire for trial. You have my word."

Nef thought for a moment, nodding his head up and down while chewing his lip. "Alright," he finally said. "If she were to go to anyone ..."

Chapter 35

"No. Get that wood over to the other side of the wall right away. Whoever was reinforcing it yesterday did a piss poor job, and I'll be damned if it collapses due to some shoddy carpentry." Corduvan had taken over directing a team of workers assigned to reinforcing Plainsview's eastern wall.

He had been working since before sun up. Now that his wife and son had left for Sun Spire, it was easy for him to wake up early. He hoped his family would be okay on the road, his wife had trouble living in Plainsview as it was. Corduvan pushed the thoughts away, he couldn't worry about that right now, he wouldn't worry about it.

The guardsman looked along the wall and saw a young boy foolishly tapping a hammer against nails. All along the board, they were bent and warped. Absolutely useless, the plank would come off the moment he let go.

"Hey!" Corduvan called, "You there!"

The boy turned, a look of confusion on his face.

"Yes, I'm talking to you!" As Corduvan approached he grabbed the shoulder of a passerby. The man was a carpenter, an experienced one. Leaning in, Corduvan whispered: "Can you give that damn fool a hand? The boy would see this wall destroyed before the day is done."

The carpenter nodded, then marched over to the struggling youth.

Though some parts of the wall were mangled beyond belief, Corduvan had to admit he was impressed at how much the Valley Wall, and Gate, had grown in recent days. The structure had almost doubled in height and thickness. It had been reinforced with lumber brought in from the surrounding forests, and that was covered with treated leather.

The wall looked strange now to him: he had lived in Plainsview most of his life and had grown accustomed to the site of the Valley Wall on a daily basis. He had walked its battlements more times than he cared to count. But looking at this new structure had Corduvan feeling a mixture of both nervousness and excitement.

There was a commotion: the Valley Gate opened and several soldiers came stumbling through, bloodied and exhausted. Corduvan moved to meet them.

"What happened?!" he cried.

"Sir!" a man from atop the wall called down. "Scouting party, sir!"

Corduvan nodded in affirmation as he knelt with the wounded. "What happened?"

"Threg scouting part, sir. Six of 'em, took us by surprise. We lost Harr and Yul just outside the swamps."

Corduvan brought his gaze up to the gate, as if looking beyond it. "Were you followed?"

"No, sir, they pulled back into the swamp. By Gwendall's Blade, I think it's safe to say that it's their territory now."

Everyone around agreed, even Corduvan. It would be time to keep scouts from the swamp, it wasn't worth the risk.

"Get a report ready for Bronwin," he said. "He'll want to know what's going on."

"Yessir, Corduvan. It shall be done."

"Good. Now go, get some rest."

The scouts picked themselves up and hobbled towards the centre of town. Whether they'd be looking for ale, pleasure, or sleep, Corduvan didn't know, nor did he care. So long as their report was handed in with haste.

In the meantime, Corduvan wanted to look at the situation of the wounded, to see who needed to be evacuated to Sun Spire, and to see what civilians remained, if any. The call for evacuation was not a forced order, but one that would be foolish to disobey. Folks who stayed were not to be protected by the Sovereign Guard. The Guard's purpose was strictly the defence of the country, should a commoner stay behind, they were responsible for their own safety.

As far as Corduvan knew, the vast majority of the town had left. He knew Ashlin had stayed, Steena and another of the tavern staff; and a few oddballs that decided to deny the existence of the Threg threat altogether.

Making his way over to the wounded, he saw a number of men and women he had known from the town guard. Though many of the guards had been killed in the first battle with the Thregs, a fair number of them had survived. Corduvan was impressed, both at himself and at the others. They hadn't received the same kind of training as the Sovereign Guard, nor did they share the same equipment. They were small compared to the might of the rest, yet here some of them still stood. Reduced to a third of their former strength, but they stood among some of Valenfaar's best.

Velamir strode over to him, his blond hair dirtier than usual. "We have lots of wounded. Doesn't help that the scouts from this morning were hurt too."

"Aye," Corduvan agreed. "How are your men?"

The mercenary shook his head. "We're down in number, and we had to send some off to Sun Spire. The magister can only help so many, you know? The poor man is doing the best he can, but the Thregs don't make life easy for anybody."

"No, they certainly don't."

Velamir continued. "The rest of my men are well and ready to fight. Our armour is a tad dirtier than we like. But it's something we'll have to live with."

Velamir ran his hand over a dent in his chest plate. "You know Corduvan, I never thought, that as a mercenary, I'd be asked to defend folks from Thregs. And yet, here we are fighting against a damned army of the things!"

Both men laughed.

"I know how you feel!" Corduvan agreed. "I was supposed to look out for merchants, criminals, and guard the prison. None of this stuff was up to me, or any of us. The striders took care of most issues past the Valley."

"The striders ..." Velamir's gaze dropped a moment. "That was a damned blood bath ..."

"Aye. It was. I had a lot of friends with them. Hard to believe they're gone. I try not to think about it, there will be time to grieve once the fighting is done." Corduvan bit back tears, he wouldn't let himself grieve, not yet.

"And when do you think that will be? When do you think the fighting will be over?" The mercenary looked uncertain. "I mean, don't get me wrong, the Highfolds are paying us very well for this contract. But, I'm starting to think it might be my final one. And I'd rather not have it last longer than it should."

Corduvan looked to the early morning sun, just peeking into the world. "That's a question I don't have an answer to, my friend. And I don't think we'll have an answer for a while yet. Unless we win it right here in the coming days."

Velamir gave a nervous laugh. "And do you think we'll actually do it? Hold off the Thregs *here*, at Plainsview?"

A shocking question, one Corduvan hadn't even asked himself. He had been following orders the entire time: fight here, help them, make sure this is done, go do that. He didn't even stop for a moment to consider if their fight could be won. And it didn't take much thought at all to realize he didn't like the answer.

"No, I don't think we can hold the Thregs here. We'll be pushed back. If not the next assault, the one after that. We'll lose a lot of lives, and if Bronwin is as smart as everyone here thinks he is, we'll fall back to Sun Spire. Leave traps behind to slow them down and cross our fingers that Esmirla, Gwendall, Jo-een and Daylen favour us more than their gods favour them."

Velamir nodded solemnly. "I think you and I see eye-to-eye on that. Holding will not go our way."

More silence as the two of them watched the wounded, the old magister jumping from one soldier to the next, running his glowing hands over each patient. The poor man looked exhausted, when was the last time he slept? When would he let himself sleep?

The mercenary broke the silence. "May I ask you something, about what you said?"

"What did I say?" Corduvan turned to match the man's eyes.

"You mentioned the gods. Do you think they have gods?"

"I don't see why they wouldn't." He shrugged. "Before this whole ordeal, we thought them nothing more than savages. We've been proven very *very* wrong on every front. They have an army — which implies leadership — they take prisoners, scout, and follow the stars for guidance. I feel we'd be fools to assume they don't have something they worship."

Velamir said nothing, only nodded thoughtfully.

And if they do have gods. Corduvan thought. *May they be lesser than ours. For our sake.*

Another commotion, this time coming from the direction of town, amongst the movement of people and the voices, he could have almost sworn he heard someone say his name. Then he heard it again, louder this time and much more clear.

"Where is Corduvan?!" a voice called, carrying over the squabbles and through the early morning air, "I said, where is **Corduvan?!**"

The crowd dispersed and Bronwin stood tall, Algrenon and many other officers behind him. Algrenon pointed a finger in Corduvan's direction.

"I'll leave you to it then." Velamir ducked his head down and scurried away.

Corduvan said nothing to the mercenary, he raised a hand towards Bronwin, letting him know that he was open for discourse. Not that he would have had much choice.

It didn't take long for Bronwin to be standing before him. His eyes spoke of pleasantries: they were calm and almost serene. As if all the worries he had were put to rest, like the last pieces of some puzzle had finally found their places.

"The wounded, how are they?" the Pale Bull asked.

Rubbing his chin with the palm of his hand, Corduvan was surprised to find his stubble was growing into something more. "They're surviving," he said. "Getting better every day. Especially with the help of the magister. But the poor man is exhausted."

"Good. I've tried to give the magister some rest, he's no use to us dead. But he insists on staying."

"Any chance Alistair will requisition us a couple more?"

Bronwin shook his head. "No, I've asked. He says they are needed elsewhere."

Corduvan sighed as he turned to watch the magister as he left a wounded woman. The priest-mage looked as if he had aged ten cycles in the past half-fortnight alone.

"Has the scouting party returned?"

This was unusual: Bronwin never asked this many questions, nor took such an interest in what Corduvan thought. The hair on the guard's neck stood on end: something felt off. He wasn't sure, but he could have sworn Algrenon and the others had spaced themselves out behind him. He couldn't tell without turning.

"No," he finally answered. "Er, yes. Sorry, sir. My mind wandered. They have returned. Wounded by Threg scouts. Two are missing, assumed dead. The rest have gone off to rest and fill out their reports."

"Thank you, Corduvan. You have done your duties well."

Now, what in Gwendall's Blade was that supposed to mean?!

"I beg your pardon, sir?"

Bronwin turned to look at the wounded. "You are under arrest for suspected aid in a conspiracy to commit treason and murder."

Corduvan's mouth dropped. He was speechless. When, in the name of Daylen, did he even have the time to consider such a thing?

"I'm sorry sir, I just ... what are you talking about?"

The Pale Bull looked back down at the guardsman. "I've been informed by a very reliable source that there is a plot in Plainsview to kill me. You have been named as a likely accomplice."

"I haven't heard anything, sir. I-I've been here, at the wall from morning until sun-down! I swear it." Corduvan knew what Rel wanted to do, but he knew nothing more. He didn't even agree to get involved. It was best to play it stupid; lean in on the fact that he really didn't know anything.

"And I want to believe you," Bronwin added. "You are only being arrested. You have not been charged with anything yet. You are only suspected to have been brought into this scheme. I have no evidence to execute you. This is a precautionary action, you have served me well recently. I award such dedication."

"I beg your pardon, sir. But how is arresting me an award?" Corduvan was shocked. He began to feel hands on his shoulders, they took away his weapons and brought his hands behind his back. He could feel iron shackles.

"Normally I would have killed you without a second thought," Bronwin said flatly. "I am being generous right now."

Corduvan's mind flashed back to Kol's execution. It had almost been murder ... almost.

"Where are you sending me?" The guardsman didn't bother to resist.

"You will be sent to Sun Spire, for a time. Then to Valen where you will either be cleared of your potential charges or tried if evidence is found to convict you."

Though Bronwin's words seemed to inspire hope, Corduvan couldn't help but feel that even though there was no evidence — how could there be, he didn't know a thing — the Pale Bull would make something up to have him tried. The man was a fiend, he didn't deal well with insubordination, and he was stubbornly petty. Those traits didn't mix well for those around the Shield of Northwood.

#

Rel had left that morning in a hurry, hardly saying a word to her before storming out the door. Ashlin was worried; Rel hadn't eaten much, came home late, tossed and turned all night, and woke up earlier than usual. Nothing felt right, something was wrong, very wrong. She already knew what had happened to the other striders. Rel told her that much at least. She supposed that Rel was grieving and going about it in her own way. But there still felt like something was missing, she didn't know what, and it was driving her crazy.

Regardless, she needed to finish packing up anything valuable. She wanted to be out of Plainsview by the next morning. She hated the thought of not being near Rel with everything going on, but her lover had insisted, it was safest and when everything was normal again, they would be together.

Oh, how Ashlin had bawled when Rel had told her of this. The final point that sold her was when Rel had said: "Look, I need to have a clear head when I'm out. I can't have that if I'm worried you've been hurt, killed, or lost. I would be distracted because I love you and I would be so worried about your safety. Please, for your health and for mine, I need you to go to Sun Spire as soon as possible."

That was what had convinced her. As much as she hated it, as much as it made her cry, she knew Rel was right. It was the sensible thing to do. By Esmirla's Winds, she would be distracted knowing Rel was in town if the roles were reversed.

Ashlin bit back tears as she opened a cupboard and pulled out a small knife, she placed it in her bag and continued to rummage through her home. A fresh pot of stew sat over the hearth, making the air smell of meat and pepper. She had finally remembered the black pepper.

She would only take the essentials: she grabbed a sack of salt from another cupboard, and two waterskins for the road ahead.

She paced, grabbing whatever she could fit in her bag that might have been of some use on the road. Now, looking at the small home that was theirs, Ashlin began to have a feeling of loss. Leaving their home behind, leaving Rel behind, even leaving Plainsview behind felt like the worst thing in the world. The pit she felt in her stomach was a hole. She hated this, but she knew it was the right thing to do. But still, something felt off…

A knock on the door, and a flutter in her stomach. Who was knocking? Who might have needed to see her? Rel might have forgotten something. Ashlin stepped towards the door as the knock sounded louder and harder. Her stomach fluttered more, whoever was on the other side of that door wasn't Rel, she already knew, she would have come in already. Could it be Nef?

Upon reaching the door, Ashlin had a wash of cold bathe over her. Taking a deep breath in, she reached for the handle and opened it. Her breath caught in her throat. So many things came into view all at once. The first thing she had noticed was the behemoth standing in front of her home: Bronwin, the Pale Bull and Shield of Northwood. He was looking down at her, a cold stare that shook her to the core. Behind him were two guards, and behind them, she saw Rel's friend Corduvan in chains, with three more guards standing with him. Even further behind, peeking over the roofs of other buildings she could see the town's famous willow tree had its leaves turned to a stark white, and what little of the branches she could see within them shone a thick, almost velvety, black.

She noticed Corduvan staring at her, wide-eyed and shaking his head. She looked into his eyes and realized there was something very wrong happening.

"Are you Ashlin?" Bronwin finally asked, breaking the silence.

The fluttering in her stomach froze into a molten core with an icy shell hiding its flare of heat and anger.

"No," she lied. "You have the wrong place. My name is Lana, Ashlin left town not more than two nights ago. She lived right over there." Ashlin spoke calmer and cooler than she had thought possible. She raised a finger and pointed at an empty house across the street. In truth, Lana used to be the person who had lived there, and she had left not more than two days ago.

Bronwin craned his head to the side.

"Is something the matter?" Ashlin asked, giving him a look of genuine confusion. He suspected something.

"Ashlin," he said flatly. "Do not lie to me. My men saw Rel leave here not long ago before heading to the longhouse. We know who you are. There is no point in hiding it."

She froze for a moment and started to feel that shell of ice inside her crack and break, her anger wanting to slip out.

"Rel is a dear friend of mine," Ashlin was shocked that words were coming out of her mouth. "She stopped by to make sure I would be out of town on the morrow. Always such a caring woman, she is. I can even show you my bag as proof, I'm just about finished packing for the day."

She caught a glimpse of Corduvan, his eyes were opened wider than they had been before. Like great balls of snow had settled there. He was shocked, and his skin grew paler by the moment. Oh, what had they been dragged into?

"Show me," Bronwin gestured into the building. "Show me your bag. Then we'll be taking a look around. This is a matter of security, Lana."

He didn't believe her entirely, she knew, it would take more careful lies to get the mountain of meat out of her home.

"Come on in, my bag is on the table there." Ashlin turned, waving them in. She gestured towards her bag.

It didn't take the soldiers a moment to start wandering through her home, poking and prodding at things. Lifting up whatever they could to look underneath. They opened drawers and closets and cupboards. Ashlin searched her mind for anything that might have been incriminating that Rel had lived here. Her eyes went wide: the trunk in their bedroom, her uniforms and some weapons were there; they bore Rel's name. A soldier walked into the bedroom and Ashlin's core froze completely. She couldn't breathe, couldn't move. She heard the trunk open.

"Sir!" the voice called from the bedroom, "I think I found something."

Bronwin moved across the home and ducked into the bedroom. Ashlin stood frozen. There was no way for her to lie her way out of this one, not convincingly.

The Pale Bull returned from the room with one of Rel's uniforms in hand, and one of her long knives in the other.

"These belong to Rel. Don't they, *Lana?*" Bronwin took another step forward. "If you stop your lies, you might be treated less harshly."

Ashlin's head dropped, she stared at the ground. "Yes. They're Rels."

"So you are Ashlin?" he asked again.

"Yes," she said, defeat in her voice. "I am her lover," The shell of ice inside her exploded. She glared into his eyes, letting that molten core pour forth. "What is it to you?!" Her blue eyes blazed with scarlet energy.

Bronwin had actually staggered, he took half a step back as he looked down at her. "Rel is believed to be planning an act of treason upon myself and our good country. We have reason to suspect you are involved in this matter. I am placing you under arrest for the suspected conspiracy to commit murder and treason."

He knew about Rel's plan?! Who had told him? The only other person who knew was Nef, and he was loyal to Rel. It would explain why Corduvan was in chains, he was also suspected. But she knew as well as he did that he didn't know much, but it wouldn't be a stretch for an outsider to think he had. Corduvan had spent a lot of time with Rel recently, ever since he had begun his training with her.

That molten core had permeated itself through Ashlin's very being, she felt as if her body radiated heat. Her skin tingled, froze, and burned all at once. "No!" she screamed, "I will not go with you!"

If she went with him, it would mean death for her and for Rel.

"Grab her," Bronwin ordered.

"Bronwin, please, don't." Corduvan tried to plead, but he may as well have said nothing.

A soldier reached forward for Ashlin's arm, leaving Corduvan behind him. She turned with fury and swatted the man's hand away, then drove her fist straight into his nose. His head snapped back with a loud crack as blood streamed down his face. The man yowled, holding his face as he fell back into the wall. Another guard reached for her, but she was already beyond his grasp, a third pushed as she tried to put space between her and them. Ashlin stumbled and nearly fell to the floor in the kitchen. She turned and lashed out with her nails as the man who pushed her closed in. She raked his face and felt the wets of an eye under her nail. He yelped and brought a hand to his injury, furious.

When he removed his hand, there was a small chunk missing from the whites of his eye. Ashlin nearly flinched. The wounded man lunged forward reaching for her again. As Ashlin turned to clear more distance, the guard grabbed a handful of hair and pulled back hard. Ashlin yelped and turned as he did this, reaching forward with both hands she grabbed onto his face and plunged her thumbs into his eyes.

"Let me go!" she roared, "*Let me go!*" As Ashlin drove her thumbs in deeper her victim screamed and let go.

By now, the last two guards who weren't injured rushed her. One grabbed her in a bear hug from behind bringing her off the ground while the other guard tried to grab her legs. Ashlin flailed her feet out, catching the chin of the guard in front of her. His head snapped back as his teeth clacked together. He cursed, then tried again. Ashlin lashed out and caught him once more, breaking one of his teeth in half.

The guard that held her, put her on the ground so she couldn't kick. When he did this though, Ashlin began to walk backwards as hard and as fast as she could. The guard behind her wasn't ready and began to stumble while trying to keep his grip. He crashed backwards, hitting the back of his head off a cupboard. His grip loosened and Ashlin broke into a dash for her bag.

She and the guard with the broken teeth clashed at the table where the bag sat. He threw a punch and caught her in the side of the head. Stars appeared briefly in Ashlin's eyes before vanishing. She retaliated with a punch of her own and caught him in the chin. He recoiled as she dropped her hands into her bag, searching. Then she found it, she grasped a wooden handle and pulled out the knife she had packed earlier.

The guard from the bear hug was back on his feet, stomping up behind her, smoke practically pouring from his pores in anger. He didn't know she had the knife, and as Ashlin turned she slashed the blade out across his face. Not once, not twice, but three times before driving the tip into his throat. His screams died away into gurgles. There was a hard blow against the back of Ashlin's head, her vision faded in and out.

That bastard! She thought.

Recklessly she turned, slashing the knife through the air blindly. It caught the final guard in his open mouth, splitting his cheeks in a grotesque false smile. He grunted and then drove his foot into her leg. It almost broke. Ashlin slashed out again and caught the man's arm. It bled fast, very fast. She must've caught an artery.

She looked around her house. Chairs had been knocked over and broken in the struggle, blood stained the ground and spread across the walls in a morose display of passion. Corduvan stood with his eyes spread wide, unable to believe what he had witnessed. The guard with the broken nose remained sat against the wall, his hand on his bloodied face. The man with the gouged eyes lay on the ground moaning, hands covering his wounds. Another lay dead behind her whilst the final was bleeding out on the floor.

She felt a trickle of blood from where her hair had been pulled, could feel the throbbing in her brain from the blow she had taken, and the bruise where she had been kicked in the leg. But none of that mattered, the Pale Bull stood in front of Corduvan, his mace now drawn at the ready.

Ashlin's lip began to quiver, her eyes watery as she looked at the Pale Bull. "Look at my home ... Look what you made me do to my *home*! All I wanted was to leave, to get away from everything ..." her voice was shaky and cracked. "But you had to come waltzing in here. You couldn't have just listened to me when I told you I was Lana could you? Could you?! Now, these men are all dying!"

Ashlin stopped again to look around, her tears mixing with the sweat on her cheeks. "Rel was right about you, you know." her voice cracked again. "You just throw soldiers at whatever problem is put before you." She pointed the knife around the house, at each of the casualties. "Four men, for little old me?

Do you think they'd say it was worth it? Their wives? Mothers? Children? They'll paint me as a criminal. And to a point, they'd be right! But it didn't have to happen this way, you could have let me leave, spare these men the pain. But no, Bronwin has a job to do, Bronwin needs to see it through. Bronwin isn't allowed to make mistakes like a *normal. Fucking. Human!!!*"

Ashlin charged across the house, ignoring the pain and throb in her leg. Bronwin braced himself and as Ashlin got close, stepped to the side, swinging his mace.

Chapter 36

Rel had never been in chains before and never thought she'd let it happen without a fight either. But when Bronwin strolled in with Corduvan in chains and Ashlin crippled, she had lost her will to fight. The sleepless nights, the stress of her plot, her wounded lover and chained friend took that away from her. The final stick to break the rhenhardt's back was finding out from both Bronwin and Nef, that her Right Hand was the one who sold her out. The final strider under her command had betrayed her to a brute such as the Pale Bull.

Rel's rage wanted to grow, to fester and breed inside her. But it couldn't; she didn't have the mind or body to do so. She was broken, defeated, and sat in a wooden jail cart with Corduvan across from her, staring at his feet, and Ashlin laying in the corner unconscious. The guard with them said nothing, he sat at his post and stared up and away from them all. It was clear he wasn't happy with his posting.

They were off to Sun Spire, then to Valen to be tried for treason. They were lucky Bronwin hadn't killed them. When she asked why, the answer's he gave were surprisingly logical for a man such as him. If Alistair had heard the Pale Bull had executed not one, but two Plain's Wardens he would surely have been tried himself. He hadn't killed Ashlin, he wanted her alive to get to Rel. Corduvan was a simple matter, he was suspected, but there was no evidence against him, he had never agreed to aid her, and didn't know of the newer plot that Nef had been let in on. When Rel tried to speak in his defence, she was ignored. In truth, she couldn't fault that either, she wouldn't have listened to one who had plotted to kill her, especially after their lover had thrashed her men.

What a mess she was in; it was almost laughable. She chuckled to herself and shook her head. Corduvan and the guard looked at her with concern before she stopped and leaned her head back, closing her eyes. Not much she could do but get some sleep. Though Nef's final words rang in her mind: *I'm sorry, Rel.* He had said. *But it's for Valenfaar, our home. Bronwin can help keep it safe. I feel it in my bones. Go free my sister, and leave as one.*

How dare he use the Strider's Endless Range to send her off to prison. If she ever saw that man again, she'd gut him on the spot, it didn't matter if all she had was a mouldy shoe, she'd find a way to make it work.

#

Alistair couldn't believe what his brother had just told him. Cullen had asked to meet and brought back troubling news from both the west *and* the east. How his brother was able to find out these things faster than he could, Alistair had no idea, but his brother's intel had never been wrong before.

In the west, the Central City of Moreen had fallen, overwhelmed and occupied by enemy forces. A mass evacuation had taken place with Arlin Grey, the Shield of Moreen falling victim to the enemy. Cullen was certain that Varen's Right Hand had made it out alive. That raised some questions, but nothing he could look at at the moment, too much was still unknown.

In the east, Bronwin continued to prepare for a Threg attack but had killed Saffron and arrested the replacement warden and their lover, as well as another soldier known to be close to them. The striders had only one man left standing, some fellow named Nef, the new Plain's Master, and now Plain's Warden, he presumed.

The country was a mess, Varen was off working on something in secret, the west was being taken over by an overwhelming enemy and an invading army threatened to attack Valen borders at any moment. He was lucky to find sleep.

Alistair's generals were not entirely sure what to do. Theofold would advise him to focus on the Thregs, so he had sent more men while Wylandt vouched to support the west. So Alistair had split his men, half to one, half to the other. Then they fully realized the scale of what they were dealing with.

Wylandt recommended removing Bronwin from Plainsview and deploying him out west. That was, of course, a ridiculous idea, Bronwin knew the Thregs, he was needed against them, not their other enemy. Now that more troops were needed to the west, Alistair could do no more than send Bronwin scraps from the bottom of the barrel. He hated doing it, but the Threg army proved to be the lesser of two evils. They had hardly even breached the Halo.

The war room had never seemed so small, and to think he was the only person standing within. He felt like the gods themselves were in this room, watching him, judging him, blaming him for the misfortunes that would fall upon the country in the days to come. His father had said as much to him.

"The west is falling because of your inability to act!" he had roared, while Vera looked off into the void, quiet and within her own thoughts.

Alistair tried to explain himself, but his father's bullheadedness would have none of it. The king had very little to do with the country; it had always been down to the royal siblings; Alistair saw that now. The king and queen were but the faces of Valenfaar; a conjoined doorman. They welcomed other nations to their politics, then showed them the door to meet with the royal siblings.

Alistair had come to realize that his parents hadn't received any morsel of training in regards to military, finances, religion, or spying. The siblings had received all of that, while the king and queen were pampered and taught how to put on a nice smile for other nations.

The Arch General swept his hand across the war room table and watched as a chalice of water clattered to the ground.

"Agh!" he bellowed, "Just what in Daylen's name is stopping me from leaving this fucking country!"

"You're family and your good heart." the voice was sheepish but caring.

It was Maryam, she must've come in while he was occupied with his thoughts. Alistair turned to face her, tears threatening his eyes.

"Look at me, Maryam! Valenfaar's Arch General, and here I am on the verge of tears!"

Maryam took a step forward and placed her hand on his shoulder. "I can see that. Is it what father said to you?"

Alistair chuckled, despite his mood. "No. Nothing to do with what that old prick said. It's stress, Maryam. I can hardly sleep, and the country is falling apart. There is not much more I can do." His lip quivered. "I am Valenfaar's Arch General, I should not be close to tears!"

His sister cupped his chin and brought his eyes up to hers. "How many pitched battles have you fought in?"

He looked into her eyes and saw something cold and calculating there. What was she up to?

"Countless." he finally answered.

"No," she said, giving his head a small shake. "Do not count the battles where you stayed in a tent or the ones where you sat on a ridge overlooking them. How. Many. Battles?" She gave his head a shake with the last word, not strong, but stern.

"One ... maybe two." he finally answered, sheepishly.

"And," His sister looked at him with a raised eyebrow. "How many enemies have fallen to your sword? Were these the battles where you were being escorted through the battlefield as the tides began to turn?"

Another odd question, what was she getting at? "Yes, those are the battles. I slew maybe five men during each ride. Ten men have fallen to my blade."

Maryam gave him a kind smile, but her eyes remained fierce. "You are not a hardened soldier, dear Brother. You are not tempered by the throws of battle. You are a strategist, a scholar. You are talented with a blade, that much is true, I've no doubt you could slay most any man who would draw against you, but you do not have the thick skin of soldiers, the thick skin of your generals. You are not weak, but you are also not tempered. You are a strong young man who seeks to do his job well. Your hide is still soft, but your mind remains sharp. It is okay to feel the need to cry, Alistair. But be sure not to be fearful in front of your men. You are doing the best you can, we all know that. But sometimes even the best we can do is not enough."

"How-how will I know that?"

Maryam cast her gaze down to the side. "Unfortunately, dear Brother, we only ever know if it's not enough once everything has fallen apart in our hands."

#

Cullen had spent the night stargazing. The day had proved interesting, *very* interesting. He watched as Corduvan had been arrested, lamenting to himself about the man. He would have risen to higher ranks if he were to survive the coming battles. Cullen was sure of that. It was difficult, but not rare, to find soldiers like Corduvan. Thankfully, Valenfaar had their fair share of them, but they were seldom put in positions of power and were often sacrificed for a less-than-noble cause. Cullen chewed his lower lip behind his mask, inhaling the scent of grass and nighttime air. Bronwin was the kind of man to sacrifice those soldiers, but Cullen's duty as a Highfold and as Valenfaar's Spymaster kept his blades sheathed.

Cullen had also watched from a nearby alley as the Pale Bull and his men stormed Rel's home in an effort to take Ashlin hostage. In the end, they succeeded, but the girl had done a surprisingly good job at bloodying them, even killing two. Again Cullen's duty had him stay his blade, though much of his being told him to draw and protect the innocent.

It was true that he had learned of Rel's plan. He was Spymaster, after all, listening in on conversations and noticing glares and trends were a profession of his. Rel was to make an attempt on the Pale Bull's life; this was treason, as clear as crystal. Ashlin had known and had willingly abided by it, she did little — if anything — to stop her lover. Thus, she too was guilty of conspiracy. Corduvan knew almost nothing, he was logically suspected, but he would be set free as innocent in due time. He would see to that.

As much as the Spymaster agreed with Rel in her assessment of Bronwin, he would stand by his duty. The Pale Bull wanted to play a numbers game, but this game he could not win. They may have more than the Threg's reduced forces, but a good sum of these men were conscripts, prisoners or reserve troops never meant to see combat. By the Spire, Cullen was more than certain a good two and a half thousand troops were formally retired. Still, he could not fault his brother for sending them, the fresher, and more talented soldiers were sorely needed in the west. But with the fall of Moreen, he supposed they would be brought to the Capital instead.

Hordes of men and women were camped in the plains and forests outside of Plainsview to the west and could mobilize with relative ease. The terrain wasn't harsh, hilly or marshy. The Sovereign Guard would be ready for a fight; 50,000 troops spread between the walls, the town, and the surrounding areas. It would be a gruesome battle.

Enjoying the scent of the night air was needed, sorely so. But yet, something felt off, it almost made his skin tingle. Cullen scrunched his face and opened his eyes. He watched as red streaks flared through the air, from east to west. He sat up, looked to his left and watched as a pair of scouts began moving through the darkness and back towards Plainsview. The Thregs would begin moving, they would be at the walls on the morrow. Cullen bit back a curse, he needed to help with Plainsview, give some of their people time to escape should the likely event of failure come to pass. He would have to keep an eye on Rel's carriage too, she could be targeted on the road by bandits, and she was tired. Too tired.

A puff of smoke, and he was gone into the dark like the scouts before him. For a moment, he was pleased Rel, Ashlin, and Corduvan had made it out of Plainsview. He was hoping he would be able to say the same about himself in the coming days.

Chapter 37

They had begun deploying troops before Moon's Peak. Two scouts had come scurrying back, panting like hounds; they spoke of a star shower. Bronwin had sent them back out immediately, and shortly after Moon's Peak, they had returned with confirmation that the Thregs were moving. That they would be at the gate by morning.

The sun had yet to crest the horizon behind them, the sun would be at their backs, and in the enemy's eyes. A blind enemy, Bronwin was once taught, was a great enemy to fight. He knew the Thregs, he had fought them time and time again. They would attack as soon as possible. It was their way.

Many archers lined the wall of Plainsview. Conscripts and prisoners had been escorted outside of the gates and had formed lines beyond the wall. They were to be slaughtered like the expendable fodder they were. It would buy the rest of the troops time, but mostly, would tire out the first wave of attackers.

Plainsview was almost unrecognizable. The sprawling town was now home to machines of war; catapults and trebuchets dotted the town's various squares, everything aimed east to Valen's Passage, ready to rain all manner of death upon their foes. Bronwin grinned wolfishly. He even had ballistae loaded with scattershots mounted on several of the larger, flatter buildings in town. He had them primed to be lit a flame and fired with oil jars mounted on the heads. The bolts would drive into the ground as the oil jar fell from its fastenings. When the jar broke on impact it would ignite the ground with pools of fire. And with each ballista able to fire a bundle of these at a time, it would create havoc.

Bronwin knew the wall would fall eventually and that was fine. He would be impressed, but not surprised if it remained standing when the battle was over and the Thregs were routed. But in the likely event the wall was breached, they had laid traps all through the town, buildings set to collapse with an easily placed ballista bolt, holes with men waiting beneath, to spring forth from the earth like the living dead. Bronwin's grin widened. He had been waiting for this day to come for a long time now. He would be promoted to General. And it would be about time too.

The Pale Bull stood at the base of the wall, taking one last moment to examine the structure for any large flaws. The wall had doubled in size, at the least. Wood planks and scrap metal pieces had been fastened on in all manner of ways. It looked cobbled together, but there were no issues large enough to be a problem, not in his expert eyes, anyway.

"Sir!" Algrenon called down from above, "You might want to come up here!"

Bronwin said nothing as he climbed the wall. He found himself resenting the size of the thing as he stepped. He arrived at the top to be greeted by Nef and Algrenon, standing among the rows of archers.

"Pardon the crowd." Algrenon approached, clearing a way for Bronwin to come through.

Nef stayed at the battlements, leaning forward as he watched something in the distance. "Sir, come take a look, they'll be here soon!"

Archers shuffled and looked nervously at one another as they heard the announcement. Fools, they had no need to be nervous, the sun was at their backs, the Thregs wouldn't even be able to see the archers until they were nearly at the walls.

"What do you see?" Bronwin leaned against the battlements too, Nef at his right. Wooden battlements felt strange to him, he had grown so used to the stone of the Central Cities.

"Look," The strider pointed above the trees of the swamp. "Smoke stacks. Not far off. I'd wager we have very little time before they breach the treeline." Nef looked up to Bronwin. "What do you think they'll do, will they attack right away?"

"Of course they will. They're savages."

Nef nodded, a new glint of confidence in his eyes.

Just then, out of the corner of his vision, Bronwin noticed Algrenon signal to an officer at the base of the wall. The lines of conscripts and prisoners began to form up, tighter now. Shields in the front, spears behind them, shock infantry at the rear.

The shock infantry was a last-minute idea, Nef took some of the more nimble prisoners and conscripts and gave them very brief lessons on how to manoeuvre the lines like the Plain's Striders had. Softening up and distracting the Thregs for the sterner troops to score swifter kills. The shock troops were the striders' replacements, there was no hiding that. If any of them survived, maybe they would be made into official striders with the blessing of the new Plain's Warden.

The lines formed up, and the archers were ready. Everyone stood on edge. Behind them, in the town of Plainsview, squads of men and women waited behind buildings, in alleyways, in small dugouts covered with camouflaged hatches, and beyond Plainsview, Bronwin's last resort: another contingent of troops, 2,000 strong, a shield wall. If any troops were to flee they would be denied passage and cut down without warning.

"There! There they are!" An archer was pointing like a toddler towards the treeline.

"Lower your hand, you idiot!" Bronwin bellowed, "I'll tear it off if you don't!"

The archer flinched and dropped his hand without a word.

Bronwin roared to his soldiers. "Sovereign Guard!" He raised his mace into the air above him, shield at his side. "Brace yourselves!! Soon, the enemy will be here! Gwendall favours us this day, fight and we shall keep our country safe!"

Bronwin and his officers readied themselves for the oncoming charge, archers stood nervous, and conscripts stood terrified. Everyone was ready, everyone was nervous, and everyone waited.

#

Nef hadn't expected to wait half a day. But they did. The Thregs had formed their lines at the edge of the swamp, shifting formations randomly as time passed. They hadn't done what Bronwin had been so sure they would: they hadn't attacked while the sun was in their eyes. Apart from their formation, the Thregs hadn't shown any indication they were going to attack at all.

The Plain's Warden could feel it in the air. Everyone was nervous. What they had all been assured would happen, didn't, the unease was infectious, dangerous even. Nef swallowed hard. His stomach was in knots, the unease and anticipation of the battle didn't help, the amount of sleep he had lost made things worse, and his ongoing guilt about betraying Rel to Bronwin refused to leave his mind. Part of Nef wanted to help her, but he couldn't risk being labelled a traitor too.

The weather held, the skies remained clear and the sun shone down peacefully into the green fields between Plainsview and the swamp of Valen's Passage. Soldiers stood at the ready, rows upon rows of shields, the tips of spears and swords poised between.

Nef looked to Bronwin next to him and saw, for the briefest of moments, the confusion in his eyes. He didn't know why the Thregs hadn't attacked, but Nef thought he had an idea as to why: they didn't want to fight with the sun in their eyes, they were smarter than Bronwin had given them credit for.

"They didn't want to fight while the sun was at our backs." the strider said to Bronwin.

The Pale Bull grunted with resentment. "It means nothing. They attack soon." He raised his mace and pointed a finger towards the swamps.

Nef squinted his eyes, and even from where he stood, he could see the agitation in the Threg lines. They were itching to move, itching to kill, yearning to slaughter.

They breached the treeline in a dash, rows upon rows of the horrors coalesced into a scattered horde of troops, like insects along a forest floor they swarmed through the field.

A horn sounded and the shield line moved up, one step at a time, swords and spears pointed towards their foes. They moved as a wall, creeping closer to the onslaught.

A command, nearly wordless, rolled over Plainsview's wall as the archers nocked their arrows and raised their bows. The first row fired, and as they loaded, the second row fired, then the third. The cycle repeated itself, thousands of arrows raining down into the Threg masses ceaselessly.

Nef grinned as he watched the Thregs become little more than pin cushions. They were nearly a third of the way to the shield line. Their troops fell, but slowly. The thick hide and relentless anger of the enemy drove them further than any human troop would have been able to endure. The shield wall ceased: they had advanced a quarter of the way through the field. Any further and they would be hit by …

#

Artillery fire.

Cullen watched from the northern slope of the passage as stone flew over the Sovereign troops. Trebuchets and catapults, built with haste, fired one after the other. The Spymaster was impressed at Bronwin's ability to keep sustained fire on his enemies: arrows rained ceaselessly, and now boulders and large swaths of stones did too.

Cullen arched an eyebrow as he watched a bundle of logs fly overhead. Each projectile spread out from the singular clump and slammed randomly into the approaching horde. The creatures were taking an astounding amount of punishment. He watched as one of the monstrosities took three arrows to the chest, fall down, and get back up, only to have its head smashed in by a projectile log.

Why use logs? he thought.

Wood was a precious commodity during siege time. It was needed to build fortifications, make weapons and arrows, to make the very artillery that was firing them. People needed it to cook, to create fire. *Fire.* That was the answer he sought: *fire.*

With that thought Cullen watched as some of the more forward ballistae fired their flaming scattershots at a low angle, causing many of the Sovereign troops on the Plainsview wall to flinch and reel, their gazes being cast upwards as the bolts nearly sheared the heads from their shoulders.

The ballista bolts crashed into the ground, belching flaming oil into the battlefield, igniting flesh and bone, grass and log, metal and leather. The Thregs continued their dash, undeterred by the losses they sustained.

And the losses were great, but nothing compared to what a human army would have suffered. The invaders were almost upon the defenders now; their shields poised, but even from here Cullen could see they wavered. Sunlight reflected off of them in a nervous shimmer.

In a blink, Cullen was gone, a puff of gold-flecked black smoke existed where he once stood, filling the void he left in existence as he moved down below. Another puff further down the slope, then another, and another until he appeared along the wall with Bronwin and Nef. His black boots silent against the wooden ramparts.

"A formidable defence, Bronwin," Cullen spoke clear and calm, his voice penetrating through the chaos below.

The Thregs clashed against shields and were met with sword and spear. For conscripts, they did a passable job at coordinating their strikes. A portion of the wall would open for a moment as weapons lashed out from within, then would seal again.

Bronwin nearly flinched at the sudden appearance of the Valen Spymaster. "Your praise is appreciated. But the battle has only just started."

"Cullen!" Nef was shocked, he gained his thoughts a moment later then looked around at the archers as they fired their volleys into the depths of the enemy. "Men, a Highfold is here with us! Take note of the royal family! Their blessing is upon us, the gods fight with us!"

Cullen grimaced behind his mask. He would let the boy and the soldiers think what they wished, but no gods were fighting with them that day, and their Highfolds didn't know their Spymaster was present at the battle itself. They didn't know where he was, they never did, and if they ever possessed such information, it would be because he had let them gather it.

"Your words are true, Bronwin. The battle *has* only just started. And though you have begun valiantly, I fear the battle will be a bloody one for your defenders." Cullen raised an outstretched arm and pointed to a section of the shield wall on their right. It was crumbling.

When that section of the wall had opened up for a counterattack, the Thregs launched themselves into a mass tackle at the men there, driving many of the shieldsmen to the ground. The Thregs that had launched this brazen attack were slain but had opened the way for those behind. The Thregs had begun to breach that section as men and women rushed to fill the gap.

Skulls were crushed and shields were tossed aside as Thregs stomped into the lines of conscripts. Cullen watched as one woman thrust forward with her spear, getting the point stuck in the shoulder of the enemy. The Threg looked at her with a sneer, roared with its spindle-tongue and grabbed the weapon. It tugged on the shaft and ripped the wielder forwards as an old rusted hatchet landed between the woman's eyes. Cullen couldn't hear the sound it had made from where he stood, not over the roar of battle, but he felt his stomach lurch anyway.

"Your soldiers need help on that flank. The line will start to fall, otherwise." Cullen leaned forward, his gaze stern behind his mask.

"And what would you have me do? They're conscripts and prisoners, they're meant to die."

Cullen said nothing, he only vanished in another puff of smoke, leaving Bronwin and Nef standing there, mouths agape.

They are still people, Bronwin. Cullen thought as he travelled, reality swirling into and out of existence as he did. *And if saving them can save more, it'll be worth the effort.*

The Spymaster's final manoeuvre brought him straight into the thick of it. A quick glance around and Cullen could see the panic on the troop's faces as they rushed to fill the line against the advancing horde. A sharp turn and a Threg stabbed out towards the Highfold. He twisted out of the way, and in half a blink of an eye, one of Cullen's daggers had breached the Threg's head, stabbing up and into its jaw, sinking deep inside the creature's skull. There was hardly a sound.

Cullen tugged his dagger out, and as if he were throwing a playing card, launched the weapon through the air, catching another Threg in the chest. Another puff of smoke and he was standing on the handle of the weapon, the point of the other jabbed between the eyes of his target. Cullen pushed off, removed his weapons in a single motion and twirled away.

#

Nef watched in disbelief as puffs of black and gold smoke appeared and disappeared at the broken line. The man moved far too fast for the strider to comprehend every movement. Each blink, and two or three more Thregs began to fall, then three more before they had even reached the ground. It was madness, it was chaos, the Thregs would swing and roar in anger as they slashed through smoke before thick daggers punctured their bodies.

"His daggers ..." Nef said astounded. "They look as if they could puncture plate mail!"

"Yes, it is impressive," Bronwin admitted, "Though his folly there will make little difference."

As the Pale Bull uttered those words, Nef could see the commander being proved wrong. Soldiers rushed to grab the fallen shields as Cullen stabbed and vanished through the Threg mass. One blink and three more flashes of smoke could be seen, and another half a dozen bodies with them. The way the Highfold killed was impossible to understand, impossible to begin to comprehend. How had he learned that type of magic, that type of speed, that type of endurance?

Then it was done, the line was reformed, though not as capable of counterattack as it had been, but there it stood. Several conscripted men and women holding shields, weapons poised between them, holding the Threg advance. The line began to fall back, but it did not break. Soldiers moved to fill in gaps where shieldsmen had fallen, and reinforcements actively strode out of Plainsview to try and replenish the lines where they could.

Nef knew Bronwin had the numbers to hold the line, but the loss of life would be catastrophic. Fire burned and acrid smoke billowed up and into the air. One bad gust of wind and the smoke would be in the eyes of the Sovereign Guard. One good gust of wind though, and it would be in the face of the oncoming Thregs.

Nef could see Bronwin watching the smoke with an intensity he didn't think was possible. Then it happened, the Pale Bull signalled to his men as a breeze began to blow east and into the invaders' front. Another horn sounded and the shield line began to advance. Nef watched as his would-be striders began to move forward. The Sovereign Guard broke their shield wall and charged. With smoke in the faces of their enemies, now was the time to strike.

The fires had weakened the Thregs coming to strengthen the assault, and with the aid of the shock troops, those that had made it to the shield wall began to fall to sword and spear. Sovereign troops engaged in combat, two to a Threg with shock troops slashing through the lines, distracting and toppling the enemy where they could. Though the battle was tilting in favour of the Sovereign Guard, Nef was not blind to the fact that for every Threg that fell, three or four guardsmen had fallen. They were winning, but the losses were staggering, almost crippling.

The archers had stopped firing, so too did the artillery, Nef wasn't sure when this had happened. They had exhausted a lot of ammunition, the warden wondered if they would have enough to hold off another assault.

The sun had stopped shining now, cloud and smoke had blotted it out and cast the fields below them in a slate grey. Armour, dented and bloody, littered the ground like leaves in mid-autumn. It was so easy to miss, but as the troops moved forward and pushed the Thregs back into the swamps, the massacre had become clear. They had saved Plainsview another day, but they did not win the battle. Bronwin played a numbers game, but even numbers could be traitorous bastards.

. .

Chapter 38

The night after the first attack, rain had swept into the sky and began to dot the ground with moisture. Wounded soldiers were rushed off the charred fields to receive aid. Weapons, armour and shields were placed back into circulation as troops worked to replenish ammunition for both the archers and the artillery. They had exhausted much of their supply, and though the final death toll hadn't been counted, there was no doubt that the Sovereign Guard had lost almost four times as many troops as the Thregs had.

Nef began to grow worried. He looked around at the men and women surrounding the town, dotted on the walls, and the dead being carted away. It was bad, and they couldn't go on with their defence in the same manner they had been. Their numbers would dwindle, and the Thregs would break through. If not this moon, then surely the next.

He had been looking for Bronwin and with little luck. Spying Algrenon, Nef quickly wormed his way through soldiers going about their business.

"Algrenon!" he called, "Algrenon, where is Bronwin?"

Upon reaching Bronwin's Right Hand, Nef could see that stress was taking a toll on the officer. His normally sharp features were sallow and sunken, the skin of his face — now paler — looked to be hanging off his skull. His eyes were yellowed and bloodshot. He looked at Nef without seeing and pointed over to the Strider's Respite.

"The tavern?" the warden asked, "What is he doing in the tavern?"

Algrenon blinked wearily, then blinked some more, some semblance of who he once was coming back to him. He shrugged. "Not drinking. I know that much. Might be talking with the rest of the officers. Fuck if I know."

Nef didn't reply; only turned away and began his trek towards the tavern. The battles were becoming more and more pyrrhic as time went on. The first battle at the mouth of the passage had been bad, but even that he had deemed a worthy sacrifice. The previous engagement was nothing short of a farce. The defenders had thrown so much at the Thregs, only to lose more soldiers to the invaders than they could have imagined.

It wasn't just the loss of lives, no. Nef couldn't help but focus on the amount of ammunition they pumped into their foes. Ceaseless arrows and constant artillery. And for what? A near victory? A good portion of that victory was owed to the good graces of Esmirla, rushing the wind in their favour. The warden shook his head, regret settling in. Maybe Rel was right: maybe Bronwin's methods were too harsh, too simple. They needed to fall back.

The tavern rose to meet Nef. The rough wood looked more worn than usual. He looked around, *everything* looked more worn than usual. Nothing looked untouched by the fatigue of war. The once smooth finish of the tavern looked rough and coarse, mud, dirt, soot and Daylen knew what else had been rubbed into it. A shame, the town had once stood so tall, a jewel on the way into Valenfaar and now it crawled, tarnished and wounded, hardly holding onto its borders.

Nef remembered seeing the sprawling town for the first time, as travellers from beyond the Halo arrived. Many of them had stood with mouths hung open, and those gaping maws would only grow bigger once they saw the walls of Sun Spire, and even further still at the sheer scale of Valen. Yet now, and to no one's fault but the Thregs, Plainsview stood in mire, and soon would sit in ruin. Doors hung open as people had abandoned their homes, dirt, grime, blood, ash and even shit had been spread on the walls and ground. Former shop stalls stood empty with fruits and vegetables rotting, some overturned into the dirt and mud.

Another shake of his head and Nef pushed the door to the tavern open. Inside he saw Bronwin and a lean man, clad in black: Cullen. The two were deep in a discussion that neither of them looked pleased to be having. Neither of them looked up at the warden as he walked over.

"Nef. Please, sit." Cullen motioned to him without a glance. "Perhaps you can try to talk some sense into Bronwin. He refuses to see reason."

The commander snorted. "I see plenty of reason, Spymaster. But you are not my superior, you are not a soldier as Alistair is, you do not command me. You play with tricks and information, you do not understand a battlefield as I do, you do not understand our foe as I do."

Nef sat, saying nothing. Now wasn't the time.

"I do not claim to be your superior, but my brother would have some words for you if he saw how you throw lives to the wind as if they were ashes." he kept his voice calm and level, without a hint of anger or frustration. "Do you not realize that the Thregs have arrived at our country with an army that numbered upwards of 50,000?"

"That is why Alistair has given me 70,000 men since we began, Spymaster."

Bronwin was restraining himself; his tone was calm and flat but the words felt muffled, their true desire withheld.

"My brother may have given you 70,000 troops but you lost 10,000 in the passage, and another ten this very day. The Thregs have lost, in estimate, 7,000 troops. Of your 50,000 remaining troops a large swath of them have had little to no training, are wounded, or were retired before being summoned. You cannot hope to beat more than 40,000 fresh Thregs with scraps from Valenfaar's waste bins."

Cullen's gaze shot out of his mask towards the Pale Bull, and the way the larger man had flinched, Nef would have sworn he had just been slapped.

Nef went to speak but was cut off.

"We will hold our ground." Bronwin struggled to match the Highfold's gaze. "Plainsview will remain secure and the threat to our country will be repelled. I understand your concern, Spymaster, but this battle is mine to fight, not yours."

"With all due respect, sir." Nef finally said, a flutter in his stomach. "I'm beginning to believe that Cullen may be right. We've already lost so many sold-"

"And what would you have me do, Plains Warden?!" Bronwin slammed a fist down as his words seeped venom. "I can lead armies! I can send those Thregs back into the Endless Plains with their tongues shoved firmly down their throats. You lead a faction of *one*. You know nothing of what we face. You will fall in line with the other officers."

Nef bowed his head. "Sorry, sir,"

The warden was beginning to think that maybe Rel had been the lucky one: getting out of Plainsview when she did. She may have been in chains, with an uncertain future, but she didn't have to worry about the invaders anymore.

The Plains Warden sat and listened to the two men debate for most of the day. The room had begun to smell of sweat and body odour: sour and wet. The tip-tap of rain that had existed earlier in the day had now swelled to the constant hammering of a downpour. Outside, the dying and wounded would be moved into the abandoned homes of Plainsview to keep them dry, to try and hold infection and illness at bay.

Cullen had, not once, lost his temper. He remained calm and steadfast at all of Bronwin's flawed arguments. While the Spymaster continued to speak with logic and concern, the Pale Bull could only speak in circles, always coming back around to the idea that he was the best suited for the operation because of his past, and that he had everything under control.

Twice Bronwin had lost his temper, and in both those moments Cullen sat back in his chair, his hands folded neatly in his lap and waited for the man to say what he wished to say. The Highfold would begin to speak again, ignoring the previous outburst and would again point out more flaws in the operation: wounded and ill soldiers needed to be vacated from town else a pandemic would be on their hands; the reinforcement of the defensive wall was also a point of contention; it was cobbled together, in a hurry, as most of the fortifications had been. If the Thregs were to reach them, they would topple with little issue. Finally, before Cullen had called the debate finished, he had pointed out how even a good portion of the artillery that had been hastily built had crumbled shortly after the battle, some even during the battle. Between that and the low ammunition, Nef was puzzled to see why Bronwin held to his opinion so stubbornly. They won once, but at a staggering cost. They would not win again, not without a miracle.

Cullen pushed himself back from the table, his chair grinding into the wooden floorboards. He stood, looked at Bronwin, then to Nef. "I will stay to help you with this fool's errand. But make no mistake, when I feel the battle is lost, I will leave, one way or the other. Best of luck to you, Plain's Strider." He looked at Bronwin, regret in his eyes. "And to you, Shield." Then the man vanished, a fistful of black and gold smoke lingered where he had been standing.

Bronwin sat at the table, wordless, staring into the centre of the wood. "We will succeed here," he said, dryly. "I will see to that, Nef. Of that, you have my word. Now go, I need to be alone."

Nef didn't speak, rose from his seat and stumbled as he left the tavern. As the door swung shut behind him, the day stood cool and grey, rain came down in sheets from the darkening skies above. The ground was now caked and muddy, deep footprints marred the landscape and deep ruts from wagon wheels traced lines through the once lively streets of Plainsview. He could hear the coughing and dying of the wounded from the abandoned homes, he could hear the ring of hammers as arrows were made.

Nef took a step and felt his boot sink into the wet ground, he pulled it out with a squelch and grimaced, step after step he moved, taking in the sights and sounds of this new Plainsview, the Doomed Plainsview.

He wandered until after sundown, where the night air grew thick and damp with darkness and death. He found himself standing before the great willow tree at the centre of the town. Its bark now a deep black, and its long tangles of leaves a stark white.

A bolt of lightning lit up the area, and as thunder rolled through his mind, Nef began to weep. Even should he not die, the omen of a Shadewood tree was not a welcome sight. They would lose Plainsview, and he would surely die. He hoped for, at the very least, that he would die with his blade in the enemy, and not with shit in his pants.

It was only when his tears dropped into the puddle at his feet that Nef realized the gods did not hold the Sovereign Guard in favour for this war. No. The Shadewood tree told of ill omens and death. And the rain, oh the rain, so often a sign of life. But now, Nef knew that Esmirla was weeping, for there was nothing that she could do to help them. Pray as he might, it would not make any difference.

A rush of adrenaline filled the Plain's Warden as Bronwin's words echoed in his mind.

"We will succeed here. I will see to that, Nef. Of that, you have my word."

Even if the gods thought the defence of Plainsview was a lost cause, Nef would fight and prove the gods wrong.

#

After two full days of the goddess' tears, sickness began to spread through Plainsview. The dying had become ill and had quickly shared their ailments with those around them. Soldiers visiting their friends were returning to their posts coughing, spreading the sickness further. Everyone was tired, everyone could hardly eat. Their bodies were not prepared to fight off a sickness *and* an invasion in tandem.

After considerable consul, Cullen had been able to convince Bronwin's officers to speak to him about the wounded and the sick. They had convinced him, after strenuous debate, to begin evacuating them for the health of those that remained able to fight. The Pale Bull had foolishly fought these ideas saying that the men were fine, that the Sovereign Guard could deal with the common cold without needing to dedicate manpower to evacuating the sick and wounded.

Cullen had an inkling of an idea that Bronwin wanted to leave these troops behind, as fodder or distractions for the Thregs should they breach the wall. They would spend time killing the wounded instead of pursuing the lively. Cullen's gut told him this was more accurate than he would have liked to admit; he could tell by the look in the Pale Bull's eyes. It was cold, heartless and savage. He would do whatever he could to assure victory. Everything but retreat.

The Spymaster could understand a portion of the man's thoughts. If the Thregs breached Plainsview and made it deeper into Valenfaar, the campaign could be considered a failure. Bronwin didn't accept failure, he had never "failed" in his duty before, and he wasn't keen on the idea of starting with Plainsview. But, Cullen had to admit, the number of men the Pale Bull had lost in skirmishes, and in Plainsview had been obscene. He couldn't continue to operate the way he had been, not with things going horribly wrong in the west. They would need all the soldiers they could get.

Cullen was not surprised to find himself walking along one of the ridges that scaled the side of Valen's passage. Here it was more stone than mud, a tad slippery, but nothing Cullen couldn't compensate for. He sat down and watched as the rain continued to fall. He sat and looked out over the fields from the previous battle below him. Still marred with charred flesh and soot.

How far the Crimson Plains have stretched. he thought, looking at the carnage. He shook his head and looked back to Plainsview. Wagons of bodies turned this way and that through the town as they transported the dead. Where Bronwin had those bodies going, he did not know, and Cullen wasn't about to allocate resources to find out.

The smell of wet stone, grass and mud reached his nostrils. He inhaled deeply, ignoring the ashy tinge that clung to every scent of his country in recent days. In the west it reeked of flame and death, and out here, in the east, it wreaked of flame and mud. Nowhere he went could cleanse that scent of ash from his nose. These were dark times for Valenfaar, and Cullen could feel it was about to get much, much worse.

Another three days of rain came to Plainsview as Cullen mulled about, watching and waiting. He wasn't entirely sure what he was watching for, so he watched everything he could. On the fourth day of rain, illness had spread rampantly through the town, infecting soldiers and the few peasants who had yet to leave their homes. The magister had taken ill and had promptly passed on to the Soul Spire, where he undoubtedly was given a hero's welcome. The old man had hardly slept, hardly ate, and worked himself beyond the point of exhaustion to help the sick and wounded. His body and spirit could not fight off the infection and he succumbed to it far more hastily than those who had before him. The magister had been given a proper burial by many of the sick that he treated day in and day out. They saw him off with sober looks and anxious tears.

Cullen saw Bronwin flex his command and order troops to work through both Sun's Peak and Moon's Peak to make arrows and ammunition. The Sovereign Guard was exhausted, the conscripts too. Whenever the Thregs decided to arrive, it would be a total defeat for them all. Bronwin had pushed his men and women to their limits, even in the face of illness and defeat. They had almost resupplied their ammo stores, but Cullen knew that wouldn't be enough. He breathed out a heavy sigh whilst sitting on the wet rooftop. He wasn't sure he'd see the end of the battle himself.

Plainsview now rested in a boggy mess of land. Mud covered every surface and orifice. Even the ground from atop the passage, flanking the city, had grown caked with mud. Eastern Valenfaar had not seen so much rain in the last four cycles. The last time this happened the swamp had flooded and started to seep into Plainsview itself. Thankfully, the aftermath of the battle did a lot to stem the tide of water rising out of the swamp. Flooding would not be a concern this season.

Cullen walked the town as he had done every day since the previous attack, looking for anything he could think of that might give them an advantage in the battle ahead.

"Nothing," he said to himself. "Of course, there isn't anything here, we've nothing but farms and food." Cullen shook his head. The Thregs would likely march the full might of their army on Plainsview after their defeat five days ago. There was no guarantee of this, but the looming Shadewood tree at the centre of town seemed to speak of evil to come. Soldiers were seen giving the monument a wide berth, as their skin prickled when passing by.

The spider holes scattered about town had filled with water up to the waist for most of the men standing within. They would spend a good portion of each evening and morning bailing out the water in the event of an attack. Cullen did not envy them. The use of spider holes, in the event of the wall becoming breached, was a smart one; even if the men dwelling inside the constructs were cramped, wet, tired, and scared.

That fifth day of rain went by in a blur: Cullen walked and wandered through town, getting lost in his own thoughts and ignoring the scent of war as best he could. As night fell, Cullen looked up at the cloudy night sky, seeing nothing beyond. No stars, no moon, only inky darkness and a few flashes of red, hidden deep within the clouds. The battle for Plainsview would be fought on the morrow. The certainty he felt at such a thought brought the Spymaster a cold sense of peace. The waiting was finally over.

He had slept soundly that night and was thankful. The morning was grey and overcast, the rain slowed to a smattering, the clouds hung like corpses in the sky as the white light of the sun tried to peek through in scant rays. How long had he slept? Looking at the clouds Cullen tried to guess as to what time of day it was, perhaps mid-morning? He felt that was likely.

As he squinted into the clouds something began to look off, wrong even. A greenish hue tinted the bottoms of the clouds. Cullen quickly snapped his head from side to side and saw the green tint reflected on everything around him. Everyone looked upwards to the skies in wonder and amazement ... then horror.

The Spymaster's eyes shot open. "Everyone, down!" he roared.

Green crackling fireballs laced the air in a horrid hue, arcing like artillery through the skies. Several missiles struck buildings, casting wooden splinters into the surrounding town with fiery hatred. A small cluster of soldiers had been standing in the wrong place at the wrong time and took the brunt of the explosive head-on. Their bodies scattered and their limbs were tossed to the side. A dozen impacts landed through Plainsview. Men and women ran, grabbing their equipment and tending to the wounded.

A horn reverberated through town, like the call of some melancholic beast. A second volley of green flame cracked through the air and detonated within Plainsview once more. The ground shook and mud shifted and slid underfoot. A third volley impacted against Plainsview's eastern wall with little effect. The fourth volley of green fire screamed and crackled under the clouds with a deathly staccato. Each explosive slammed into the reinforced Valley wall and tore open a hole wide enough for two carriages to fit side by side.

The fifth volley of mage-fire proved to be the worst. They hadn't landed in Plainsview, they had landed on its flanks, along with the drops and walls of Valen's Passage. The explosions shook the rocky structures, loosening the mud. Cullen watched in stunned horror as mudslides from both the north and south of Plainsview began to tumble and undulate their way down the slopes.

The Battle for Plainsview had begun.

Chapter 39

Bronwin stormed out of the small bunkhouse he had been sleeping in to the sound of explosions and trembling ground. He had slept in his armour, it was uncomfortable, but he was thankful he did. A cluster of crackling green fireballs streaked through the sky above and smashed into Plainsview and its defending wall.

Bronwin swore to himself and watched as two great mudslides from the mountain walls converged on the town with rolling death. Buildings were taken from the very ground they were built on. Homes with wounded men were washed away into the muck, their screams hardly reaching his ears.

The very earth revolted against them. Sodden land rolled and reached out to Plainsview with slovenly lust, devouring soldiers and structures alike.

The Pale Bull turned back into his quarters and grabbed his shield and mace before marching into the mud. His feet sank deep as the weight of both himself and his equipment dragged him down. It took an effort to pull each step from the ground. Looking around, soldiers were doing their damnedest to get to the gates to launch their defence. They were taking planks of wood from destroyed buildings and using them to try and cross the mud faster, laying them out to use as small bridges.

Bronwin continued to stomp through, now able to see the tops of the wall. Arrows rained out from portions of it in a mockery of their previous efforts. Step after step the Pale Bull closed in until the Valley Wall was in full view. To the right, a gaping hole burned in the structure. Through the smoke and rain, Bronwin could see the Thregs making their advance. They were more than halfway to Plainsview from the swamp. He quickened his pace.

With every step the Shield of Northwood's anger grew, sweat broke free on his brow and a red haze began to creep into his vision. He watched as Cullen and Nef made it to the breach with a small group of shieldsmen. The Highfold and strider shouted out orders in sequence, forming the line as fast as they could before settling back behind the shields. Cullen disappeared in a puff of smoke and appeared on a part of the wall that had not yet sustained damage. Then vanished out of sight again.

"I hate that fucking trick of his," Bronwin muttered as he pulled his boot free from the mud once more. He began to find more solid ground and hastened his pace. He turned around for a moment and watched as the mudslides continued to roll in. Much slower now, but still in motion. Much of their remaining artillery had been swept up and rolled lazily along with the rest of the debris.

"Esmirla's Cunt!" he bit the curse into the sky, trying to direct it at the goddess herself. Bronwin turned and trudged up to the shield line where Algrenon had now joined.

"Sir!" Algrenon cried, "Sir, what do we do!"

"Hold the fucking wall, you fool." Bronwin pushed past the two men and shoved his way into the shield wall. "If any of you can hold a shield-" he roared, "Grab it and get your asses to the breach *now!!*" He turned, added his shield to the line and crouched down with his mace at the ready.

#

"He'll get himself killed!" Nef found himself grabbing onto Algrenon's shoulders. He looked scared, confused and panicked. "Won't he listen to you?!"

"He never listens to me." Bronwin's Right Hand said with a flat, almost dazed tone. "If he felt it was right, he wouldn't listen to me if I told him to not fuck his mother." Algrenon's gaze lingered over Nef's shoulder before the sound of weapons on shields brought him back to the present. "Where are your striders?" he said almost confidently, his gaze snapping onto Nef.

The warden shook his head. "I've no idea. Everyone is scattered, we don't even know if they're alive right now."

They both turned to look at the mudslide ruefully, it was finally coming to a halt. More than half the town was buried. Anyone unlucky enough to be in the spider holes would surely have been buried alive.

"They'll make their way here if they're alive." Nef continued, trying to give himself some hope. "You can be sure of that."

Algrenon nodded, then looked back to the breach, Bronwin had smashed a Threg in the chin with his shield and brought his mace down onto the creature's skull. The troops around him rallied at the sight.

They could hear the ring of weapons on the wall and on the shields defending the breach.

"We need to get higher," Algrenon finally said. "Come, to the wall."

Both men turned and pushed their way through troops and over debris. The smell of ash and flame, once almost retired, had blown back into the air with a force that was almost overwhelming. Nef and Algrenon coughed, and for a moment, Nef wasn't sure if the cough was from smoke or from illness.

The officer's made it to the top of the wall in little time, the wood slick beneath them, but they managed to keep their balance. Squeezing between two panicked archers, Nef and Algrenon gazed into the plains below them and stared in stunned amazement. The entirety of the ground spanning the distance between Plainsview and the swamp had been filled with Thregs, some with ladders as they approached the walls.

"It's their whole fucking army ..." Algrenon spoke the words with a fatalistic fascination.

Another mess of green flame and a group of archers to their right were flung into the air. The explosion rocked the wall. Nef braced himself on the nearby battlement and looked with horror at the burning corpses that had been strewn about.

"Come on," The warden placed his free hand on Algrenon's shoulder. "That could have been us, we need to get off this damned wall, *now!*"

Algrenon said nothing, he nodded in agreement and the two men returned from the way they had come, ladders clattering onto the wall behind them as they left. The officers stepped over bodies and charred wood, down the steps and finally onto the cold and muck-ridden ground. Another explosion of green fire, this one next to the breach. Bronwin came stomping away from the wall, having the same realization they did.

"That shield wall won't hold if one of those fucking things hit them." The Pale Bull was drenched. Mud streaked his armour where soot and blood didn't.

Another explosion and they flinched, bowing their heads low. Bronwin raised his shield to protect himself from an incoming piece of debris, it bounced harmlessly away.

"What do we do?" Nef looked at them incredulously. "What is our plan? We're caught with our pants around our ankles here!" He noticed a few of his shock troops had made it to the wall, maybe a dozen, possibly a couple more. "Hey, get away from there!"

Another green fireball crackled into existence and slammed into more archers atop the wall. Burning bodies were cast aside and rolled over the edge, some down the stairs tripping up soldiers as they tried to make their way up or down the structure.

"Fall back!" Nef pointed to a row of buildings outside the reach of the mudslide.

His troops nodded before moving to safety, as they stepped away Nef called back out. "And be ready to move on my order!"

"We fight," Bronwin said. "Get every last man and woman and get them stationed. Behind buildings, in alleyways, creating choke points. They can fight from rooftops, use the mud to our advantage."

"Sir!" Algrenon called over another explosion, "The wall is breached, the town is half-buried and our artillery is *fucked!* They've taken us by surprise, we should pull back to Sun Spire!"

"He's right!" Nef called, his throat pained as he tried to be heard over the chaos, "We need to retreat!"

"One more word of retreat and I'll kill you myself. Is that clear?" Bronwin's tone came through the carnage clear and crisp.

Both Nef and Algrenon looked at each other, worried, then back to their commander.

"Yes, sir," they said.

The Pale Bull nodded. "Good, now get the Sovereign Guard prepared for skirmishes. Go!"

Both the strider and Bronwin's Right Hand moved into Plainsview, trudging through the mud and flagging groups of soldiers down to their positions for reassignment. Groups were dispersed through the town, on top of buildings and in the remains of alleyways.

#

The shield wall fell before Cullen could assist. He had been preoccupied with pulling soldiers out of the mud. Bronwin slogged over with a score of men in an attempt to contain the flood. The Thregs stomped through the grime without care, snarling their evil grins as they cut into the flesh of soldiers. A single Threg cut away at one, two, three conscripts before being felled by a spear.

Bronwin and his retinue had circled the breach now and fought back tooth and nail. Soldiers parried, blocked, countered and struck. Sickness was almost forgotten among the troops, the sheer panic and adrenaline-fueled need for survival superseded all.

Cullen moved to join the containment team, but someone had grabbed his shoulder.

"Sir!" the familiar voice called from an unfamiliar face, "Sir! Where would you like the Anvil's Hammer?!" Another explosion rocked the ground beneath them.

The Spymaster gazed into the man's eyes before him and saw it to be Velamir. His eyes were sunken and dark, hair caked with mud, no longer resembling the golden locks he had prided himself with before. Velamir's armour was dented and smeared with muck. And Velamir didn't seem to mind. That was good.

"Fall back to the central square! Start setting up a fallback there!" Cullen ordered as soldiers ran past them to aid with the breach.

The mercenary looked at the soldiers sprinting past with a look of longing, he turned back to Cullen. "What of the breach, sir?"

"Forget the breach! The wall is lost, get that defensive line up as soon as you can, we might be able to buy some time."

"Will he order a retreat?" Velamir nodded his head towards Bronwin, his eyes pleading Cullen to tell him the answer was sensible. The Bull had just brought the tip of his shield up and into the sternum of a Threg. It doubled over so his mace could land the killing blow to the back of the head.

Cullen turned back to the mercenary and shook his head, despair in his eyes.

"Yes, sir. I understand." Velamir gazed into nothingness for a moment, as if remembering something somewhere. "We'll get that line sorted. You can count on us." The captain turned, raised his sword into the air and roared: "Anvil's Hammer, to me!"

Cullen puffed through the air leaving behind golden-flecked smoke until he appeared at Nef's side, behind Bronwin's containment troops.

"Nef! What is Bronwin planning?" Another explosion rocked a section of the wall. It was about to give way. Soldiers tried to scream as green flames began burning the oxygen in their lungs. A body, charred and lifeless, was tossed aside, smashing into another man who cried out as he fell back, head striking wood with a meaty crack.

"Not sure, sir!" Nef pulled out his bow, nocked an arrow and drew. "I think he hopes to hold Plainsview!" He released and the missile flew through the air, striking a Threg in the throat, the beast went down. Bronwin looked over his shoulder, nodded, and turned back into the fray. He caught a Thregs arm with his mace, then a knee and finally caved in the Thregs chest in a series of swings that nearly left Nef stunned.

"They're going to breach the wall again!" Cullen pointed as green mage fire soared overhead, missing the wall and smashing harmlessly into a mound of black mud. Soaked earth exploded outwards, revealing two bodies hiding underneath.

"Try telling him that!" Nef yelled, releasing another arrow.

Cullen didn't reply, he focused on where he wished to go and in the blink of an eye, he was there, the partial moment of silence during his travels gone and the chaos of battle once again batted at his eardrums. He was behind Bronwin.

"They're about to breach the wall again, Bronwin! There!" Cullen pointed past Bronwin's head and followed the wall towards the northern slope of the passage. It rocked and cradled, the stairwell fell as the wood began to splinter. "You cannot hope to hold another breach, you can barely hold this one! Fall back to the town square, a defensive line is already being formed!"

"Who the fuck are you to redirect my troops?!" The Pale Bull turned and seethed as he glared at the Highfold.

Another massive glow of green and the northern section of the wall exploded. Wooden planks, splinters, and corpses flew into oncoming soldiers. Several were skewered by the wreckage, more were cast aside by debris.

"Take it up with my brother!" Cullen yelled back, "We need to move. *Now!*"

Bronwin roared in anger, turned and with a single, anger-fueled, manoeuvre crashed his mace into a Threg's chest. The beast rose from the ground and was tossed back into its allies.

"Fine!" the Pale Bull agreed. "We pull back." the words oozed hatred.

They broke away from the breach and began working their way back. Bronwin ordered any soldiers he could reach to fall back to the town square and help with forming the defensive line. Then, he did something that Cullen actually considered smart. The Pale Bull had reached out to Algrenon and gave him a stern order to get the troops stationed outside of the town to advance into the town centre; they were to be their primary muscle.

Cullen was pleased, this opened the way for retreat, and gave the town another 2,000 well-trained, healthy men. It was likely they wouldn't have been caught up in the sickness that had spread through Plainsview.

The mud was horrendous, soldiers were forced to use wooden debris to cross the mud without losing their boots or getting stuck. Once the final group of soldiers made it across, they began removing their makeshift bridges in hopes of slowing the Thregs down. The mud would buy them some time, not much, but maybe enough for the troops from outside of town to make it to the line. Bronwin left behind whatever troops were already at the wall, considering them casualties of war.

Time stretched past in segments of blinding speed, and of aching lag. Algrenon had moved fast through Plainsview, climbing over whatever he could to hasten his movement. Cullen had watched as he got on horseback at the far side of town and rode out to meet the troops. They had arrived in time, but the wait was excruciating. From the centre of town, when Cullen had gone back, he could hear the cries of soldiers and the explosive splintering of wood as the Thregs began to move methodically through the streets of Plainsview. The tavern lay in cinders, a singular dwarven body within, charred and barely recognizable.

The longhouse the striders had called home had half-collapsed in on itself, mud licking up the walls. Rain fell harmlessly into the fires that had once been the eastern side of Plainsview. Soldiers, who had spent most of the battle digging their way feverishly out of the spider holes, breached the surface to find inhuman faces staring at them.

Cullen's posture shrunk from his perch. Something out of the corner of his eye forced his hand. For the briefest of moments, everything went quiet, his sight went dark, and he could taste nothing. Then he was on the ground, watching as the rooftop he was just perched on explode in green mage fire.

Another moment of nothing, then another, and another. Half a dozen of these null moments and he was back in the centre of town, standing behind the defensive line as Algrenon's fresh troops filed in to reinforce the fallback.

The town square was large, open and made for a well enough battleground. Nef had been smart and moved squads of guardsmen to the flanks, blocking off any potential off-shoots. They were not worried about artillery fire, it had seemed the Thregs had kept their artillery at the rear of their assault.

Bronwin paced up and down the rear of the defensive line. Shields in the front, spears in behind, shock troops further back. They only had a score of archers left, fresh from outside of town. The rest were either dead or fighting for their lives at the wall and Cullen wasn't sure which was worse.

Chapter 40

When Barragan had woken up the previous night, he was groggy and sore, but the fatigue from a day standing atop the wall had thankfully vanished upon opening his eyes. But now that fatigue had returned in spades. His arms and shoulders ached fiercely with every pull of his bowstring, but he continued to loose arrows into the oncoming horde. Great green balls of fire had rendered the wall useless as Thregs stormed through the openings their artillery had provided. Soldiers struggled to keep ladders off the wall, preventing the Thregs from climbing into their lines, the wall was as good as gone.

He was lucky, Barragan thought, lucky that he hadn't burned to death. He knew as soon as he saw Bronwin pull back, ordering troops away, that he was a dead man. But there had been a kind of peace with that. Suddenly everything was simple. He didn't have to worry about what was right or what was wrong anymore. He didn't need to worry about what he would eat that night, or how his commanders would scold him for marching too slowly. It no longer mattered how well he kept his equipment or how well he kept his posture. He was a dead man, he would die on the very wall he stood.

With all the weight of a soldier's day-to-day off his shoulders, he found his arrows flying truer than they had ever before. Soon he would be sleeping in the cold, and he was surprised to find himself fine with that. He nocked once more, pulled back, aimed, and released. The arrow caught a Threg in the eye, much to his surprise, and the creature dropped. There was a call behind him.

"Barragan, help me!" it was his friend Brand. "Barragan!" he cried once more.

The archer turned from the plains below and looked behind him. Through the smoke, he could see Brand and four others struggling to hold the stairs leading up to their section of wall. They had the high ground and they used it well, jabbing down with spears and pushing back with shields. But they were being overwhelmed and overpowered. The Thregs gained purchase with every passing moment.

Without thinking, Barragan dragged his supply of arrows with him to the opposite side of the wall and without so much as a second thought he began pulling them and firing. He didn't have many arrows, but by Esmirla's Glorious

Cunt he would see them fly. He nocked, pulled, and loosed arrow after arrow. Thregs dropped not with each one, but they were dying by his hand.

Brand had stopped his yelling and had fallen into a sharp focus as he jabbed and prodded at the Thregs mercilessly. Another arrow flew and caught its target in the neck, forcing the Threg's attention away. Brand's spear took hold in the distracted Threg's jaw and it dropped back down the stairs.

The spearman was tugged off his feet as his weapon failed to free itself from his foe. He fell forward, catching one of the shieldsmen. The two of them tumbled into the invaders and were buried within moments.

Barragan expected himself to feel cold and to freeze up in fear as he watched his friend disappear into certain death. But he did not, his arms did what they knew and his hands followed suit. He kept firing until he reached for another arrow and grabbed nought but air. He looked down, eyes cold, and found the small container of arrows held nothing. Barragan grinned, his teeth caked in mud, but he had not taken notice.

No rest for a soldier. he thought.

The Thregs had made it on top of the wall now and Barragan turned to face them, he held the bottom of his bow in both hands, ready to use it as an awful club. The first Threg came in range and he swung and batted at it. Each blow rocked with a loud, thudding slap. The bow shook in Barragan's hand and he grimaced with every vibration. Fatigue came through stronger, making his hands ache. They opened without his consent and the weapon fell to his feet. He looked up at the Threg. It looked back, its smile had Barragan thinking that its what a vulture would look like if it had teeth.

He shuddered for the last time.

#

It fell silent in the square as the sounds of battle from the wall wilted away. The last of the defenders had lost. The final confrontation would take place in the centre of town, among the streets and buildings that had once been homes to so many.

Nef knew defeat drew nearer with each passing moment. Mud had buried and killed a portion of their soldiers, the Thregs had killed even more. Where they sat now, in the town's central square, under the canopy of the famed willow tree, now darkened with black bark and white foliage, they watched as Thregs began to trudge through the mud towards them.

They watched as the invaders took one step at a time, the ground pulling and sucking at their feet. But the enemy was not phased, their eyes were locked on the Sovereign Guard.

The town square was safe from most mud. The buildings surrounding it had done much to slow down the tide, and managed to stop it before it had travelled too far. Some soldiers stood at the edges and beyond the square to try and keep flanks secured, knee-deep in wet earth. Nef did not envy them.

Bronwin raised his shield as the Thregs approached. He brought his mace into it, connecting with a loud *bang*. The line of soldiers moved up one step, striking their shields in return. Bronwin scored his shield again. Another step, another resounding *clang* shook the air. The rain stopped.

Esmirla finds hope yet. the warden thought to himself.

Clang. Another step. ***Clang.***

With every step, every echo, Nef's heart began to beat faster. Adrenaline coursed through his veins, his face red with the heat of it.

Clang. Another step. ***Clang.***

The Thregs had gathered in a scattered line at the edge of the muddy grounds, watching the troops move in their new ritual. Anger left their gazes, Nef noticed, and it was replaced with respect for a few moments. This show of unity and strength seemed to speak to the enemy.

Nef stepped alongside Bronwin with every clash of his weapon, drawing his sword and long knife as he went. The Thregs still stood and their front row began to shift colours in sequence. Their trademark green, then to a dark brown, slate grey and then blood-red, before becoming green again and repeating the process.

Nef spoke through clenched teeth. "I was wondering when they were going to show up."

"A Threg all the same," Bronwin said flatly, commanding another step.

Clang. Another step. ***Clang.***

Another Threg stepped to the forefront, standing taller than those shifting their shade in a strange show of companionship. It stood a head taller and wore more than a simple loincloth. It wore large boots and wielded a two-handed axe. Its hair held a multitude of colours braided into it. Only the initial shade was its own, Nef guessed. The rest were prizes, woven into its own hair as a show of strength.

The Threg donned plates of smooth bone, strung together with rough twine, in place of traditional armour. Nef could see a patch of skin here or there, a strand or two of hair hanging limply. No armour on its legs. That made it weak.

"Bronwin, it's legs."

"I see it."

Clang. Another step. ***Clang.***

"Think we can take him?" Nef brandished his blades, a predatory grin stretched across his face. The adrenaline held his body in a tingling blaze, his heart pounded in his throat with anticipation. The smell of the mud no longer bothered him.

"Do we have much choice?"

Clang. Another step. ***Clang.***

Clang. No step this time. *Clang, clang.* Still no step. *Clang clang clang.* The troops returned it. ***Clang. Clang clang. Clang clang clang.*** Then a roar of anger as the Sovereign Guard charged, Bronwin and Nef leading the assault.

Time stretched in odd ways that Nef had never experienced before. He became aware of every movement in front of him, of every piece of rubble in his path. His senses felt heightened and his perception of time became sharper; he tapped into things he never would have thought possible for him. Maybe for Bronwin, but not for him. There was a puff of black and Cullen was at his side, running with them.

That predatory grin stayed on his face, savage and unyielding. The feeling of defeat fled with every passing step.

Then it happened: the clash.

Nef ducked below a Threg club and sliced at the creature's sternum as he carried forward. The sounds of thousands of shields on thousands of bodies rang out behind him, men and women roaring over the carnage. Swords cleaved into thick flesh, bones broke in return. Shields were battered like drums. Nef screamed as he drove his sword home through the stomach of his target, severing the spine on the other side. He pulled back hard and watched the body crumple.

Movement in the corner of his eye; he side-stepped just out of reach of a rusted axe; turned to counter and swung, nearly taking the creature's arm off. His sword was caught, and he couldn't pull it out. Using his long knife he struck the top of his blade hard. It drove the rest of the way through. Nef unleashed a flurry of blows, alternating his weapons as he fought. The Threg fell with their body in ribbons.

Onto the next one.

#

Cullen blinked in and out of existence more rapidly than he ever had before, his feet hadn't touched the ground in his last dozen kills. He'd move, stab, move, stab, move, stab. He repeated this process, picking his moments carefully and his locations even more so. He caught a moment to breathe and let his feet find the dirty cobbles beneath him. He looked around and let the rush of battle guide his eyes. Nef was doing fine, superbly fine. The man moved with a speed he hadn't thought him capable of. Even from where he stood, the Spymaster could see Nef was picking up on the subtlest movements of his foes. The slightest hesitation a Threg could possibly make, the Plain's Warden exploited with lethal efficiency. Bronwin too.

The rest of the troops fought better than Cullen had ever seen them. Their slow approach drove away many of the fears the soldiers had felt. They no longer wanted to just put up a fight, they wanted to *fight back*. And by Gwendall's Blade, they were doing it.

Cullen vanished again and appeared next to Algrenon, who had just finished dispatching two Thregs with the help of three others.

"How are you holding up?" Cullen called above the carnage.

Algrenon didn't meet his eyes; he kept them focused on a red-hued Threg ahead of him, they were locked in a staring contest that only blood could end. "As well as I can be, sir. Care to join me?"

"Oh, of course. I've always hated that shade of red." The Spymaster disappeared again, his senses leaving him for the briefest of moments.

When the sights, sounds and smells of Plainsview returned, Cullen was standing beside the red Threg, he thrust out with his daggers, yet the creature twisted and avoided the blow. It swung a blacksmith's hammer in retaliation. Cullen ducked and stepped forward driving his shoulder down into the creature's stomach. It lurched back as Algrenon came through with his sword. He swung and caught the Threg's hip. Black spindles of tongue shook with rage as their foe roared. It swung down at Algrenon who had his shield raised to block the blow.

Cullen vanished, reappeared behind the Threg and launched himself into the air for a puncturing strike to the skull. The Threg turned, ignoring Algrenon and hitting Cullen with its empty hand. The Highfold felt the blow drive some air from his lungs and before he could be driven too far off course, he vanished again. When he came back, it was a struggle to gather his breath but he had placed himself opposite where he was before, driving a dagger into the beast's side. Algrenon came forward and struck along the back of the Threg's knees where the flesh looked soft.

The beast dropped to its knees, and not a moment later the officer had driven the tip of his sword into its spine. Bronwin's Right Hand withdrew the blade and pushed the body over with the flat of his foot.

"Thank you, Cullen. Are you alright?"

Cullen chuckled, finally getting a lungful of air. "As well as I can be."

Algrenon grinned, the last emotion he would ever display. A great two-handed axe cleaved deep into the man's body from behind, nearly splitting him from shoulder to hip.

Cullen said nothing, he blinked from existence once more and appeared above the battle on the slick rooftop of an abandoned home. The scent of mud and blood wafted up to meet him, earthy and iron-like. He grimaced behind his mask as he looked down at the large Threg. It stared back at him with an unsettling calmness. No anger hid in its eyes, its strange vertical nostrils didn't even flare in frustration. It looked at peace, calm and collected. Cullen recognized this look, it was something that religious folk wore after mass. That they were right because they were doing whatever it was they believed a god had told them. The Threg believed the same: that it was right because something had told it so.

The Spymaster's heart sank. He looked at the other colour-shifting Thregs in the battle, they wore the same sense of peace. Cullen hadn't noticed this with the one he and the late Algrenon had fought, as he had been moving in and out of reality. They were martyrs, not savages. And they began to cleave Sovereign troops in spades, paving the way for the rest of their troops.

The soldiers near Algrenon had begun to falter with the death of their officer. Their lust for battle drained from their bodies with every swing and every death. A weakened link in the chain. They would fall and that would break the line, dooming them all to the depths of the Soul Spire.

#

Bronwin had been keeping track of the big Threg as he fought. His mace was bloodied, hide and sinew hanging in morbid clumps. He had watched as his Right Hand was sent to death with one fell swing of an axe. Hatred did not boil up within him, however, he felt calm, his goal clearer than it had been before: Bronwin needed that Threg's head.

With each swing of his mace, Bronwin cleared himself a path towards his quarry. Nef followed close by, realizing what it was that Bronwin meant to do. The two men moved in tandem, when Bronwin would block, Nef would strike. When Nef dodged, Bronwin would bring death upon the invaders. The two of them moved with ease through the chaos, almost unstoppable.

Then they reached it: the towering Threg, standing taller than the Pale Bull and wielding an axe larger than he had ever seen. The beast turned to face the two men, calmness in its gaze.

"It thinks it's already won." The warden brandished his blades.

"It hasn't." Bronwin stepped forward shield ready.

"Shall we?"

Bronwin said nothing as he rose to meet the Threg. It swung its axe down hard. The Pale Bull's shield rocked with the blow. He grunted with the vibration and pushed upwards, driving the axe into the air, as he did this he swung his mace in a flat curve trying to crush the horror's ribs. It stepped back avoiding the blow.

Nef swept in behind and cut at its legs, the Threg raised a foot and stomped down hard onto the strider's blade. Pinning it in the dirt. An empty hand came down and struck the warden across the cheek, casting him into the mud.

Bronwin lowered his shield and charged forward. He might need the strider's help; at the very least as a distraction. Metal met flesh as the Pale Bull charged into the rear of his foe, causing it to stumble forward. It turned and blindly swung its axe in a wide arc. Bronwin stepped back to avoid it. But in doing so lost his chance to strike. He closed the distance again, lashing out with his mace, the Threg swatted the blow aside and was met with the flat of Bronwin's shield to its chin.

It reeled back, then fixed its gaze onto Bronwin with a grin, nostrils flaring with pleasure.

Nef scrambled on his knees to grab his sword, but the Thregs axe was brought down hard and fast onto the weapon, bending the blade out of shape.

Bronwin couldn't hear it, but he could see the words "Esmirla's Cunt" on the strider's lips. Nef was out of the fight.

It was a duel between the Pale Bull and the large Threg. Other invaders had kept clear of the fight, as had the Sovereign Guard, some kind of agreement made without a spoken word: no one was to interfere.

They charged towards one another, blows clashing back and forth. Bronwin's shield rocked and shook at every strike, the metal growing dented and weak. Every blow he returned was met with either air or had been swatted away.

The Threg moved with grace and agility. Again Bronwin swung and the Threg dodged, then countered. He raised his shield to block the first blow and stepped back to avoid the second. The Pale Bull advanced with carefully aimed strikes, trying to exploit anything he could. A miss, another then another, the next parried, he blocked, felt his shield start to give, and roared back with another body check. The Threg staggered, never having fought someone large enough to use a manoeuvre so effectively. Bronwin continued the charge. The Threg staggered back further and further until they crashed through a closed door.

At some point during the struggle, the Threg had lost its axe and Bronwin his mace. They stood in the abandoned home staring at one another, the Pale Bull feeling small for the first time since he was a child.

The Threg smiled again, like a vulture with teeth, and looked to the shield Bronwin still held: it was warped and bent beyond use, hammered almost to oblivion. The Bull tossed it aside, and charged towards his opponent, dropping his shoulder into its sternum. The Threg responded by hunching over the man and hammering its elbow down and into his back. It caught plate and chain mail harmlessly.

They slammed into the building's rear wall with a loud crack as wood splintered from the force. Bronwin launched a series of punches into the Threg's gut, smashing its bone armour into splinters and hammering home blow after blow into its thick hide.

The Threg reached out with an open hand and grabbed Bronwin's face, pushing him back with all the force it could muster. The Pale Bull began to lose his footing.

"You sorry, fuck!" he roared and reached up for the outstretched arm with both hands.

He realized his mistake as the Threg's other hand came up in an uppercut that caught his jaw. Bronwin's head snapped back as he staggered into a table.

The Threg stepped forward, throwing a wide punch. Bronwin blocked it on the elbow, feeling his foe's fingers crash against metal. He launched a jab with his backhand feeling it sink into the Threg's diaphragm. Another punch came from the other side, Bronwin brought his fist back up; blocking the blow with his elbow, his other hand now circling around for a hard punch to the side.

The Threg dropped its forehead for a headbutt as the Pale Bull's punch landed. Stars exploded and Bronwin's nose broke. He could feel the blood rushing out of his nostrils. Everything circled and swam around him and he staggered back, nearly falling.

The Threg stepped forward, seizing Bronwin by the throat. The commander reached for the arm, but every time he did, the Threg's free hand rained another series of punches into his nose, causing fresh stars to explode in awful abundance.

The Pale Bull could taste his blood, feel it running down his throat. The strength left his arms as he heard a voice call to him in the doorway.

"Bronwin! Flee you damn fool!" it was Cullen, blinking out of existence again, and appearing behind the large Threg, daggers at the ready.

#

Nef came through the door shortly after Cullen had performed his disappearing trick. Bronwin was beaten and bloody, his face already starting to bruise where his nose had been smashed in.

"Come on, we need to get out of here. The battle is lost, our numbers are spent."

While Bronwin had been in a brawl with the largest Threg Nef had ever seen, the battle had skewed poorly. The Sovereign Guard were pushed back, slowly at first, but as the battle waged and the battle-lust faded, fatigue and illness began to pull at the troops. Even the fresh-faced guard had grown tired and began to fall in greater numbers.

Bronwin struggled to bring his gaze to Nef, but when he finally did, he nodded, struggling to place his feet beneath him. Nef reached down to help and waved another soldier through the door to give him a hand.

Cullen was engaged in a deadly dance with the Threg. Taking what few strikes he could afford, but the thing's reach kept him at bay, even as he moved about in his magical ways. Then Nef realized, he wasn't actually fighting the Threg, nor distracting it, he was blinding it. With every disappearance and reappearance, Cullen was filling the house with a thick cloud of black-gold smoke. In a few fleeting moments, the Threg wouldn't be able to see any light shining through the door.

The Plains Warden and the Sovereign Guardsman got Bronwin to his feet and carried him out. Rain began to fall as Esmirla continued to weep. The Battle of Plainsview had been lost. Whoever would make it out of Plainsview would rendezvous at Sun Spire, and that was where Nef intended to bring Bronwin. It was time to leave home behind.

Chapter 41

The door to Alistair's war room swung open. He expected to hear it slam shut in its own disembodied way, but that moment never came. Silence seeped from the open door like steam from a kettle. The Arch General cast his gaze up, his eyes opening wide, mouth hanging as open as the door itself.

"Cullen?!" he gasped, "Cullen, by Gwendall's Blade, is that you?!" Alistair's knees grew weak, but he pushed himself to stay standing. He walked over to his brother, who had been leaning silently in the doorway, his face hidden behind a clean black mask, his green eyes showing fear. His clothing was spotless, even his travelling boots were clean.

"Yes, it is me, Brother." Cullen stepped forward and into the war room. The door slammed shut behind him. Alistair felt everything had settled back into normalcy.

The Spymaster placed his hands on the Arch General's shoulders. Alistair returned the gesture, a smile forcing itself to be shown. He couldn't have fought it if he wanted to.

"It-" he stammered, holding back tears of joy for the first time he could remember, "it's been cycles, Brother. How big you've grown, how big we've both grown! Come," He turned, reaching his hand out into the messy room that was his headquarters. "Take a seat, please."

Cullen placed a hand on his brother's. "No. I cannot stay long. There is much to be done. So very much to be done."

Alistair turned to see his brother's eyes full of sorrow. "What is it? What has happened in the west?"

"It's not the west." The Spymaster met his brother's gaze as if asking for forgiveness for what he was about to say. "It's the east."

"You can't mean ..."

"Yes. Plainsview has fallen. Bronwin and the Plain's Warden have retreated with what forces they could muster, but the Thregs will begin their advance. Within the next moon, possibly the moon after that. They are ransacking Plainsview thoroughly for whatever it is they can get their hands on."

"When?" Alistair swallowed hard. "When did Plainsview fall? Were you there?"

"Plainsview fell two days ago, Brother. I was there, I watched it with my own two eyes as I watch you now."

"How did y-"

Cullen turned away, cutting off his brother. "Do not worry yourself with me. You and I will be seeing a lot of each other very soon, and if I find the time, I may answer your questions. Right now, prepare to try and save Valenfaar. The threat in the west slows with their conquest of Moreen, but they will make haste once again. The enemy in the east is the lesser threat, but a threat nonetheless. Sun Spire stands before them, but I understand it is defended by a fraction of its former might. You may wish to call a meeting with our siblings and their Hands. And our parents, if you so wish."

Alistair said nothing as he watched his brother vanish. He felt tears pull at the corners of his eyes. The wide array of emotions he now felt threatened to send his mind into a spiral of anxiety-induced panic. The east was being invaded and would soon be pillaged and raped. The west was crumbling, slower now than during the past moon, but still crumbling. He had finally been able to see his brother for the first time since the family was elected, and already he was gone. Now he would have to call the most difficult meeting of his life, and the Highfolds would have to find the best way possible to keep their country safe.

#

Leaving Plainsview behind as a sodden, burning, mud-ridden shadow of itself was one of the hardest things Nef had ever had to do, seconded only by his decision to turn his back on Rel. The small group of men and women that had made it out of Plainsview were sick and wounded. Only a dozen or so remained in one piece, or as close to one piece as they could be.

They had managed to find Velamir amongst the chaos, whirling his blade at foes wildly. He fell back with them, him and the last two remaining men of the Anvil's Hammer. The rest were stragglers, those who knew the battle was lost and saw that a retreat was in order.

It had been half a fortnight, and Bronwin was looking better. His face was a black and blue mess under the bandages and rags that covered much of his face. He could stand and speak, and that was good enough for now. There would still be another fortnight before they reached Sun Spire and got proper assistance. By Nef's best guess, they still had plenty of time before the Thregs began to come close to the central cities. It was a lot of land to cover, and they would be ransacking everything they came across.

Every town the ragtag band of soldiers passed was warned of the coming danger. Supplies were offered to them as thanks, and as a sign of sympathy for their sorry state, but only the bare minimum was taken. The people needed their supplies. Bronwin had disagreed at first, claiming the life of a soldier more valuable than that of a peasant. But he ultimately relented and let Nef and Velamir deal with the commoners. It wouldn't be long before Sun Spire saw an influx of refugees.

The sun and moon rose day in and day out as the survivors of Plainsview travelled further into Valenfaar. The few horses they made away with were shared amongst everybody in shifts; the sick and wounded carted along behind them. They didn't have the look of survivors, they had the look of prisoners or convicts. But the people helped them, recognizing the armour of the Sovereign Guard, even through all the blood and grime.

On the days when the rain poured, Nef felt himself wanting to add to its torrent with his own tears, and on the days when the sun blazed in the sky, he felt his anger match its heat. Anger he felt towards the Thregs, towards Bronwin, even towards Rel and Kol. So much had gone so wrong so fast, and now he was a Plain's Warden issuing command over no more than three dozen soldiers. He shook his head as a spraven flew overhead. He watched its feathers flare emerald in the sunlight and followed its flight path to the horizon, the direction they were travelling.

In the distance, peeking over the hilltop, Nef could see a line of *something*. It was too straight to be a natural phenomenon. His eyes opened wider with every passing step as they drew closer. It was Sun Spire, stretching up to the sky with a posture so mighty the Plain's Warden felt like whooping into the wind around them.

He did.

The other soldiers joined in. For the first time in a fortnight, they had finally found some semblance of safety, somewhere they could rest their heads without fearing death. The sick would find medicine, the wounded would find care, and Nef would find Rel.

#

Bronwin would never have admitted it, but even he almost joined in the whooping cries of their company upon seeing the walls of Sun Spire. The gates opened to them without a word. Magisters, looking a little out of their prime, swarmed over the wounded and sick, only stopping to take a passing glance at the Pale Bull's broken nose before saying that he would be fine, and to sleep with his face to the stars for the next half fortnight.

He and Nef marched through Sun Spire, looking for the person in charge, the Shield of Sun Spire would be wanting an update. Finally, they found the woman named Harpp: the Shield of Sun Spire, the commander of the guard for the towering city that met the sun every morning.

"Bronwin," she said, reaching out a hand, forefinger extended.

"Harpp," he replied and copied the gesture as they clasped each other's forearms.

"It is a pleasure to see you again." She released his arm. "What news do you bring of Plainsview?"

The Pale Bull looked down and matched her strong gaze as best he could. Saying what he was about to would be the hardest thing to admit since he was a child sneaking candies from his mother. He was a stranger to failure on the battlefield, a man who had never lost, only won.

"Plainsview has fallen. The Thregs will travel our way soon. Be prepared."

Harpp let out a sad chuckle as she stared at their feet. "Take a look around you, Bronwin. My city is staffed with nothing but dregs and lads who've hardly had their balls dropped for more than a moon." She shook her head. "I can run scouts, but when they get here? I fear we're only going to be a very pretty wall for them to gawk at. They won't get in, I can assure you that, but they'll go around us, they will, I tell you that right now, so I do. We won't be able to stop them. Where are my troops?"

"Where, ar-" Bronwin was cut off.

"West of here, Bull. They are west of here, deployed to Valen, accompanied by prisoners and anyone who could swing a sword faster than this lot." She chuckled again. "And I fear you'll be heading that way too."

Bronwin had noticed the lack of proper soldiers. Harpp was operating with a skeleton crew. The streets seemed barren, only the elderly and children remained. All able-bodied individuals had travelled west, presumably. And he would be too?

"Why am I to travel west? The Thregs are here in the east, I am needed here."

Harpp held out a piece of parchment with the royal seal of Alistair Highfold broken upon it, the scar covering her mouth twisting as she smiled with sad irony. "These were the orders I was to pass along to you."

Bronwin took the note in his hands, fumbled with it, then finally got it open. He swatted at a passing fly as he read. A few lines stood out to him more than the others:

Send Bronwin west, to Valen, with his men and with all due haste. They may rest for the night. Leave those too wounded to fight behind. I order his audience with my council as soon as possible.

It was in Alistair's hand. And sure enough, he was ordered to Valen.

"Esmirla's Cunt," he bit into the air, "that man better have a damn good reason for pulling me away. I could turn your skeleton crew into a force the Thregs would fear."

Harpp nodded solemnly. "I don't doubt that, my friend. Not one bit." Her scar looked like it had almost twitched. "But I reckon the Arch General is right, I tell you that right now, I do. Right as he ever could be. The west is in shambles, they need you there more than they need you here, I tell you that right now, I do. I'll do what I can here. By Jo-een I will see it done."

"You use the name of the God of Death?" Bronwin found this odd, very few outside of a small cult openly gave praise to the God of Death. "Why?"

Harpp laughed loudly, almost manically. "Death is all around us, my dear Bronwin! It sits in the east, and in the west and it wishes to drive its way into the heart of our country! I tell you that right now, I do. There has never been a better time to praise Jo-een himself, for now, his harvest is plentiful and he will be oh so generous to those that speak kindly of him, I tell you that right now, I do!"

The Pale Bull said nothing in response to this, he supposed it made as much sense as it could.

By the Veil Strider, he needed sleep. "Alistair has given us leave to rest until the morning. Where will we stay?"

Harpp grinned widely, the scar that stretched down her face moved and twisted as her skin did. "Why anywhere you like! Almost all of our barracks are empty and are begging for someone to be inside them as a whore does a cock!" She laughed loudly again then fell sombre. "Go, get some rest. You all need it."

They slept like no other night that night, as their heads lay, their consciousness left them. Bronwin had no dreams and awoke the next morning feeling as if he had only blinked. The fatigue in his arms and legs felt more pronounced now than it had been in more than a moon.

Nef had arisen hoping to head to the dungeons to see Rel before they left. Bronwin relayed the news she would have been transported to Valen.

"I suppose I'll find her in Valen, then," he said, his gaze downcast.

"She's a traitor, Nef. You need not worry yourself with the likes of her."

"She's still a friend, Bronwin. She's done much for me, and I feel it's time I thanked her properly for all those cycles she was my mentor." His sorrow left a bit at that thought. "Yes, I'll find her and thank her, with Gwendall's Blessing she may just listen."

Bronwin had said nothing whilst the strider turned to leave the small barracks they slept in. They would be back on the road soon, himself Nef and Velamir with six others. The rest were not cut out for travel, not yet. But they would be on the road before the fortnight was up, shortly before the Pale Bull anticipated his arrival in Valen.

Once there, the way in which he participated in his campaign would change drastically, he could feel it on the wind and in his bones, and as Bronwin rode out from the western gate of Sun Spire he felt his flesh prickle with anticipation and something completely alien to him. It had taken nearly two days to pin down what the feeling was: it was fear. What he had seen at Plainsview had not scared him, his failure had not scared him, nor did the prospect of admitting his failure. It was in the west. Whatever had happened in the west, he knew nothing about, and yet on the winds that blew from there; if he closed his eyes and listened, especially in the dead of night, the Pale Bull could swear he heard the faint laughter of children in a strange sing-song rhythm that chilled him to the bone. This children's song spoke worse things than the roar of a Threg ever could.

Epilogue

The council meeting room was cramped, smelled of sweat, and glowed a low orange in the candlelight. A fortnight of non-stop travel and the Pale Bull had been denied his first night of rest. He was escorted from Valen's eastern gate to the palace immediately. He hadn't even a chance to remove his armour, as beaten and bruised as it was.

When he walked in, Bronwin looked around the large rectangular table where the historic meeting would take place. He saw Alistair seated to the right of the head, his two ageing and useless generals at either side, a chair open to the left of one. His seat, he correctly guessed. Alistair made eye contact with him and gestured him over.

Moving carefully around he could see the Master of Coin, Maryam and her Right Hand sat opposite the Arch-General, next to her more nobles and their assistants. Bronwin passed Varen Highfold, his Right Hand sitting to his right, next to the Pale Bull's own spot. Something was off, Varen's Right Hand, the Hand of Magus looked as if he were a beggar. He wore rags, his hair longer than most and running loose down his head.

He turned in his seat, brown eyes looking up into the Pale Bulls. "Well aren't you a big one!" he said with a chuckle. "You must be Bronwin, the Pale Bull and Shield of Northwood!" The strange man spoke with playful mockery in his tone, implying that the number of titles Bronwin held, were far too many for one man.

The Pale Bull stopped his movement and looked down, he saw something strange therein. This man had seen something, had fought something that left him with a faint look of constant caution behind the jovial flash in his eyes.

"That would be me, yes. And you are?"

A handsome grin flashed up, erasing the caution that Bronwin had seen mere moments ago. The beggar reached out a hand, forefinger extended. His hands were clean, which was more than could be said for his clothes, thank the Veil Strider.

"Jo-een Tolshin," They clasped forearms. "The Hand of Magus." They released.

Bronwin pulled away, feeling a slight tingle where Jo-een had gripped him.

"You bear a strange name, Hand."

"Aye, that I do! A bit of a long story. I'll gladly share it though, but not tonight, too many serious things to speak of, I fear. But you and I will be seeing quite a bit of each other I imagine. You're going to hear a lot of stories, my large friend."

"We're not friends," Bronwin said flatly. He watched a mischievous glint cross Jo-een's face.

"Oh, but we will be! I can feel it." He gripped his hand tightly, close to his chest. "We won't have much of a choice, and I would much rather work closely with a friend than a foe. Now, come," He patted the empty chair next to him with his palm. "Take a seat, the king and queen should be here soon."

The Pale Bull did so, he sat, pulled his chair in and leaned forward, his armoured elbows landing on the table with a small thunk.

"So much armour. How do you move in all that? I like to keep things light." the Hand of Magus quipped next to him.

The meeting was going to be a long one if he had to deal with jokes, and by the Veil Strider, he hoped the dirty man was wrong about working together. Bronwin's patience had been tested enough recently, and the look in this Hand's eye spoke volumes in more ways than one.

Silence fell across the room as the doors to the meeting room opened, standing before them were King Roth Highfold and his wife, Queen Vera Highfold. Their gazes were cruel and sharp, noses lifted high as if smelling the room prior to entering. The king and queen walked slowly around them, silently judging those within as they worked closer to their twin chairs at the head of the table, miniature versions of the thrones they sat on regularly.

Finally, as Roth and Vera took their places, they looked around at those before them. The room began to feel increasingly small, almost suffocating. Their gaze filled the room with a presence that had everything and nothing behind it at the same time.

The doors to the meeting room opened once more, nobody entered and then they shut of their own accord. Bronwin craned his head before he heard the voice of Cullen reach out from the walls around them, from everywhere and nowhere all at once.

"Sorry I am late, I had other urgent matters to attend to."

The queen replied, her voice cool but motherly. "That is alright, my son. You are here now, that is all that matters."

Bronwin wanted to look around for the Spymaster but didn't want to appear daft.

Jo-een leaned in close, the Pale Bull expected to smell a stench from him. There was nothing. "It's a neat little trick, eh?" he whispered, "Wonder if I'll figure something out like that, one day."

Bronwin didn't respond, instead, he looked to the king who cleared his throat. Jo-een leaned away, sitting properly.

"Now then," Roth Highfold announced, "our son, your Arch General, has gathered us here today to speak of the future of Valenfaar. What is it you wish to say, my son? I trust the situation in the west has been dealt with?"

Bronwin's heart froze, the king and queen knew nothing. The fate of Valenfaar was placed in the hands of their children, their peons, the young ones that didn't know tit from toe, cock from nose.

The Veil Strider worked in strange ways. At this realization of the king and queen, the Pale Bull's skin went stark white, his flesh prickled on end and he began to shudder and shiver. What had happened to the country he worked so hard to defend? That he had sacrificed so many to keep safe? He looked to his Arch General and saw Alistair wringing his hands anxiously.

Alistair took a deep breath. "Well, Father ... you see ..."

Bronwin looked to Jo-een sitting next to him. They met each other's eyes with the same look of worry. The king and queen were none the wiser.

As Alistair began to speak, the Pale Bull's own thoughts summarized the situation perfectly: *"Valenfaar would crumble."*

About the Author

I am a Canadian writer who loves a good story. I was raised as an only-child thus allowing my imagination the opportunity to run free to keep myself occupied on my days home alone.

I would also write horror stories during my spare time in an attempt to freak out my friends. I am proud to say it worked. Daniel, I'm sorry (not really).

I'm still "young and budding" with my writing, but with more than forty novels planned, I hope to continue to provide the worlds of my imagination for many years to come. And I hope you will come to be as immersed while reading my stories as I was while creating them.

(I also want to say thank you to the lovely Laura of Riverview Photography for the wonderful picture you see above)

Manufactured by Amazon.ca
Bolton, ON